# Through the Mist: Restoration

C. Renee Freeman

.

# PROLOGUE

*Gleann A'bunadh*
*Scotland*
*1601 A.D.*

MORAG LEANED against the freshly-hewn wood of the paddock as she watched her husband Ailig tend to the calf recently delivered by their shaggy Highland heifer. He cooed to the animal and whispered endearments in Gaelic. Shaking her head, she realized they were the same words he said to her last night. "You silly man, you love that wee cow more than you do me," she chided.

"My love, you had no complaints when I petted you," he said, laughing heartily.

Despite her advanced years, she blushed like a

maiden. "Lower your voice," she said. She glanced around to make sure her grandchildren were not lurking nearby. "I do not want the whole village to know our private business."

He strode to her. With a hand battered by age and hard work, he tucked a strand of her white hair behind her ear. "We do not want to cover that lovely face," he whispered. He placed a warm, gentle kiss on her lips. His white beard tickled her face.

She sighed. Even after all these years, he made her weak in the knees. "How much longer will you be?" she asked. She plucked a piece of straw from his kilt. She noticed that the shirt she made for him had grown thin. She should make him another one soon.

"I am almost finished," he said, wiping the sweat from his bald head. He opened the gate and joined her. "I must gather more wood for the fire."

"Then, hurry. Dinner is almost ready."

They walked in companionable silence toward the thatched-roof hut he built for them. Ailig patted her on the bottom when she entered their hut. She watched him pass through the village and was happy to see one of the men join him.

While her husband and she believed themselves to be forever young, they were not. They both moved a little slower than they once did, their bodies aching from the unstoppable march of time. She was grateful they had settled in this valley after years of wandering. It was a perfect spot. The valley backed against a thick, green forest filled with red stag and was surrounded by gently rolling mountains. A stream with the clearest water she had ever seen flowed nearby. Yes, this valley could provide everything they needed. Perhaps they could stay and watch their grandchildren grow here.

A shriek interrupted her thoughts. She raced to the doorway and frantically scanned the area. She spotted a woman who was pointing toward the forest. Squinting, she could see her husband and his companion running back to the village. A horde of men on horseback were in hot pursuit. "MacDonalds!" Morag cried, recognizing the tartan of the attackers.

She rushed into the hut. With some effort, she removed the silver shield from above their bed and grabbed a sword that always rested beside the door.

When she ran outside, she found the village in utter chaos. The women dragged their children into the huts. The men collected whatever weapons they could find and prepared to do battle. She searched among them for her husband but did not see him. She looked across the valley and saw that the

MacDonalds had surrounded Ailig.

"No!" she screamed as she charged toward them. She could hear the men running behind her, a small comfort. She would have taken on the whole group by herself if it meant saving her beloved.

"Morag!" her husband shouted when she drew near. "Go back, woman!"

The MacDonalds laughed when they saw her. They probably thought she was a frail, old crone who was no threat to them. *That will be their undoing,* she thought darkly.

She clutched the shield and sword, reaching the intruders before the villagers behind her. She could still move fast when the need demanded. "You will leave this place now!" she yelled.

The MacDonald chieftain dismounted from his horse and drew his sword. Walking toward Ailig, he raised it high and swung wide. Just when the blow would have connected with her husband's head, Morag lifted the shield in front of his face. Her arm shook when the sword hit the silvery metal but did not yield.

Winking, Ailig took the sword and shield from his wife. He gave her a quick peck on the cheek and said with a wicked grin, "Thank you for bringing my weapons, my love."

She heard him yell a grievous insult when he turned and attacked the chieftain. The men from the village fought in hand-to-hand combat with the other MacDonalds, using fists when their weapons failed them. She crouched low on the ground and pulled a small dagger from her woolen stocking. While she was no warrior, she was prepared to defend herself.

It quickly became apparent that their group was no match for the MacDonalds. They were outnumbered. Their crude farm implements were no equal for broadswords. Morag watched three men fall in front of her. She ruefully admitted she was glad that none of them was Ailig.

To her surprise, the sound of thundering hooves filled the air. Fearing the arrival of more MacDonalds, she clutched the knife and readied herself for the attack. This new set of men came from the opposite side of the valley. Had they been waiting for the right moment to join their party?

Then, she realized they were not part of the MacDonald clan. On the contrary, they were Campbells. She spotted the distinctive navy color in their tartan as it flapped in the wind. She counted twenty men in the group and noticed the furious look upon its leader's face.

They attacked immediately upon arrival, viciously slashing the MacDonalds with their mighty claymores and hurling insults that were almost as brutal as the blows. They were relentless in their assault. They sliced through the group without mercy. Morag smiled, an odd thing to do in battle, but she was glad that survival no longer seemed like a bleak prospect.

She scanned the tangle of fighting bodies, desperately searching for her husband. It was hard to see in the furious struggle so she rose from her crouched position. At last, she found him and screamed. He was lying in a heap ten feet in front of her.

She pushed her way through the mass of men until she reached his side. She rolled him onto his back and saw that he was still alive, though barely. A wicked slash at his temple gushed with ruby red blood. Using her blade, Morag sliced a piece of the tattered grey dress she wore and pressed the thin fabric against the wound. She felt the blood soak the cloth. It did not staunch the bleeding. Her beloved had suffered a mortal blow.

Tears tumbled down her wrinkled cheeks. Clutching his face in her hands, she leaned over him and stared desperately into his eyes. "Stay with me," she pleaded. "Stay with me, my love."

She was oblivious to the battle that ended almost

as quickly as it began. She looked up when a tall, auburn-haired man in a Campbell tartan kilt approached them. She raised her blade in case he meant them harm.

Lifting his hands, he said, "My name is Colin Campbell. I am not a foe."

She lowered the blade and returned her attention to her husband. His breathing was shallow, yet he looked at her with a steady gaze.

The man bent beside them. Ailig grabbed his hand, tightly gripping it. He stared into Colin's green eyes. "You have saved the lives of my clan," he said. "I thank you."

"My name is Ailig," he continued. "I am the chieftain, and this is my bonny wife, Morag."

She nodded to Colin. Her eyes filled with fear, she whispered words of comfort to her dying husband.

"Rest ye now," Colin said, trying unsuccessfully to remove his hand from the old man's firm grasp.

"Nay, I do not have much time," he protested. "I wish to bestow a blessing, if you will accept."

Morag leaned forward. "Save your strength, my heart," she urged. She gently caressed his forehead. She could not contain the tears that fell from her eyes.

Ailig caressed her cheek with his free hand. He forced a weak smile and said, "Take care of our family. Know that I am with you always."

He turned to Colin. "Take my shield as a reminder of this day," he said, lightly touching the battered object beside him. "You fought so that others may live. Remember that when you look upon it."

Gazing lovingly at his wife, he added, "May it also remind you to fight for love. I die this day knowing that I fought for love." Looking at the dusky sky, Ailig said, "To know love is to know God."

Colin covered the man's hand with his own and squeezed hard. "Sir, I solemnly vow to honor you," he whispered.

Ailig drew one last shuddering breath. He was gone.

Morag wailed and collapsed upon her husband's chest, her long white hair spreading across it. Hot tears burned her cheeks. She thought her heart might shatter and silently hoped it would. How would life continue without Ailig by her side?

The other villagers assembled around them, word spreading of their chieftain's death. One of the women carefully supported Morag when she tried to stand. Colin helped the other men carry Ailig to the edge of the forest.

Someone had already constructed a crude funeral pyre for the bodies of the MacDonalds. Morag watched the villagers toss the dead attackers into the fire. She spat onto the body of that clan's chieftain. In the long-forgotten language of her mother's people, she damned them to a restless afterlife and cursed their descendants to a life of ruin. All that they loved would be ripped from their grasp one day, just as her husband was taken from her.

With great reverence, Ailig's clan dug graves for their fallen chieftain and comrades underneath a mighty oak at the entrance to the forest. Morag appreciated the great respect Colin and his men showed as they stood off to the side, heads solemnly bowed.

Night descended, the only light provided by the crackling funeral pyre. The villagers ignored the approaching darkness for a few more moments as they bid a final farewell to those lost in battle.

After a time, Morag separated from them. She firmly grasped the shield and approached Colin. She handed it to him. "Remember him when you carry it," she said. "My husband was a fine man."

He took it from her, his hands shaking. Overwhelmed with emotion, he humbly dropped to his knees before her. She placed a gnarled hand upon his head and closed her eyes. Tilting back her head, she lifted her face to the night sky and reached her arm toward the heavens. A thin mist rose from the forest floor, and clouds moved over the full moon and twinkling stars.

She inhaled the crisp air. She spoke again in the foreign tongue, summoning heaven and earth to watch over this man and to bring him health and happiness. While he had not saved Ailig, he rescued their village. For that, she was eternally grateful.

She was amused to see Colin swallow a lump that had apparently formed in his throat. She suspected he thought she was a witch. Perhaps she was. Or maybe she was not. It was of no consequence now. Her one true love was gone.

Raising his head, he stared at Morag. "I will protect your family," he promised. "I make this vow in Ailig's memory."

A ghost of a smile formed on her lips. She extended her hand and helped him to his feet. Patting him on the cheek, she said, "I know you will, son. If you do not, his soul will haunt you forever."

Colin laughed uneasily. He offered his arm to her.

As they walked toward the village, the moon

slipped from the clouds. A silvery beam of light struck the shield. Morag smiled when she noticed four symbols briefly flash in each quadrant of the armament's surface. They disappeared, unseen by her companion.

*So it begins*, she thought.

# *One*

*Asheville, North Carolina*
*June 2018*

TILLY MUNRO STOOD ON THE CONCRETE
SLAB OF THE PATIO, her eyes closed and face
tilted the sky. She savored the warmth of the sun on
her skin. After a long, cold winter, it felt wonderful to
have a spring day. She inhaled the smell of grass,
trees, and plants, all waiting to burst forth with new
life. It was a time for new beginnings for everyone,
including herself.

She lowered her head and opened her hazel eyes.
She stared at the tiny handprints on the patio's
concrete floor. Bending down, she gently traced the
outline and could not resist a smile. Her husband

Alex spent two hours smoothing the surface to perfection. He was angry at first, then he burst out laughing at the joyful expression on the twins' faces. Their children John and Anna giggled at the squishy feel of the cold concrete between their fingers. Who can be angry when confronted with those innocent, smiling faces?

She caressed her ring finger on her left hand. It felt odd not to feel the platinum wedding band there. Would the feeling go away some day? Did she want it to disappear?

"Sweetie, it is a time," her best friend, Beth Madison, yelled from the kitchen. "We will miss our flight if we don't leave now."

Sighing heavily, Tilly took one last look at the backyard. She wanted to burn the sight into her memory - the gleam of the stainless steel grill where Alex cooked many a meal, the bright reds, blues, and yellows of the children's jungle gym. So many evenings spent here.

She hastily wiped away the tears that slid down her cheeks before she strode into kitchen. Silently, she looped her arm around Beth's and made her way to the front door.

Beth's husband Randall met them on the porch. "Cathy Rogers is here," he whispered. He cast a pointed look toward his wife. "Be nice."

As they descended the brick steps, Cathy rushed to greet them. She leaned forward and air kissed each of Tilly's cheeks, a habit that always made Tilly cringe. Cathy liked to say she picked up the practice when she spent a year in France as an exchange student. Tilly knew it was yet another attempt for the Young Urban Professionals League doyenne to appear superior to everyone else.

Of course, she did not need air kisses to do that. From head to toe, the woman oozed money. Her icy blond hair was a color that she maintained with weekly visits to a posh salon downtown. Cathy's navy sheath dress and red stiletto heels cost more than Tilly's first car. She always wore delicate pearls around her neck, a present from her physician father when she graduated from Wellesley College. Cathy kept none of these things secret, for she liked to maintain her elevated status in the community.

Tilly suddenly felt very self-conscious. She ran her fingers through her straight, brown hair which held hints of grey she did not bother to dye. She tugged at the bottom of her dull grey t-shirt and wished she had picked a pair of nice pants or a skirt, instead of the faded jeans she wore. And, was that a chunk of red clay mud stuck to the side of her right sneaker? She shifted her foot behind her to conceal the mess.

"Such a beautiful home," Cathy said, scanning the exterior of the two-story white farmhouse. "I can see how much care Alex and you put into restoring it. Rest assured, I found the perfect family who will be just as respectful as the two of you were."

"I appreciate your help with selling the farm," Tilly said. She nudged Beth in the ribs. Without looking at her friend, she knew a biting comment from Beth was imminent.

Cathy dismissively waved her hand. "Oh, honey, it was my pleasure!" she exclaimed with false warmth. A smug smile formed on her red lips. "I am glad I could be there in your time of need."

"Time of need?" Beth asked, cackling acidly. "The first time you set foot in this house was the day you heard she wanted to sell it."

Tilly smothered a laugh as Cathy's face flushed most unbecomingly. She stepped between the women, glancing at Randall for help. She was glad to see that he too noticed the impending fight.

As he guided Beth toward the car, Tilly turned to Cathy. "Thank you for working with the buyers so I could see the house one last time," she said. Reluctantly, she placed the keys in Cathy's outstretched palm.

The woman stared angrily at Beth's back. Leaning

close so only Tilly could hear, Cathy said, "If you decide to return to Asheville, you give me a call. Your friends are always here to help you."

Nodding absently, Tilly shook Cathy's hand. She watched the woman hop into a silver Mercedes convertible. She forced a smile and waved with more enthusiasm than she felt when Cathy drove away. It greatly pained Tilly that the woman was the best real estate agent in town. It likely would have been more pleasant to work with Lucifer himself than with that rich bitch.

"Come on," Beth called from the car. "Let's get the hell out of here and start having fun!"

Casting one last look at the farmhouse, Tilly made her way to the car. Would she ever be able to have fun again?

# *TWO*

HOURS LATER, TILLY FOUND HERSELF ON A PLANE bound for Scotland. For nearly the entire flight, Beth lost herself in the latest book from her favorite author. It was a series, and she had been waiting for three years – three *long* years, she moaned – for the next installment.

Beth gave Tilly a copy of the author's first novel and encouraged her to read too. The story was set in Oban, a place they planned to visit on the trip. Wasn't she interested in reading about it?

Tilly snickered when she saw the cover. A rugged, shirtless Scot in a very short, garish red kilt held a bosomy woman with luxurious brunette locks in his heavily muscled, tan arms. The woman's ruby red lips parted in invitation, and he looked at her as if he was ready to ravish her *right now.*

Tilly doubted the book would provide useful information about Oban's history and folklore. Instead, she would probably learn one hundred new words to describe a man's penis without saying the actual word itself. She closed her eyes and feigned sleep until they touched down in Glasgow.

At the baggage claim carousel, Tilly and Beth saw a tall, thin man wearing a tattered brown kilt of undeterminable tartan. He held a sign bearing their names. Beth waved wildly at him to get his attention. The smile on her face was a thousand watts.

After the long flight, Tilly was too tired to muster up such enthusiasm. She watched the man heave their bags into an ancient, green Land Rover. She had an uneasy feeling but pushed it aside. Surely, Beth's careful travel planning would result in a nice trip.

They zipped through the now darkened streets of Glasgow. Unfortunately, they arrived so late in the evening they would not have an opportunity to explore before bedtime. It was just as well. When the Land Rover stopped in front of the hotel, Tilly took one peek out the car's window and had no desire to tour the area. Judging from the look of dismay on her friend's face, Beth shared the opinion.

The online reviews for the hotel were positive –

and largely false. They were in a shabby area of town. In this case, "shabby" did not refer to old, quaint buildings from the 1600s. With its grey, uninspiring stone façade and dingy, narrow windows, the building did nothing to improve the dreary street. Its rickety sign hung limply from a black iron hanger that was broken at the end. A sticker on the dirty front door proclaimed the hotel was voted "Best in Glasgow" – in 1964. Beth and Tilly exchanged a worried glance as they exited the vehicle.

Their driver ushered them into the hotel after he piled their luggage onto a brass cart with a wobbly wheel. He banged a bell at the abandoned front desk until an elderly gentleman shuffled from an office in the back. The innkeeper very nicely explained that they had arrived too late for the evening refreshments. Breakfast would be served promptly at 6:00 a.m.

Tilly and Beth were too tired to question the arrangements. They took the keys to their rooms and hauled their luggage up three flights of stairs. The hotel lacked both a bellhop and an elevator.

After struggling up the stairs, they found their rooms. The women hugged tightly and wished each other goodnight.

∞

TILLY EXPERIENCED SOME DIFFICULTY with the sticky lock on her door. She managed to open the door and walked into the dark room. It took a few moments to find a working lamp. When the room was illuminated, she wished it had remained dark. The comforter on the twin bed had a psychedelic floral print that probably hid decades of stains. A small nightstand beside the bed was the only other piece of furniture in the room. Spartan would have been a generous description.

She walked into the adjoining bathroom and found a white pedestal sink with two faucets. "What the hell is that?" she asked aloud as she switched on the water to one of the faucets. Tentatively, she stuck a finger underneath the stream of water. It was hot. Switching on the other one, she found it produced cold water. Shaking her head, she wondered how she was supposed to get lukewarm water.

Tilly continued her inspection of the cramped bathroom. The shower was barely large enough for one person and had some sort of contraption that would produce hot water. The toilet was an old-fashioned model with the tank suspended above the bowl. It appeared that one pulled a rusty chain to flush it. While the bathroom lacked modern décor, it was at least clean.

She decided to unpack only the bare minimum of her belongings and left her clothes in the suitcase.

Tilly checked twice the zipper on the bag, ensuring it was closed. She was afraid of what might crawl into it if an opening was provided.

Sitting on the edge of the bed, she switched on her cell phone. No messages. She flopped back onto the bed and closed her eyes. After the long flight, sleep came almost immediately. Unfortunately, so did the dreams about her family.

She awoke in a cold sweat a few hours later and spent the rest of the night staring out the dirty window that overlooked the deserted street below. She waited patiently for dawn to come and, as always, hoped it would be the beginning of a better day.

∞

BETH AND TILLY MET IN THE LOBBY. Beth arranged for them to tour the city with a group that convened outside the hotel. They only had time to grab a piece of toast and hop onto the waiting motor coach. Their tour guide was a middle-aged woman who wore too much makeup and not enough deodorant. She pursed her lips as she watched them board the coach with their dry crusts of bread. "In future, please refrain from bringing food on the bus," she said testily. "We like to keep the vehicle clean."

Beth lifted an eyebrow at Tilly. They took their seats without argument. The tour company's dedication to cleanliness was apparent in the condition of the sticky floor and soiled seat fabric.

Tilly surveyed their fellow inmates. All the people on the coach were easily thirty years her senior. The ladies must have raided the souvenir shops. They wore baggy sweatshirts emblazoned with Gaelic sayings. Not to be outdone, some of the men sported scarves of fluorescent plaid she was sure had never been any clan's actual tartan.

Beth glanced at her. "Don't," she said, holding up a hand. "I know."

∞

BETH AND TILLY ENDURED THE TOUR for all of an hour. The guide's knowledge of Glaswegian history was as poor as her hygiene. Tilly elbowed Beth in the ribs so many times she was certain she left bruises. She was afraid her friend would either laugh out loud or argue with the woman whenever the supposed expert proclaimed some "fact" about the locations they visited.

They abandoned the tour outside a church. Hailing a taxicab, they made their way back to the hotel.

"Now, you get some rest, sweetie," Beth said as they walked toward their rooms. "This is just one little bump in the road. The rest of the trip will be fabulous. I promise."

Tilly said nothing. She went to her room and stretched onto the bed. She fell into a deep sleep brought on by jet lag and, if she was honest, a little bit of depression. *Was it a mistake to come here?* she wondered before she drifted off to sleep.

# THREE

WHEN TILLY DESCENDED THE STAIRS with her luggage the next morning, she found Beth waiting for her in the lobby.

Holding out her hand for Tilly's key, she took it and gave it to the clerk. "We are checking out early," Beth told the clerk. She motioned for Tilly to follow her out the door.

Outside, a compact, blue rental car was parked in front of the hotel. Beth opened the boot of the car and shoved the suitcases into the tight space. "I planned for us to spend some time in Glasgow," she said. "Well, that might not have been a good idea. Let's head out today."

Tilly climbed into the passenger's seat without comment. Beth thrust an itinerary into her hands. "It is actually not the worst thing," she said as she started the car. "Now, we should have plenty of time to explore the Highlands."

Tilly absentmindedly listened to Beth, who talked almost nonstop about all the places she planned for them to visit. Researching family history was her hobby. Before they left, she presented Tilly with a detailed record of her Scottish ancestry and especially excited to announce they both had ancestors who hailed from the western shore of Scotland.

Their itinerary included stops at places where long-dead relatives once lived. Tilly was not sure how visiting such places would lift her spirits but said nothing. Beth was so enthusiastic about the trip that surely some of the excitement would rub off on her.

They exited the city on a busy, four-lane highway. Though it was a common view in the States, something about seeing the highway and nearby industrial sprawl in Scotland made it special. Even the landfill looked exotic. Of course, the giant silver Kelpie sculptures truly were a sight Tilly did not see every day. She wished they had time to stop for a closer look, but Beth refused. They were on a strict schedule.

In the distance, she glimpsed rolling hills and flat countryside. The view held the promise of more beautiful scenery. Despite her gloomy moody, she felt a stirring of excitement.

∞

EVENTUALLY, THE BUSY FOUR-LANE HIGHWAY GAVE WAY to a two-lane road as they headed further north. They did not stop until they reached Loch Lomond. On the way there, Beth played the song of the same name and told Tilly the story about it.

The song told the tale of two brave Jacobite Highlanders who were captured after a battle. Written from the viewpoint of the soldier who would be executed, the ballad talked about how his friend would survive. The soon-to-be executed soldier lamented that he would not see his true love or the shores of Loch Lomond. Always the history buff, her friend eagerly recounted the tale to prepare Tilly.

Unfortunately, the car park at the loch was crowded that day with tourists who were busy snapping pictures or boarding little boats for tours around the loch. A cruise was a popular thing to do, or at least the guidebooks said so. "We don't have time," Beth said before Tilly asked.

Instead, they stared at the glistening water of the famous loch. A thick forest of trees climbed toward the bald mountain tops, with Ben Lomond jutting toward the cloudy sky. They snapped pictures of the scenic view. In one of them, Beth and Tilly managed to squeeze close together for a photo, both women smiling. Though Tilly's heart ached, Beth's enthusiasm was contagious. It was impossible to be unhappy for long when she had her best friend by her side.

The friends climbed back into the car and continued their ascent into the Highlands. At every turn, they saw a vista more stunning than the previous one. "Can you believe how tall the mountains are?" Tilly asked as she pressed her nose against the car window.

"It is incredible," Beth said. "The pictures don't do it justice."

"They really don't."

Living in Western North Carolina, she was accustomed to mountain views. Scotland's mountains, though, were a thing of beauty and wonder. Soaring high into the sky, the mountains appeared to be chiseled from solid granite. Devoid of vegetation, the craggy peaks loomed over them at every turn.

"So, where are we heading?" Tilly asked.

Beth said with a sly grin, "Some place very special."

"Ok, I guess I am just along for the ride," Tilly mumbled. She resumed her study of the incredible landscape. If the breathtaking views were any indication of how the rest of the country would look, she knew she was in for a real treat.

∞

A SMALL SIGN advertising a soon-to-come Highland games was the first indication that they neared a village called Deoch. After driving for three hours on two-lane roads and through mountain passes and rural countryside, Tilly was relieved to finally approach something like civilization.

"We are almost there!" Beth exclaimed. Within minutes, they crossed an arched, stone bridge. Tilly looked to the right and saw a magnificent castle perched on a small hill. Unlike the steep peaks they saw along the way, this area was surrounded by gently rolling mountains covered in green trees.

"That's Castle Fion!" Beth said excitedly. She pointed to the building as they crossed the bridge. She announced that they would visit it the next day. A guidebook declared it was not to be missed. It was built in the 1600s after the original family home fell into disrepair.

They travelled further down the two-lane road that led into Deoch. The little village stood on the shores of a loch bearing the same name. The expansive body of water reflected the grey sky and surrounding mountains. The loch's water seemed as smooth as glass. A few white-and-black buildings stood along the shores. As they made a quick drive through the village, Tilly saw an imposing, three-story limestone building at the top of High Street.

Beth and Tilly stopped at a pub in the village. It was late afternoon, so the castle was closed for the day. When Beth informed the bartender that they intended to spend the night at a local bed-and-breakfast inn, he gave them directions to it.

"The inn isn't far from here," Tilly said, her stomach rumbling. "Why don't we have an early supper?"

Beth ordered pints of cold, locally produced beer. Tilly suggested they share a plate of fish and chips. "After all, isn't that quintessential pub grub here?" she asked in a whisper. She didn't want to seem like tourist, though her Southern accent gave her away.

They took a table near a floor-to-ceiling window that faced the street. "Can you believe we are in Scotland?" Beth asked, practically squealing with delight.

Two children and their mother passed in front of the window. Tilly felt a deep pain in her heart. "No, I cannot believe it," she said. She looked away.

Beth reached across the table and held her hand. "Hey, it's alright," she said.

Tilly managed a brave smile. "I know," she said. She took a deep breath. "So, tell me about this castle we will see tomorrow."

As expected, Beth launched into a thorough history of Castle Fion, the site of their future visit. She already knew which treasures they could see at the castle and where the best spots would be for pictures. She shared loads of tiny details gathered from hours of late night searches on the Internet.

*Good,* Tilly thought. She desperately needed a distraction.

# *FOUR*

THEIR STOMACHS ACHING FROM THE FRIED FOOD, Beth and Tilly jumped into the car and headed for the inn. It was at the end of a dirt road near the entrance to the village. The neat, white cottage with a black slate-shingled roof stood in the middle of a green field. An ancient rock wall ringed one section, keeping in a few scraggly sheep. The area was surrounded by thick forest.

Apparently, the pub's owner called ahead to alert the innkeeper. As Beth parked the car, a plumb woman passed through the doorway and into the car park. She waved a hand, beckoning them inside. "Welcome, dears, I am Mrs. Emma Douglas," she said, with a huge smile on her face. "I am so happy to see you."

She called to a young man who rushed to collect their luggage. They all walked inside, where she produced a large, red ledger book. "My son tells me I should use a computer registry, but I like the old ways," she explained. She handed Beth a pen and asked her to write her name in the ledger. Then, she swiped Beth's credit card through a very modern card reader.

The formalities of registration handled, Mrs. Douglas motioned for them to follow her. She led them to their rooms down the hallway. She explained that the front of the house was built in the 1750s. Additional rooms were added over the decades. When Mrs. Douglas took over in the 1980s, she completely renovated the house.

"It might have been the last time the inn was redecorated," Tilly whispered to Beth. "I doubt the 1700s were known for combinations of mauve, teal, and brass."

Mrs. Douglas stopped in front of a door on which hung a brass number eight and waved a plastic card over the electronic lock. Turning to Tilly, she said, "Mrs. Munro, I have placed you in the garden room."

The innkeeper swung wide the door and strode into the room. Its main feature was a large, four-poster bed with heavy pink velvet bed curtains. A warm fire danced in the fireplace, chasing away the slight chill in the air. Above the mantel hung a silver shield that looked to be much older than the inn itself. A cross spread across the front of the object, with intricate Celtic knots stamped onto each point. Tilly stopped in front of the fireplace for a closer inspection.

When she noticed Tilly staring at it, Mrs. Douglas said, "This cottage stands upon Campbell lands and was originally built by its gamekeeper." She looked up at the relic and smiled. "We have a few bits and bobs on loan from the family. They have been very generous to us. I hope you plan to visit Castle Fion while you are here. This branch of the Campbell family calls it their ancestral home."

The ladies nodded which seemed to please Mrs. Douglas. She crossed the room in four quick strides and flung open a set of doors. She beamed in delight when she showed the ladies the garden. Clearly, it was her pride and joy.

The little garden had a variety of colorful flowers and shrubs. Tilly and Beth admitted to the innkeeper that they were terrible gardeners. Mrs. Douglas smiled when they complimented her on the beauty of the garden.

Tilly surveyed the field, old stone fence, and forest. The fuzzy heads of the sheep bent low as they plucked the emerald green grass. The scene was idyllic. She took a deep breath. "It is a peaceful spot," she commented, with a smile. "I haven't felt this good in months."

"Mrs. Douglas, can we venture there?" Tilly asked, gesturing toward the woods.

"Oh, aye," Mrs. Douglas said. "If you would like to stroll around the property, there is a nice set of trails in the forest. Walk just past that first stand of trees, and you will see a lovely stream. We placed a bench there if you are of a mind to sit and take your rest."

Turning to Beth, the innkeeper informed her that her room was just across the hall. The women left the room, providing Tilly with a few moments of solitude.

She took a seat in a chair beside the garden doors. Closing her eyes, she savored the silence.

∞

THE NEXT MORNING, Beth and Tilly gorged themselves on the most delightful scones they had ever eaten. Tilly would have been content to sit in the garden, fat as a tick, but Mrs. Douglas had other plans for them.

The innkeeper prepared a picnic basket and a set of directions. While there was a more direct route to the castle, she explained Beth and Tilly could enjoy a better view by taking an old service road behind the cottage. She deposited the picnic basket into the car and cheerily told them to have a wonderful day at Castle Fion.

Tilly realized the innkeeper was right. As promised, the one-lane, gravel road offered spectacular views. It cut through the rolling hills and, at the turn of every curve, revealed fine vistas of the surrounding valley that were even more stunning than the last. Deoch was nestled along the loch's shore and a few farms scattered around the area. There was a distinct lack of habitation.

"Even in the 21st century, it remains a remote, untamed place," Tilly commented to Beth. "Still, it is so beautiful here."

About ten minutes into the drive, they found an old stone bridge so narrow Tilly worried their car might not fit. Beth carefully drove over the bridge, checking the sides of the car. Fortunately, there was just enough room to slide by without incident, and they continued their journey.

As they drove through the verdant forest, Tilly wondered if they would make it to the castle before dark. Finally, they approached a small hill. The trees were cleared to reveal a striking view of the castle below. Beth stopped the car in the middle of the road.

They both climbed out, mouths ajar.

"It is like something from a fairy tale!" Beth exclaimed.

Tilly agreed. Castle Fion was impressive. It sat on a slight rise below them. The forest bracketed the building on the left and right. A garden rested behind the castle. Filled with shrubs and wildflowers, it looked like a great place to take a relaxing stroll.

The castle was the real jewel, though. Its crenelated roof conjured images of men in full armor, standing guard and ready for action. The dove grey stones did little to soften the formidable image of the two-story structure. And yet, there was something very romantic about the ancient home. Tilly half expected a fair maiden to drop her long, flowing hair from one of the many windows that lined the exterior.

Her children would have loved it. Her daughter Anna would have expected a princess to be waiting for her in the castle. Her son John would have insisted upon climbing to the battlements so that he could survey the knight's kingdom. Tilly felt a sharp pain in her heart.

"Excuse me, misses," a gravelly voice bellowed from the forest. "You cannot block the road."

Tilly turned to find a short, elderly man hobbling

their way. He carried a gnarled walking stick almost as tall as he was. He would have been imposing if he did not look like a kindly grandfather. His thick, white hair was barely held in check by a tweed fedora that matched the jacket he wore. She could not resist smiling at the sight of him.

"You will want to bear right just there," he instructed, pointing to a fork in the road. "It will take you to the car park."

"Thank you, sir," Beth said. "Where are you headed?"

"To yon castle," he said.

Noticing his difficulty in walking, Tilly asked, "Can we give you a lift?"

He gratefully accepted. As they drove down the hill toward the castle, he informed them he was the former groundskeeper. When arthritis made it difficult for him to work, the Campbell family generously offered him a job as general supervisor. Beth asked him what that meant.

"Nothing really," he said, chuckling. "I stroll around the grounds and offer suggestions to the staff when I see something that needs fixing. It keeps me out of my wife's way, so I guess it is a good thing."

"Oh, I am sure your wife would not mind having

you help around the house," Beth said.

"No, no," he said. "She says she has enough to do, what with running the inn and all. She prefers it this way."

"What is your wife's name?" Tilly asked, leaning forward. She had climbed into the backseat of the car, knowing the old man would have difficulty managing it.

He looked flustered. "Oh, beg your pardon, ladies," he said. "I have forgotten my manners. My name is Robert Douglas. My wife is Emma Douglas. We own the inn down the way."

"What a coincidence!" Beth said as she parked the car in the empty lot. "We are staying there. Your wife has taken excellent care of us."

Mr. Douglas seemed pleased by her remarks. He leaned toward them and whispered conspiratorially, "Would you ladies like a personal tour of the castle, including all the good areas that guests are not supposed to see?"

"Absolutely!" they exclaimed in unison.

# *FIVE*

THE CAR PARK WAS LOCATED in a paved area beside the castle. As they exited the car, Mr. Douglas pointed to the heavy, wrought iron awning that extended from the building. "This is not the original entrance," he informed them. "Around 1900, they added the awning and cleared the space so carriages could pull right up to it. The ladies were tired of getting wet in the rain, ye ken."

Beth and Tilly followed him to the front of the castle where a large, circular drive swept toward the stone steps of the original entrance. "You ladies entered the estate from a road we use to maintain the property," he said. Mr. Douglas waved his hand toward the tree-lined drive in front of them. "This is the actual entrance. It was built to impress visitors as much in the 1600s as it does today."

"From this vantage point, the castle seems so grand," Tilly said. The left and right sides of the building jutted forward, drawing her eye toward the recessed center section where thick wooden doors marked the entrance. The face of the building was covered with windows. The architect obviously intended to dispel any gloom inside with light from the outside.

Turning to Beth, Tilly whispered, "This building was someone's home. It looks nothing like any house where we've lived." Her friend nodded, equally awestruck.

In the center section, just above the second floor, Tilly noticed "Fion 1645" chiseled into the stone. On each side, the mason added a carving of a hairy boar with fearsome tusks. Underneath each boar, a Latin inscription read *Ne obliviscaris*.

Noticing her puzzled look, Mr. Douglas pointed to the words. "It is the Campbell family's motto. It means 'Do Not Forget.' And, the boars are part of the Clan's crest."

He slowly climbed the worn steps. "The doors are made out of timber from our own forest," Mr. Douglas said, tugging open one of them. "You will see many original items, for the family take great pride in preserving this place."

The ladies gasped upon entering the castle. Massive white marble pillars rose on either side of them, set in a gleaming parquet floor. Looking up, they saw a barrel-shaped ceiling of dark wood. In front of them, a sweeping, mahogany staircase wide enough to accommodate ten people bisected the foyer and led to the second floor. On the right, they saw an antique clock. It featured a hand-carved woodland scene and resembled a large tree trunk. Their eyes bounced from object to object. Unaccustomed to such grandeur, Beth and Tilly could only stand there with their mouths ajar.

"In the old days, the main floor was reserved for family use," Mr. Douglas said. He guided them to a room on the left. "The Campbells have restored a few rooms for the public to view. This is the first."

They strode into what they discovered was the family's dining room. While it may have been reserved for personal gatherings, it was very opulent. White marble fireplaces stood on opposite sides of the room. A rectangular wood table that could easily accommodate twelve people had been placed in the center. Ancestors stared disapprovingly from the ornate, gold-framed portraits that covered the walls.

Beth whipped out her camera and snapped several pictures, even though a sign politely asked that guests refrain from it. Mr. Douglas did not stop her. He seemed to be pleased by her eagerness.

"If you will follow me, we shall visit what you Yankees call the laird's chambers," he said, holding open the door for them. "He would not have been called the laird in his time, though."

"Wasn't the clan system destroyed after the '45?" Beth asked. She winked at Tilly, who smiled in return. Beth's minor in college was history, though Tilly often thought it should have been her major. She was passionate about the subject.

"I see the lady knows something about Scottish history," Mr. Douglas said approvingly. "The Act of Proscription effectively eliminated the clan way of life. The men who managed the estates after the Act would not have dared for anyone to call them 'lairds,' but I know the term carries a certain romantic association with you Yankees."

Tilly lightly touched the man on the arm. "Sir, you should know that calling a native of the southern United States a 'Yankee' can be offensive to some people," she said. "It would be similar to telling a Scot that he is English."

"Oh, I did not know!" Mr. Douglas exclaimed in horror. "Please accept my sincerest apology." Shaking his head, he mumbled, "No wonder that couple from Alabama seemed so angry last year."

They walked to the end of the hallway and stopped

outside a room with a tall set of oak doors. The same crest they saw on the exterior of the castle was carved into the wood. "The chamber was last used in the 1800s by Malcolm Campbell," he said in hushed tones. "His heirs have never used the rooms."

"Why?" Beth asked.

"His son Benjamin felt his father represented the old ways. I suppose all heirs who followed must have agreed," Mr. Douglas said as he pushed open the doors to reveal a small, windowless room. A rather ordinary fireplace sat to the right, with two chairs beside it.

Beth raised an eyebrow and glanced at Tilly. "Perhaps Malcolm's heirs were wise to eschew the austere accommodations," she murmured.

Mr. Douglas overheard her comment. "Oh, lasses, do not despair," he said, grinning. "This is merely the antechamber. Mr. Campbell believed in making it difficult to reach him. He would have posted guards here in times of trouble."

They walked through a doorway at the left and entered a study. The shelves along the walls were filled with old books and ledgers. An oak desk sat near the fireplace. "He would have conducted all of the estate's business in this room," their guide noted.

The next room was a private receiving room. It

was very masculine with its brown leather wallpaper, deep navy rug, and burgundy velvet chairs. Heavy, green curtains hung over the sole window in the room, allowing only a tiny sliver of light to pierce the darkness.

They followed Mr. Douglas into yet another room that served as a dressing room and closet. While plainly furnished with two overstuffed chairs, a looking glass, and storage for clothes, the room was still larger than the master bedroom in Tilly's house.

When they entered the bedchamber, they were surprised by the massive size of the room. Arched, floor-to-ceiling windows flooded the room with light. Looking up, they noticed an elaborate mural painted onto the ceiling. It depicted nymphs and fairies romping in the forest.

Pointing to the ceiling, Tilly commented, "It seems rather fanciful for a man's room."

"Mr. Campbell personally commissioned an Italian artist to paint the scene," Mr. Douglas said, shaking his head. "He was a lover of nature, though not of much else."

Two green marble fireplaces were probably necessary to warm a room of this size. Tilly noticed the oil paintings that hung above each fireplace. "His wife Eleanor," Mr. Douglas said, pointing to the portrait on the left.

The woman in the portrait sat rigidly in a burgundy velvet chair. The inky blackness behind her gave no indication of the location. Her auburn hair was arranged in an elegant chignon. The emerald color of her gown accentuated her pale, smooth skin and green eyes. Save the simple coral cameo on her ring finger, she wore no jewelry. The expression on her face was very sad.

"It was not a happy marriage," Mr. Douglas said. "Malcolm married her for the dowry and inheritance, and she knew it."

Tilly stared at the portrait above the opposite fireplace. "And, this must be the infamous Malcolm Campbell."

"Aye, he was a hard man," Mr. Douglas said with a shiver. "According to historical accounts from the time, the artist captured his likeness very well."

Malcolm's portrait had been painted in the study through which they just passed. He stood behind a brown leather chair, a large ledger open on the desk in front of him. His hair was as black as a raven's and neatly held in place by a stiff, black bow. The rest of his dull grey garb was nondescript. Judging from the stern expression on his face, his ensemble was of little consequence to him.

*But, those eyes*, Tilly observed. His steel blue eyes were unyielding. They challenged anyone who dared look at the picture. She shuddered involuntarily.

Tilly turned to find Mr. Douglas standing beside the bed. Apparently, it was the real showpiece of the room.

"This is called an angel bed," he said proudly as he patted the red velvet bedspread. "Only the wealthiest of men owned something like this."

Tilly did not quite understand the significance of the bed. Frankly, it looked downright gaudy. Its square, red velvet canopy hung from the ceiling by thick gold chains. Ostrich plumes dyed red and black protruded from each corner. She peered underneath it and saw the family crest emblazoned in black velvet on the inside lining. Malcolm must have been very proud of his family's history.

"Is it just me, or does it feel as if we are not supposed to be here?" Beth asked, easing closer to the door. She glanced at the portrait of the former occupant and shook her head. "Dead all these years, and he still has the power to intimidate."

As they exited the last room, Tilly noticed the courtyard directly in front of her. She was so excited about entering the private suite that she completely overlooked the wall of windows that led out to the courtyard. When she commented on it, Mr. Douglas informed her that Malcolm added the windows during a renovation.

"The whole castle was much different when Mr. Campbell inherited it from his father," he said, guiding them upstairs. "The man used every penny of his wife's sizeable dowry to transform it from the original stone fortress into a fine country retreat worthy of any English aristocrat."

"Why was it important?" Tilly asked. The man in the portrait did not seem like the type who cared for creature comforts or the opinions of others.

"He believed the English were the key to preservation of the estate. He sought their favor in everything he did and often hosted hunting parties on these grounds."

"Did it work?" Tilly asked.

"Aye. Within ten years of completing the renovations, he became an Earl. Within twenty, a Duke. The title has passed through the generations to the current duke."

The second floor was even more ostentatious than the entrance. Tilly felt as if she stepped onto pillows when her feet touched the fine, jewel-toned rugs that lay on top of the honey-colored oak floors. She scanned the family portraits in their ornate, gilded frames that lined the walls. She could not fathom how much money it must have taken Malcolm to create this incredible display of wealth.

Mr. Douglas ushered them into the formal state dining room. Again, the ladies were stunned at the show of riches. The long, rectangular table easily seated twenty-four guests and was set for a very elegant dinner, with fine china, crystal, and silverware. Enormous floral arrangements stood in the center of the table. Tapestries portraying a banquet for Greek gods lined the walls on one side, protected by a panel of Plexiglas. Though the colors were faded now, it was easy to imagine how vibrant they must have been at one time. Mr. Douglas noted that the dye was likely made from vegetables and lost color over the years, for the tapestries were very, very old. Made in France sometime in the 1500s, they were from the original castle and were quite valuable.

He pointed to the chandeliers hanging over the table. "Malcolm commissioned these from the finest glassmakers in Italy," Mr. Douglas said. "We found them in a storage room in the basement. It took us five years to restore them to their current beauty."

"It was worth the effort," Tilly said, moving closer to study them. The chandeliers were delicate with dainty red roses and clear glass flutes. She imagined the room looked lovely when candles were alight.

"I want a copy of your pictures," she murmured to Beth, who was taking photos of nearly every object in the room.

"What could be more magnificent than this room?" Beth asked, examining the thick gold molding that surrounded a family portrait. "If he wanted to impress his guests, Malcolm certainly succeeded here."

Mr. Douglas clucked. "Oh, lass, you have not seen the best parts yet," he said. "You must see the state bedchamber and guest library. Once you see those rooms, I fear I will have to lift your chin from the floor."

He was right. The state bedchamber was meant to be the finest suite in the house. It was ambitiously reserved for a royal visit. Mr. Douglas said that, unfortunately, Castle Fion was never graced with His (or Her) Majesty's presence so the rooms always stood empty.

Like Malcolm's chambers, they traveled through a series of rooms before entering the bedchamber. It was far more extravagant than anything they had seen. The room featured a four-poster bed with silk bed coverings that looked like liquid gold. Arched windows along two walls offered the best view of the garden below and mountains in the distance. Two fireplaces were framed with creamy marble mantels that resembled the frosting from a wedding cake.

Mr. Douglas pointed to the gilded, coffered ceiling. "It cost a bit o' money to restore that lot," he said, shaking his head. "The workers used sheet after sheet of gold leaf. The current duke and duchess wanted the ceiling to look just as it did over two hundred years ago."

He did not object when the ladies took turns posing for pictures in front of the bed. He even volunteered to take a picture of them together.

"What a waste!" Beth said. "They should have enjoyed that room instead of letting it sit unused all those years. Was it really this grand?"

"We believe so," Mr. Douglas said as he led them from the suite. "People with fancy degrees were consulted when the family restored the room. It seems that Malcolm spared no expense. The state bedchamber was meant for royalty. It would have been the most glamorous part of the castle."

They followed Mr. Douglas to the library. Tilly could not imagine anything more spectacular than the rooms they just left. She was wrong. When she entered the library, she thought she had died and gone to heaven.

A wall of windows produced soft light for reading. Overstuffed chaises underneath each window gave the reader a perfect spot to enjoy all of the books lining row upon row of the mahogany shelves that climbed to the ceiling. At one end of the room, two chairs were placed in front of a stone fireplace, providing another cozy place for curling up with a book.

She sighed with pleasure, gliding her fingers over the leathery spines of the books. She wanted to grab a book from the shelf and curl up on a chaise by the window. She feared that Mr. Douglas would be reluctant to grant her that liberty, though.

She spotted several gaps in the collection. "Has the current family squirreled away the best volumes for themselves?" she joked.

Mr. Douglas lowered his head. "It is a sad thing to part with one's treasures," he said. A hint of sadness crept into his voice. "Over the years, the family needed money to keep the estate running, particularly during times of heavy taxation. It hurt them dearly to part with the books, but they had no choice."

He gestured toward a small oak display case on a table in the center of the room. After producing a brass key from his pocket, he unlocked the case and gently plucked the volume inside from its emerald green home. "Benjamin Campbell – Malcolm's son, ye ken – was a visionary. He collected a lot of valuable works that financed a great many endeavors for his heirs. His foresight saved the family on more than one occasion." He handed the book to Tilly. "I believe you will find this one to be especially dear."

Beth peeked over Tilly's shoulder and exclaimed in awe. "Is that what I think it is?" she asked, a hand to her mouth.

Beaming brightly, Mr. Douglas nodded. "Aye, it is the Kilmarnock edition," he said. "It is rare to find one that is in its original form. Most people bound the book to suit their own preferences."

Tilly glanced between them, thoroughly confused. "Will someone please explain the significance to me?" she asked, delicately returning the book to its home.

"It is the first book published from Robert Burns, the Scottish poet," Beth said, unable to tear her eyes away from the yellowed pages. "The cover would have been blue, right?"

Mr. Douglas carefully locked the cabinet. "Aye – and the pages would have been uncut," he added.

"Is that an autograph?" Tilly asked, pointing to the stained parchment.

"The work was valuable without it," Mr. Douglas said. "The autograph makes it priceless."

Shaking her head in disbelief, Beth said, "Benjamin Campbell had the good fortune to acquire an amazing book." Her eyes swept the other books stuffed into the bookcases. "He seems like an interesting man. What do you know about him?"

"He is credited with saving this great place," Mr. Douglas said. He motioned for them to take a seat on one of the chaises by the windows. He tucked his hands into the pockets of his tweed coat and proceeded to give them a history lesson.

After the Battle of Culloden, the English confiscated land held by clans loyal to the Jacobite cause. Some families like the Campbells had remained loyal to the Crown and were rewarded by being able to keep their estates. However, it was difficult to survive. After he inherited the estate from his father, Malcolm faced pressure to sell but preferred to keep the estate intact. He knew it would be more valuable on the whole than in pieces. But, how do you maintain such a vast enterprise?

By shaping the castle into a hunting lodge, Malcolm created a retreat for English nobles who came for sport and fine Scottish hospitality. He could be charming when it worked to his advantage, so he was known as an excellent host. The plan worked brilliantly. He formed important alliances that advanced his own interests and made him a very wealthy man.

Malcolm was ruthless in the management of the

property. In his mind, the end justified the means. He kicked off the crofters to make way for various hunting and sheep-raising operations. He cut down trees and cleared land wherever it proved convenient for him. Anyone who stood in his way was promptly moved. He was rough with the local folk, showing little respect to the generations of people who made the estate into what it was.

His son Benjamin did not approve. He too fought to keep the family property intact. Unlike his father, he cared for the crofters who leased its land and won the support of the locals, something that would prove valuable when times were difficult.

"The attitude of service before self was drilled into each son that followed Benjamin and even exists today," Mr. Douglas declared with pride. "The castle and surrounding lands remain, because of what Benjamin started."

"He sounds like a great man," Tilly observed.

"By all accounts, he was," Mr. Douglas said. "We have a portrait of him. It hangs just down the hall from this room. Unfortunately, we do not have a portrait of his wives."

"He had two, didn't he?" Beth asked.

"His first wife was named Mary and bore him five children before dying in childbed," he said. Mr.

Douglas bowed his head in respect. "Sadly, many women died that way back then."

"And his second wife? What was her name?" Beth asked.

"Her name only appears as 'Mrs. Campbell' in family records," Mr. Douglas said regretfully. "We know stories passed down over the generations. She was a good woman who brought happiness to Benjamin, and she was a champion of education for all. If you venture into the village, look for the great building on High Street. The second Mrs. Campbell established a school there in 1802."

"Can we see his portrait?" Tilly asked. She was very curious to see who inspired such devotion all these years later.

∞

THE DASHING MAN who stared down at them from the portrait in the hallway looked every inch the Scottish laird, even if he could never use that title. Benjamin Campbell stood in the forest, the castle behind him in the distance. He looked comfortable in the setting, as if he spent many a day wandering through those woods. His left hand rested lightly on the hilt of a lethal-looking claymore strapped to a thick black leather belt around his trim waist. The tartan kilt seemed to move from a soft breeze that also ruffled long, unchecked auburn hair that fell to his shoulders. The white, billowy shirt he wore was partially open, revealing a hairy, muscular chest. It looked like something straight off the cover of a steamy romance novel.

"Oh, my," Beth sighed, placing a hand to her chest. "Now, *that* is a fantasy."

Tilly laughed, moving closer to examine the picture. The man's eyes were a beautiful mossy green shade that matched the lush foliage in the background. Lucky for him, he looked more like his dear mother than his overbearing father. His strong jaw, high cheekbones, and broad shoulders gave the impression of strength, yet his soft, steady gaze hinted at a sweetness of spirit. "The portrait is lovely," she said. "Do we know if it is a fair resemblance of Mr. Campbell?"

"It is said Benjamin was a very handsome man," Mr. Douglas said. He cocked his eyebrow and smiled at the ladies. "My dear wife is a great admirer of this portrait."

Tilly and Beth exchanged a look but said nothing.

"I thought it was forbidden to wear a kilt after the Act of Proscription was enacted," Beth said. "When was the portrait painted?"

"Aye, it *was* forbidden until the Act was repealed in

1782," he said. "We found an entry in a ledger that suggests the painting was commissioned in 1802."

"Why did he decide to wear a kilt?" Tilly asked. "Wouldn't it have been rather passé at that point?"

"Wearing a kilt would not become popular until many years later, when King George IV visited," Mr. Douglas said. "It is rather strange that he chose this garment."

"And, who is that woman in the background?" Tilly asked. She pointed to the figure who sat on a rock some distance behind Benjamin. The woman's long, straight brown hair was undone and covered her face. The mystery lady wore a simple green dress that matched the moss of the granite rock on which she sat. She faced the castle, not the painter.

"We think she is his second wife but cannot be sure," Mr. Douglas said. "The ledger entry says the style of the portrait was her idea. It follows that she might be included in the painting. We are not certain, though."

He leaned closer to the ladies and said in a low voice, "Mr. Campbell's room has not been restored yet. They do not let tourists see it." Mr. Douglas glanced from side to side, making sure no one was near. "We could sneak inside the room if you like."

The ladies nodded eagerly. As Tilly followed her

companions, she glanced back at the portrait. *I bet many a fair maiden swooned over him*, she thought wryly. *No wonder* **his** *name was not lost to history.*

∞

BENJAMIN CAMPBELL'S SUITE was located on the ground floor, to the right of the entrance. It was similar to the other areas they visited. They passed through a series of rooms until they reached the bedchamber. Even though much of the furniture was covered with cloth to protect it from dust, the room seemed grand.

The coffered wood ceiling was easily twelve feet high. The rough, hewn wooden beams did not have gold leaf or any sort of embellishment, unlike the ceiling in the state bedchamber. It lent a distinctly masculine air to the room.

Upon entering the bedchamber, Tilly was drawn to a massive fireplace. Lacking the ornate trappings of other fireplaces throughout the castle, a thick oak timber served as the mantel. Rugged, grey granite climbed the wall to the ceiling.

She could not resist running her fingers across the cool rock. How much work went into creating such a humble fireplace? "This room is so rustic, compared to the others," she said. "I hope it will retain that character when it is restored."

She looked down at the oak floors, dusty and worn. The floors would shine beautifully when they were refinished.

Beth made her way to the large, four-poster bed that stood on the opposite side of the room. Navy brocade curtains hung above a mattress so high that a stepping stool was needed to enter the bed. She patted the matching bedspread, and a huge cloud of dust rose from it.

As she strode around the room, something about it unnerved Tilly. Maybe she was simply tired from the continuous history lesson. Or perhaps it was just too stuffy. The air was deathly still. The room seemed to be waiting, but for what? Or whom?

Whatever the reason, Tilly decided it was time to explore the garden and said as much to her companions. She noted Beth's reluctance to leave the room but was happy when her friend relented. As they left, Beth whispered in her ear, "Makes you wish for a dashing laird of your own, doesn't it?"

"Beth, if you see one, let me know," Tilly replied. "A hot Scot seems like the perfect salve for the soul right now."

# *Six*

MR. DOUGLAS WAS AS WELL VERSED WITH PLANTS AS HE WAS WITH CASTLE LORE. Beth and Tilly enjoyed a lovely stroll through the gardens as he spent a full hour talking about the formality of the original design, which would have featured carefully manicured shrubs and a small maze. After all, taking strolls through the garden was a fashionable pastime of a bygone era.

Their guide informed that Malcolm had the finest garden in all of Scotland when Castle Fion enjoyed its popularity as a retreat for the English. With appropriate chagrin, Mr. Douglas admitted that the current, relaxed style suited his simpler taste.

Upon hearing Tilly's growling stomach, though, he insisted he had taken enough of their time. Fumbling around in the pockets of his jacket, he produced a scrap of paper and pencil. He hastily wrote directions to where they could find the perfect picnic place. He said it combined history and beauty, since a monument marked a spot where a Campbell ancestor experienced an important event. It also overlooked the prettiest valley in the area. After confirming Beth could find the way and securing a promise from them that they would return tomorrow to finish the tour, he said goodbye and headed into the castle.

On the drive to the picnic spot, Beth talked incessantly about the wonders they saw at the castle. "And, just think, Tilly, there's so much more to see tomorrow!" she exclaimed. "We didn't tour the basement where the old kitchen and servant quarters were located. And, I read that an old chapel is hidden somewhere in the forest. I am sure Mr. Douglas would know exactly where to look."

Tilly rolled her eyes and stared out the car window as her friend carefully threaded her way through the forest down an old dirt road. She feared the trip would be an endless history lesson.

∞

FORTUNATELY, MR. DOUGLAS' DIRECTIONS WERE VERY GOOD. Beth had no trouble finding the spot. Unfortunately, he failed to mention that the ladies would have to climb a steep, rocky hill to get to the picnic spot.

"Damnation!" Beth huffed, shifting the heavy picnic basket to her other hand. "Do you think there is a piece of ground in Scotland that isn't covered in rocks?"

"If there is, I haven't seen it yet!" Tilly cried, gasping for air.

When they reached the top of the hill, they discovered it was devoid of vegetation. The only marking was a granite monolith in the middle of the clearing. It stood ten feet high, with words carved onto the surface of the rock.

Tilly guessed the words were written in Gaelic, because the words looked a lot like the road signs they saw on the drive to Deoch. Above the words, she spotted symbols – a fish, triangles, a strange caldron with legs protruding from it, and the horizontal number 8, which was meant to represent infinity.

"What do you suppose it says?" Beth asked. She traced the carvings with her fingertips. "We should ask Mr. Douglas tomorrow. I bet there's a story here."

Tilly nodded absently. Her attention was drawn away from the rock and toward the expansive view of the valley below. "Look, that's our cottage!" she exclaimed, pointing to Mrs. Douglas' inn.

It was indeed their temporary home, the little white cottage that stood in the middle of the field. The lush green forest surrounded it. Tilly noticed that a gently flowing stream sliced through one section of the woods. She hoped the trails Mrs. Douglas mentioned led to that area. It looked like a tranquil spot.

She glanced at the grey sky, a gloomy sight that thankfully did not threaten rain. The air was cool but not cold. While it was not the balmy weather to which she was accustomed in the South, it was a nice day for Scotland.

Beth spread a blanket onto the ground and began disassembling the picnic basket. "Oh, bless the woman!" she squealed with delight when she found a bottle of wine. She grabbed a corkscrew from the basket and deftly plucked the cork from the bottle. She filled two mugs with the ruby red liquid, offering one to Tilly.

She took it and joined her friend on the blanket. The wine was really good. Closing her eyes, she savored its flavor.

"Try this," Beth said. She shoved a sandwich into Tilly's other hand. A fast eater, she had already consumed half of her own sandwich.

Tilly mused that a simple repast of wine and farmer's cheese wedged between two slices of homemade bread seemed very exotic when eaten on the top of a Scottish hill. It was delicious. Buttery shortbread cookies nicely finished the meal.

The friends stretched onto the blanket as if they were sunbathing on a warm beach, their eyes closed. They lay there for several moments, lost in thought. Beth broke the spell. "How do you feel?" she asked.

"Fat! I ate too much!" Tilly exclaimed.

"That is not what I mean, and you know it," Beth said, lifting herself onto one elbow. She ran her fingers through her wavy, dirty blond hair, a nervous habit, and said, "It has only been a year. You sold the house. That was a big step. No one would blame you if you wanted to take more time to recover. Are you sure you are okay?"

Tilly opened her eyes. "It has been difficult," she said. "For the first few months, I felt like a shell of a human being. I didn't know what to do. The life we planned was over. I didn't know what I should do next."

She hesitated. Tilly had never told Beth the story. "I went to a meeting for a support group about six months ago," she said. "I met a lady there who was a wreck. She didn't have a job. She had few friends beyond the other wretched souls in the group. She told me she sat in a room in her parents' basement, crying every day. Her life was completely destroyed."

Her eyes filled with tears. "When I asked her how long it had been, she told me twelve years," Tilly said. "Twelve years, Beth! In a flash, I pictured Anna. Would I want my daughter to stay frozen like that? Would I want her life to end because of what happened? How would I feel if she spent the rest of her life crying in a basement?" She shook her head. "A mother always wants her children to be happy and to lead wonderful lives. Yes, it has only been a year. I feel it in my bones, though. I must start now, even if it is just one small step at a time. I would expect nothing less from my own children – or Alex, for that matter."

Tilly squeezed Beth's hand. "Thank you so much for everything Randall and you have done. I could not survive without your support," she said. "It has been hell this past year. I can never tell you how much you have meant to me."

The mood was far more serious than Tilly wanted. She grinned slyly. "And, thank you for this trip. What a treat! Of course, it would have been nice to travel somewhere warm," she teased. "We could be at your house on Sullivan's Island, basking in the sun and sipping a fruity cocktail."

"I thought about going there," Beth admitted. "Then, I remembered all the happy times your family had there, all the summers we spent playing on the beach and swimming in the ocean. I was afraid it would bring back too many memories for you. Scotland seemed so far from anything you ever experienced with your family. It might be the one place we could go where you could create new memories."

"I appreciate everything you have done," Tilly said. Sweeping her arm wide, she added with a chuckle, "This is definitely unlike anything I ever saw with Alex and the kids."

"I truly appreciate it, Beth," Tilly said with a sigh. "After the accident, I was afraid I could never be happy again. Thank you for showing me that it is possible to find a little joy in life."

Now seemed like the right time to share the news. Taking a deep breath, she announced, "I sold the restaurant."

"No! It was Alex's dream! When?"

"Last week. Remember the investors who wanted to expand it?" she asked. At Beth's nod, she continued, "Well, a few months ago, they approached me about buying it instead. I discussed the sale with the staff. Everyone agreed it was the right thing to do.

The money will settle some debts. Combined with the proceeds from the house, I should be able to make a fresh start somewhere."

"Somewhere? Are you leaving Asheville?"

Tilly lifted herself from the blanket. It was clear that her friend needed brutal honesty. "I cannot afford to stay," she said. "I don't even have a job. I will burn through the money so fast there. I have a better chance if I move to a new city."

"Oh, you know Randall and I can help you. You don't have to leave."

"I appreciate that, but it is not the answer. Sooner or later, I must face reality." She wiped a tear that trickled down Beth's face. "Hey, it will be fine," she said reassuringly. "I will figure this out."

"I know. The whole situation just sucks, though."

"That's putting it mildly! It helps to know that you will be there to support me through whatever happens. And, I don't plan to go far. I still need to be near you."

They hugged tightly. "You are right," Beth whispered. "They would want you to go on with your life. Just promise me you will take care of yourself. I want to see you happy again."

Tilly forced a weak smile. "I will," she said. "I

promise."

# *SEVEN*

LATER THAT EVENING, Tilly finished a relaxing bath in the antique claw foot tub in her suite's bathroom. She slipped into a soft, cotton nightgown and donned a warm, blue polar fleece robe. It wasn't a sexy outfit by any means, but she didn't plan to entertain any gentleman callers. Comfort triumphed over fashion.

She settled into one of the chairs beside the fireplace and sipped a glass of whisky. She found a bottle of the soothing liquid and a set of crystal tumblers on a small table beside the fireplace when she returned from dinner. Apparently, it was customary in this house to have a wee dram before bedtime.

She knew Mrs. Douglas and probably the whole of

Scotland would be aghast at her frivolous behavior, but Tilly could not resist the urge to fling open the double doors that separated her room from the garden outside. It felt good to breathe fresh air.

From her seat, she looked outside and admired the evening view. She watched as a white mist glided over the field, softening the light of the full moon that hung in the sky. She felt the moisture tickle her cheeks and cling to her eyelashes.

It reminded her of the last night at the farmhouse. Tilly spent that evening staring out into the garden, trying to remember every last detail and watching a cool breeze move the mist across the green blades of grass.

She breathed deeply, inhaling the crisp Scottish air. This trip was the first step in her grand plan to start a new chapter in her life. She knew some people would think it was silly to dash off on an adventure with Beth. Now that she was here, she realized she needed the escape. She would politely tell the naysayers to go screw themselves. The memories at home had been overwhelming, reminding her with every passing second that her family was gone.

It was time to pick up the pieces and start a new life. Sadly, Tilly never imagined she would have to do it. Her husband Alex and she planned everything so carefully. She worked very hard to earn that master's degree, knowing it would help her secure a better teaching position. After her first interview, she felt certain she would get the job at the same school her kids attended. Everything was falling into place. They never planned for *this*, though. What was she supposed to do?

She refilled the glass. She tilted the tumbler, admiring the way it sparkled in the dancing light from the fire.

Out of the corner of her eye, she spotted intricate symbols on the shield above the fireplace. They resembled the symbols carved into the stone monument on the hill above the cottage. She supposed the symbols were there all along, and she simply failed to notice them. So far, Tilly had seen enough old relics to last a lifetime. She could only imagine what sights Beth planned for them to see in the coming days.

She stared at the shield. It looked very old, with its rough edges and deep cuts in the silver metal of its surface. She wondered how many times it was used in battle. It seemed a shame to use a beautiful piece in such a violent way when someone obviously took great care in creating the knots on the cross and etching the symbols into each quadrant of the armament.

What did the symbols mean to its creator? It

seemed like an odd mix – an infinity symbol, two triangles joined at the point, a fish, and a weird caldron with two sets of legs protruding from it. That last one was incredibly creepy. Was it a warning against witchcraft or something?

Sighing, she dispelled all thoughts about the object as she stared at the amber liquid in her glass. Tilly was so tired. And yet, the sheer luxury of sipping whisky by a fire made her feel pampered and safe in a way that she had not felt in months. *I could get used to a wee dram every night,* she thought.

She placed her glass on a table beside the chair. With the warmth of the liquid filling her belly and the heat from the fire spreading across her limps, she felt herself melting into the chair. Her eyes grew heavy until she stopped fighting it and eased to sleep.

A low, pain-filled moan drifted across the field. Was it real or a little fragment from a dream forming in her mind? She heard it again. Tilly slid her feet into fleece slippers and rose from the chair. She walked over to the doors leading into the garden. Squinting, she tried to find the source through the swirling mist but could see nothing.

She listened carefully. Surely, she did not imagine it. *There it was again.* This time, it sounded as if the moan came from the forest. Was she awake? Was this all a dream? Tilly was so tired she could not tell the difference, yet she knew she had to find the source of that sound.

She pulled her robe close to her body and folded her arms across her chest. Cautiously, she stepped outside. She moved carefully across the field, afraid she might plant a foot in a steaming pile of sheep dung. As she drew closer to the forest, the sound became even more heart-wrenching. She hoped a poor sheep was not in distress.

She noticed a flickering light a few feet ahead. It looked like a camp fire. She slowly walked closer to the edge of the forest and hid behind an oak tree. Tilly saw a man sitting by the fire, his back to her. He rocked back and forth, crying softly. Every now and then, the low moan she had heard before would burst from his lips.

As quietly as she could, she moved within a few feet of him. She did not want to disturb him, but, at the same time, she felt drawn to him. *Why was he crying?* she wondered.

She jumped when he stood abruptly and faced her. He dropped the dirk he retrieved from God knows where. He took a step towards her, then stopped. He seemed wary of her.

Tilly stared into his green eyes, which were rimmed red from crying. She did not know why she did it. She closed the distance between them and lifted her hand to brush a tear from his cheek.

She did not resist when he grabbed her, roughly pulling her against his chest. He bent low and kissed her. At first, it was a slow, soft kiss, each tentatively exploring the other and enjoying the deliciousness of it.

The heat rose between them, and the kiss became urgent. Tilly pressed herself against him as his hands explored the curves of her body. She felt his tongue probing the depths of her mouth. *I should stop drinking,* she thought. *Vivid dreams brought on by excessive alcohol consumption must be a bad sign.*

She wrapped her arms around him, clinging to him. He was so warm, so solid. She did not realize how much she craved physical contact until she found herself in his arms. Feeling loved again, even if only in a dream, was a powerful feeling. She choked back a sob.

She broke free from his kiss and tugged at his shirt. Tilly looked for buttons but found none, so she lifted it over his head. Her breath caught in her throat. She marveled at the beauty of him. She stretched her fingers across the coppery hair of his muscular chest and ran them down his rock hard stomach.

*If you are going to have a wild dream, at least the guy is ripped in it,* she thought wryly. She must remember to thank Mrs. Douglas for that whisky.

She did not resist when he slipped the fleece robe down her arms and knelt before her, lifting the hem of her nightgown. His warm, calloused hands cupped her buttocks. His lips burned a trail up her legs. Tilly worried he might see the scar from the C-section or the stretch marks and cellulite, all battle scars from having twins. Then, his lips found her, and all thoughts left her brain. Her knees buckled with every swirl of his tongue, her body rocked with desire.

Tilly pulled the nightgown over her head and tossed it to the ground. The night air chilled her skin, but his fiery touch rapidly drove away the cold. He continued his slow ascent up her body, stopping at her breasts. He gently caressed one breast with his hand and delicately stroked the other with his tongue. She ran her fingers through his wavy, auburn hair. His lips and tongue travelled up her neck, sending the most extraordinary sensations down her spine.

After what seemed like an eternity, his lips met hers. She pressed her breasts against his chest and sank into his embrace. He pulled her down to a plaid blanket already spread onto the ground. His hand travelled from her thigh to her warm center. His fingers swirled and teased her, leaving her gasping. He seemed intent upon giving her as much as pleasure as her body could endure. She guessed she would be driven insane by the urgent want of him.

Just when she believed she could take no more, she felt an exquisite explosion deep inside her. She convulsed involuntarily, wracked by wave after wave of bliss. "Please," Tilly pleaded. "Please…."

He knew exactly what she wanted. She was astonished at how quickly he removed his boots and shed the beige breeches he wore. His well-sculpted body glowed in the orange firelight. She opened her arms, and he returned to her side. He gently stroked her cheek, asking, "Are ye real, lass?"

Before she could answer, he pressed his lips to hers and plunged deep inside her. They both trembled with each thrust and clung to each other. She desperately wanted to be connected to him. She needed to feel every inch of his body. Tilly wrapped her legs around his waist, urging him deeper inside her. She could not get enough of him.

By the sound of his ragged breath, he could not get enough of her either. Again, he murmured, "Are ye real, lass?"

"I hope so," Tilly exclaimed, her world exploding into a million shimmering stars. She arched her body against him, wanting the moment to last as long as possible. She screamed in ecstasy. She held onto him as if he was her only lifeline in the raging tempest of her desire.

His body responded in kind to her urgent need. His pace quickened as his primal urges took over. His eyes closed, he tilted back his head and moaned with pleasure after each thrust. It was obvious he could not have stopped even if she begged him. He was lost in the passion of the moment. At last, when his body could endure no more, she felt him surrender to the sweet abandon of release.

To her surprise, he began to cry. He wrapped his arms around her and rocked her gently. Tilly stroked his hair and whispered words of comfort. She did not know what loss he suffered but guessed it was deep. Soon, her tears mixed with his. She knew that pain all too well. This stolen moment of heaven hurt so much more because of the profound loss that preceded it. *What an odd way to end a dream,* she thought.

They held each other tightly for some time before he raised his head and looked deeply into her eyes, "Please do not leave me, lass," he begged. "Please stay with me 'til the morn."

She nodded, unable to speak.

He folded his arms around her and tugged the plaid blanket over them. She settled close against his chest. Tilly had not felt so warm and content in a long time. She closed her eyes, and her world turned to black.

# *EIGHT*

TILLY AWOKE SLOWLY AND PAINFULLY. It felt as if the cold seeped into her bones. Shivering, she realized every muscle in her body ached. Her head throbbed from drinking too much whisky the night before.

She did not remember feeling this way the previous morning. Granted, she did not get stone cold drunk then. Why were the bed covers so threadbare or the bed so uncomfortable? Was she so exhausted the first night that she did not notice these things?

And, she was naked. How did that happen? She did not recall drinking *that* much whisky.

As she slowly emerged from the fuzzy world of sleep, she remembered she was not at home but staying at a B&B in Scotland. She tugged at the comforter, trying to cover herself. She did not remember the covers being so scratchy and thin. Why did the mattress seem to be rising and falling as if it was breathing?

It *was* breathing, Tilly realized in horror. She shot bolt upright and discovered a nude man lying beside her.

At her sudden movement, her companion leapt to his feet and looked around the campsite, clearly addled. She watched him come to his senses and notice his state of undress. To her relief, he hastily donned his discarded clothes.

She tugged at the plaid blanket to cover her bare flesh. She looked away, trying not to stare at him. She mumbled, "You aren't a dream. You are real…."

"I might say the same thing about you, lass," he said gruffly. He walked to the remnants of the previous night's fire. He tossed wood onto the pile of orange coals and angrily poked the embers until the fire reignited.

While he tended the fire, Tilly grabbed her nightgown and slipped it over her head. Unable to find her robe and slippers, she tightly wrapped the blanket around her body and stumbled barefoot toward the fire. She continued to mumble, "You are real…."

"Aye, I am real," he stated flatly. He was so irritable. *Definitely not a morning person*, she thought.

She surveyed her surroundings. The mist had lifted. She looked around the campsite and saw the trees of the forest and an open field in the distance. The inn was gone. She spun in place. *Where the hell was it?* she wondered. She only walked a few feet into the forest. The inn should be *right there*!

He watched her spin in circles and shook his head. She knew she must look insane to him. Tilly was thankful he did not share the thoughts that were so clearly written on his face. Instead, he said, "You must be cold. Come, warm yourself."

She sat on a rock opposite him. She warily eyed the handsome stranger and did not know what to say. Memories of the previous night flooded her mind, making her very uncomfortable. She believed it was all a dream. Was she wrong?

She noticed his Scottish accent was not as thick as it was last night. Tilly spotted other little details that she missed. His thick, auburn hair fell in soft waves to his shoulders. *Women would kill for that hair*, she thought.

His green eyes were a lovely shade, resembling the moss that grew on the granite boulders around them.

Staring at him, she realized he looked vaguely familiar. Hadn't she seen that handsome face somewhere recently? She stretched her hands toward the fire to warm them. Was he a patron at the pub they visited in Deoch? She had an uneasy feeling.

The man walked toward a nearby rock on which rested a saddle and saddle bags. He plucked apples from one of the bags and strode toward two horses that were tied to a tree. He murmured something she could not hear as the horses eagerly grabbed the apples. Smiling, he walked back to the bags and retrieved a bundle.

Returning to her, he carefully unfolded a blue cloth and held it in front of her. He offered a crusty pastry. She accepted with a smile. She nibbled the treat and tried not to stare at the man.

She glanced at the horses. Her anxiety grew. Who rode horses in this day and age? Tilly attempted to quell her growing concern. As remote as the area was, it was probably more practical to ride a horse than take an all-terrain vehicle or truck in the dense forests and rocky mountains.

"Thank you," Tilly said belatedly. "I was starving."

He absently nodded while he ate the pastry. He stared at the ground, seemingly lost in thought.

She was deeply offended. After their passionate

encounter, he could at least do her the courtesy of being civil. She could have smacked him. Tilly was not one to have sex with strange men. Of course, she firmly believed she was dreaming last night, and everyone knows you can do whatever you want in a dream. No consequences, just fun. Now, in the cold light of day, she was downright mortified and feared there would definitely be a price to pay for her wanton behavior.

"Sir, I appear to have gotten lost in the woods last night," she said. "I am staying with Mrs. Douglas at her inn. I do not believe I walked very far." She pointed toward the field and added, "The cottage was right there."

"Madam, no cottage has ever stood in that field," he said. He stared at her in confusion. "The nearest inn is in town, certainly not in the woods. You must be mistaken."

It was her turn to be confused. "No," Tilly argued. "I walked from the inn to the woods, to you. It was only a few yards."

Something was very, very wrong. She studied his clothes. His untucked, white linen shirt had billowy sleeves and looked like something a pirate would wear. His khaki-colored pants were tucked into brown, worn boots that reached to his knees. Instead of a zipper, she saw a flap in the front of the pants, with little buttons down each side. She felt an icy chill sweep down her spine.

She glanced around the campsite. The horses enjoyed a breakfast of fresh, green grass. No car. Save the small campfire, there were no other smells of hearth fires burning. And, oddly, the cottage that stood in the field was gone.

"Sir, if I could borrow your cell phone, I can call my friend Beth. I am sure someone at the inn can guide her here."

He did not seem to comprehend what she was saying. "Madam, what is a *cell phone*?" he asked. He shook his head and poked the fire with a gnarled stick.

*Geez, leave it to me to meet the most primitive person in Scotland,* she thought. "Well, I have heard you Brits call it a *mo-bile*. You know, a mobile phone?"

Judging from the look on his face, he had no idea what wireless phones were. Tilly had no desire to explain them. "Well, there must be a house nearby that has an old-fashioned landline telephone," she said in exasperation. "I can call the inn from there."

"Madam, have you recently suffered a blow to the head?" the strange man asked. He walked around the fire and knelt in front of her, a look of concern on his face. "You are incomprehensible."

"There are no homes near this site," he said. He swept his arm wide, encompassing the area around them. "The closest home is my own, and it is a good ride from here."

"Do you have a telephone at your house then?" she asked. Hopefully, the matter could be cleared up with a quick phone call. The situation grew worse by the minute. Tilly just wanted to get back to the inn and pretend the whole evening never happened.

He gently placed a hand upon hers. "Madam, have you suffered some injury to your person?" he asked. He looked at her as if she had sprouted a second head.

She guessed that the man was one of those people who preferred to live "off the grid." Telephones must be one of the many modern conveniences he eschewed. The conversation was getting nowhere.

"I assure you I am fine," she replied. She patted his hand. "I just want to return to the inn as soon as possible. I remember seeing a telephone at the White Rose, the little pub in Deoch. Do you know it? Perhaps you could take me there?"

He stood abruptly and towered over her, his arms firmly crossed over his broad chest. "Madam, there is no such establishment in Deoch," he said testily. "What kind of game are you playing?"

"Fine," she said. Tilly rose from her seat and glowered at him. "Show me where the road is. I will find my own way to the village."

"An old trail to Deoch winds through the forest, and I fear you would be lost within minutes," he said. He shook his head at what he seemed to think was an unreasonable request. "Or, you could take the alternate route to Castle Fion. From there, you can find a road that leads to town."

*An old trail?* What happened to the road? She distinctly remembered a road from the village to the inn. It must be near here.

She took a step away from the stranger. She was positive she did not walk far from the cottage. Could the man have carried her to another campsite after she fell asleep, to confuse her? No, Tilly dismissed that idea. She was a light sleeper. She spent too many nights listening for the faint call for Mommy.

She looked across the field and thought she saw the hill where Beth and she picnicked. Tilly needed a closer look. Was there a monument located at the top of the hill? If she was in the right area, the hill should overlook the inn. *The inn that was not there….*

"If you will tell me your name, we could find your family and return you to your home," he interrupted her thoughts. Bowing slightly, he said, "I apologize for my lapse in manners. My name is Benjamin Campbell."

Her worry deepened. The Campbell clan was the largest in Scotland. It must be a coincidence.

"My name is Matilda Munro," she whispered. Clearing her throat, she said louder, "Everyone calls me Tilly."

"It is a *pleasure* to make your acquaintance, Miss Munro," Benjamin said, with a cocked eyebrow. A devilish smile teased the corners of his mouth.

She stared back at the man, deciding to ignore his sly comment. He said the nearest home was his own, and she knew Castle Fion was near the cottage. And, what should she think of his name? Perhaps Benjamin was a popular name, especially if the original owner from the 19th century was so well regarded. He did bear a striking resemblance to the man in the painting, though. Despite her best judgment, she felt a sinking feeling in the pit of her stomach. *Oh, this is silly,* Tilly thought. *Just ask him.*

"Are you the Benjamin Campbell who lives in Castle Fion?" *Please say no.*

"Aye, I am."

Tilly thought she might vomit. *This was not real.* Yesterday, her head was filled with stories of the dashing man, and she was still dreaming. Beth would shake her awake any moment now, telling her they were late for breakfast.

But, she never dreamt anything like this. The sights and feelings were all so vivid. She eyed the stranger. He did not seem to be a figment of her imagination. Carefully, Tilly extended her hand and placed it on his taut chest. He certainly felt as real this morning as he did last night.

She closed her eyes. Maybe the current Campbell family who lived at Castle Fion had a Benjamin Campbell in their fold. *Yes, that must be it,* she frantically thought. The alternative was beyond all comprehension.

"Sir, what year is it?" she asked. She feared the answer as she withdrew her hand.

"Why, 'tis 1801, Miss Munro."

She collapsed to the ground. She tried to place her head between her legs to avoid fainting. It must be a dream. It must! She felt him beside her. Tilly looked up and found him gazing intently at her.

"Madam, are you unwell?" Benjamin asked, his voice filled with worry. He carefully covered her hands with one of his massive ones.

His hand was so warm. She could feel a small

callous on his thumb. Dreams could never be that detailed, could they?

It was true that Beth and she loved Scottish romance novels where the handsome laird rescued the desperate damsel in distress. They even read those historical romances where a heroine fell through a crack in time and landed hundreds of years in the past, usually in the arms of a dashing Scot. They never believed any of it could be true. Time travel was the work of fiction, right?

With growing certainty, Tilly knew this was not a dream. She was indeed a damsel in distress, yet nothing about her current situation felt sexy. Something very bad happened to her. She slipped through a rip in the fabric of time, or she was driven mad from grief, and her mind created a new reality. Either way, she was royally screwed.

She looked deeply into his eyes. "Please help me," she implored. "I don't know how I came to be here. One minute, I was sitting in my room, and the next…."

She did not finish the sentence. Tilly could see he guessed that she referred to their night of passion, not the shift in time. She did not correct him.

Benjamin helped her to her feet. "Show me where this cottage is," he said.

∞

IT WAS A GREAT IDEA. If Tilly had travelled back in time, she might find where the magical transport spot was in the field. She could just slip right back to the 21st century. If she was lucky, she could return to her room before Beth noticed she was gone. She would take this little adventure to her grave.

They walked side by side in silence until they reached the center of the field where the cottage should have stood. Tilly looked around and saw no trace, no remnant of the house. On the bright side, it proved that cottage definitely was not built in the 1750s, as Mrs. Douglas said.

She stood perfectly still, listening for some slight humming or disturbance that would alert her to an enchanted place, some – oh, she didn't know what! Shouldn't she feel a tug back to modern times?

Instead, Tilly was met with deathly quiet, save the sound of her companion's breathing. She glanced at him. He watched her closely, probably expecting an answer. She had none.

"You say a cottage stood here?" Benjamin asked skeptically. "I have lived here all my life. I have explored every hill and valley. No dwelling has stood in this spot for as long as I can remember."

She began to tremble. *How am I going to get myself out*

*of this mess?* Tilly asked herself. *What can I say? Would he think me deranged if I told him the truth? Could people in this time comprehend the concept of time travel? Hell, I don't know if I understand it!*

Her discomfort must have been clear to Benjamin, yet he could not know the true reason for it. He bade her stay where she was, a laughable request. She had nowhere else to go.

She watched him prowl from one end of the field to the other, searching for her trail. She hoped he would find some sign that would lead her back to her own time, even though she questioned her sanity.

Turning her attention away from him, Tilly inspected the area. The field lacked both fence and sheep, and the grass was knee high. Mustering her courage, she looked up at the hill. At the top, she saw the monolith that Beth and she examined the previous day. While there were hills aplenty around them, this was the only one thus marked. It was undeniable proof she was in the right spot, just not the right *time*. She silently prayed for the millionth time that this was all a dream from which she would soon awaken.

At length, Benjamin returned to her side. She noticed that he looked a little pale. He took her hand and led her back to the campsite.

After stoking the fire and ensuring she was as comfortable as one can be on a seat made of granite, he took a seat on a rock opposite her. He seemed to be searching for the right words to say. She understood the feeling.

"Let us speak plainly," Benjamin said. His voice was shaky. "My father's factor taught me how to track nearly anything. I saw your footsteps leading toward the forest. They appeared from nowhere. Of a sudden, your trail began from thin air."

He stared at her a moment before continuing. "There is no sign of another's footprints so no one carried you," he said aloud, obviously reviewing the facts more for his own benefit than hers. "I did not see hoof prints, so you did not ride a horse. You could not have ridden in a wagon or carriage, for the trail is too narrow in this section of the forest."

"Tell me, woman!" he said, gulping hard. "Did you spring from the mist like a wee fey?"

She could see his mounting distress as he spoke. If it was 1801, were they far enough away from centuries of superstition and illiteracy so that he might not consider her a witch? Did Benjamin place great stock in the legends of the wee folk? Would he believe in time travel? He sounded like an educated man. Perhaps she could reason with him.

Tilly was not sure if she herself understood what had happened. She hoped she might awaken at any second, even if it was in a mental institution. Since she had no idea when that awakening might occur and presently had no means of returning home, she forced herself to face the truth. She was stuck here for an undetermined amount of time.

She needed help, and he might be able to provide it. Mr. Douglas said Benjamin Campbell was a good man. Would he be willing to help her? She decided to take a chance and hope for the best.

"I'm not a fairy or other supernatural being," Tilly said. She noted the relief on his face. "I really was staying at a cottage in that field. I heard someone moaning in the woods."

"I was afraid a poor sheep was hurt. You see, the field was filled with the animals when I was there," she said. She could not tell from the blank look on his face whether or not he understood her. "I found you and…well, you know what happened."

"But, I told you no cottage has ever stood there, lass," Benjamin argued. "How did you come from a place that does not exist?"

"In my time, an cottage stands there. It is a cozy inn now, and I was a guest there."

"In your time?"

"Somehow, I have traveled from the 21$^{st}$ century to…well, *here*."

Benjamin let out his breath in a rush and leapt from the rock. She thought he might run away in horror. He stayed, though he paced around the fire for several minutes. He raked his hands through his hair, making it stand on end. He looked positively wild.

"Woman, what the hell are you trying to tell me?" he asked. He flung his hand into the air, not giving her time to answer. His accent grew thicker as he became more agitated. "Am I supposed to believe you somehow dropped out of the sky in your journey from the future?"

It was her turn to pace. "I have no idea how I got here," Tilly said. Stamping her foot in frustration, she pointed an accusing finger at him. "It's your fault! If I had not heard you moaning, I never would have crossed that damn field! I would be sleeping in my soft, *21st century* bed right now!"

They both stopped moving and glared at each other across the fire. Clearly, it was more than either one of them could fathom.

"We need water," Benjamin said softly, bending to retrieve a bucket beside the fire. "I shall return in a moment."

# NINE

BENJAMIN WALKED TO THE STREAM near the campsite. He took his time while he filled the bucket with icy cold water. Then, he sat on a rock to think.

His deep sense of honor dictated that he should take the woman as his wife. He could not believe he had succumbed to the pleasures of the flesh. He was taught to be a respectable gentleman, not a man who could enjoy the delights of a whore. Of course, he did not believe she was one. Still, he took advantage of her, and that was unacceptable.

The more primitive part of him knew he had another choice. They were on Campbell land, and he was the only son of the current owner of Castle Fion. He could smash her head with a rock and bury her lifeless body. No one need ever know about their tryst.

No one, except him. Killing someone who harmed one's family was one thing. Killing an innocent woman in cold blood was another. Could Benjamin live with the knowledge that he killed her simply because she might tell everyone about their illicit affair?

He refused to yield to such evil thoughts, no matter how convenient the deed might be. He loathed himself for even allowing the idea to enter his brain. No doubt, some small part of his father's dark nature lived inside him.

He could not help but think if she was insane. She said she travelled from over two hundred years in the future. What madness was that? Benjamin read many books of science and philosophy. New discoveries were being made every day, for they lived in an exciting age. He supposed it could be possible, but how?

*Examine the facts*, he thought sensibly. He was an excellent tracker. He found no sign that anyone had been there except for the clear trail that started in the middle of the field and led to the forest.

What of the strange clothes she wore? He recalled the spongy feel of her blue coat, so unlike any fabric he ever touched. Her plain gown was not suitable for trekking around the countryside and, like her shoes, was not fashionable or practical. In fact, Benjamin could not imagine anyone walking more than a few feet in that outfit in the rough terrain of the area.

Also, her manner of speech was very different. She spoke with him so informally and looked him directly in the eye. Frankly, she unnerved him with her boldness.

Even more troubling was the fact she knew who he was and where he lived. He remembered the startled expression on her face when he confirmed his ties to Castle Fion. That part disturbed him the most. How could someone from another time know about his home? Who *was* this woman? Could she be a fortune seeker?

Benjamin snorted in disbelief at the idea. He knew women like that existed. He did not think one would be so desperate as to wander in the woods, hoping to stumble upon a rich man. While he stood to inherit the Campbell estate, it did not yet belong to him. His father did not seem inclined to leave this earth anytime soon, so it could be years before he gained his family's modest fortune.

His heart was heavy. If she was a fortune seeker, she gained her wish by bedding him last night. She would shout from every rooftop that he took advantage of her if he did not offer to marry her. It greatly vexed him that he might bring a potential enemy to the castle where she would be in easy reach of his children. In a moment of loneliness, he let a wolf into his home.

Benjamin shook his head. As remote as the possibility might be, she could be an innocent woman alone in a strange place. After all, he did not perceive guile in her manner. She truly believed she was from another time. Perhaps she was suffering from some ailment of the mind. Maybe she did not have devious plans to claim his hand in matrimony and steal his supposed fortune. She might be confused from a recent trauma.

*Yes, that must be it*, he thought. The way she rambled about a cottage and the town – why, she must have suffered some accident in the woods. She may have been lost and frightened for days before stumbling upon him. Her mind could be as battered as her body.

He saw no evidence of injury on her person, though. With a broad grin, Benjamin recalled the thorough examination he gave her body the previous night. Her milky skin was unmarked and smelled of vanilla. And, her clothes were cleaner than his. Someone who spent days lost in the forest would have looked and smelled like it. That explanation was just as implausible as the others.

Groaning, he realized he had little choice since violence was not an option. Benjamin could not leave a helpless woman in the forest. The decision made, he rose from his seat. He would open his home to her and offer her refuge.

At least, until he knew more about her.

∞

TILLY SAT BY THE FIRE for several moments after Benjamin left. Her mind reeled. Time travel was not possible. It was the stuff of fiction. She must be dreaming.

She spotted a small rock on the ground. She picked it up and threw it hard at her foot. She swore in a most unladylike fashion when hot pain shot across her foot. "Maybe this is not a dream after all," she said through clenched teeth.

She stumbled to her feet and looked around the campsite. She spotted her shoes and robe and donned them.

She still held the plaid blanket. She studied the material. Her mother went through a sewing phase when Tilly was a child. She wore enough of her mother's creations to recognize a handmade garment when she saw one. The stitching on the edge of the blanket was not made by a machine.

Holding the blanket to her nose, she inhaled deeply. It smelled funny. Examining the fabric again, she noticed how thin and worn the material was in spots. If it was illegal to have tartan for many years after the '45, could the blanket have been stored in a trunk somewhere?

Shaking her head, she wrapped the blanket around her shoulders to chase away the chill. Tilly looked around the area and desperately wished for a proper bathroom. Unfortunately, the urgent demands of her bladder overrode the need for modernity, so she made her way behind a boulder.

While she attended to personal matters, she recalled a failed family camping trip. Her late husband Alex insisted upon taking the kids and her camping – once. Both her daughter Anna and she refused to ever go camping again. Ladies were not physically equipped for "roughing it" in the woods.

Her morning necessity resolved, she walked to the horses. The animals briefly stopped picking grass to examine her, then returned to their meal. Tilly ran a hand over the neck of one of the horses and whispered soothing words to it. Both horses very healthy and had shiny chestnut-colored coats. They seemed accustomed to the current time, even if she was not.

She checked that Benjamin was nowhere in sight.

She made her way to the stack of baggage on the boulder. Carefully, she undid the thick, metal clasp of one of the brown leather saddle bags and slid her hand inside. She found a cloth bag of root vegetables along with bread and the crusty pastries they enjoyed for breakfast. Returning the articles to the saddle bag, she checked the other bag. Again, she found additional food items.

She walked around the rock and checked the other saddle bags. She discovered more items there – a small bowl, a spoon, a spool of twine. Tilly found a tattered book by an author whose name she did not recognize. Tucked inside it were folded pieces of thin paper, a letter. Reading someone else's private correspondence might be forbidden, but desperate times called for drastic measures.

She gently unfolded the document. Tilly gasped when she saw the date at the top: *April 17, 1801*. She read:

> *To My Son Benjamin,*
>
> *I have been travelling for many months and found your letters waiting for me upon my return to Tinberry Hall. I was deeply saddened to learn of dear Mary's passing. She was a sweet girl who bore you healthy sons and took great care of your home.*
>
> *I am pleased the bairn survived. Fortunately, your wife*

*gave you four male children before delivering the last child, a female. The girl will be of great help one day in your old age.*

*By my calculation, your mourning period will not be much longer. When the appropriate time has passed, you must take another wife. I know the subject is not agreeable to you now, yet I am confident you know the wisdom of my words. You have a family and, when I have left this earth, you will have estates that require your attention. You need a suitable lady by your side.*

*I sometimes wish I had married again after your mother died. I have found myself in many social situations where a wife would have been exceedingly practical. The right match could even further one's prospects, which I wish you would understand.*

*I question your ability to find a suitable match in the country. Women of genteel birth are in such short supply there. Since you are in mourning, it would be inappropriate for you to begin the search on your own. I shall begin discreet inquires amongst my acquaintances, including my connections in London. I will find a woman of good breeding and character, and I will travel to Castle Fion with your future wife when she has been located.*

*I can picture your face when you read my words. You are furious with your father. Benjamin, you were always a stubborn boy who hated me. Do not deny it.*

*The time has come for honesty.*

*You are a father. You are the future keeper of the Campbell name. You have responsibilities that are more important than any romantic notion of love. I indulged you when you met Mary because I saw the strategic advantages of your union.*

*You were young then. You are a man now. Put aside your foolish pride. Your father can guide you in matters about which you have no knowledge. Consider my offer, Benjamin. It is for the good of your family.*

*Before I end this correspondence, I want to discuss the education of your eldest son. Mrs. Donnelly is a capable governess for the younger children. Allan should receive advanced education at his age, though. I have found an excellent tutor for the task. His name is Daniel Ramsey. He is originally from Edinburgh. He is knowledgeable about a great many subjects and speaks several languages. He is well suited for the task.*

*I have given him funds to purchase suitable materials for Allan's instruction as well as books that could benefit the other children. I anticipate his preparations will take a fortnight. On his way north, he will visit with some old acquaintances. It might be at least two months before he reaches Castle Fion. My letter should reach you in time. I gave him a letter of introduction so that you will not turn him away.*

*The hour grows late, and I have other matters that require my attention. I shall write again when I have found a prospect for you.*

*Your father,*

*Malcolm Campbell*

Tilly's hands trembled violently. She refolded the letter and placed it in the book. She returned the book to the saddle bag, careful to refasten the clasp. She hoped it would not appear that she had been rummaging through Benjamin's things.

Would the terrified look upon her face betray her? She hoped not as she made her way back to the rock beside the fire and took a seat before her legs gave way. The letter was filled with all the facts she learned about Benjamin Campbell during the tour of Castle Fion. The first wife, Mary. The overbearing father. And, the date on the letter – how could she forget that?

Tilly closed her eyes and took a deep breath. The paper was new, not yellowed with age. It was rough, unlike the manufactured paper she knew in her time. *In her time.* No one could have planted that letter in an attempt to deceive her, and no dream would ever last this long or have so many details.

It was time to accept that she had somehow travelled back to 1801. *What am I going to do?* she thought as she buried her face in her hands.

∞

BENJAMIN WAS GONE so long that Tilly began to panic he might not return at all. At last, he slowly walked back to the campsite with a bucket of water. He lifted a small pot from its place beside the fire and poured the water into it. He then placed the pot over the fire and set the empty bucket nearby. His tasks complete, Benjamin delayed the continuation of their conversation long enough.

He scratched the light beard that had formed on his face. She failed to notice it earlier. She recalled with a blush that her attention was focused on other parts of his body last night.

He sat on a rock beside her. "Miss Munro, I consider myself to be a learned man," Benjamin began. "My father sought the best tutors for my instruction. I have read a great many books and travelled extensively. Despite all of this, I have neither heard of nor seen anything like the events of the last few hours."

"I am also a gentleman. You are a lady in great distress. Do you have any connections or family in the area?" he asked.

After the slight shake of her head, he continued, "I sincerely apologize for taking advantage of you last night. It was despicable, and I intend to make right the wrong that I have inflicted upon your person. Rest assured, we will be married after what occurred between us. Your reputation will not be sullied."

"Do you believe me, Benjamin?" she asked, choosing to ignore the marriage part of that speech.

"I am very certain of my abilities as a tracker," he said confidently. "The marks do not lie. It would seem you did indeed appear from the very mist itself last night."

*Well, that's all I can expect right now*, she thought. Tilly extended her hands toward the fire. She felt awfully cold, even though she was wrapped in the plaid blanket.

He lightly placed his arm around her trembling shoulders. She did not know this man, but his presence brought her enormous comfort in a very, very difficult situation.

"Why were you so upset?" she asked, studying his face. He looked away. She could tell he was slightly embarrassed at his show of emotion. "I confided my tale to you. You owe me an answer."

"My wife Mary died in childbed nine months ago. I loved her dearly. I came here to spend some time alone." Benjamin paused, appearing to carefully weigh his words. "It is a great responsibility to manage

Castle Fion. I have not had time to properly grieve the loss of my wife."

When Mr. Douglas told the family's stories yesterday, it seemed like a history lesson from the distant past. Now that the depressed husband sat beside her in the flesh, the painful loss of Benjamin's first wife seemed all too real.

Tears sprang into her eyes. She realized they shared something in common. "My husband and children died over a year ago," she whispered.

She did not resist when he pulled her into his arms. To her surprise, Tilly began to cry. Sure, she shed a tear here and there, but she had not cried like this in months. The pain poured from her. She knew some of the tears also stemmed from the confusion of her current situation.

Benjamin stroked her hair and asked, "How did you lose your family, if you do not mind telling me?"

"There was an accident. They died instantly," she said. Tilly did not want to explain that her husband's car swerved in front of a tractor trailer after a tire blew on his car. The vehicle was crushed like a tin can. She could barely comprehend it, so she doubted a 19th century man who had never even seen an automobile would understand.

"You were a guest at the inn," he said. At her nod,

he asked, "Were you travelling with family?"

She wiped the last tears from her cheeks. "I came here with my friend Beth," she said. "I wanted to get away. I sold the home I shared with my family. I couldn't stand to be there for one more day. Too many memories, you know?"

"I do. Even though my home is filled with servants and children, I feel so lonely without my precious Mary," he said. He hesitated. "If it is not too painful for you, can you tell me how many bairns you had?"

She stared at the mother's ring she wore on her opposite hand. It was to be a birthday present. Tilly found it when she cleaned out the closet she shared with her husband. It stung to see the sparkling diamonds and garnet, which was her children's birth stone. "I had twins – John and Anna," she replied. She struggled to suppress a sob as she exclaimed, "And, I cannot have more children!"

"Oh, lass, do not fret," Benjamin said, trying to reassure her. "You are young and can have many children."

"No. I mean, I had…I cannot…." Tilly could not say the rest. Two years ago, Alex and she agreed that two children were plenty so she had her tubes tied. She never believed she would regret the decision.

"Oh, you are barren then?" he asked uncomfortably.

She did not know how to explain sterilization to a 19th century man. "Yes, in a manner of speaking," she replied. His guess was close enough to the truth.

"Well, I have five – four boys and a baby girl," Benjamin proclaimed proudly. "You are welcome to spoil all of them as much as you like."

She noticed the shadow that fell over his face. He probably did not mean it. How could he? Would she want a crazy person around her children? Of course not – and she knew that is exactly what he thought she was. Time travel was as preposterous in 1801 as it was in her time.

Tilly worried he might want to discuss the subject of marriage again. She did not understand why it was so important. In her time, it was not a big deal for a man and a woman to have what obviously was a wild, one-night stand. Granted, she had never done it, but she honestly believed she was dreaming.

She pushed away from him. "The only people who know what happened are you and me," she said. "I promise not to breathe a word to anyone. You don't have to marry me, Benjamin."

"Miss Munro - or should I say *Mrs.* Munro," he corrected himself. "I do not know how men act where you live. I assure you: we Scots are honorable. You are without family or connection, so what will become of you? I offer you safety and a place to stay. What will happen if I leave you here?"

She knew full well the dangers of being alone and penniless in *any* age, yet she had no intention of marrying him only because they shared a night of passion. She desperately clung to the futile hope that this was all a dream. When she looked around an area devoid of all habitation, it felt less like a dream, though. The situation felt increasingly real with each passing minute.

"I thank you for your offer of marriage," Tilly said, in a manner calmer than she felt. "Unfortunately, I cannot accept."

Before he could protest, she pressed a finger to his lips. "If you are an honorable man, you will help me," she said. "I am not lying. I *am* from the future. Is there any way you can help me *without* marrying me?"

He stared at her for several moments. After some thought, he nodded in agreement and said, "You will have my full protection and can stay at my home as long as you wish. I will not tell your tale *if…"*

She finished the sentence. "…I will not share ours."

Benjamin studied the grey sky. "A storm is

brewing," he said, at last. "We can either bide here a bit longer or take a wet horseback ride to my home. Which do you prefer, Mrs. Munro?"

She looked at the sky. It was so overcast that she could not see the sun. Of course, it looked that way ever since she arrived in Scotland. She was not sure how he knew a storm was imminent. "Let's stay here," she said, not relishing the idea of traveling on a wet horse.

He set about making a rough shelter for them. Benjamin gathered tree limbs and pine boughs and weaved them together to make a crude roof. He propped the makeshift structure against a large granite boulder. When he was satisfied with his efforts, he moved the saddle and bags into the shelter. He told her to wait for him there before he set off into the woods.

She wrapped herself in the plaid blanket and curled into a ball on the ground. As she fell asleep, Tilly fervently hoped she would awaken from this surreal nightmare.

# TEN

TILLY DID NOT HEAR the sound of rain hammering the glass on the windows, so the storm must have passed. Her eyes still shut, she inhaled a delectable scent that made her mouth water – garlic, onion, potato, some kind of meat? She was starving. She hoped she had not missed Mrs. Douglas' fabulous breakfast spread. She was surprised Beth let her sleep so late.

She slowly opened her eyes and saw the campfire. Then, she noticed Benjamin hovering over it, carefully stirring a pot. She squealed in surprise as she flung away the plaid blanket and sat upright. She banged her head into the low roof of the makeshift shelter he created for her. Rubbing her sore head, she managed a weak smile.

He jumped but otherwise maintained his composure, choosing to ignore her little outburst. "I was afraid you would sleep through the meal," Benjamin teased. "It is nearly one o'clock."

She stumbled to the fire and took a seat beside him. He filled a wooden bowl with contents from the pot and handed it to her along with the spoon. He had prepared a watery stew that contained morsels of mystery meat and the vegetables she found in his saddle bag. She sniffed it, detecting the scent of onion and garlic that interrupted her sleep. "What is it?" she asked.

"It is rabbit stew," Benjamin said. "I suggest you eat it quickly. The sky will open again at any moment."

She took a tentative spoonful of the stew and sighed in satisfaction. The onion and garlic gave the broth a savory taste. Chunks of potato and carrot mixed well with the rabbit meat. The stew was delicious.

Tilly was a good Southern girl who had also been married to a chef. This was not her first experience with rabbit. Of course, as hungry as she was, she would have eaten a rock if he sautéed it properly.

"I found that I was absolutely ravenous for some reason," he said, dipping a dirk into the pot and eating a piece of skewered meat.

She noticed the corners of his mouth twitched. She would not dignify that comment with a response.

"We should discuss certain matters before our arrival at my home," he said, taking advantage of her silence while she ate. "I recommend that you do not share the tale of travelling through time with anyone else."

She nodded. She had no intention of sharing her story or discussing their romantic interlude.

As predicted, fat drops of rain began to fall from the sky. Tilly scrambled into the shelter, with Benjamin rushing behind her. He had the forethought to bring the pot of stew with him. He took a seat beside her, placing the pot in between them.

"The best lies involve elements of the truth," he said while he continued to eat. "You have no family or connections in the area. You are alone and lost in a strange land."

With a sinking feeling, she realized the seriousness of the situation. She added, "I was, until I met you."

"Aye. That part of the story will require some embellishment," he said. He paused for a moment, considering their quandary. "Listen to my tale, and let us see if it is reasonable."

They would say he found her in the woods in the early morning hours. Her party was set upon by men of evil nature and intent late one night. Her husband urged her to run, promising that he followed her. She did as he bade but knew not what happened. She ran so far and so fast that she found herself lost and alone in the forest. She hid there until dawn, when she happened upon Benjamin.

They trekked back to the camp and discovered the bodies of the servants and, to her great sorrow, her husband. The money and belongings were gone.

Being a gentleman, Benjamin offered his assistance. They travelled for one day's time to reach the safety of his home. That should place them far enough away from the scene of the alleged attack. The idly curious might be willing to ride an hour or two, but certainly not a day, to investigate on their own.

He stared expectantly at her when he finished his yarn. Tilly knew the area was remote in her time. She assumed it was even more so in 1801. "Why were we travelling so far from a major city?" she asked.

He pondered her query for a moment. "Your husband longed to explore the western shore," he said. "Your guide was in league with your attackers and thus led you astray."

"Is an attack plausible?"

"Aye, very."

"What about my friend Beth? What if I slip and tell someone about travelling with her? Will that arouse suspicion?"

"Aye, it would. If you like, we could say that you were travelling with your husband *and* a friend. We found both of their bodies."

Tilly shook her head. "I don't want to say that Beth died too," she said. She saw the frown on his face. "Look – I can deal with telling people my husband is dead. I mean, he already is. But, I cannot say Beth is dead too."

Benjamin sighed. "We cannot say that your friend lives. It would raise too many questions," he said practically. "Why are we not searching for her? Should we not alert families in the area, in case she is found? We want people to hear the story and then forget it just as quickly. You must take care in what you say, Mrs. Munro. We tread on dangerous ground."

She knew he was right. "Yes, we do. I will be careful," she promised. She handed the empty bowl to him. "Thank you for the stew."

"It was my pleasure, madam," he replied with a

grin. He carefully cleaned the dirk on his breeches before returning it to the leather sheath on his belt.

"Benjamin, do you think I am insane?"

"I am not sure. Your tale is incredible. I could almost believe you are a fey. If you are, you have a voracious appetite. I fear you might eat me next."

She thought he was serious until he flashed her a huge grin. Tilly laughed, despite the gravity of the situation. She playfully poked him in the ribs. "If I was a fey, I would gladly return to my own people now!" she exclaimed.

"Does my company offend you?" he asked. He looked hurt by her comment.

"No!" Tilly said, lightly touching his arm. "You have done so much for me already. I don't know what I would do without your help." She gave him a serious look. "Please know this - I want to go home, Benjamin. I don't belong here."

"I understand, Mrs. Munro."

"Why won't you call me 'Tilly?' I call you 'Benjamin,' after all."

He shook his head. "When we arrive home, please do not address me thus. It would not be proper for us to address each other by our Christian names" he said. "We do not want people to think our connection is as intimate as we know it to be."

She was surprised. "May I call you 'Benjamin' in private?" she asked, her tone slightly mocking. What an uptight society!

"Aye, I suppose you may."

"Is your home far from here?" she asked. She extended her hand outside their makeshift shelter. The rain was but a drizzle now.

"It is an hour's ride, maybe a little longer if the trail is muddy from the rain," Benjamin said. Climbing from the shelter, he looked at the sky. "Aye, 'tis nearly spent."

He helped her exit the shelter. He frowned as he examined her from head to toe. Defensively, she pulled the plaid blanket tighter around her body.

"Mrs. Munro, you do not look like a woman who was lost in the woods," he said. He ripped one sleeve from the shoulder of her robe. Then, he bent low and rubbed mud onto her shoes.

"Stop it!" she demanded. Tilly attempted to step away from him, but Benjamin prevented her escape by grabbing the hem of her gown. Before she could protest, he swiftly tore a small slit in the garment. He lightly smeared mud on the hem.

"What the hell?" she yelled. "You are ruining my

clothes!"

"Stop your havering, woman!" he exclaimed angrily. "You cannot look as if you stepped straight from the bath. You are too clean to have spent days in the woods."

Much to her irritation, he stroked her cheek with a grimy finger. "I am sorry if I have offended you," Benjamin apologized, softening his tone. "You have no idea how extraordinary your appearance will be. Everyone in the village will know about it within an hour of our arrival. Let us not give them any doubt that the story is true."

Shaking his head, he slowly moved around the campsite. He gathered his things and readied the horses.

As she examined her torn garments, she acknowledged to herself that he was right. Tilly should have known her appearance was incongruous to the tale they concocted. *He did not have to tear my clothes, though,* she thought irritably.

She pulled the plaid blanket tightly around her shoulders. She was sure he did not believe her but hoped he was a man of his word. Benjamin was her lifeline – and it scared her.

# ELEVEN

THE RIDE TO CASTLE FION took much longer on horseback than it had in an automobile. The journey seemed particularly long because Tilly was unaccustomed to riding on a horse. Benjamin was surprised to learn that his guest did not know how to ride and therefore insisted that she share a horse with him.

She rode sidesaddle, a totally unnatural position, with Benjamin behind her. She maintained good posture for about fifteen minutes, twisting slightly to the front so that she could take in the view. That position eventually proved most painful to her lower back. She relented and leaned against her companion who seemed quite at ease.

After an hour, she could not handle another

moment in the saddle. Tilly hurt in places she did not know had muscles and was certain her spine was severed. She was about to say as much to Benjamin when he stopped the horse. She looked up and gasped.

In front of them, she saw the old stone bridge she crossed with Beth. In her time, it stood near a disused road that led to Castle Fion. In this time, the trail appeared to be well travelled. The dusty path was worn, with tracks from horses and carts.

She discovered that the bridge was wide enough for the conveyances of 1801, not the modern automobiles of her day. A farmer led a rather stubborn horse that pulled a rickety cart across the bridge. He nodded to Benjamin as he passed them and headed down a road to their right.

Tilly ignored the pain in her back and turned to face forward again. The forest was much thicker than it was the previous day. She decided they must have chopped down a lot of trees over the last two hundred years.

With great interest, she studied the landscape. If she remembered correctly, she should see a small building on the right. Yes, there it was – only, it looked much newer and was surrounded by more trees. Beth told her it was one of the old stables. In this time, it was likely in use. *We must be getting closer to*

*Castle Fion,* she thought.

"Do you see the clearing?" Benjamin asked, interrupting her thoughts. "You will have your first glimpse of Castle Fion there."

The road wove through the forest and into an area that was cleared of all trees. The opening offered a fine view of the valley, loch, and, most importantly, Castle Fion. The building looked more intimidating with its deeper grey color stone. Two hundred years of weather exposure must have dulled the stone to the softer hue she saw during her tour of the grounds.

She surveyed the area. Tilly did not see the electrical power lines and wind turbines that dotted the hills the previous day. Instead, she saw gently rolling mountains covered with trees, heather, and rocks.

The garden also showed a great difference between the times. In her day, the style was relaxed. The shrubs were not as heavily manicured as they appeared to be now, and she did not see any wildflowers. Every plant appeared to be carefully selected for its location, without a single weed in sight. And, didn't Mr. Douglas say something about a small maze? She could see that it existed in the 19th century version of the garden.

She glanced at Benjamin. He seemed very tense.

"What are you thinking?" she asked.

He stared at her for some time before he answered, "When I cross that threshold, I wear a heavy mantle of responsibility. The lives of everyone in the castle and on our lands are my concern. It is an extraordinary burden to bear."

"You are worried that I will create a problem for you," she said. "A strange woman found in the woods, unaccompanied, without family or connection."

He nodded, urging the horses forward. "Do you remember the tale?" he asked. "You must not deviate from it, Mrs. Munro."

"I remember. I will do my best not to be a problem for you, Benjamin."

He winced at the use of his Christian name, yet he said nothing. She could tell he was donning a mask that he no doubt wore all the time. When they met, it must have been a rare, unguarded moment for him. Now, he would assume the role of manager of the estate.

They rode in silence. The forest grew thick once again, obscuring the castle from view until they were within a few feet of it. They traveled along a dirt trail to the area that would one day become the car park. She noticed the wrought iron entrance on the side of the castle was gone. Mr. Douglas said it was built in the 1900s, if she remembered correctly.

Benjamin guided the horses to the front of the castle. She spotted a tall, thin man hurrying down the stone steps. The man barked orders to unseen servants behind him and seemed eager to be the first to greet his liege. When Benjamin commanded the horses to stop, the servant bowed deeply and smiled. The smile vanished when he saw Tilly.

Clearing his throat, he straightened his black jacket and rose to his full height. "Milord, I see you have brought us a guest," he remarked, as if it was an everyday occurrence to ride up with a bedraggled waif.

Benjamin whispered into Tilly's ear, "Mr. Murphy is the butler. Remember our tale, Mrs. Munro."

He deftly dismounted and raised a hand to assist her. She was not as graceful as he. She slid from the horse and crashed into him. Her legs were like jelly. He scooped her into his arms and carried her into the castle.

"Mr. Murphy," Benjamin said, glancing back at the flustered butler. "My companion is most weary from our travels and the great troubles she experienced on her journey. I am taking her to the Rose Room. Will you please ask Mrs. Keith to attend her?"

"Aye, milord!" the butler cried, scurrying away to find the woman.

"That should keep the servants occupied for a bit," Benjamin whispered in her ear. He strode through the grand entrance hall that captivated her on the previous visit. The portraits of long-dead ancestors seemed to glare at her as he climbed the stairs with ease. He turned to the right at the top. She recalled that the guest rooms were located on the second floor. Since they only saw the state bedchamber, she was curious to see what a guest room looked like in 1801.

He gently placed her on her feet outside an oak door. He made sure she would not fall before he opened it. Then, he ushered her into what she realized must be a receiving room. The light from the hallway cut through the darkness of the room. She could see that the walls were painted a shade of soft pink, giving the room a distinctly feminine air.

He placed her in an overstuffed, gold-colored chair that felt like a piece of heaven after being on the jarring horseback ride. Benjamin expertly laid several logs in the hearth and built a cozy blaze in no time at all.

He took a chair opposite her. Glancing at the door he purposely left open, he explained, "When the servants come, they will be very curious about you.

Everything you say will spread around the castle and in the neighboring village faster than the plague."

"I am sure I will be quite a novelty for some time."

"Aye, you will. You must realize how highly unusual and improper this situation is. Normally, an unmarried man and woman would not be alone without a chaperone."

Tilly sighed at the silliness of the social convention. Still, she did not want to arouse suspicion or create further trouble. "Tell me what to do, Benjamin," she said, folding her hands primly in her lap.

"Say nothing to them about our journey. I will share our tale when the time is right."

He glanced toward the doorway. They could hear the servants coming toward the room. As he rose from the chair and placed a great amount of distance between them, he hissed another warning, "And, please refrain from addressing me by my Christian name when others are present."

A woman with a distinct air of authority entered the room first. She wore a black gown with a thick leather belt around her waist. A large set of keys dangled from it and jingled with her every movement. Her white hair was neatly held in check underneath a lacy cap. Her face was set in a very serious expression, yet her grey eyes seemed very kind.

She crossed the room and opened a door for the two maids walking behind her. They carried a large copper bathtub. The women disappeared into the room next door.

Tilly could hear them move into what sounded like other rooms but could not be sure. It suddenly became a beehive of activity when an army of maids descended, carrying steaming buckets of water. She could hear the women pouring the water into the tub. Someone set about building a fire in what must be yet another fireplace.

When their work was completed, the maids quietly scurried away. They averted their eyes when they passed. Tilly suspected any scrutiny would earn them great condemnation from the formidable woman who stood in the doorway to the adjoining room, hands on her hips.

"Mrs. Keith, will you allow me the honor of presenting you to Mrs. Munro?" Benjamin said formally. He extended his hand to Tilly, which she gratefully accepted. She doubted she could have stood without assistance. "Mrs. Keith has been the head housekeeper here for as long as I can remember."

Mrs. Keith must have noticed Tilly's wobbly legs. She rushed across the room and took Tilly by the arm. "You look as if you could fall flat on your face, milady," she said, amusement creeping into her voice. "Let's get you in the bath straight away. Everything is better after a good soak."

As they walked toward the next room, Mrs. Keith glanced at Benjamin. "Milord, Iain has been pacing the floors all day," she said. "You might find him in the kitchen or your study."

Benjamin nodded and slipped from the room, careful to close the door behind him. Tilly chuckled to herself. *I doubt many people can order the king of the castle to leave.*

∞

MRS. KEITH SMILED at Tilly as she ushered her into the next room. "Mistress, I welcome you to Castle Fion," she said warmly.

The housekeeper led her through the room. Tilly noticed a mahogany, four-poster bed. It was very grand, with silk brocade curtains of rich gold. She did not understand the fascination with four-poster beds and bed curtains, but she supposed there must be a purpose. She imagined sinking deep into the bedcovers and sleeping for days. The bed certainly looked comfortable, especially after spending the previous night on the hard ground. She had little time to consider it, though, because Mrs. Keith urged her forward.

It was in the next room that the maids had prepared the gleaming copper tub for her. Placed in front of a roaring fire, it looked most inviting. Tilly glanced at the woman and said belatedly, "It is a pleasure to meet you too, Mrs. Keith."

The woman nodded absently. "A proper soak will soothe your soul," she said, bending low to remove Tilly's soiled slippers. "You look as if you have had quite an adventure."

"Ahh, Mrs. Keith, I…" Tilly said uneasily. She looked around the room. They did not have modern bathrooms yet, so what was she supposed to do?

Fortunately, the housekeeper guessed her need. She led Tilly to a screen in the corner. "You will find what you need here," she said. "I am not sure if it is as fancy as what you may be accustomed to in…."

Clearly, the woman expected her to reveal from where she came. Tilly smiled faintly, ignoring the unasked question. She doubted Mrs. Keith would believe her tale anyway.

A small chair with a hole in the center stood in front of her. She stepped behind the screen, not wanting Mrs. Keith to see her confusion. She had just enough room to tilt to the side and look underneath the chair. She saw an ivory-colored chamber pot tucked on a ledge directly underneath the opening. The pot had hand-painted roses along the gilded rim, a fancy touch.

"What the hell?" she mumbled to herself. Sighing, she realized the needs of her bladder were stronger than her curiosity.

That unpleasant experience over, she emerged from behind the screen and tried to look as if she did that sort of thing every day. Before she could ask what should be done about the chamber pot, the housekeeper pulled her toward the steaming tub.

As she removed Tilly's robe and gown, Mrs. Keith said, "Mr. Campbell's father thought it was very rude to have chamber pots underneath beds. He believed a person needed a bit of privacy during such a vulnerable moment."

Tilly stifled a giggle. She slipped into the tub, gritting her teeth against the boiling hot water. After the initial sting, she felt the heat ease her aching muscles and exhaled in pleasure.

"Would milady like to soak a bit before I wash her hair?" Mrs. Keith asked, producing a bar of jasmine-scented soap from her pocket.

"If you don't mind, I can wash my own hair," Tilly said.

Mrs. Keith seemed unnerved at the prospect of a lady attending her own needs, but she relented without protest. Handing Tilly the bar of soap, she said, "Very well, milady, I shall see where the boys are with your belongings."

The method of her arrival had probably spread throughout the castle. She appreciated Mrs. Keith's tact. "I am afraid I lost my belongings," she said, careful to stick to the official story.

"Well, do not worry, milady. I can find something for you to wear while we launder your…gown." The woman stopped talking as she examined the unusual garments. The nightgown was long, but Tilly knew it was not at all the fashion of the time. The torn fleece robe was made from what was most likely an odd material to the housekeeper. She hoped the woman would not question her choice of garments.

Deciding a change of subject was in order, she asked, "Have you been employed at the castle for a long time, Mrs. Keith?"

"Aye, for some thirty years now. I joined the family when Mr. Campbell was still a wee boy, barely two years of age."

"How interesting! What was he like?"

"He was a sweet, quiet boy. His older brother Allan was always the rambunctious one. Benjamin was like Allan's shadow. Wherever Allan went, Benjamin followed."

"Does Allan live here?"

The housekeeper turned away. She busied herself by lighting candles throughout the room. She glanced at Tilly. "Allan died when he was only two and twenty," she said mournfully. "It was a great tragedy."

Tilly thought she heard a sniffle and noticed the woman dabbing her nose with a handkerchief.

Mrs. Keith cleared her throat. "If it pleases milady, I will leave now and find a gown," she said, edging toward the door.

Tilly nodded and watched the woman leave the room. She sank deeper into the tub and savored the intense heat that relaxed every muscle in her body. She scrubbed away the dirt that had accumulated on her skin and in her hair. With luck, the soap would cleanse her of the horse smell she probably held in her very pores. Travelling in the 19th century was a very nasty business.

∞

WHILE SHE ENJOYED HER SOAK, Tilly looked around the room. She was no fan of pink, yet the color worked well in this room. She was amazed at how smooth the plaster looked. It must have taken the workmen hours to achieve the effect.

She noticed another door. Based upon what they saw of the castle yesterday, she guessed it led to another part of the bedchamber. What more could one need? *A time machine would be nice*, she thought sarcastically. Tilly decided further exploration would be done later. For now, she would be satisfied by familiarizing herself with the current room from the comforts of a relaxing bath.

She was happy to see that the pictures on the walls were of forest scenes, not frowning ancestors. She spotted a large wardrobe that lined half of a wall. How many dresses could you fit into such a substantial piece of furniture? A gold-colored chaise lounge was placed beside the wardrobe, along with a floor-length mirror. Was dressing so stressful that the wearer needed to take a nap afterwards? She hoped not.

Tilly peered over the rim of the tub to get a better look at a small, mahogany table with an overstuffed, gold-upholstered seat underneath it. An oval mirror with petite pink roses around the frame was attached to the table. She assumed this was a dressing table, based upon the assortment of sparkling glass bottles arranged upon its surface. If she remembered correctly, the cosmetics to which she was accustomed would not exist for many more years. What could the bottles contain? Shrugging, she deduced that she must be in a dressing room.

Most importantly, she looked for the telltale signs of modern life. She did not see electrical sockets or light switches. No electric lamps, only ivory candles in silver candlesticks. No telephone. No WiFi router. No television. She could deny it as much as she liked, but all signs pointed to being trapped in 1801.

She propped her feet on the edge of the tub. She could not forget where – or should she say *when* – she was, if she had traveled back in time. Maybe it was all a dream. Maybe she was in a mental institution. Whatever the truth may be, she knew there was only one thing she could do right now. Closing her eyes, Tilly tried to enjoy a few moments of silence. Chaos would return soon enough.

# TWELVE

MRS. KEITH RETURNED TOO SOON with a pretty gown embellished with delicate, rose-colored flowers. Tilly thought the dress would look better on a younger woman. However, she knew she could not parade naked around the castle so she graciously accepted the garment.

She reluctantly submitted to the housekeeper's assistance when she climbed from the tub. While the hot bath may have soothed her aching muscles, it failed to strengthen them. She doubted that she could stand without help for days. She drew the line, though, when the woman attempted to dry her wet skin with a piece of cloth. She could handle that task on her own, thank you very much.

When she saw all the underpinnings that

accompanied the gown, she was exceedingly grateful Mrs. Keith would help her. *It must take forever to dress and undress in this century,* she thought in exasperation.

Mrs. Keith offered Tilly a pair of flesh-toned pantaloons that stopped above her knees. To her amusement, they resembled 70s-style culottes.

She recognized the next garment as a shift, a thin white muslin slip with tiny pink roses along the hem. She would like to have admired it, but there was no time for contemplation. Getting dressed in the 1800s was serious business.

"What is that?" she asked when Mrs. Keith slipped a diaphanous half shirt over her head. She watched the woman tie it closed with ivory-colored ribbons that ran down each side of the garment.

"It is a chemisette," Mrs. Keith replied. "I fear the gown may be immodest without it, milady."

She nodded, even though she had no idea what the woman meant. She remained silent while she was forced into a corset, partly because she did not want to seem ignorant and partly because she could scarcely draw breath. She thought corsets went out of fashion sometime in the 1800s. To her chagrin, she must not have travelled far enough in time for that event.

Mrs. Keith next placed the gown over her head

and seated her in the chair at the vanity table. "I confess that I have always enjoyed arranging a lady's hair," she commented, grinning broadly. She swept Tilly's hair into a very becoming up 'do.

"Now, stand up and let me see how you look," the woman said. She critically examined her charge from top to bottom. "Milady, you look very fine."

The corset gave her a buxom bosom for the first time in her life. Mrs. Keith adjusted the chemisette, making sure the plunging neckline of the gown was not too revealing. Tilly would have left it alone, so that she could admire her never-before-seen cleavage. Of course, it was improper. The last thing she wanted was to offend.

The housekeeper frowned when she stared at the hemline of the dress, which was easily three inches too short. While the shift closed some of the gap, it did not completely cover her ankles. "That will not do," Mrs. Keith mumbled as she crouched on the floor and examined the hem. She looked at the underside of the dress and shook her head.

She produced a pair of small scissors from her pocket. She deftly snipped a few threads, releasing an inch or so of fabric. Mrs. Keith tugged the hemline.

"I apologize, milady," the housekeeper said, rising from the floor. "If you please, I will take the gown from you and try to fix the hemline." She removed the garment and was halfway to the door before Tilly could register what was happening.

Tilly did not understand why it was a problem but did not protest. The woman seemed knowledgeable about proper fashion, so who was she to argue?

Realizing Mrs. Keith meant to leave the room, she asked desperately, "Could you undo my corset before you leave?"

"Does milady require further assistance?" Mrs. Keith chuckled as she freed Tilly from the constraining article.

She shook her head, blushing slightly. She wondered if she should have known how to remove her own corset. She thanked Mrs. Keith for her efforts, fully aware that the head housekeeper had more important tasks than being her personal stylist.

Mrs. Keith promised to return with the altered dress before dinner. "You must be very hungry. I will have a maid bring you a tray," she said. "Then, you may take your rest."

∞

WITHIN MOMENTS OF THE HOUSEKEEPER'S DEPARTURE, two maids appeared at her door. One maid, a girl who could not have been more than twelve, bobbed a quick curtsy and swiftly moved through the doorway leading to the adjacent room. The other maid carried a silver tray and had a robe draped over her arm. She followed the other maid into the room. Tilly watched her place the tray on a round table near the fireplace.

The senior maid returned to the dressing room and helped Tilly into the robe. "Milady, I will be happy to help you to the bedchamber if you would like to retire there," she said, gesturing toward the doorway. "I am sure the fire is prepared by now."

At that moment, Tilly was more curious than hungry. The previous bedroom seemed very elegant. She was eager to see how the main bedchamber would look, especially since the guest rooms were not part of the tour Beth and she took.

She was not disappointed. As she slowly walked into the room, she was struck by the quiet elegance of the decoration. Whoever designed this room's décor had a light touch. The pale pink wallpaper nicely complimented the oak floors. Thick brocade curtains in a rich shade of gold hung from massive windows that climbed from the floor to the ceiling. They offered a view of the dense forest through which she rode to the castle with Benjamin.

As promised, the girl built a roaring blaze in the marble fireplace opposite the bed. Since it was not quite cold enough for two fires, the hearth in the other fireplace between the windows was untouched. Tilly surmised that the lack of a modern heating system necessitated the need for as many fireplaces as a room could accommodate. She shuddered to think how cold winters would be here. She sincerely hoped she was home before she could learn firsthand.

Settling into one of the pale gold arm chairs that faced the hearth, she watched the maids work. The girl handled the menial task of sweeping away the debris from starting the fire while the other maid poured a hot cup of tea from the silver teapot.

The fireplace maid, as Tilly called her, curtsied and swiftly left. Turning her attention to the other maid, she noticed how pretty the woman was. Her blond hair was tucked into a white cap that complimented her clear skin. Large, blue eyes gazed critically around the room as the woman made sure everything was properly arranged for the comfort and ease of the castle's guest. The crisp white apron tied around her simple, navy dress accentuated her petite, hourglass figure.

If Tilly remembered correctly, it was customary to hire pretty women for the maids who dealt directly with guests. Did Benjamin personally pick this blue-eyed beauty? Did he prefer blonds? To her surprise, she felt a pang of jealousy.

"Milady?" the woman repeated, staring expectantly at her.

"I am sorry. I was lost in thought. What did you say?"

"I asked if milady requires anything further for her stay."

"No, thank you. You are free to go."

The maid curtsied and left the room. Tilly felt like such a snob. *You are free to go – what the hell was that?* she thought, shaking her head.

She turned her attention to the tray. Steam rose from the cup of tea as she poured a tiny bit of milk into it. She carefully stirred the beverage, savoring the welcoming aroma. She took a sip and almost gagged. The tea was bitter, nothing like the smooth teas to which she was accustomed.

She hastily grabbed a buttery scone from a plate on the tray and took a big bite. Its sweet goodness eliminated the harsh taste of the tea. Easily 50 grams of fat, but Tilly did not care. She was starving and consumed the scone in seconds.

Her belly full, she rose on shaky legs and stumbled toward the bed. In design, it was very similar to the one in the other room. This bed, however, was even grander, something she did not think possible. Each of its four mahogany posters were as thick as tree trunks. The bed curtains that hung on this bed were a thick, gold fabric that felt like velvet. The matching bedspread was embroidered with thousands of tiny pink roses.

She flopped ungracefully on top of the bedspread. She did not realize how exhausted she was. She closed her eyes and could feel herself sinking deeper into the fluffy, goose down pillow. In seconds, Tilly fell into a deep sleep before she could even bother pulling the covers over her body.

# THIRTEEN

BENJAMIN WAS A BUNDLE OF NERVOUS ENERGY. He paced restlessly in his study, trying to sort out the events that had happened in the last twenty-four hours.

Suddenly, the heavy oak door to the room swung wide. A burly man with a thick red beard burst into the room. "Thank God you are back!" he boomed, closing the distance between them. He pulled Benjamin into a bone-crushing embrace.

"I have not been gone *that* long, Iain," Benjamin said, gasping for air. He shoved the man away from him and frowned. "Why are you acting like a lovesick lass?"

Iain MacIver punched his friend in the shoulder and settled into a chair beside the fireplace. He had been the estate's factor for many years. It was the man's job to worry.

"I take it you have not heard the news," Iain said, handing Benjamin a piece of battered parchment that he retrieved from his coat pocket. He grabbed a scone from a tray on a nearby table and took a bite, an enormous smile of satisfaction lighting his face.

"It cannot be," Benjamin whispered as he read the message. He collapsed into a chair beside Iain and stared at the man in disbelief.

"Aye, the wily bastard died. A boy delivered the letter a few hours ago. I was about to assemble a search party before I heard you were back. I feared the worse."

"The debt was paid in full sixteen years ago."

"You believe they paid a debt owed to you," Iain replied thoughtfully. "I suspect Richard MacDonald feels *you* owe a debt to him."

"His father swore the feud was over."

"The father is gone. The son may have other designs."

"When did it happen?"

"Three weeks ago," Iain answered between bites of scone. He licked the crumbs from his fingers and deftly dusted his beard. "The weather has been fair. Richard could be here."

Iain's calculations troubled Benjamin so he shared the tale about how he found Tilly. He spared no details. The man was also his best friend and would not share the story, not that anyone would believe it. It was too incredible.

"Are you absolutely certain there were no other tracks in the field, Benjamin?" Iain asked thoughtfully.

"None. It is as if she appeared from the mist, just as she claims."

He could almost see the wheels turning in Iain's head. His friend probably worried Tilly might be a MacDonald spy. The timing of her arrival was all too convenient. Still, she did not have a Scottish accent, and her ways were so foreign. He said as much.

"Let us say nothing to the lass and watch her carefully," Iain said at last. "If she is indeed a MacDonald spy, she may reveal herself."

"What if she is not a MacDonald spy?"

"Do not forget you have other enemies besides the MacDonalds," Iain replied. "Your father is the worst of them all!"

Benjamin tossed his hands into the air. "As long as

the money continues to flow, he does not care about me."

"The man has his fingers in everything," Iain said, shaking his head. "Have you forgotten the contents of his recent letter? He means to see you married as soon as may be. You do not know who she is, so pray hold your tongue around that woman."

Something in his heart made him dare to believe that she was not a threat. He did not share the thought, realizing it was madness to trust too soon. Reluctantly, he agreed, "Aye, we will sit quietly and watch her." Taking a deep breath, he said, "Now, Iain, tell me what else has happened since I have been gone."

The factor proceeded to inform him about the mundane activities of the estate. All the while, Benjamin continued to ponder Tilly's mysterious appearance. Before he learned about the MacDonald, he was convinced she was a deeply troubled widow who invented a fantastic story to deal with the pain. Now, he could not help but wonder if the truth was far more sinister.

# FOURTEEN

TILLY WALKED TO THE WINDOW and saw her son John playing with her husband Alex in a lush garden that was filled with vibrant flowers and blooming shrubs of every color. She squinted against the bright sunshine that beamed upon them. It must be warm outside since her family wore short-sleeved shirts and shorts.

She tapped the glass to get their attention. They had better put on sunscreen. Alex got sunburns so easily. They did not hear her, though. They were too busy pretending their sticks were swords. Father and son were locked in an epic battle. *Whack, whack, whack.* The sound of each strike carried all the way through the thick walls of the castle in which she stood.

Her daughter Anna sat on a bench near her brother and father, combing the golden locks of the doll in her lap. She was too engrossed in her task to hear Tilly calling her name. The little girl smiled sweetly as she styled her doll's hair.

A handsome prince walked into the room and put his arm around her shoulders. "What are you doing?" he asked.

"Watching them," she replied, pointing to her family.

"It is not real, you know," the prince said. "None of it is real."

Tilly awoke with a start, her heart pounding. Like all of the dreams about her family, it *did* seem so real. She wiped the tears from her eyes. As the prince said, though, none of it was real. No matter how much she wanted to return to the halcyon days with her family, they were forever out of reach.

She stretched her arms high above her head and opened her eyes. Her gaze fell on the gold bed curtains. Then, turning her head, she spotted the fireplace. Her memory flooded back to her in a rush. She groaned. It seemed as if her new reality was as nightmarish as the one she left behind in the 21st century.

She slowly rose from the bed, her muscles aching

from the tortuous horseback ride. If she needed further proof of her situation, there it was. Had she suffered some sort of spinal injury? She stumbled to her feet and used the bed as support until she steadied herself. Modern transportation usually did not involve so much pain.

She managed to make her way to a window and peered outside. The idyllic scene from her dream was not there. If she pressed her face against the cool glass, she could glimpse the sun setting over the loch. It painted the sky in vibrant purples, oranges, and blues. Even in the dim light, she recognized where she was in the castle. She should be overlooking the car park. Instead, she saw the forest through which they rode earlier that day.

Tilly took a deep breath. Her friend Beth would say it was time to put on her big girl panties, figuratively, not literally. *Did they even* have *big girl panties in 1801?* she wondered.

Shaking her head, she decided musings about undergarments were not helpful to her plight. She was likely stuck here until she could figure out how to return. If she had travelled back in time, she would be in a similar period as Jane Austen's novels.

After seeing the BBC mini-series of *Pride and Prejudice* – the good one with Colin Firth – Tilly and Beth went through a Jane Austen phase. They read every book. They watched the mini-series again. And again. And again. Regrettably, Austen's books were set in the English countryside, not in Scotland. She hoped that Scottish manners were comparable so she would not embarrass herself. *What would Eliza Bennet do?*

Tilly decided Eliza would make sure her appearance was fine for dinner. She ran to the dressing room and took a seat in front of the dressing table. Studying her reflection in the mirror, she almost did not recognize the person who stared back at her. She never wore her hair that way, all swept high upon her head with little wisps dangling on the side. She tucked a few errant strands of hair in place and smoothed her eyebrows. Thankfully, her pale skin and hazel eyes looked clear even though she did not have a trace of makeup.

Satisfied that her hair and face looked presentable, Tilly examined the state of her dress. She hoped Mrs. Keith would be able to work her magic. Of course, even if the housekeeper managed to make the hemline the proper length, the style was questionable. The little pink flowers set onto a field of soft ivory were a bit daintier than her usual, somber wardrobe, which was comprised of black and grey knits. She decided that beggars cannot be choosers.

What was she to do? She did not want to draw attention to herself by acting in an unusual way. The

Austen novels were the only source material she had for the current era. Sighing, she stared at her reflection. *Think, Tilly,* she commanded herself.

As she recalled, the characters moved in a constrained world where saying or doing the wrong thing could bring disgrace upon you and your family. She certainly did not want to create trouble for her host or, to be honest, herself. What did she remember about that world?

She spread the fingers of her right hand and began to count. One, the use of a person's first name seemed to be a big deal. Was it reserved for parties with whom she had a close relationship? How long did she have to know someone before she could use the person's first name? The issue seemed so complicated. Benjamin already cautioned her so she should take his advice.

She supposed number two was to avoid any hint that she engaged in sinful behavior. It was wildly scandalous when Lydia ran away with Wickham in *Pride and Prejudice.* Tilly snorted in a very coarse manner. She did with Benjamin the very things Lydia probably did with Wickham, so she was already a wanton woman. No one else knew about it, though. She must endeavor to act as if it never happened.

Three, she should curtsy whenever she saw Benjamin. Should she address the servants that way too? The maids had curtsied to her. Was she supposed to do the same? It seemed a bit rude not to acknowledge them. She did not want to be dismissive of their presence the same way those rich snobs back home were with the wait staff in their restaurant. Should she nod? Could she address them by name? If so, which name? Their first or last name? Would Mrs. Keith's reaction be a suitable guide? Of course, the housekeeper would correct any unsuitable behavior, right?

*Moving on*, she thought. Four, women of genteel birth had no occupation, save marriage, household management, and child rearing. Days seemed to be filled with leisure, not work. This concept was completely foreign to her. How would she fill the time? Should she embroider pillows or take strolls around the garden? Actual work seemed out of the question.

Did Benjamin sit idly while his servants took up the difficult tasks? Tilly could not envision him spending his days reading books or making calls to other gentry in the area. Images of his naked body glowing in the firelight danced before her eyes. He did not get those muscles or calloused hands from leisurely pursuits.

She mentally shook herself. Now was not the time for steamy memories. What else?

Five…she hesitated. This was the most painful thing of all. Women with no connection or money did not belong in proper society. The plight of the Bennet and Dashwood daughters was most grim. They were wealthy compared to her present situation. She literally had no money or connections in 1801.

This realization was depressing. She sincerely hoped her host was a man of his word. Otherwise, she had no idea what she would do. If he did not offer her assistance, where would she go? How could she get back to the 21st century?

She shook her head. Why was she thinking so much about Benjamin? He seemed to constantly pop up in her brain. Didn't she have more important concerns right now? He probably was not thinking about *her*.

She folded her shaking hands in her lap, sitting straight. She crossed her ankles and tried to arrange her face into a demure expression. Tilly assumed this is how she must be – a tumult of emotion on the inside, a blank canvas on the outside. Glancing at her reflection in the mirror, she was pleased to see that her countenance did not betray the terror she felt.

"Milady, I have mended the gown," Mrs. Keith announced from the open doorway. "I tried my best, milady. You are a tall woman."

Tilly groaned when Mrs. Keith forced her into the corset. Then, she donned the gown and realized the woman was too modest. With a bit of lace and satin, the housekeeper managed to fashion a longer and very attractive hemline that covered her bare feet. If she did know better, she would have sworn the new hemline was part of the original design.

She sat at the dressing table and slipped on a pair of matching satin shoes. They were a bit snug but manageable. Impulsively, Tilly hugged the surprised housekeeper. "Thank you so much!" she exclaimed. "The gown is beautiful."

Mrs. Keith appeared flustered at the show of affection but smiled nonetheless, a most becoming look for her. Tilly guessed the woman was once a great beauty and did not understand why she settled for a housekeeping position. That would be a story for another day.

"Milady, if you please," Mrs. Keith said, motioning to the door. "It is time to join Mr. Campbell for the evening meal."

*Show time*, Tilly thought.

# FIFTEEN

BENJAMIN WAITED FOR TILLY outside the formal state dining room on the second floor. She was taken aback at the sight of him. The man cleaned up well.

He looked as if he too had bathed, the grime of travel removed from his brow. He had shaved the light beard that formed on his face and looked as ruggedly handsome in real life as he did in the portrait she saw during the castle tour. Tilly lowered her gaze and decided to focus on his outfit. It was dangerous to stare into his green eyes.

His coat was navy and resembled a tuxedo jacket with tails. The shirt was more formal than his previous pirate shirt, as she called it. It was crisp, white linen with a fancy knot at the neck. Benjamin wore what appeared to be a light blue vest underneath his coat. It was embroidered with tiny gold leaves. His beige pants clung to his muscular legs and stopped at the knees, where they skimmed the tops of well-polished, brown leather boots.

She was so taken by his appearance that it took a moment for her to realize he offered her his arm. Tilly was perplexed at first then pretended he was Mr. Darcy, and she was Elizabeth Bennet. She wrapped her hand around the crook of his arm and allowed him to lead her into the dining room.

As he helped her to her chair, she tried to remain calm. She sat in the same dining room where Beth took a ton of pictures during their castle tour. The crystal chandeliers she admired were now lit with a multitude of candles and looked just as beautiful as she imagined they would. Several silver candelabras that were carefully arranged on the table and sideboard provided soft light to the room.

From the gleaming silver of the candelabras to the sparkling chandeliers, Tilly was amazed at the extravagance on display. Even the tapestries looked richer. Since they were over two hundred years younger, it seemed appropriate. The scene depicted in the tapestries was easier to see without the protective layer of Plexiglas, and the colors were not muted. The vivid blues, greens, and gold practically glowed in the candlelight.

The shift from one time to another gave her a headache. She spotted a glass of wine in front of her and took a healthy gulp.

She tilted her head to the side so she could see around the candelabras. Benjamin sat at the opposite end of the long table. He was too far away for conversation and, judging from the look on his face, did not seem inclined toward it.

She surveyed the vast spread of dishes in front of her. Tilly saw more food than one would find on the brunch buffet of that fancy hotel in Asheville, the one where Beth and Randall always celebrated their wedding anniversary.

The butler, Mr. Murphy, marched into the room with three footmen. Dinner began with military-like precision when he announced the menu for the evening. The meats were a haunch of venison and a loin of pork. A variety of sauces were available for the other offerings of salmon, mutton, and chicken.

One of the three smartly-dressed footmen ladled soup from a gleaming silver tureen set in the center of the table into the most delicate bowls of china Tilly had ever seen. With great care, the footman handed the bowls to the other footmen, who ceremoniously placed them in front of Benjamin and her.

"What is it?" Tilly asked the footman. She hoped it

was not a breach in protocol to ask questions about the menu.

"Rabbit soup, milady," the servant answered with a nod.

Benjamin coughed and gingerly wiped the corner of his mouth. He barely concealed the smile on his lips. She choose to ignore him.

They ate the soup in silence. The footmen stood beside the tapestries, gazing fixedly at a spot on the wall. She found their presence unnerving.

When they finished with the soup, the bowls and tureen were whisked away under the watchful eye of Mr. Murphy. He supervised the pouring of the next varietal of wine, ensuring that not a drop touched the white table cloth.

He instructed the footmen to serve the fish and complimented milord at the choice of accompanying sauce. He scowled at the men if they were too slow in bringing a serving of whatever morsel his liege desired. With so many bowls and plates of food spread across the table, Tilly need only glance at a dish, and Mr. Murphy made sure someone promptly brought it to her plate.

The rest of the meal was a blur. She could not relax and enjoy the food under the dull look of the footmen or withering gaze of the butler. She nibbled at the endless offerings, wondering how someone did not gain lots of weight from eating so much food this late in the evening. Judging from the darkness outside, it had to be at least eight o'clock.

She had no problems with the delicious wine, though, drinking more than she should. She noticed that Benjamin drank small amounts from each glass and did not drain his as she did. She should follow his example but found it difficult to do at that moment.

When the footmen cleared the table, she thought the meal was over. She groaned inwardly when they returned with more food. This time, they brought trays of cheese and salad. It was delicious, but she was near the point of bursting. The previous dishes were so rich, unlike her usual diet. They weighed heavily in her stomach. *Do they have antacids in this time?* she thought, putting down her fork.

The table was cleared again. The footmen delivered another round of savory dishes. They looked expectantly at her, ready to dole out whatever she liked upon her plate. She dared a glance down the long table at her host.

Benjamin ate his food in silence. She was somewhat annoyed that he did not bother to make small talk or even look at her. And, Tilly observed that he did not seem to suffer the ill effects of too many entrees. In fact, he seemed to be enjoying the meal.

*Well, I cannot eat another bite,* she decided. She placed her napkin upon the table and rose from her chair, surprising the footmen. They exchanged a worried glance. Would Mr. Murphy be angry with them? She hoped not.

"Mr. Campbell, I thank you very much for your great hospitality," Tilly said, moving away from the table. "I fear my travels have made me most weary. I shall retire for the evening."

She attempted a weak curtsy and moved toward the door. She would have hurried back to her room but heard Benjamin walking behind her. She paused.

He took her by the elbow and led her into the hallway. In hushed tones, Benjamin asked, "May I speak with you privately? I can come to your receiving room in an hour."

At her nod, he said in a louder voice, "I am sorry to hear you are tired from your journey. Please have a pleasant rest, madam." He bowed deeply and returned to finish the meal.

∞

ONCE TILLY WAS IN HER ROOM, she pulled the pins from her hair and let it cascade down her back. She was curious about why Benjamin wanted to speak with her. He seemed so distant during dinner.

She could not ponder the matter further, for a maid knocked on her door. The servant was not the blue-eyed beauty who attended her earlier. This woman – or girl, to be more precise – was fair in complexion with dark brown eyes and hair. She kept her head down and spoke so softly that Tilly repeatedly asked her what she said.

It seemed a lady expected a maid to attend her when she prepared for bed. The girl was sent to help. Tilly ruefully admitted she had no idea how she was supposed to remove a corset without assistance.

Once in the dressing room, the maid disassembled Tilly in far less time than it would have taken by herself. She was happy when the girl presented her with a comfortable night gown. *At least the bed clothes are not confining*, she thought, slipping the garment over her head.

She thanked the maid for her help and once again felt a bit elitist. She never had servants. It felt wrong not to thank them at the very minimum. It felt stranger still when the maid curtsied as she exited the room. She did not feel worthy of a curtsy.

Shaking her head, she understood how ignorant she was about the ways of this age. Of course, she did not plan to be in 1801 long enough to learn any lessons.

∞

SOMETIME LATER, BENJAMIN KNOCKED UPON TILLY'S DOOR. She warily cracked open the door, then broke into a relieved smile upon seeing him.

"I apologize for intruding upon your evening," he said. Seeing her bedclothes, he blushed slightly. "I wanted to speak with you but see you have already prepared for bed. Please forgive me, madam."

Tilly rolled her eyes. She grabbed his arm and pulled him into the room. She locked the door, fearing another maid would appear to tuck her into bed and read her a bedtime story. "Propriety be damned," she said in frustration. "After all, it is your house. You should be able to do whatever you want."

It was clear from the expression on his face that he wanted to protest, but, to her relief, he did not. She motioned for him to join her in one of the chairs beside the fireplace.

"I would prefer it if you called me by my Christian name, if that's how you say it," she said. She held up her hands. "I know it is not proper, but can we dispense with the formalities in private?"

Benjamin nodded, a sly smile tugging on his lips.

"Given our history, it seems fitting," he said. He took a seat by the fireplace and stretched his long legs toward the fire. Undoing the knot around his neck, he sighed with pleasure.

"Mrs. Munro – Tilly," he said. "I am sorry we could not speak freely during our meal. The servants are always a concern, particularly Mr. Murphy."

She sat in a chair opposite him. "Why is Mr. Murphy a concern?" she asked, curious.

He seemed to struggle for the right response, which seemed odd to her. Benjamin finally relented and answered honestly, "He was hired by my father. He reports everything that happens in this castle to the man. I must be careful about what I say in front of him."

Tilly was surprised. She assumed everyone in the castle was loyal to the "laird." She said as much.

"We do not use that term anymore," he said, chuckling. "However, if we did, that title would have belonged to my brother Allan. I am the second son. I was never meant to be the manager of the estate."

She knew in the old days...or rather, *present*... the first son inherited everything, leaving the rest of the children to find their way in life. "What were you supposed to do?" she asked.

"I planned to be a soldier. Then, my brother died. My plans changed."

"How did he die?"

A shadow fell upon Benjamin's face. "He was murdered by the MacDonalds," he said. "It is an infamous affair. I am surprised you are unaware of it."

"How would I know?" she asked defensively. "I told you that I am not of this time. It certainly was not mentioned during the tour."

"What tour?" he asked suspiciously, his eyes narrowing. "Have you been in my home before this day?"

"Yes, I have. The castle is a tourist attraction in my time," she said. She smiled at a memory. "Beth was so excited to see it. We were fortunate that the former groundskeeper, Mr. Douglas, gave us a personal tour. We saw all sorts of interesting things the general public could not see."

"Such as?"

"Well, not all of the rooms are available for viewing."

"No, they are not."

"What?" she asked, cocking an eyebrow. Tilly had a feeling Benjamin was not pleased about her prior visit but did not understand why.

"Pray, forgive my interruption," he said, waving his hand. "What did you see during your tour?"

"Well, we saw a few rooms. The ones that impressed me the most were the guest library and state bedchamber," she said. Tilly paused, noting the serious expression upon his face. "Are you alright, Benjamin?"

"Aye, I am well," he said distractedly. He leaned forward. "You saw the state bedchamber? No one is allowed access to that chamber."

"Maybe no one can visit *now*. It has been fully restored in my time, so it is an important area of the castle."

Suddenly, she remembered something from the tour. "Oh, and what is up with your father's bed?" Tilly asked. "That is the gaudiest thing I have ever seen!"

He stared at her for some time before he spoke. "You saw my father's bed?" he asked. "Is that how you came to be here?"

"What?!" she exclaimed in disbelief. "What the hell are you saying?" She had an inkling that he implied something unflattering yet wanted to hear the words from his mouth.

"I find the situation fascinating," Benjamin said, leaning back in the chair and tenting his fingers in front of his face. "You are a strange woman who appeared in the middle of the night. You claim no connection to 'this time,' as you say. You wore unusual clothes when I found you. And, now you tell me that you know the look of my father's bed, even though his room is only seen by intimate relations. How extraordinary!"

Tilly rose from her chair and angrily tossed another log on the fire. She grasped the poker in her hand, prodding the logs and sending orange sparks into the flue. She allowed the tears to tumble unchecked down her cheeks. "I know you do not believe me," she sobbed. "I really am from the future. I know these things because it was all part of the tour."

She turned to face him, unconsciously clenching the poker. "I swear to you that I am nothing more than a lost person," she said. "As soon as I can figure out how to leave this place, I will."

Benjamin joined her beside the fireplace. He carefully took the poker from her hand and returned it to the stand. "I am sorry that I made you cry, Tilly," he said, brushing the tears from her cheeks.

She shrugged and tried to turn away from him. He placed a gentle hand on her cheek and forced her to look at him. "I am truly sorry," he said. "Rest assured, you are welcome to stay here as long as you need."

It was annoying the way he said "as long as you need," as if she had a choice in the matter. She fumed over his remark.

He must have mistook her silence for melancholy. "You must be thinking about your family," he said. "I miss my dear Mary so much sometimes that I can hardly breathe. I think about her all the time."

She met his gaze. Despite the confusion she felt about her present situation, she could not ignore the fact that they both suffered recent loss. "I do, very much," Tilly whispered. "It feels as if a giant hole has opened in my chest. I don't know if anything will ever fill it."

Despite her better judgment, she wrapped her arms around him. She felt such comfort whenever he held her. She pressed her face against the rough linen of his shirt and asked, "Does the pain ever go away?"

He stroked her back and held her close to him, saying, "I am told it will." With a humorless chuckle, Benjamin added, "It certainly does not feel that way. Why do people fall in love when its loss is so devastating?"

She had no answer for him. Instead, she held him tighter.

They stood that way for many minutes, drawing comfort and strength from each other. Whatever the circumstances of their meeting, they both ached. In each other's arms, perhaps they could enjoy a brief respite from the pain.

It eventually became apparent, though, that the close proximity called to mind memories of their torrid first meeting. Tilly felt a growing heat that had nothing to do with the fire by which they stood. And, she could tell that he felt it too. Reluctantly, they pulled away from each other. Benjamin pressed her hand against his lips, bade her good night, and slipped from the room.

Once again, she was left with the sensation that it was all a dream. She fervently hoped she would awake tomorrow to find herself in her comfy bed at Mrs. Douglas' inn. And yet…Tilly wished he had kissed her goodnight on the lips, not her hand.

∞

MRS. KEITH RUBBED HER ACHING NECK as she strode by the kitchen in the basement of the castle. She waved at the cook who grunted a greeting and returned to punching the unyielding bread dough. It had been a long, strange day.

She checked the lock on the door to the hallway leading to the maids' rooms. They were threatened with death if they did not keep that door locked, so she was happy to find that the women compiled. The last thing she needed was a pregnant servant.

The housekeeper unlocked the door to the hallway that led to her own suite. She shared the area with Mr. Murphy, the butler. Their section of the basement was quite spacious and comfortable, a nod to their elevated rank among the other servants. They each had an office and private bedchamber, in addition to a shared receiving room. It was the most luxurious arrangement she had ever had in her many years of service, and she was most grateful for it.

Naturally, the wine, spirits, china, and silver were kept in rooms along their private hallway. His Grace considered the contents to be too precious, so they were kept well away from the sticky fingers of unscrupulous staff. As Mrs. Keith walked past the wine and spirit room, she noticed the door was open. Peering inside, she found Mr. Murphy taking inventory of the wine supply. "How are you this evening, sir?" she asked courteously.

The butler frowned, placing a bottle of wine on the shelf. He lifted the candlestick from its resting place on a small, round table and moved toward the door. "I am most agitated, madam," he replied. He closed the door and locked it.

They moved toward the receiving room. "Milord

asked you to attend our visitor," Mr. Murphy said, opening the door and gesturing for her to enter. "What can you tell me about her?"

Mrs. Keith took her usual seat in a simple wooden chair beside the fireplace. She stretched her weary hands toward the fire and sighed contentedly as the heat eased the ache in her bones. "We did not converse beyond the usual civilities," she answered. "She seems to be a pleasant woman."

Mr. Murphy placed the candlestick on the mantel and shook his head. "I do not like it," he said. "Did you notice her peculiar appearance when she arrived? It was thoroughly disreputable."

Guests would not enjoy the butler's esteem unless they arrived in a splendid carriage and were members of the peerage. Despite his own lower rank, Mr. Murphy believed himself superior to most people. It was why the servants resented him so much. "It is not for us to cast dispersions upon any guest milord brings to Castle Fion," Mrs. Keith said tactfully. "I am sure all will be explained in due time."

"His Grace would not approve," the butler said, snorting derisively. "Let us hope her visit will be of short duration."

Mrs. Keith stared at the man and listened as he continued to grumble. The butler was a spy for His Grace, Malcolm Campbell; everyone knew it. For

Mrs. Munro's sake, she hoped he was right about the length of the visit. It was best not to make an enemy of Mr. Murphy or His Grace.

# SIXTEEN

TILLY WAS STARTLED to find that she had overslept. Even after the accident that took her family from her, she could not bring herself to sleep late. A habit was already formed. She spent too many years with the alarm always blaring too early every morning. If she didn't get a jump on the day, how would she prepare everyone for theirs? Her children John and Anna must go to school. Her husband Alex often left early in the morning so that he could meet with his staff. Those few precious moments before the rest of the house awakened were her only opportunity to enjoy a little peace.

She stretched in the bed before tossing back the bedspread. She tugged at the bed curtains that had successfully blocked the morning sun and probably contributed to her deep sleep. Squinting against the sudden appearance of light, she looked around the room and noticed that the same maid who attended her the previous evening stood silently in the doorway.

Upon seeing that Tilly was awake, the girl curtsied and strode to the bed, robe in hand. If she needed any reminder of her new reality, being greeted by a servant gave it to her. Lately, back home, she began each morning in the empty bed of an empty house.

Pushing that devastating thought out of her mind, she reluctantly allowed the girl to help her into the robe and guide her to the dressing room. She noticed that a warm blaze was already prepared in the room's fireplace.

Since it appeared the young girl was assigned the task of helping her, she thought it was rude not to know the girl's name.

"I am Sarah Poole, milady," the maid responded to Tilly's query, her eyes downcast.

She tilted the maid's chin upward so that Sarah was forced to look her in the eyes. "Your face is too lovely to hide," she said, smiling warmly. Her compliment brought a blush to the girl's cheeks. She guessed Sarah was from England but was not familiar enough with accents to know from which part.

The maid was a pretty girl of maybe fifteen or

sixteen years of age. Her dark brown hair and eyes were a sharp contrast to her porcelain skin. To some, she may have appeared mousy. Sarah's smile made her eyes sparkle, and the little dimples in her cheeks were most becoming. Tilly imagined all the male servants must be infatuated with the shy girl.

Sarah interrupted her thoughts. "If it pleases milady, I can help her prepare for the day," she offered.

Unfortunately, she needed all the help she could get. She had no clue how she was supposed to don the many layers of clothing without assistance. Also, what kind of hairstyle was considered proper? Ponytails were probably inappropriate.

Sarah helped Tilly into the same dress she wore the day before, since she possessed no other garments. Taking a seat at the dressing table, she stared into the mirror and watched Sarah arrange her hair into a very becoming chignon.

When the maid finished, Tilly admired her reflection. "You are amazing," she said. "Where did you learn to do that?"

"Our mistress' maid was from France," Sarah said. "I reminded her of her little sister, so she was kind to me and taught me things. I have always dreamt of being a lady's maid one day."

Tilly recalled reading somewhere that the lady's maid was in the upper echelon of servants. "Where is the lady's maid now?" she asked.

"She left when our poor mistress passed," Sarah replied sadly. Apparently, Benjamin's wife Mary was beloved by others besides her husband.

"What do you do then?"

"I am a housemaid, although I have been asked to attend you," she said. Suddenly, she looked guilty. Was the maid asked to do more than assist her with dressing or hair styling?

She let it pass. To her surprise, she was starving. While the extravagant spread the previous evening left her stomach bulging, it was the only substantial meal she had that day. She asked Sarah if she might have a bite to eat. The maid seemed flustered, as if she had forgotten something important.

Tilly was escorted to a breakfast room down a short hallway near her suite. It was at least half the size and less formal than the state dining room, to her delight. Arched windows along one wall allowed the morning sun to flood the room with bright sunlight. A cozy fire burned in the fireplace. The sage green walls complimented the rich wood of a rectangular dining table that seated a smaller party of eight. Only one portrait hung in the room, a nice landscape scene that dominated an entire wall. She had grown weary of the scowling visages of deceased Campbells that typically decorated the rooms.

She was surprised to see that she would dine alone. Sarah told her Benjamin frequently dined at dawn and was immediately off to attend matters as lord of the estate.

The meal was less elaborate than the multi-course affair of the previous evening. One footman arrived, delivering a modest meal of bitter tea and an assortment of fresh bread and rolls. As she nibbled the food, she longed for bacon and eggs. It was mid-morning, though. Perhaps heartier fare was served earlier if she had awakened at a normal hour.

Her thoughts drifted to Benjamin. Did he have a large breakfast before he left to attend the needs of his tenants? She shook her head. He should be the last of her concerns right now.

After she ate breakfast, she had no idea what to do. Finding herself without any occupation at all was just as unsettling in 1801 as it was in her own time.

Sarah returned and offered to give a tour. Tilly readily agreed. Since her previous tour was limited to the few rooms that were restored, she was eager to see the house in all its 19th century glory. She felt a sense of déjà vu when the maid guided her around the second floor.

Just as she was in her own time, she was in awe of the grandeur. Sarah first showed her the drawing rooms in which ladies and gentlemen separately retired after dinner. Each sex had a small room located near the state dining room that provided convenient spots for après dinner refreshment. Furnished identically in ornate, gilded pieces, the rooms did not seem comfortable at all. She could not imagine sitting for long periods in the stiff chairs or relaxing on the chaises by the fire. *Give me a flat-screen TV, a cushy sofa, and a bowl of popcorn any day,* she thought wryly as they exited the rooms.

Guests could also entertain themselves in the adjoining music room, where a pianoforte and harp could be used by the refined ladies of the day. The room had an airy look with its soft green walls and white crown molding. Tilly admired the celestial scene painted onto the ceiling. Rosy-cheeked cherubs played flutes and harps while a heavenly angel choir sang. It lifted her spirits and made her wish she knew how to play an instrument.

She immediately smelled tobacco upon entering the adjacent gentlemen's billiard room. Deep burgundy-colored walls and heavy navy-colored drapes of rich velvet lent a distinctly masculine feel to the room. A massive billiard table sat in the center of the room, with four leather chairs arranged in a ring around the fireplace.

Pointing to low-slung mahogany table in front of the chairs, Sarah said, "The gentlemen usually have a glass of whisky here and discuss the goings on of the day. It is a good place to entertain male guests."

Sarah guided her from the entertainment rooms to a long hallway. Placing her hand on a wooden door, she said, "Eight guest rooms are located here. Usually, the single men in a party stay in this area." She took a few steps forward and pointed to another door. "We have another hallway of rooms where the single ladies may stay. That door has a lock so the ladies can feel safe."

She waved her hand toward the end of the hallway, where Tilly spotted the door to the state apartment. Sarah shook her head and informed her that no one would dare enter the room. "It is for the king," she whispered. "Only Mr. Murphy and Mrs. Keith are allowed in those chambers. They keep the rooms clean for His Majesty, should he ever wish to visit us."

They returned to the front of the house and crossed the hallway opposite the grand staircase. Sarah indicated that, in addition to Tilly's room, there were seven other suites of rooms for guests down the same hallway.

"Why are there so many rooms in each suite?" Tilly asked. "It seems like a huge waste of space for one person."

"It was Mr. Malcolm Campbell's design – His Grace, that is," she clarified. "He wanted the rooms to be used by married couples or single persons of distinction. The first room is a receiving room for visitors. The next room is the lady's bedchamber, or it may be used by a personal attendant, if her ladyship desires. Then, you have a dressing room. We could rearrange that room into a private sitting room for the gentleman and his wife, if they prefer. The last room is the main bed chamber. The gentleman usually sleeps there, although we have had some married couples who prefer to sleep together," Sarah blushed.

Was it scandalous for a husband and wife to share the same bed? "So, the married couple does not always sleep together?" Tilly asked.

Sarah laughed. "Not always." She added in hushed tones, "I heard His Grace once brought a couple here who refused to share a suite. The lady stayed in a suite on one end of the hall. The gentleman stayed in a suite at the opposite end!"

"You said the suites were also used by single persons of distinction," Tilly said, recalling something that Sarah mentioned. "What does that mean?"

"Do you remember the hallway of rooms with the locked door?" the maid asked. At Tilly's nod, she continued, "Usually, single ladies stay there if they do not possess a title or fortune. His Grace intended the suites to be used by persons of noble birth." Sarah tilted her head to the side. "If I may be so bold, milady does not sound English. Are you from an important family in a foreign land?"

She keenly felt the honor Benjamin bestowed upon her by placing her in a suite called the Rose Room, yet she had no desire to discuss it with the inquisitive girl. Clearing her throat, she was uncertain how to reply. She glanced up and noticed that they stood in front of the door to what she hoped was the library. "What room is this?" she asked, desperate to change the subject.

Sarah swung open the door to reveal a room filled with light. With a smile, she beckoned Tilly to follow her.

"It is wonderful!" Tilly exclaimed. The oak shelves were stuffed with books. It seemed that the family had not yet sold selected volumes to raise needed funds. As Mr. Douglas indicated during the tour, that unfortunate event would happen in the future. For now, the collection was intact.

She strode into a room that was arranged for reading and relaxation. When she toured the castle in the 21$^{st}$ century, it had a few tables and a chaise lounge or two. It was arranged for presentation. In this time, though, the guests were expected to enjoy the room so chairs were assembled around the fireplace. Chaise lounges lined the walls underneath the windows. Two tall tables stood in the center of the room, in case a guest wanted to closely examine any of the books proudly displayed upon the shelves. Tilly was in heaven.

"Can you read, milady?" Sarah asked.

"Yes. Can you?" Tilly inquired. She turned to see that Sarah's face had turned a shade of crimson. "What's the matter?"

"It is not your concern. Would it please milady to spend some time in the library?"

"Yes, very much."

Sarah seemed relieved. "I will leave you alone to enjoy the room then," she said.

She smiled and sent the maid on her way. Like Mrs. Keith, Sarah probably had other tasks besides babysitting her.

It did not escape her notice that the tour was restricted to the second floor. Mr. Douglas said the family used the first floor. If that was true, it was probably off limits to a guest like her.

"A guest like me...." Tilly said aloud. She suspected she was the first time traveler to walk the halls. She hoped her stay would be short.

∞

ENJOYING HER SOLITUDE, Tilly strolled around the library. She itched to open every book. She could only imagine what fantastic treasures lay on the shelves.

She selected a book and walked toward one of the chaises by the windows. She faced the front of the castle, which offered her an impressive view of the gravel-lined entrance that was flanked by majestic oaks. The view was wonderful, no matter the century in which it was seen. No wonder guests were impressed by the majesty of the castle. Surely, the approach captured the fancy of many a visiting noble.

Sighing with pleasure, she decided to open the book – and then promptly shut it. She closed her eyes. *This cannot be*, Tilly thought.

She opened her eyes and the book. With great care, she turned the first few pages. Yes, it was true. The book was a first edition from Robert Burns. It was the same book she saw in the 21st century, except now the pages were white and uncut. The cover of the book was light blue, not the dull, weathered grey from the modern day.

*Well, in 1801, the book is relatively new,* Tilly scolded herself. She glanced at the first page and saw the autograph, though she needed no further confirmation of its authenticity.

She tried to read a few pages but struggled with the text. She was unfamiliar with the flow of the language and guessed some parts might be in Gaelic. Even if she was fluent in that language, she doubted it would have mattered.

Her mind reeled at the dramatic shift in time. How could it be that she held the <u>same</u> book? The pages were untarnished by time, unlike its future, ragged self. She eventually gave up and returned the book to its home on the shelf.

She heard a faint noise behind her. Turning, Tilly discovered she had an audience. A little boy with fiery red hair and piercing blue eyes peeked from the hallway. He smiled at her, revealing a set of adorable dimples in his chubby cheeks.

She returned the smile. She noticed he carried a small book. "Would you like me to read to you?" she asked.

The little boy nodded and emerged from his hiding place. He walked into the room, clearly wary. He clumsily pulled himself onto one of the chaises and patted a spot beside him. Grinning broadly, he offered the book to her.

She happily joined him. He leaned close to her so that he could get a better look at the book. "What is your name?" she asked.

"Stephen," he replied softly. Now that he was closer to her, she noticed the gap in his upper teeth. Did the tooth fall out naturally, or was knocked out by another child?

"It is nice to meet you, Stephen," she said, throwing caution to the wind and using his first name. "My name is Tilly."

"Silly?" Stephen asked, grinning wickedly.

She laughed. "No, *Tilly* – with a T," she said.

The little boy giggled and pointed to the book. "We look?" he asked.

She nodded. She discovered it was a picture book that told the story of a great knight. The illustration was remarkable. The artist who drew the pictures captured every detail in the richest colors she had ever seen. Tilly watched while he studied each picture. The book was obviously a favorite.

The last page showed the brave knight riding off with the beautiful, fair maiden. Stephen pointed to the flame-haired woman and exclaimed, "Mama!"

Tilly felt a lump form in her throat as she drew him into a hug. He smelled so good – of green grass, dirt…little boy things. She had almost forgotten that sweet smell. Her heart broke a little. Memories of her beloved John and Anna rushed forward, deepening the ache in her chest. How many times had she read stories to her children while she held them close?

She heard someone call his name. She noticed the guilty look upon his face and suspected he slipped away from his keeper. Stephen slid from the chaise and grabbed the book from her lap. He dashed toward the door, then stopped abruptly. He spun around and offered her a most courtly bow. "Thank you, milady," he said, flashing a huge smile before running away.

She chuckled at his precociousness. Benjamin said he had five children, four boys and a baby girl. Was Stephen one of his children? She did not notice a resemblance in coloring. That mischievous smile reminded her of his father, though.

Shaking her head, she strode to the bookshelves and scanned the titles. While a happy moment, the little boy's visit was a distraction from what should be her real purpose. Her mother always told her, if she did not know the answer to something, she should search for it in a book.

She removed whatever science books she could

find and placed them on a table. She did not expect to find a practical guide to the use of wormholes. That would truly be a revelation. It was improbable that the books held some secret to her situation. However, she desperately wanted to find *something*, *anything* that could be useful in explaining what happened to her.

She had no other ideas but knew one thing for certain: she must find a way home. *After all, that's what you were supposed to do, right?* Tilly asked herself. She hastily pushed aside the thought that no family anxiously awaited her return since she was just as alone in this world as she was in her own.

# SEVENTEEN

AFTER SEVERAL HOURS, Tilly succeeded in covering her hands with the dust and dirt that had accumulated in what must be a little-used library. The elegant hairstyle was long gone, replaced by her usual disheveled look. Her nose and eyes were red from repeated sneezes from the decades' old accumulation of dust on the books and shelves. It was in this state that Mrs. Keith found her.

"Mrs. Munro!" the housekeeper exclaimed upon seeing her blackened hands. "What have you done?"

"I wanted to read the books," she said. "The library is very impressive."

"Well, 'tis a sad thing how filthy this library has become," Mrs. Keith said. She shook her head. "I shall have some maids thoroughly clean it. In the meantime, we should get you tidied up. You are a fright!"

Mrs. Keith ushered her to her room. As she scrubbed Tilly's hands and face with jasmine-scented soap and water from the basin in the dressing room, the housekeeper said, "I am most sorry, Mrs. Munro."

"Oh, it is all right," Tilly replied, drying herself with the proffered towel. She assumed Mrs. Keith was embarrassed by the dust. "It must be a daunting task to maintain the household."

"Oh, aye, but I was referring to your loss," Mrs. Keith said patiently. She plucked at the sleeve of Tilly's gown. "I wish you would have told me. I could have searched for a more suitable gown. Rest assured, we will have something more appropriate for you before the meal this evening."

Tilly was thoroughly confused but simply nodded her head. For the first time, she noticed a black shawl draped across one of the chairs beside the fireplace.

Mrs. Keith followed her gaze. She strode across the room and returned with the garment, delicately placing it upon Tilly's shoulders. "We women bear great burdens," she said. "We can always handle them better than men, aye?"

"Thank you for your kindness."

The housekeeper nodded. She glanced at a little watch that dangled from a gold chain attached to her leather belt. "Shall I send up a tray for you?" she asked.

"Yes, thank you."

With that, the woman scurried from the room. If Mrs. Keith knew the tale Benjamin and she crafted in the forest, Tilly speculated that the other servants were privy to it too. She would know soon enough, for the looks were all too familiar. People would murmur apologies, then look away. Hopefully, people would not be as bold as they were in her time, always asking prying questions.

She chuckled softly. Tilly would not mind it, though, if someone would bring a nice chicken casserole and some peach cobbler.

∞

INSTEAD OF PEACH COBBLER, Sarah appeared with a tray of dainty sandwiches and a dull grey dress. Before Tilly could sample the food, the maid slipped her into the new garment. Sarah fussed at the hem just as Mrs. Keith did the previous evening. Shaking her head, she pulled the dress over Tilly's head in a flash and set to work fixing the gown.

Thankfully, a cup of ale was provided instead of the bitter tea. She was no great fan of ale, but it was far more appealing than the unpleasant tea. She nibbled on a cold ham sandwich and surveyed the tray of food. The selection was small. At this rate, she would easily drop ten pounds in a week. Apparently, ladies in this era were not expected to have appetites.

Sarah worked silently beside the fireplace while she made the necessary adjustments to the gown. After about an hour, she managed to produce a garment deemed worthy of wear. She helped Tilly into the dress. Placing the black shawl around her mistress' shoulders, she proclaimed her to be presentable.

The maid took the empty plate of sandwiches and cup of ale, heading for the door. "Please take your rest here until the meal," she said. "Someone will fetch you."

As she watched Sarah leave, she realized the maid's request was more of a command. "Don't go wandering around the castle," she said aloud. "We don't know if we can trust you yet."

Tilly shook her head and made her way to the bedchamber. With nothing else to do, she may as well take a nap.

∞

THAT EVENING'S DINNER proved to be much livelier than the previous one. When Tilly walked toward the entrance to the dining room, she saw

Benjamin speaking with a brawny man. He was the personification of the stereotypical Scotsman. He stood head to head with Benjamin, who was a tall man himself. His thick, red, wavy hair fell unchecked to shoulders. He had obviously attempted – and failed - to tame the wild beard sprouting from his face. In further efforts at domestication, he managed to squeeze into a navy jacket that probably belonged to his liege. His simple tan trousers were clean and reached to his simple brown shoes. They were not the elegant knee britches that Benjamin wore. He looked very uncomfortable in the attire.

When they saw Tilly approach, both men stopped talking. Benjamin turned to his friend and said, "Mrs. Munro, please allow me to introduce you to my factor, Mr. Iain MacIver."

She attempted a clumsy curtsy. He offered an equally awkward bow. The social graces observed, the party walked into the dining room.

Benjamin helped Tilly with her chair. He looked startled when Iain took a seat to her left. He sighed and took a chair beside the factor.

Mr. Murphy seemed most put out by the change in seating arrangements. The butler scurried to the opposite end of the table. Along with the three footmen, he gathered the china and silverware for both men. He apologized profusely for inconveniencing Mr. Campbell. Benjamin waved a hand in dismissal after the new settings were placed in front of Iain and him.

"Mr. Campbell tells me you were beset by great troubles during your travels," Iain said, placing the linen napkin in his lap. "I am surprised to find you so far from Edinburgh. Most people do not venture this way without a purpose."

She decided to stick to the story upon which Benjamin and she agreed. "We were in Glasgow, not Edinburgh," she said. "My husband wanted to see the countryside. I fear our guide took us farther than we intended."

"Oh, you have a husband?" Iain asked, feigning surprise. "Of course, you do! Where is my mind? Mr. Campbell addressed you as 'Mrs. Munro,' after all."

"I *had* a husband," Tilly said, looking him in the eye. "He is dead."

Iain murmured condolences. She nodded her head and glanced sideways at the servants. She could tell Mr. Murphy was very interested in the conversation. Apparently, only Mrs. Keith was aware of her story until that moment.

"I fear everyone in your party met an untimely end," Benjamin interjected. "Robbery seemed to be the motive. The evidence would suggest it."

She pretended to be upset by the news. "I wish I stayed behind with them when the attack occurred," she murmured. For dramatic effect, she placed a trembling hand upon her chest and said, "It vexes me greatly to think about how they must have suffered."

She swallowed hard, remembering the car crash that killed her family. She often prayed her family *had not* suffered. Suddenly, the little ruse did not seem like a fun game anymore. Lowering her head, Tilly whispered, "Can we please change the subject?"

Iain glanced at Benjamin, cocking an eyebrow. She noticed a subtle shake of his friend's head quelled a comment that obviously formed on the factor's lips. Did he intend to press the matter?

"Your accent is strange, if I may be so bold as to say," Iain remarked. "You cannot be from Scotland."

"No. I am from America," she said. Did he know where she meant?

"Ahh, I have a cousin who fought against the English in their little war over there," Iain said. "I believe he lives in Philadelphia now."

She was thankful that Mr. Murphy and the footmen interrupted them. As the food and wine were served, she was spared from further conversation. Iain was a man of hearty appetite. His attention turned away from her and toward the feast that spread before them over many courses. Tilly marveled at the quantity of food the man ate. It was as if his stomach was a bottomless pit.

Unlike Iain, her stomach was confined by a corset and layers of clothes. She took a lesson from last night's meal and choose to nibble the wide array of dishes. She had no desire to experience another evening of gastrointestinal agony.

She also had no desire for Iain to resume his interrogation. When the dessert was served, she decided to excuse herself and retreat to her rooms. The conversation may have been for the servants' benefit, but she worried that they tread on dangerous ground. She did not want to contradict anything Benjamin told Iain or anyone else, for that matter. And, she definitely did not want to give Iain any reason to be suspicious of her. Something about the way he looked at her revealed that he was very protective of Benjamin and his family.

"Oh what a twisted, tangled web we weave," Tilly muttered to herself.

# EIGHTEEN

BENJAMIN AND IAIN RETIRED TO THE GENTLEMEN'S DRAWING ROOM. The servants already prepared a cozy blaze for them. They took chairs near the fireplace and sipped whisky in silence, each lost in his own thoughts.

"That was an interesting evening," Iain remarked, shattering the quiet. "Mrs. Munro is a peculiar woman. I am not convinced she speaks the truth about traveling through time, though."

"It is beyond all comprehension. And yet..." Benjamin paused. While he found her remarks about touring the castle and seeing his father's bed to be most alarming, no one could feign the deep grief he saw in her eyes. Whoever she was, she definitely was a widow and an anguished mother. He knew the look well, for he saw it on his own face every time he gazed into the looking glass.

"Surely, you do not find yourself believing her?" Iain asked, incredulous. "It is madness!"

Benjamin ran a tired hand through his hair. "I do not know what to believe," he replied. He was exhausted from thinking about the matter. "She speaks in a strange accent. Her manners are not those of someone raised in society, yet she is not displeasing. She is…unusual."

He rose from his chair to refill his glass. He decided to change the subject. "Thank you for the little performance," he said. "I know it was for Mr. Murphy's benefit, but I appreciate it nonetheless."

"That old geezer would have nosed around 'til he learned the story," Iain said, with a shrug. "Better to give him our version."

Benjamin returned to his chair and stared at the liquid in his glass. He sighed, "Pray he does not contact my father."

"He will – eventually," Iain said. "The man is wily. Before he alerts His Grace, Mr. Murphy will make sure there is just cause. He would not risk incurring your father's ire for someone who will not be here long."

Benjamin said nothing so Iain asked in disbelief, "Do you intend to let the woman stay?" Shaking his head, he said, "You must send her away as soon as can be. You have no idea about her intentions. For all you know, she could be working with Richard MacDonald."

"I do not think she is a spy for the MacDonald," Benjamin said. He held up his hand to stop the factor's protest. "But, I am not convinced she is innocent. She may work for my father. You saw the letter. Could he have sent her to watch me? The man means for me to marry – what was it he said – *the right prospect*. He would not want me to run away with the governess."

"If Mrs. Donnelly had her way, you would!" Iain laughed heartily.

"Aye, it would serve the man right," Benjamin said, grinning broadly. "After all, it was his idea to employ her. He would be shocked about what happened."

Turning serious again, he leaned forward and said, "While Mrs. Donnelly made her desires very clear, I do not know what Mrs. Munro's intentions are. She could be innocent. Her mind could have created a bizarre tale so she can deal with the loss of her family. You saw how disturbed she became when we talked about her husband's death. I do not believe you can pretend to have that kind of pain."

Looking down, he added, "She told me she lost her children as well. I know how a mother looks whenever she speaks of her children. I see it in Mrs. Munro's eyes. She could be attempting to escape some extraordinary loss, not perform a task assigned to her by my father or Richard MacDonald."

"I am worried about you," Iain said. "You have been lonely since Mary's passing." Before his friend could disagree, he said, "I understand. It was sudden and devastating. Please do not settle your affections on Mrs. Munro merely because she fills a void. If she is working for your father, you must be on your guard. You have accomplished so much since the man left. You do not want it to be undone."

"I am reminded on a daily basis of all the work I have done, and that is yet to be done," Benjamin said indignantly. "Do you have any idea the damage my father did? Do you understand the task that lay before me?"

"Aye, more than others."

"How is your father, Iain?"

"He is doing better now that we have found a little farm for him to tend. He missed the life so much. It does him well to be outside, watching over a few cattle and tending a wee garden."

"My father did not have the right to do what he did."

"Many men in his position think they do," Iain replied thoughtfully. He rose from his chair and placed his glass upon the table between them. "Right is right. You will prevail in the end."

He made his way toward the door. His hand on the doorknob, Iain turned abruptly, "Remember the past and think of the future, Benjamin. You cannot trust the lass."

The silence that followed Iain's exit was deafening.

∞

THE CANDLES BURNED TO THE HALFWAY POINT before Tilly heard two faint knocks on the door. Since Sarah already helped her prepare for bed, it must be Benjamin. When she opened the door, he hurriedly stepped inside the room without comment.

He sat in the same chair as he did on the previous visit. She took a seat opposite him.

"Did you enjoy the meal this evening?" he asked.

"Are you referring to the food or the interrogation from Mr. MacIver?" Tilly asked, tilting her head to the side.

"Both, although I suppose the food was more

pleasant than the company."

"Iain's inquisition was troubling. Did he do that for the servants' benefit or his own?"

"Again, both. We grew up together. He is my best friend. He always has my best interests at heart."

"Judging from the look on Mr. Murphy's face, the servants have been gossiping about me since my unusual arrival. Our evening performance may have been meant to quell the rumors. That is unlikely. People have a habit of forming opinions long before the truth is known."

"Aye, it is much more interesting to believe a juicy lie than the boring truth. Still, I wanted to lessen the gossip if we could."

Deciding a change of subject was in order, she said, "Thank you for sending Sarah to assist me."

"She is a nice girl. I hoped she might be helpful to you.

Tilly was puzzled by his response. Wouldn't it be Mrs. Keith's responsibility to assign servants? Why would Benjamin be bothered with such trivial matters? "Does she have other chores besides tending to me?" she asked.

"Aye, of course," he said. "She was a housemaid before your arrival. Mrs. Keith carved out time in her day for the additional duties of attending you. We have need for every servant who is here. I am sure she is very busy with all the work she must do."

His answer bothered her, not only because it meant extra work for Sarah but because he made her feel like another chore. "I don't want to create trouble," Tilly said. "I can take care of my own needs."

"It is no trouble at all, madam."

"But, you just said she has regular chores to do as well as help me. That hardly seems fair."

"It is not a bother. Sarah is capable of handling the work."

Tilly stared at Benjamin. "How would you know?" she asked. "Do you often speak with Sarah about her workload?"

"Sarah is a servant," he replied testily. "It is her job to do whatever her employer asks. I assure you she was most happy to have the extra work. She has been fairly compensated for any *inconvenience* you may cause her."

"If I am such a problem for you, then why the hell did you bring me here?" Tilly asked, bristling at his tone. "Why didn't you just leave me in that damn field?"

"What is bothering you? I do not believe you are greatly vexed by a girl taking on extra chores."

She reflected upon his question. She was genuinely upset about Sarah's added work. However, if she was honest with herself, something far greater had been gnawing at her. Tilly dared to ask, "Do you trust me, Benjamin?"

He slowly rose from his seat and crossed the short distance between them. He placed his hands on the arms of her chair and leaned forward, his breath tickling her face. "My children are the most important people in the world to me," he said. "You are a stranger. You say you are from another time. Iain thinks you are a spy. I question whether or not you are suffering from some mental ailment caused by your family's loss."

Pushing away from the chair, he towered above her. "Until I know who you are, I will take whatever measures I deem necessary to protect my children," he said. He stared deeply into her eyes. "Would you have done anything less for your family?"

Tilly exhaled, not realizing she had been holding her breath. "No."

Benjamin bowed slightly and left the room without bidding her goodnight. She shivered, despite the warm fire.

# NINETEEN

BENJAMIN'S COMMENTS STILL STUNG the next morning. While Tilly could understand his protectiveness, it hurt that he did not believe her. Of course, would she have believed anyone who claimed to have travelled from another time? Unlikely.

It also bothered her that she might be creating more work for Sarah. She endeavored to be of little trouble to her maid or Benjamin. To that end, she confined herself to either her room or the library for the next several days. Servants delivered meals to her room, where she dined in solitude. She allowed Sarah to help her dress in the morning and did not discard her gown until bedtime, a small thing that she hoped would lessen the maid's chores.

In the library, she desperately searched for any clue

that might tell her how to return to her own time. She began her search in the science books. Finding nothing there, Tilly moved on to fairytales and legends. It gave her a deeper understanding of wee folk and witches yet provided no fresh ideas for escaping 1801.

On the fifth day of her quest, Sarah found her pouring over a beautifully illustrated, 15th century book about alchemy. The drawings inside were magnificent and completely useless to her. It was a welcome distraction from her situation, though, so she chose to study them. After all, if she found a way home, she would never have an opportunity to examine a book like that.

"Milady, why are you here?" Sarah asked, her hands on her hips. She shook her head in disapproval.

Tilly's jumped at the question. "Pardon?"

"You should be outside," Sarah said, pulling her from the chair and wrapping a black shawl around her shoulders. She offered a bonnet, but Tilly waved it away. "You need fresh air."

"But, I am reading!"

"Enough!" Sarah said, raising her voice. Blushing slightly, she apologized, "Milady, I am sorry for my boldness, but what you are doing is not healthy. You need fresh air and exercise."

Sighing, she glanced out the window. It did look like a nice day outside. It might be helpful to clear her mind for a bit. "Alright, but please leave these books where they lie," she said. "I want to finish reading them later."

"As you wish, milady."

∞

TILLY SLOWLY WALKED DOWN THE STAIRS for the first time since she entered the castle. She made sure none of the servants could see her as she slipped out the front door. Once outside, she was not sure where she should go.

She knew the gardens were behind the castle. She wanted to avoid Benjamin and the servants. Would she bump into any of them there? Perhaps. Beth and she did not explore the rest of the grounds, so what else should she see?

Hearing voices behind her, she decided that she should not linger at the door. Tilly descended the stone steps and turned to the left. When she reached the corner of the castle, she noticed a little trail leading into the forest and decided to follow it.

It appeared to be a path through the trees. It was just large enough for people, not horses. It was not the trail on which she rode with Benjamin. Judging from the smoothness of the dirt, people frequently travelled it, so it must be a favorite.

She inhaled deeply and smelled fresh pine. The birds sang happily in the trees above, making it impossible to feel gloomy. A light breeze rustled the leaves that lay upon the forest floor. She felt herself relax. For a moment, Tilly forgot about the *when* and relished the *where*. It seemed like ages since she felt at ease.

A few feet ahead on the path, she discovered a stone building. Didn't Beth say there was an old chapel somewhere on the property? Of course, in this time, it might be in use.

The building looked fairly new with its white paint and thick thatched roof. She pushed hard on the heavy oak door and cringed at the metallic creaking of the hinges. Inside, Tilly saw four rows of wooden pews leading to a primitive pulpit. Beams of soft light filtered through the multi-colored glass in the arched windows. Save the shuffle of her slippers on the flagstones, no other sound disturbed the peace of the little chapel.

She took a seat at the first pew. She always liked visiting empty churches, regardless of the denomination. She felt such tranquility there.

Tilly closed her eyes. "Why am I here?" she repeated aloud the question Sarah asked her, only this time the meaning was much different. "Why did you send me to this strange place? Why??!"

She opened her eyes and stared at the wooden cross mounted on the wall in front of her. "I am not a bad person," she said. "I have always tried to live a good life. Why did you send me here?"

She gathered the courage to ask the question that burned her to the core. "Why did you take away my family?" she asked, clenching her fists. "The children were innocent. My husband was a decent, hard-working man. Why did you do it? Why?!"

She cried, "Why did you punish us? What did we ever do to you?!!" She fell to her knees and sobbed.

Suddenly, a handkerchief waved in front of her face. Gasping, Tilly looked up and saw a tall boy standing in front of her. "Madam, please do not cry," he said. He looked to be on the verge of tears himself.

She took the handkerchief and climbed back onto the pew. Dabbing her eyes, she thanked him for his kind gesture. She closely examined him. He wore a crisp white shirt with a simple knot at the throat, black jacket, and black breeches tucked into black leather boots that brushed his knees. His auburn hair was held in check with a somber grey ribbon.

He joined her on the pew. "Why were you talking to God like that?" he asked. "I have never heard anyone dare to say such things."

Tilly squirmed in her seat. "Well, I –"

"Are you the lady my father found in the woods?" he asked, not giving her time to respond. "The one whose husband was killed by bandits?"

She could not believe that she missed the resemblance. The boy had Benjamin's auburn hair. His eyes were blue, not green. Still, they had the same strong, steady gaze that belonged to his father. His overall manner seemed much more mature than she thought he was. Realizing that she was probably staring, she looked away. "Yes," she said. "I was very fortunate that your father found me."

"My name is Allan Campbell," he said. "I presume you are Mrs. Munro?"

She wanted to tell him to call her 'Tilly' but recalled what Benjamin said about being so informal. "Yes," she said. "It is a pleasure to meet you, Mr. Campbell. Your father spoke about you and your siblings. You are the oldest, aren't you?"

He held his head high. "Aye. I am ten years old," he said proudly.

"Well, you are almost a man, aren't you? Do you look after your brothers and sister?"

"I try to manage the wee mongrels as best I can,

but they are a rowdy bunch," Allan said, with a sigh. "Stephen is the worst of the lot. I believe you have already met him."

Stephen was the young boy she met in the library. "Is he much younger than you?" Tilly asked.

Allan spread his fingers and lightly touched each one as he named the siblings. "Angus is 8. Michael is 5. Stephen, the wee rascal, is 2." He paused. "Maggie is almost one. She is a baby, so I do not know if she is good or bad. Do you have any brothers or sisters, madam?"

"No, I am an only child."

"That must be nice. My brothers will not give me a moment's peace. I had to sneak away from the castle to come here."

"Why did you come here?"

The boy pondered the question a moment before answering. "I visit the chapel to be closer to my mother," Allan said. "She brought us all here from time to time. She said it was a quiet place."

"I am sorry about your mother."

"And, I am sorry about your family. You must be very angry to talk to God like that."

She was unsure how to handle the situation. It

could certainly be misconstrued as sacrilege, especially in the 19th century. "I hope I did not offend you," Tilly said sincerely. "I do not understand why my family is gone and am very upset. Sometimes, people say things when they are distressed that they might not say under other circumstances."

"I was very angry too when my mother died. My father said God sometimes needs angels in heaven so he takes good people like my mother." Allan leaned closer to her and added, "I do not believe him."

She was surprised. "Why?" she asked, genuinely curious.

"If we only experience happy times, how would we appreciate them?" the boy asked. He smiled faintly. "Sometimes, bad things happen to good people. It does not mean God hates us. I believe it teaches us that we should appreciate the good moments and people in our lives."

She dared to wrap her arm around his shoulders and gave him a light squeeze. "Well, that is as good an explanation as any other I have heard," Tilly said, moved by the boy's candor. "We just endure and hope there is a meaning to what happened, don't we?"

"Aye," Allan said seriously. "It is a great mystery."

She held back a giggle, knowing he would be

offended. He was the most mature ten-year old she had ever met. "I fear we are becoming too gloomy, Mr. Campbell," she said. "Why don't we return to the castle? The cook may have prepared a fresh batch of scones."

The boy's face brightened at the prospect of hot pastries. He gallantly offered her his arm as they exited the chapel.

"Aren't you afraid to walk in the woods by yourself?" Tilly asked when they headed down the woodland trail.

"No. Someone is always watching," he said, pointing toward a tree a few feet ahead of them. "You can come out, Robbie. I see you."

A young man emerged from behind the tree. "Please do not tell your father that I did a poor job," he said, looking quite embarrassed. "He was most cross the last time you told him."

"If you would learn to properly conceal yourself, then I would have nothing to report," Allan said mischievously as they passed the sentry.

She enjoyed the banter between the boy and his guard. Apparently, this was a daily game between them. She wondered why the other man who followed them did not teach Robbie his tricks. She only saw a fleeting glimpse of tartan before he disappeared into the woods. She decided not to mention it, lest Robbie be embarrassed even more.

When they reached the castle, they parted ways. Allan was ready to conquer a plate of scones. And, Tilly was ready to thank Sarah.

∞

TILLY FOUND THE MAID in the rose-hued bedchamber that had become a second home. Sarah sat by the window, sewing a piece of fabric to the bottom of a black dress.

Impulsively, she wrapped her arms around the startled girl and gave her a hug. "Thank you," she said. "You were right. The walk did a great deal to restore my soul."

"Oh, you are most welcome, milady."

Tilly pinched the fabric of the dress and asked, "Don't you have something more colorful?"

Sarah seemed shocked. She explained that, in Deoch, it was the custom to wear mourning clothes for at least a year after a husband's passing. It was preferred to mourn for two years, but sometimes, necessity dictated a speedy marriage to a new partner.

"You should wear black for the first six months, then grey for the last six months. I regret that you have been wearing a grey gown so soon after his passing," Sarah said, gesturing toward the dreary dress Tilly wore. "It is all that we could find, but we shall remedy it with this gown. Do they observe such customs in America?"

As she examined the dress, she nodded absently. Protest was useless. She glanced at the grey gown she wore. While the empire-waist dress was very flattering and was certainly better than going naked, Tilly grew tired of wearing the same gown day after day. Any change in wardrobe was welcome, even if the color would be a boring, somber tone.

"May I speak freely with you?" she asked as she took a seat beside Sarah.

"I do not understand the customs in this country," she began, careful not to say *in this time*. "We do things somewhat differently in America. I do not wish to offend anyone here."

Sarah sat on the edge of her seat. It was obvious that the maid was uncomfortable with the prospect of sharing confidences. Still, she seemed slightly relieved. Tilly's revelation would explain some of the rumors that were probably spreading throughout the castle.

"Milady, it must not be very different in America," Sarah said. "You only need a few bits of advice here and there."

"Will you please help me? I need guidance."

"Aye, milady, but I am certain you will be fine."

"I will be in your debt."

"Well, milady, if you wish to return the favor.…"

Sarah was suddenly shy.

"Is there something I can do for you?" Tilly asked.

"I noticed that you spend time in the library, reading," Sarah said, her voice low. "A proper lady's maid should know about literature and art, so she is a good companion to her mistress."

"Would you like me to teach you about those things?"

Sarah was flustered. "No – I mean, aye – eventually," she sputtered.

Tilly could see how ashamed the maid was. Then, she guessed the secret. "Do you want me to teach you how to read?" she asked. She tried not to sound surprised.

Sarah eagerly nodded. "Oh, please, milady!" she exclaimed. "It would change my life!"

"It is a marvelous gift. You can expand your mind in ways you never imagined."

"Do you think you can teach me, milady?"

"Yes. I have taught many children how to read. I am sure I can teach you in no time at all."

"Were you a governess?" Sarah asked, her brow knitted in confusion.

Tilly silently cursed her slip of the tongue. Then, she remembered that it was not uncommon for governesses to marry their charges' father. Didn't Jane Eyre do it? *I should tell Sarah some scandalous story of stealing away with my mistress' husband*, she thought wickedly. Instead, she replied, "I was a teacher before I married my late husband."

Sarah did not question her story. She seemed thrilled about the prospect of learning how to read, a skill that would provide her with greater job opportunities. The maid asked when they could start the lessons.

Tilly shrugged her shoulders. "We can start right now, if you like," she said.

# TWENTY

TILLY WAS TIRED. Sarah and she were up until the wee hours of the morning as she began the difficult task of teaching an adult how to read. With sadness, she observed it was easier with children. After all, how many first graders worried about mending garments before bedtime?

She sat in the garden. The day was gloomy, and there was a slight chill in the air. Sarah insisted she don a coat. Tilly was surprised when the maid produced a sort of half jacket. It had long sleeves, but the hem of the jacket itself ended just below her bust line. Sarah called it a "spencer."

She plucked the cloth-covered buttons of the grey woolen garment. She reluctantly admitted it was warm, even though it was shorter than she expected.

Sighing, she stared at the page of the small blue book she held. It was the dullest book of poetry she had ever read. She supposed it might be fashionable for a lady of leisure to spend her days sitting on a bench underneath a tree and indulging in quiet time with a good book.

Unfortunately, she could not focus her mind. Tilly tried to read the same page five times, not grasping a single word. Yawning, she closed the book. Was it improper for ladies to take naps? That was exactly what she needed.

"Good afternoon," Benjamin said behind her. "It is nice to see you out of doors for a change."

She jolted in alarm. "How long have you been standing there?" she asked, slightly embarrassed.

"Long enough to see that you are not interested in that book," he replied, chuckling. He took a seat beside her and glanced at the title.

He frowned and asked, "Do you enjoy poetry?"

"I like some of Byron's work, but I really prefer novels," she said. "Is it wrong to read novels in this time?"

He lifted his brows at the mention of a different time. Tilly was glad he held his tongue. Instead, Benjamin said, "As long as you are reading appropriate material, there is nothing shameful about reading a novel."

She wanted to ask what was considered appropriate. Most likely, the "bodice ripper" romance novels of her day would be tossed straight into the fire in 1801. Trying to look prim and proper, she said, "I shall look to you for guidance about what is appropriate."

"You sound like my sweet Mary."

Her interest piqued, she took the opportunity to learn more about his late wife. "Did she enjoy reading?" Tilly asked.

"Mary would read books if I asked her," Benjamin said, shaking his head. "I tried to broaden her mind. She was content as she was, though."

She thought it was an odd response. "Were you unhappy in your marriage?" she asked. "It is not uncommon, you know, for married people to be unhappy."

He seemed taken aback at her direct query. She guessed her bold way of speaking was unsettling to him.

"I was content," Benjamin said. "Mary was a good woman and an excellent mother. She gave me a wonderful brood of children."

"That hardly sounds like glowing praise," she said sarcastically. "The same could be said of a breeding mare."

He jerked as if he had been slapped. "I did not call my wife a horse!" he objected. "I was a lucky man to have her."

Once again, her modern bluntness landed her in trouble. "I did not mean to imply that, Benjamin," she apologized. Boldly, Tilly touched his arm. "I just noticed you spoke nothing of love."

"Were you happy in *your* marriage?"

"To be completely honest, no, not always."

"You were not?" he asked. Obviously, he did not expect that answer.

"No. At the time of the accident, we were in therapy," Tilly said. "We discussed getting a divorce but wanted to give it one more try, for the children's sake."

She noticed the shocked look on Benjamin's face. "It was not an easy romance," she said. "When we met, I was 24. He was 35. That age difference may be common in your time, but it is big in mine. We enjoyed being together then, so age did not matter. We had a lot of fun."

She smiled faintly at the memory as she admitted,

"I moved in with him, and we were married six months later."

"You lived together as man and wife before you were formally married?!" Benjamin exclaimed in horror.

At first, she was annoyed at his outburst. Then, she recalled that, to him, cohabitating before marriage would be wildly improper among genteel people. Sure, the common folk may have done it in the 19th century, but he probably had never heard of "respectable" people doing it. "In the 21st century, it is very common for couples of all social classes to live together before marriage," she explained. "Don't be such a prude, Benjamin."

"If you are indeed from the future, I do not approve of the new way of thinking," he said, with his arms folded firmly over his chest.

She ignored his censure. "I was thrilled when Alex worked up the courage to propose marriage," she said. "It was happy moment for us."

"About damn time…." Benjamin muttered under his breath.

She cast a dark look his way. "We were married at City Hall," she said, recalling the location with a twinge of regret. "He did not want a big, fancy wedding. Beth and her husband Randall were witnesses. About six weeks later, I discovered I was pregnant with the twins."

"Your husband must have been happy," he said. "It is exciting to learn that you will be a father."

Shaking her head, she said, "He was devastated. He already had a son from a previous marriage and told me he did not want more children." Her voice filled with sadness, Tilly added, "He did not speak to me for three days."

"Was he indifferent to you for the rest of your marriage? Is that why you wanted a divorce?"

"No," she said. "He eventually accepted the news. It was a big shock. He did not expect to be a father again and would need to alter his plans."

Tilly shook her head in disgust. She was amazed at how much his comment hurt, even after all that had happened. "Alter his plans – that's what he said. As if I always planned to marry an older man and have two kids at once," she said. "As if my goal in life was to be up at 2:00 a.m., alone, trying to get two fussy babies to go to sleep."

Benjamin covered her hand with his. "I never asked Mary what her feelings were about having a large family," he said. "I always thought it was a woman's greatest desire to raise children. Seeing the hurt in your eyes, I recognize a woman might have other feelings on the matter. We men are very stupid sometimes."

She stared at him. That speech was awfully progressive for the 19th century. "Alex was a good man, and so are you," she said, squeezing Benjamin's hand. "He loved his children. His mistake was that he believed he needed to make a lot of money so that they could have everything in life. About a year ago, I told him what they needed – what I needed – was *him*. If he did not change his ways, I would move out with the children."

"Did he alter his schedule?"

"Yes. I told him the same thing for years, but this time, he understood. He knew I was serious."

"Men are fools. It sometimes takes us longer to understand matters that are so simple for women."

She did not refute his words. "I am so glad he did it," Tilly said. "Even though we were still struggling, he was present for our children. They had their father during that final year."

Something suddenly occurred to her. "Did I tell you he was a chef?" she asked.

"No, I do not believe so."

"He was very talented. He travelled all over the world, helping other people open restaurants. When he decided to make us a priority, we opened a restaurant in our town. It was nothing fancy, just a small place. It enabled him to be with us, yet still do the work he enjoyed."

"Had I known your husband was a talented chef, I would have endeavored to make the stew more appetizing for you," Benjamin said, feigning embarrassment.

"I was starving," she said, laughing. "It was wonderful."

"Oh, that is high praise, milady," he joked. "It was wonderful because you were starving."

"That is not what I meant," she said. She playfully poked him in the ribs. "The stew was lovely. I am very glad that you did not let me starve."

Turning serious, she asked, "How *was* your marriage, Benjamin?"

He looked down, suddenly shy. "She was a MacDougall," he said. "My father felt the union would be beneficial for both families."

"You were crying for her in the forest. You must have cared for her, despite it being an arranged marriage."

"I did not say the marriage was arranged. I fell in love with her the first moment I saw her," Benjamin said. "Her feelings were not the same. It took some time for her to warm toward me. Eventually, she relented and became my wife."

Tilly did not think any woman could deny his affections for very long. With a blush, sweet memories of their only union flooded her mind. She pushed those thoughts aside. That event would never be repeated so it was best not to dwell on it.

"Mary was a kind, gentle woman," he said. "She was an excellent mother. She was my lover and my friend. Her passing is a terrible loss."

They sat in solemn silence for several minutes, haunted by memories. Then, Tilly broke the spell by making an offhand comment. "I am surprised your father has not selected another marriage prospect for you," she said. "He seems to be involved in everything."

She immediately wished she had kept her mouth shut. She vividly recalled the letter his father wrote to him and realized just how incredibly careless and stupid her comment was. "Benjamin, I am sorry." She felt him tense beside her. "I shouldn't have said that."

"My father is always thinking about the betterment of the family," he said as he stood abruptly. "If you will excuse me, I have some matters that require my attention."

She watched him return to the castle. The letter hinted at a deep divide between Benjamin and Malcolm. She did not think it formed simply because the father wanted the son to marry well. Didn't Mr. Douglas say something during the tour, something about the son disagreeing with his father's management of the estate? Could that have caused the tension between father and son?

Tilly pondered the problem before deciding that an excellent source of information was available. She abandoned her ladylike pursuit of poetry and entered the house in search of Sarah.

# TWENTY ONE

TILLY FOUND SARAH in the dressing room, mending yet another black dress. She pulled a chair beside the maid and exchanged idle chit-chat for a few moments. She wanted to soften Sarah's reserve. From the look on Sarah's face, it was obvious the maid had no desire to engage in small talk.

"I know you are very busy, so thank you for giving me a moment of your time, Sarah," she said, hoping flattery would win favor. She guessed the maid had a great many tasks to accomplish, and lounging by the fireplace with her would not see them completed any sooner.

"Mr. Campbell speaks often of his father, yet I know so little about him," she said. Tilly tried to be coy. "You seem to know all about the family. Could you tell me more about the man?"

"There is really nothing to tell," Sarah said. She squirmed in her seat. "His Grace – Mr. Campbell's father, that is – stays at the family estate in Derbyshire or at the townhome in London. He has not visited in years."

*So, the Tinberry Hall estate he mentioned in the letter must be in England*, Tilly thought. She filed away that piece of information for later consideration. She continued her query, "Surely, His Grace was here when Mr. Campbell and his older brother were children."

"Aye, I heard he was a doting father."

"Really? Even to the younger Mr. Campbell?"

"You must understand that Allan Campbell was the first boy. His Grace devoted time and energy to his instruction. He wanted the child to learn how to manage the estate, since it would be inherited by the eldest son one day." Sarah paused as she struggled to recall information. "I have heard that milord spent a lot of time with the MacIvers, though his father did inquire after his health and welfare. It is not uncommon for those born after the first son to be treated thusly. Milord always knew he must find his own path."

Tilly considered the maid's comments for a moment. Deciding that all this formality with names made conversation nearly impossible, she boldly said, "When Allan was murdered, everything must have changed for the Malcolm and Benjamin. What happened then?"

Sarah was quiet. Tilly leaned forward and squeezed the maid's hand. "Please. I fear I offend Benjamin whenever I mention his father." She smiled encouragingly. "I would like to know why."

"Milady, Mrs. Keith would have me whipped if she knew I told you these stories." Sarah lowered her voice and said, "If I speak of this matter, you must swear on your life that you will never reveal the source of the information."

"I swear it," Tilly said, nodding eagerly.

Sarah took a deep breath and began the tale. His Grace was a hard man, born in very difficult times. He arrived in the world three years before the Rising, the eldest son of Allan Campbell.

Malcolm's father Allan placed preservation of Castle Fion and its lands above all things. When rumblings of a Jacobite rebellion began, Allan Campbell carefully weighed the matter. He even went to the Continent and met Bonnie Prince Charlie. After that fateful meeting, he decided the Scottish could not possibly come out on the winning side. He joined forces with the English and did dastardly deeds against his own people, so that he might preserve the estate. When the rebellion came to naught, he was greatly rewarded by King George II for his loyalty. Other families lost their holdings, but not the Campbells. They survived.

With such a role model, it was not surprising that Malcolm became a ruthless man. Upon his father Allan's death, he inherited the estate and promptly married Eleanor MacLean. Her dowry included a large sum of money, and it was rumored her family owned a large property in England. Upon her father's passing, the property would land in Campbell hands. Marriage was a strategic move, plain and simple. No love could ever exist in a marriage to Malcolm Campbell.

The couple had, in rapid succession, two stillborn children. Malcolm became sullen, worried his union would not produce an heir. Gossips whispered that he contemplated a divorce from his wife, so that he might seek another woman with whom he could produce a son. Then, to his delight and his wife's relief, a healthy son was born. He insisted the lad be named after his father Allan.

Benjamin arrived six years later, but Allan was Malcolm's sole focus and purpose for living. Malcolm took the boy with him everywhere, instructing him about how to run the family estates in Scotland and England. Allan accompanied his father to London so he could learn politics and business dealings beyond those of the Scottish countryside. Allan studied with the very best tutors. In Allan, Malcolm saw the future of the Campbell family.

Benjamin was left on his own. Fortunately, Iain MacIver's father, Robert, took an interest in the boy. Robert was the factor, as his son Iain would one day become. He took both Iain and Benjamin with him when he travelled throughout the Campbell lands. Robert showed them the real work that occurred in the management of the estate, the daily toil on the farms, and the hard life of the tenants. Where Allan's education was centered on abstract matters, Benjamin learned firsthand the value and struggle of the crofters who were the life's blood of the property.

The years quickly passed. Allan grew into a handsome man who was his father's pride and joy. Benjamin chased after the MacIvers and was generally oblivious to the opposite sex – and his father.

With the prospect of a great inheritance, Allan was a valuable prize for any unmarried woman. He had his choice of feminine companionship and seemed to be in no rush to wed. All of that changed when he met the beautiful Cairen MacDonald. She was bewitching. Many men sought her hand, yet she favored none. Allan never faced rejection, for no one refused the future owner of Castle Fion and its vast estate. Her indifference sparked his interest and challenged him to win her heart.

The man recklessly pursued her, even though their families had a long-standing and oft-times bloody feud. He sent messages to her and arranged clandestine meetings. Allan was deeply in love and believed her when she said the ancient feud meant nothing to her. That was his folly.

One night, Cairen lured him to the outer boundaries of the Campbell lands. It was a remote area, far from any witnesses. Allan thought they were stealing away to be married. Instead, he found her waiting with her brother James. They slaughtered him. They tossed his body into a ravine and fled to the MacDonald family home.

It devastated the Campbell family. His mother Eleanor collapsed in grief when she heard of her son's murder. She lay in bed for a week before she died.

Malcolm was inconsolable. In one fell swoop, he lost his precious son and his wife. He wanted immediate revenge, not the slow kind obtained through the legal system. He wanted swift justice served from his own blade.

In the middle of the night, he grabbed Benjamin. They rode two days to the MacDonald castle. They spent two more nights in the forest, watching the movements of its inhabitants. On the fifth night, they crept into the castle. Malcolm ran a knife through James' heart while he slept in his bed. Then, he pulled Benjamin into Cairen's chamber. Killing her was a task that the father ordered his son to complete.

When they returned, life changed for Benjamin. The naïve boy of sixteen was now a man. He was no longer allowed to accompany the MacIvers. He spent his days at his father's side, learning what would be required to run the estate. With Allan gone, the mantle of responsibility would rest upon his shoulders one day. His father meant to teach him well.

Unfortunately, Malcolm did not find an eager pupil in his other son. Benjamin balked at his father's heavy-handed ways and efforts to sculpt him into a copy of himself. He complained incessantly when his father took him to London and abroad. He had no taste for the pandering necessary to win political favor with the English. Malcolm understood, at last, that his son had been left wild too long.

However, in one area, his father prevailed: Benjamin's marriage to Mary MacDougall. It was a fortunate alliance. The family's property bordered Campbell lands. Of late, they enjoyed a friendly relationship, which would be strengthened by the marriage. For his son, it offered the opportunity to marry someone who might not slit his throat at the first opportunity. His brother's ill-fated romance hung like a cloud over the family.

Fortunately for all, Mary MacDougall was a sweet, innocent girl with fiery red hair and sparkling blue eyes. She loved to laugh and went through the world with a light heart. The couple found love and happiness with each other.

When she mentioned her former mistress, tears sprung into Sarah's eyes. "It was such a tragedy when she died," she said between soft sobs. "Our hearts were very heavy, especially milord's. He was lost without his dear wife."

Sarah rose from the chair. "He is a good man, despite the terrible deed his father commanded him to do," she said. "I have seen the great things he has done for the crofters and the kind way he treats us servants. He should not be judged harshly for the one sin he committed."

"If it pleases milady, I have other chores that require my attention," she said, looking expectantly at Tilly. At her mistress' nod, she left the room.

The 1800s were supposed to be more civilized than the restless past. Or at least, that's what Tilly believed. She grimly understood "the past" was not that long ago in 1801. It would take a couple of centuries to distance oneself from the bloody times that once existed in Scotland. She desperately wanted to leave this place soon. It was not the Highland fantasy she envisioned.

∞

WHEN TILLY APPEARED AT THE TABLE that night for dinner, Benjamin was surprised how happy he felt. Her comment about a prospective union may have been badly timed, but he enjoyed the rest of their conversation. To his shock, he admitted that he always liked talking with her. She challenged him in ways that he found refreshing. Her opinions were unusual and thought-provoking. He never felt bored by any conversation he had with her. As he helped her into her seat, he looked forward to the evening.

He heard reports that she was going through every book in the library and wanted to ask why. Given her boredom with poetry, he doubted she looked for volumes of those works. Unfortunately, her responses to his queries were limited to "yes" and "no." With the constant presence of the servants, he decided it would be impossible to engage in meaningful conservation. At length, he stopped trying, and they ate their meal in silence.

He was dismayed when she excused herself before the dessert was served and scurried away to her room. Her unusual reserve perplexed him.

"Mr. Murphy, I too shall retire for the evening,"

Benjamin informed the butler as he tossed his napkin onto the table. The man looked slightly vexed that his liege would not enjoy the dessert but said nothing.

Instead of going to his chambers, Benjamin made his way to Tilly's room. He knocked twice, hoping the maid was not attending her. Thankfully, she answered the door and let him into her receiving room.

He took his usual seat by the fireplace. "It was nice to see you this evening," he said, stretching his legs toward the fire. "I feared my company had offended you."

"No, not at all," she replied as she eased into the chair opposite him. She stared at the fire. "I thought my presence might be intrusive."

"Why would you believe that?"

"Well, you made it perfectly clear that you do not trust me. I am sure you want me to leave as soon as may be."

"Madam, I promised you refuge for as long as you need it."

"I wish I could go home but have not figured out how."

"Perhaps you could contact a distant relative?"

"I told you I don't live in 1801," Tilly snapped. "I

am from the 21$^{st}$ century. If I could figure out how to contact that time, I certainly wouldn't be in this damn place, would I?"

"When will you tell me the truth?" he asked angrily. "Why must you continue with this fiction of being from another time? You are safe here. You have no need for lies, Tilly."

She stood abruptly and pointed toward the door. "Get out!" Tilly roared. "I may have to stay here, but I *will not* be called a liar, you murderous bastard!"

He noticed she was trembling. Was it from rage or fear? "Murderous bastard?" Benjamin pronounced evenly. "What an interesting thing to say. Pray tell me, madam, why would you call me that?"

She looked down at the floor and said nothing. She reminded him of his children when he caught them being mischievous.

He calmly rose from his chair and leaned against the mantel. "I must warn you that the servants love a good story, true or false," he said, taking a moment to gather his thoughts. "Be careful what you believe."

"Then, tell me the truth."

He bade her to return to her chair. He pulled his own chair closer to her and took a seat. From the startled look on her face, he knew he surprised her by lifting her hands to his lips and kissing them. "There is only one tale that would warrant such a description of my person – the story of my brother Allan's death."

"Did your father and you really kill those people?"

He could not look her in the eyes for some time. Finally, he did. "Aye, it is true," Benjamin confessed.

Stunned, she asked, "Why?"

Hot fury coursed through his veins. "Why?!!! Why not?! Do you know what they did?!" He jumped to his feet and planted his arms on either side of her chair. "They stalked my brother like a red stag," he said. "They lured him into their trap. They slaughtered him, and then they left his body for the wolves to devour."

He pushed away from her chair. "Do you know why they did it?" he asked, breathing heavily. He struggled to contain his anger. Vivid images of his brother's lifeless, tortured body flashed in his mind. "Did you hear that part of the tale?"

She managed to sputter "no."

"During the Rising, a group of Campbells led by my grandfather attacked a village where Cairen MacDonald's ancestors lived. They burned it to the ground, killing every man, woman, and child who lived there. Her family never forgot."

"But, that must have been around 1745!" Tilly exclaimed. "It was ages ago, long before your brother was even born."

"They killed Allan forty years to the day the village burned," Benjamin said. "We do not forget or forgive. We wait for the day when vengeance is ours, even if it means waiting a lifetime."

"So much for a civilized society," she muttered.

"We try to be civilized, but sometimes we must return to our base natures," he said with a shrug. "I am not proud of what I did, but they murdered my brother for no good reason. They deserved to die." He took a seat beside her. "Now I ask you - would you want justice, if it had been your kin?"

Tilly lowered her gaze. He said softly, "Aye, it is not so simple, is it?"

He gently held her hands and took a moment to regain his composure. His head bowed, he said, "My actions will haunt me for the rest of my life. I have had many, many sleepless nights. I am tortured by dreams of what happened. Sometimes, in the middle of the day, I will jolt and shake when those images appear before me, a waking nightmare. I hate myself for doing it, yet I know -" Benjamin gulped. "I know how good it felt to avenge my brother's death."

"If you could have seen what they did to Allan…they tortured him, lass," he said, his face twisted in anguish. "They must have played with him like a cat with a mouse. It was not an easy, quick death. I cannot imagine the suffering and horror my beloved brother must have experienced. They will receive no forgiveness from me."

"My grandfather did such terrible things during the Rising," he said. Benjamin abruptly released her hands. "He slaughtered his own people, all in the name of allegiance to some faraway king he never met. He cared naught for the English cause. He merely wanted to preserve his own fortune. His brutality toward the MacDonald family brought this pain to our door."

"My father evicts people from land on which they have lived for generations," he continued as he raised his sorrowful gaze to hers. "He runs rough over anything and anyone that gets in his way, even his own son. He killed that night just as I did." He swallowed hard. "And, now, look at what I have done. I am continuing the family tradition."

He paused briefly as memories of the past flooded his mind. "When I entered Cairen MacDonald's chamber, she was awake. She twirled a finger through her brown hair and batted her eyes at me. She told me I must be a brave man to enter the MacDonald castle."

"You would not believe the things she said," Benjamin spat. "It occurred to me that she must have said the same sweet words to Allan. I have never felt such rage in all my life, and, pray God, I never feel it again. I slit her throat without the slightest hesitation. In my nightmares, I can still see the way her ivory skin parted when I ran my blade across her throat. I can hear the gurgle of blood spewing from the wound and the thud of her body on the rocks below when I tossed it out the window."

He rubbed his hands together, trying to remove some invisible stain. "We Campbells have spilled so much blood," he said, his voice filled with pain. "I try so hard to atone for my family's sins but find myself committing this terrible act. Am I doomed to repeat the evil of those who came before me? Am I a fool for hoping that I can be a better man?"

With the back of his hand, he dashed away the hot tears that fell down his cheeks. "Mary never knew my dark secret," he said. "People fear you when they know the terrible things you have done. They judge you. I could not bear to have that innocent woman think poorly of me."

He looked intently into her watery eyes. "You will think differently of me too," he said. Resignation crept into his voice. "You will see me for the monster I am."

He rose from the chair and stared down at Tilly. "You know the very worst part of my soul," he said. "It cannot be undone. I must live with this disgrace for the rest of my life."

Turning, Benjamin wordlessly exited the room.

# TWENTY TWO

TILLY SPENT THE NEXT TWO DAYS TRYING TO FIND BENJAMIN. He did not join her for any of the meals. According to Sarah, he was constantly busy, working in the stables, riding on the estate, and dealing with tenant matters. It seemed as if he purposely avoided being in the castle. Short of barging into his bedchamber in the middle of the night, she did not know how she might have an opportunity to speak with him.

Deciding she needed a moment's respite, she made her way to the little chapel in the woods. She enjoyed the quiet of the place. It was an understatement to say the last year had brought incredible change in her life. Her family was gone, and she was ripped from her own time. She felt completely adrift. Visiting the chapel always gave her a small measure of peace.

241

When she pushed open the door, she discovered she was not alone. Benjamin sat on the first pew. He did not turn as she walked toward him. She slid beside him onto the pew. They sat shoulder to shoulder for several moments, not speaking.

Tilly slipped her hand into his. She felt him tense at her touch. She did not move, though, giving him time to relax. When she heard him exhale, she spoke. "I have been looking for you," she said. "Why have you been hiding?"

"I have many matters that require my attention."

"You are afraid of my reaction to your confession. You left before we could talk."

Benjamin turned to face her. He did not let go of her hand. "Aye. I told you that people treat you differently when they know the terrible things you have done. They fear you," he said. He looked away. "Mary always regarded me with such love. She always saw the very best in people. A part of me wanted her to see only the good, never the bad, in her husband."

"It was not difficult for me to discover the story," Tilly said. "Mary probably knew. She loved you anyway. She saw your true heart and knew you are not a bad person." She gently turned his face toward her. When his eyes met hers, she repeated, "You are not a bad person, Benjamin."

"I cannot pretend that I understand what happened," she continued. "I come from a time and place where we do not react in such a violent way – well, not normally. You have been raised in a society where violence is a way of life. It might not be as lawless in 1801 as it used to be, but the undercurrent of brutality is still here. You are not a cruel man, though. I see a great determination to be a better person. I simply cannot reconcile the man you describe with the man I know. You are not a monster."

He raised her hand to his lips and kissed it fervently. She felt a hot tear splash upon her hand before he released it. He said hoarsely, "Thank you."

Benjamin placed his arm around her shoulder and cleared his throat. "I built this chapel for her, you know," he said. "She was not fond of the church in the village. She said it was too large, and the sermons were too long."

He chuckled at the memory. "She preferred to meet one-on-one with God," he said, gesturing toward the cross that hung in front of them. "I built her this wee chapel so she could have regular conversations with Him without having to trudge down to the village. She would slip away sometimes, whenever the bairns were too much for her. I would find her sitting in a pew, a little smile on her face. She told me this was the only place where she could find a moment's peace."

"I have found solace here too," Tilly said. "You gave her an extraordinary gift." Sighing, she leaned closer to him and was glad he did not move away. "Will you be my friend? I have no one else here with whom I can talk."

"Of course. You can confide in me."

"I should want to go home, but I have nothing waiting for me there. My family is gone," she said. "Still, I do not have anything here. I need to go back to my own time, right? That's how this works. What if I am trapped here, though? I am scared."

"You are an intelligent woman. I am sure you will find a way."

"Thank you for not saying I am foolish to bring up the whole time travel thing again."

"You cannot tell lies in church, or you will burn in hell," Benjamin said, winking at her.

She laughed, despite the gravity of the situation. "And, thank you for taking care of me," Tilly added. "I may not know everything that you do, but I can see how hard your life is. I never want to be a burden for you."

He pulled her close to him and rested his head on top of hers. "How could you ever be a burden, lass?"

he asked tenderly.

She closed her eyes and relaxed in his embrace. She forced herself to set aside her memories of the past and worries for the future. For this moment, she wanted to feel peace and serenity and safety. Could this man give her all of that, if she would open her heart? *Don't overthink things, Tilly,* she thought. *Just breathe.*

∞

MR. MURPHY SAT AT THE DESK in his office and reread the letter he composed. He was uncertain if it was premature to alert His Grace. However, the man had been most explicit with his instructions. If anything out of the ordinary occurred at the castle, the butler was instructed to send word at once.

Sighing heavily, he folded the parchment and carefully placed a blob of black wax to join the pages. Pressing a metal seal in the warm wax, the butler smiled with satisfaction at the impression of the Campbell crest. His Grace gave him the signet as recognition of the service he rendered to the family. Mr. Murphy used it only when addressing matters of the utmost concern to the family's wellbeing.

He added the letter to a pile of other missives for the post. With luck, the strange woman would be gone before the letter reached His Grace. He grabbed a candlestick from his desk and made his way to the door. It was time to prepare for the evening meal. He must not shirk his other duties as butler for Castle Fion.

# TWENTY THREE

SARAH WAS EXCITED when she came to Tilly's room very late in the evening. Fortunately, the maid just missed Benjamin's nightly visit. Tilly was glad she did not have to explain *that* to Sarah. It would probably be considered very scandalous.

She repeatedly asked what happened, but Sarah refused to share the reason as she led Tilly downstairs. Checking first for any lingering servants, Sarah ushered her into the family library and firmly closed the door behind them.

She was shocked to see Allan standing beside the fireplace. Suddenly self-conscious, she pulled the robe closer around her body. She was not dressed to receive people.

He cleared his throat and held a tattered book in

front of him. "Miss Sarah says you are teaching her to read," he said. "I thought you might like to use one of my books."

"That is very generous of you," Tilly said. She crossed the room and took the book from the boy. "Are you sure you do not need it?"

"No. It is a book I used long ago. I have moved to more advanced material now."

She cleared her throat to conceal a giggle at his boast. Flipping through the pages, Tilly was relieved to see the text was much easier for her task.

He strode toward a doorway on the opposite side of the fireplace. "Our classroom is in here," Allan said, opening the door. "I have prepared a fire for you. Would you like to use the room for the lessons?"

She followed him into the classroom. She saw tables and chairs as well as rows of books and maps tacked onto the walls. A gleaming slate blackboard hung on one wall. She wanted to hug him but thought better of it. "This is perfect!" she exclaimed. "Would you like to stay for the lesson?"

"I would be happy to listen, if you do not mind," Allan said, grinning shyly.

"Not at all! Please, take a seat," she said. She motioned for Sarah to do the same.

Spreading the book upon the table, they began the lesson. Her heart lifted when the maid read the text with ease. Tilly felt they turned a corner, thanks to the gift from a ten-year old boy.

∞

IT WAS SEVERAL EVENINGS LATER, AND BENJAMIN COULD NOT SLEEP. He flung aside the covers and rose from the bed. It had been three weeks since he brought Tilly to his home. He was no closer to learning her true identity than when she arrived. Despite all his queries and cross questions, the woman never wavered from her story. She emphatically stated she was from the future. He began to think she might be telling the truth, as improbable as that seemed.

At the same time, he confessed his darkest secret to her. He poured out his heart and revealed the depth of the pain he felt. He told her things he never shared with anyone else, not even his late wife. Tilly knew so much about him. What did he know about her?

Grinning devilishly, he recalled the things he knew well – the curves of her supple breasts, the silky smoothness of her skin. He could not erase their passionate first meeting from his memory. If he concentrated, he could feel the heat of her body and taste the sweetness of her mouth.

Frustrated, he decided sleep would elude him yet again. He pulled on his clothes and boots. Maybe he could find a book in the library that would distract his frenzied brain just long enough to get some much-needed rest. As he left his room, he shook his head. That woman was driving him mad.

Once inside the library, he retrieved a book he left on a table beside a window. Benjamin was about to return to his bedchamber when he noticed the faint glow of light coming from the room next door. It was the children's classroom. Considering their distaste for learning, he seriously doubted they were up late, studying.

He carefully nudged the cracked door, not wanting to be detected. He saw two women huddled over a table they had moved in front of the lit fireplace. He noticed they placed several candles around the room to provide maximum light for their task.

"Try again, dear," he heard Tilly murmur encouragingly. Looking closer, Benjamin recognized the maid Sarah by her side. As he listened, he recognized the text was from one of his eldest son Allan's books. *What the devil?* he wondered.

He sensed rather than heard someone standing behind him. He turned and found Allan hiding in the shadows. He touched his finger to his lips and motioned for the boy to follow him.

Once they were behind the closed door of his study, he rounded on his son. "Why were you out of bed at this hour?" he asked, his voice firm.

The boy stared at the floor, a guilty look upon his face. When he failed to answer, Benjamin lifted his chin with one finger. "Did I not tell you boys to stay away from Mrs. Munro?" he asked.

He noticed Allan shook slightly. He decided intimidation was not a successful tactic. Sighing, he led his son to the chairs by the darkened fireplace and deposited him into one of them. With deliberate slowness, he lit several candles around the room. His son should take some time to collect himself before Benjamin continued the interrogation.

He crouched beside the chair, lightly placing his hands on Allan's knees. "I will always worry about your safety," he said. "It is my duty as your father. I love you, son."

The declaration seemed to soften Allan's reserve. "I returned from the privy to listen to the lesson," he whispered. He cleared his throat. "Miss Sarah is learning how to read."

"Aye, from one of your books. How did she get it?"

"A few days ago, I heard that Mrs. Munro was teaching her maid to read. I knew my books could help so I gave her one and told them both they could use our classroom."

"It is a secret," Allan added, glancing anxiously at his father. "I do not want Miss Sarah to get into trouble. She always completes her chores for the day so the lessons do not interfere with her work."

Benjamin's knees were aching so he took a chair opposite his son. "Do any of the other boys join you?" he asked casually.

Allan clamped his mouth shut.

"Tell me the truth," he said, giving his son a stern look. "You know I will find out eventually."

Seeing the look upon his father's face, Allan confessed, "No, not for the lessons. One day, I saw her walking to the chapel so I decided to follow her. It is not safe for a woman to be alone in the woods. Well, Angus saw me, the little spy. He decided to join me."

Leaning forward, he blurted, "He told Michael, not me. I told them both not to come, but they joined me every time I followed her." Allan hastily added, "It was Stephen who saw her first. He met her in the library and said she was a nice lady."

"Da, do you think she is a nice person?" the boy asked innocently. "She is very kind and likes going to the chapel, just like Ma."

Benjamin eyed his son. "Have you ever spoken with her in the chapel?" he asked. He wondered if Allan was there the day Tilly and he were together but decided not to ask.

The boy shrugged. "Aye, once. We talked for a bit about her poor family," he said. He looked at his father. "Ma always said it was a good place for quiet reflection so I usually leave Mrs. Munro to it." He tilted his head to the side and repeated his earlier question, "Do you think she is a nice person?"

"Aye, I believe she is."

"Then, are you angry that I have been spending time with her, even though you told us we should not?"

"I am not happy that you disobeyed me," Benjamin replied. He swept a hand over his face. "The hour is late. Let us discuss this further in the morning. For now, I want you to go to bed. Go straight to your room. Do not stop in the classroom. Do you understand me?"

Allan nodded. He raced from the room before his father could change his mind about punishing him.

∞

TILLY BLEW OUT THE LAST OF THE CANDLES and massaged her tired neck. The new text was a blessing. It was as if she could see knowledge blossom like a flower in Sarah's brain. It was a silly analogy, but it seemed to apply.

She was just about to bank the fire when she heard a man cough behind her. She spun around and found Benjamin standing in the doorway. "Oh, you startled me!" she exclaimed, her hand to her chest. "Trouble sleeping?"

"Aye, I came to the library about an hour ago for a book," he said, slowly walking into the room. "I was surprised to see someone in the classroom."

She swallowed hard. *Busted*, she thought. Well, was there a law against teaching a servant? Gloomily, she realized, in this age, there *might* be.

She lifted her head and moved toward the door. Feigning a yawn, she said, "It is late. I believe I shall go to bed. Good night."

Benjamin grabbed her arm when she tried to pass him. "Might I have a moment of your time, Mrs. Munro?" he asked.

He bade her to follow him to the table and chairs in front of the fireplace. "I understand that you have been teaching your maid Sarah how to read," he said, taking a seat and placing his arms on the table.

"Knowledge is a wonderful thing, do you not agree?"

She sat stiffly in the chair. "Yes. Knowing how to read will open many doors for her," she said. Tilly raised her chin defiantly. "I will teach her how to write too, as soon as I can figure out how to use those damn quills."

"I would appreciate it if you would avoid teaching her your unladylike vocabulary," he said, a bemused smile on his lips.

She laughed. "I assure you that our lessons are wholesome," she said.

"For your sake, I hope they are," he said. Benjamin eased forward in his chair and asked, "What lesson did you teach my son?"

Tilly gasped. *Oh, double damn,* she moaned inwardly. She pretended to be deeply intrigued with a knot in the wood of the table. Peeking at him, she saw the serious look on his face and knew that he expected an answer. With as much feigned innocence as she could muster, she asked, "What do you mean, sir?"

"Madam, I believe that is the first time you have called me 'sir.' You must be very worried indeed," he said, chuckling. "Let me allay your concern. I confess I was most aggrieved at first. You are fortunate that I spent some time waiting for you to finish your lesson. It gave me the opportunity to think clearly."

"And, what have you concluded?"

"You are a guest of undetermined duration. It was inevitable that you would meet my children. I only wished it was on my terms, but alas, I cannot alter that direction now."

"No, I suppose not. The cat is out of the bag."

"What cat?"

"It is an expression we use back home."

"Ah, I see," Benjamin said, though he did not seem to grasp the meaning of the phrase. He leaned back in the chair and appeared to tuck in for a long chat.

"Were you a governess before you married?"

"I suppose that is what you would call it now," Tilly said. She gathered it was time for yet another discussion of her past. "I was a teacher for a year before Alex and I married. Once the twins were old enough, I completed my master's degree in education and had hopes of obtaining a job. Plans changed, though, after what happened."

Benjamin's face clouded. "I apologize if I have brought forth bad memories," he said sincerely.

"It is fine," she said, trying to sound less troubled than she was. "We made plans for our future.

Unfortunately, things did not work out. You know as well as I do how that happens."

"Yes, all too well."

They sat in silence for a few moments. She assumed the interview was over and rose from her chair. She immediately returned to her seat when she saw the look on his face.

Sighing, he said gravely, "After all that you have learned of my past, I hope you can understand why I am so protective of my family."

"I would expect nothing less," she admitted. "Please understand that I am a stranger in a different time, though. This is hard for me too."

"In your time, do people flit from one century to another?"

She shook her head. "Although scientists have theories that time travel could happen, no one has proved it yet," she said. "Of course, if someone had travelled from another time, I doubt they would admit it. They would be considered insane and locked away somewhere."

"You do not seem insane to me," he said so softly she was afraid she imagined it. "You seem quite rational."

As if he reached a difficult conclusion, Benjamin

exhaled slowly and said, "We must remedy the situation. Meet me in the family library tomorrow at 9:00 a.m."

He strode to the fireplace and banked the fire. Turning to her, he grinned broadly, "Tilly, the hour grows late. Let us away to our beds. Tomorrow will be a long day."

With that, he moved toward the door, leaving her to stare at his departing form.

# TWENTY FOUR

THE NEXT MORNING, Tilly and Sarah entered the library together, a united force against whatever repercussions might come. The maid was very upset about what happened, despite assurances that all would be well. *At least I hope so,* Tilly thought.

They found the boys lined up in front of a large window, their faces pressed against the glass. When Tilly asked what they were doing, Allan informed her they were watching their father. She looked outside and found Benjamin talking with two of the servants. When he glanced back at the house, they all scurried away from the window.

Several moments later, Benjamin walked into the library where everyone was scattered around the room. Allan, Angus, and Michael shared a chaise near a window and were studying a large atlas. Tilly and Sarah sat in chairs beside the fireplace. Stephen flipped through a picture book on the floor beside their feet. It seemed like an innocent scene, yet there was a palpable undercurrent of nervousness in the room.

Without further ado, he summoned his children to his side. They arranged themselves from eldest to youngest as if they had done this many times. Benjamin placed his hand on Allan's shoulder and looked at Tilly, "Allan is my oldest son, age 10."

She always admired Allan's lovely crystal blue eyes, the color of the sky. They were so different from the mossy green of his father's eyes. Now that he stood beside Benjamin, she noticed how tall the child was. He almost reached his father's elbow.

Benjamin walked down the line. He patted the cheek of the next boy, a short child with the same auburn hair and green eyes of his father. "This is my son Angus, age 8," he said.

Approaching the next boy, he said with a smile, "Here is Michael." He could have been Angus' clone, except he was a few inches shorter than his brother. "He may be five years old, but he thinks he can do anything his older brothers can."

When he came to Stephen, the youngest boy made little grunting noises and grabbing movements with his hands. He obediently scooped his son into his arms and said, "This wee rascal is Stephen."

The boy grinned broadly at Tilly, revealing those charming little dimples she saw during their first encounter. She noticed his blue eyes were filled with mischief. He must be a handful.

As if reading her mind, Benjamin said, "Aye, this one is the wildest of them all. My other boys managed to survive age two without burning down the castle. I am not so sure about this one."

At that moment, Mrs. Keith walked into the room. She carried an adorable, chubby girl on her hip. Benjamin nodded, and she gave the child to Tilly.

"And that is my precious Margaret," he said softly, his eyes filling with tears. "She is the spitting image of her mother."

Tilly ran a finger over the little girl's soft, rosy cheek, earning herself a little giggle. The baby was gorgeous with her thick, curly red hair and blue eyes just like her brothers Allan and Stephen. She leaned forward and planted a little kiss on the child's forehead. It felt so good to hold a little one again.

"Would you mind taking Maggie, Mrs. Keith?" Benjamin said gruffly. "The boys and I have things to discuss with Mrs. Munro."

She reluctantly returned Maggie to the housekeeper. She was confused at his sudden shift in mood but said nothing.

"Let us all take a seat," he said, motioning to the chairs around a table in the center of the room. He deposited Stephen into one of the chairs. For once, the child did not squirm.

Everyone else looked very guilty as they took their seats. "Despite my command, it seems my boys have deliberately disobeyed me, Mrs. Munro. Allan gave you leave to use the classroom and loaned you his books," he said. Benjamin gestured toward his other children. "Angus and Michael followed you in secret. And, wee Stephen was apparently the boldest one, meeting you not long after your arrival."

"It is not as if anyone was doing anything bad," Angus protested, his arms folded tightly at his chest.

"Why is it so awful?" Tilly asked angrily.

"Aye," Allan said, ready for an argument. "She is a nice lady. I learned a lot more from one lesson with her than I ever did from that old cow, Mrs. Donnelly."

To prove his point, he retrieved a book from the bookcase. Allan returned to his seat and opened it. Tentatively, he read aloud the first two pages. While he stumbled over a few of the big words, he used the techniques Tilly taught Sarah to correctly pronounce the words. When he finished, he smiled triumphantly at his father.

Benjamin took a seat at the table, a stunned look upon his face. She was thoroughly confused. She leaned over and asked Allan what happened.

"He has struggled for the last six months to read that book," Benjamin said. "Mrs. Donnelly said it was too advanced for him. What did you do?"

"Nothing special," she said, shrugging. "He overheard me reviewing the basics of reading with Sarah."

"Who is Mrs. Donnelly?" she asked. The name sounded familiar, but she could not quite remember why. She felt a little kick in the shin and looked at Sarah who gave a look that quelled further questions. She would learn more on the topic later.

Benjamin cringed involuntarily. "She was their governess and, apparently, not a very good one," he said. "A new tutor will be here any day now." Staring at Tilly, he added, "His arrival will resolve the matter of Allan's education. I still require a governess for the other children."

"Stephen is too young for formal lessons but will protest if he is not included," he said, rising from his chair. "Can you handle my active boys, Mrs. Munro?"

"Why – yes, of course." Confused, she asked, "Do you want me to be their teacher?"

"Aye. Your maid may attend the lessons as well. I will ask Mrs. Keith to assign Sarah's other tasks to someone else. She will devote herself solely to you as a lady's maid," he said. He strode toward the door, adding, "You can use the family library and classroom for your lessons. The boys know where all the materials are. Feel free to start today."

Tilly, Sarah, and the children sat in stunned silence.

∞

BY THE END OF THE DAY, Tilly was exhausted but very happy. For the first hour, the boys were on their best behavior while she assessed their levels in reading, writing, and arithmetic. Unfortunately, they rapidly grew bored. It soon became very hard to keep their attention. In that regard, it was not much different from the challenges of a 21$^{st}$ century classroom. She enjoyed herself, though. After all, had she not planned to return to the profession anyway? *Perhaps not in 1801*, she thought.

She wearily returned to her chamber with Sarah and prepared for dinner. "Are you more exhausted after a day spent with the children than spent doing your normal work?" Tilly asked, noticing the tired look on Sarah's face.

The maid laughed, a rare sound that was always pleasing. "Aye, milady," Sarah replied. "I never thought it was possible."

"They will settle by the end of the week. Children usually spend the first few days determining how much mischief they can cause."

"They were always very mean when Mrs. Donnelly was here."

Tilly hoped they would discuss the former governess. She was glad Sarah mentioned it first. "Please tell me about her," she said. "I sense a lot of animosity toward the woman."

Sarah lowered her voice, even though no one was in the room with them. "Mrs. Donnelly was sent here by milord's father, Malcolm. He knew her late husband, a merchant in London." She smirked, "Apparently, when the man died, he did not leave his wife much money. His Grace thought she could be a governess for his grandchildren."

"Oh, so she was here for a long time?"

"Aye, many years. They say she had designs on His Grace, that she took the job thinking he would be here on a regular basis. She hoped to be his wife someday if he spent time with her."

"But, he never paid her any attention. She was just another servant," Sarah continued as she helped Tilly into a clean gown. "She became very bitter. Mrs. Donnelly was nice to the children – in front of His Grace and milord and milady. When they were not about, though, she was very harsh."

"That is most unfortunate. Was she dismissed because of it?"

"Oh, no," Sarah said, shaking her head and grinning slyly. "Milord was heartbroken over his wife's death. Mrs. Donnelly saw an opportunity. She at least had the decency to wait for a few months. Then, one night, she crept into milord's room. When he retired for the evening, he found her waiting for him, naked, in his bed."

"I take it he was not happy about the situation?"

"We could hear the yelling all the way down in the servants' quarters!"

The ladies laughed for several minutes. Sarah wiped the tears from her eyes. "Mrs. Donnelly was sent away that very night," she said. "I hear she is still in the village. Some say she believes milord will change his mind and send for her."

"When did this happen?"

Sarah thought for a moment and said, "Oh, it has been a month or so. Milord was most upset. He left the castle the next day. He told everyone that he needed some time alone." She brightened. "And, then he returned with you!"

Tilly was quiet while she considered the new information.

# TWENTY FIVE

BENJAMIN DID NOT SIT at the opposite end of the table during the evening meal. Instead, he sat to Tilly's right and entertained her with stories about how his children tortured Mrs. Donnelly. She was amused by Angus' penchant for placing frogs in unlikely places. She made a mental note to be very careful in the child's presence.

When the last course was consumed, he helped her from her chair. "Mrs. Munro, would you accompany me to the family library?" he asked. Casting a sidelong glance at Mr. Murphy, he added, "I have a book I want Allan to read."

She took his arm and allowed him to guide her down the stairs toward the library. When they entered the room, they found Mr. Murphy had somehow arrived before them. A fire danced in the grate, and lit candles illuminated the room. The butler busied himself by placing a bottle of whisky and glasses on a small table in the corner.

Benjamin escorted her to a seat, then excused himself to look for the book. He returned moments later with a hefty volume that resembled the thick ledgers she spotted on the bookcases around her. He took a seat opposite her and waited until the servants left the room before he spoke, "This book is a compilation of our family's stories. A distant relative prepared it some fifty years ago."

She accepted the book from him. Its leather binding was cracked, and she could see wood peeking from the torn brown cover. She was very careful as she flipped through the dry, yellowed pages. Disappointed, she said, "Oh, no, the book is written in Latin."

"You cannot read Latin?"

"It is not commonly taught in schools, so I never bothered to learn it."

He retrieved the book from her and placed it upon a table. "We shall save it for the tutor then," he said. "Knowledge of Latin is a requirement for the position."

"Do you mean I cannot be the governess?"

"I only mean that the new tutor can supplement your deficiency. Based upon Allan's improvements alone, I see you possess many other skills."

She did not like to think she was deficient in any areas of teaching. Tilly conceded his point, though. She decided to change the subject. "Would you like a drink?" she asked. She walked to the table where Mr. Murphy had placed the whisky and glasses.

Taking his silence as assent, she poured their drinks. She handed him a glass as she returned to her seat. She noted the smile of satisfaction that spread upon Benjamin's face when he took a sip.

"How was your day?" she asked, taking a sip from her own glass and savoring the warm feeling as the liquid tumbled down her throat. In the last few weeks, she had grown accustomed to the taste of whisky. She especially enjoyed the brand served at the castle.

He seemed surprised that she was interested. Benjamin ran a hand over his face. "Sometimes, my duties require a great deal of attention," he said, his voice weary. "It can be exhausting."

"What were you doing?" she asked. She studied him carefully. He tended to be evasive whenever he discussed "castle business," as she called it

"A tenant wishes to buy the plot of land on which his farm is located. We had matters to discuss."

"I thought your father owned all of the property. Does he allow you to sell land?"

Benjamin eyed her suspiciously. "When he dies, I will inherit everything," he said. "It is important that I familiarize myself with the affairs of the estate."

"So, you cannot legally sell the land until your father dies?"

"I never said I was selling property to a tenant," he said, leaning forward in the chair. "I cannot sell that which is not mine."

"I did not mean to imply that you were," she said. She was surprised by the shift in his mood. "I was just curious." She swallowed the rest of the whisky and rose to refill her glass. "By the way, whatever your plan is, you should know it will save the estate."

He grabbed her arm. "What did you say, lass?" he asked. "How do you know what the future holds?"

Tilly winced at the pressure from his hold. She stared into his eyes. They were bloodshot from fatigue. For the first time, she noticed the deep lines on his face. "When was the last time you slept, Benjamin?" she asked. She resisted the urge to run her hand across his face.

"Answer me," he demanded, a hint of danger in his voice.

She pulled her arm from his grasp and shook it to restore the blood flow. "What is wrong?" she asked.

"You must be a spy for my father," he said irritably. He stood, placing his glass on the table between them. He glared at her. "Do you send him messages about the goings on at the castle? Do the two of you work in secret to thwart everything that I do?"

"No, of course not! I told you where I came from. Don't you believe me?"

Shaking his head, Benjamin slumped in the chair and ran his hand through his hair. "Tilly, your story defies all logical explanation. You must know that," he said. He sighed heavily. "I am so tired of worrying about everything – the estate, my family, you. I just wish I knew the truth about you. Perhaps then I could have some peace."

She strode to the table and refilled her glass, keeping her back to him. She felt a friendship forming with him. She began to trust him and desperately wished he would return the favor.

"My friend Beth planned this trip," she said. "It was the one-year anniversary of the accident. She probably didn't want me dwelling on it, so she whisked me away on an adventure."

She took a sip of whisky. Tilly heard him rise from

his seat and felt him standing behind her. "Beth gave me a thick packet of materials and several books to read before the trip. I learned more than I ever wanted about Scottish history," she said. "Many of the great estates are gone. As you know, land was seized by the English after the Rising. Some of the families who still held land sold it to the English. Others tried unsuccessful sheep or timber operations."

"Because of the lack of work and the famines that ravaged the country, families moved. They sought better lives by emigrating to England and America," she said. "Even worse, many crofters were forced off their land by greedy landowners during something called 'the Clearances.' Whole villages were wiped off the map. Even in my time, large sections of Scotland remain unpopulated."

Benjamin exclaimed in shock, "This is terrible news indeed! I always believed a brighter future lay ahead and hoped that the cruelties of the past would not continue. I am naïve. I thought people would someday see the error of their ways."

He paused, clinging to the one glimmer of hope she offered. "Did you say this estate survives?" he asked.

"Yes," Tilly replied, turning to face him. "Remember? I told you that I toured the castle the day before we found each other in the forest. We didn't tour everything, but I got the sense that the Campbells owned a lot of land in the area."

He stared at her for some time. She could see that he struggled with her story. "I desperately want to believe the castle will stand more than two hundred years in the future," Benjamin said. "It is the reason I work so hard to preserve it."

"The castle remains, although some of the rooms have not been restored yet," she said. "It takes a great deal of money to maintain a home like this."

"Aye, I know that all too well. I struggle daily with the task."

"Mr. Douglas told us your work saved the estate," she said. "You remember me telling you about him, right? His wife and he owned the inn where Beth and I stayed."

Tilly placed the glass on the table. "He said that you took care of the people. Your loyalty to them meant the survival of this place," she said. "I don't know what you are doing, but you must not stop. You are on the right path."

"I want your words to be the truth," Benjamin whispered. "Can you understand why it is hard for me?"

"It is hard for me too. Can you understand that?"

"Tell me more of this future in which you live," he said, guiding her back to their seats by the fire.

"What would you like to know?"

"Have they invented a faster means of transportation? You say you are from the former Colonies. Sea voyages are long. How did you travel here?"

"Oh, transportation is faster now – I mean, then. We flew here," she said. She caught his confused expression and giggled, "Not physically!" She could not resist flapping her arms.

"We have machines called airplanes that fly like birds. They can hold lots of people – kind of like a ship in the sky. We can travel great distances in a matter of hours."

"Travel must be a great pleasure then. I dread boarding ships whenever I travel abroad. The journeys are long and extremely boring."

Tilly considered all the inconveniences of modern travel – lengthy security checks, overcrowded planes, cancelled flights. She guessed it was better than travelling on a boat for weeks, even months, at a time. "It has its disadvantages too, as all travel does," she said.

"Pray, tell me more."

She looked at all the books stuffed into the bookshelves and said, "We have devices that can hold this entire library's worth of knowledge many times over. Some devices are smaller than a piece of paper."

"Amazing."

"It is. We also have something called the internet. It is a worldwide web of knowledge. You can search it for information about any topic."

"Would it know about time travel?"

Tilly glanced at him and realized he was teasing her. "Yes, smarty pants, it would, although time travel is more of a concept than actual practice," she said.

"I miss other things, though," she sighed. "I miss being able to take a bath every day because I don't need a team of maids to haul hot water up the stairs. I miss toilets. I miss cold, clean water." She groaned. "Oh, the food – barbecue, pizza, mochas, chocolate."

"I did not realize how unhappy you are here."

"I'm not unhappy – well, not completely. Those things are all material. If I learned anything from my family's accident, it is that you should treasure people more than possessions."

"Do you miss Beth?"

Tilly felt a small pain in her heart when she thought of her best friend. "I do," she said. "I wish I could ask her what I should do. I have tried to figure out how to go back to my time, but I haven't found a way. If I could just talk with her, maybe she could help me understand what happened. Maybe she could – "

Benjamin looked expectantly at her. "What could she do, Tilly?" he asked.

"I have spent the last year feeling lost, as if I would never find my purpose in life," she admitted. "I felt like a shell of a human being. And, now, I feel alive again. I love teaching your children. When I wake up in the morning, I don't feel depressed. I am excited to see what will happen. Maybe Beth could tell me why I feel this way. Why did I have to travel to 1801 to feel complete?"

He stood and lifted Tilly from her seat. He wrapped his arms around her. "I cannot tell you what Beth would say," he whispered. "I can only speak from my heart. I am happy you are here."

He placed a light kiss upon her lips. "The hour grows late. You should go to bed." Chuckling, he added, "You will need your strength tomorrow when you resume your lessons with the boys."

Tilly did not want to leave his embrace. She was

confused by his little kiss and profession of being happy about her presence. *What the hell does that mean?* she wanted to know. She was afraid of the answer. "You are right," she said, reluctantly slipping from his arms. "Perhaps it is time for bed."

With that, she bade him goodnight and headed for the door. She paused when he spoke.

"Tilly, please know that I want to believe you," he said. "It is very hard for me. For now, can you be content that I have allowed you to teach my children? I am trying to open my mind to what you have told me."

She looked at him. She could see his struggle but could not forget her own. "I speak the truth. I am trapped here and have no idea if I will ever return home," she said. "Instead of trying to open your mind, you should open your heart. What does it say, Benjamin?"

He joined her at the doorway. He placed a hand upon her shoulder. "You will be safe here for as long as you want to stay," he promised.

She asked angrily, "What the hell is that supposed to mean - *'for as long as I want to stay?'* Do you think I am having a delightful holiday and will soon discover how to go home?" She huffed. "Didn't I just tell you I have no idea how to return?"

She banged her fist against the closed door. She did not know which was more infuriating – that he did not believe her or that she desperately *wanted* him to believe her.

Surprisingly, Tilly realized his opinion meant a great deal to her. He was her only support, her only friend. What would become of her if his good opinion turned sour? Equally important, why did she even care about his 'good opinion?' Frustrated by the realization, she flung open the door and raced from the room.

∞

BENJAMIN CONSIDERED CHASING AFTER HER but decided against it. Instead, he went to his study. Taking a seat behind his desk, he opened a ledger and attempted to push Tilly from his mind.

An hour later, Iain MacIver entered the study, now dark save the light from the fireplace. Benjamin still sat behind his desk, lost in thought and sipping a glass of whisky.

Iain spotted the bottle on the desk and helped himself to a glass. "What troubles you?" he asked, taking a seat in a chair on the opposite side of the desk. "You look as if the weight of the world rests upon your shoulders."

"Have you heard we have a new governess?"

Benjamin asked. "As usual, the boys disobeyed me. Allan joined Mrs. Munro when she tutored her maid in private, and the other boys have followed her around the estate. My efforts to shelter my family from her have failed."

"Aye, they usually do. It is difficult to shelter those who do not think they need protection."

"What should I do? I am no closer to knowing who that woman is than the day I brought her to the castle. She does not seem dangerous. She does not appear to be a spy. Can I trust her?"

"It is too soon to fully trust her. However, contact with your family cannot be avoided. I assume you have taken suitable precautions?"

"Aye. The maid was instructed to stay with Mrs. Munro whenever she teaches the children."

"Do you trust the maid?"

"Mary liked her, and she was always an excellent judge of character."

Iain nodded in agreement. "I fear Mrs. Munro is not the only matter of business we should discuss this evening," he said. He took a deep breath. "The excise men have been in the northern part of our fair lands." Before Benjamin could voice concern, he added, "I have resolved the situation. Rest assured, they left satisfied."

"How many pounds of flesh did they take this time?"

"Slightly more coin than usual and an extra barrel of whisky. They seemed happy with the arrangement, and that is all that matters."

"This is the second time they have visited us this month. Are you concerned?"

"Any time an excise man pays us a visit, I am concerned. I have sent men to other operations in the Highlands. Soon, we will know if the Crown has increased their patrols or if this is an isolated incident with a particular group."

"Thank you, Iain. I do not want to jeopardize our little business. It is too profitable."

"I have asked the men who guard the castle to be extra vigilant for another reason."

That statement got Benjamin's full attention. "What have you heard?" he asked. "Have you learned from whence the lass comes? Is she in league with the excise men?"

"No. I have learned something more disturbing."

"Well, out with it, man," Benjamin said, flinging his hands in frustration. "What wickedness threatens us now?"

"Richard MacDonald was seen in a village two days' ride from here."

"What else do you know?"

"He inquired about the Campbell family. He asked about Mary and the children. Apparently, news of her death had not reached the MacDonalds."

"I am sure he is on his way here to condole with me."

"Aye, the MacDonalds were always known for their prodigious care for their fellow man," Iain replied sarcastically. "It warrants concern. If you will recall, the MacDonald was most aggrieved with the agreement between his father and yours."

Benjamin refilled his glass. "I do not need this trouble now," he said. He downed the fiery liquid in one gulp. "I have enough worries."

"We have friends in Deoch. We will know if he is close."

"Pray that we do not learn too late, Iain. Post a twenty-four hour watch along the castle grounds."

"Already done."

"Good."

"There is one last piece of news," Iain said, sighing. "It seems Mrs. Donnelly remains in Deoch. My source tells me she talks of her return to Castle Fion. She is under the impression you will send for her."

Benjamin massaged the aching muscles of his neck and said, "Tell your friend he should advise her against false hope. The woman was given sufficient funds to find her way back to London. She should leave."

Iain guffawed, "Oh, Benjamin, you have a mighty effect on women." Wiping tears of mirth from his cheeks, he teased, "She pines for you. It will take more than a bit of friendly advice to be rid of her."

"Deal with this problem, Iain," he commanded. He rose from his chair and moved toward the doorway to his bedchamber. "I do not have the energy to deal with a lovelorn woman."

Even through the closed door, Benjamin could hear his friend's laughter.

# TWENTY SIX

MRS. MAUREEN DONNELLY SAT AT A GRUBBY TABLE IN THE PUBLIC HOUSE. She was neither pretty nor rich, so she did not fear being approached by any of the male patrons. *At least I am honest about my situation*, she thought sullenly.

The bloom of her youth was wasted on her late husband, a man who promised he was a prosperous merchant and was, in reality, a lowly clerk. Life with him erased the rosy glow on her cheek and replaced it with a sallow complexion on her perpetually frowning countenance. Her brown hair and eyes seemed even drearier with each passing year. If she did not find her way soon, she knew her prospects were very sad indeed.

She sipped a chipped mug of weak tea and watched the door, waiting eagerly for the man to arrive. Maureen heard about him from another person in Deoch. She hoped he would pay a handsome sum for the information she possessed. She desperately needed the money. A fresh start in America just might be far enough away from this God-forsaken place. The funds that Benjamin Campbell gave her would not be enough.

The door swung wide. The tall man in the doorway momentarily blocked the light from the setting sun. He made his way to the bar and flung a coin onto the countertop as he collected a tankard of ale. Spotting Maureen, he took a seat at a table directly behind her, his back to her. "Are you the governess?" the man asked without turning his head.

"Aye," she whispered.

The man finished his ale in one thirsty gulp. "Meet me behind the stable in five minutes," he said. He tossed a gold coin to her when he walked by her table.

Maureen greedily grabbed the coin before anyone saw it. She continued to nonchalantly sip her tea, even though she wanted to race after him. It would attract attention, a bad thing. After waiting several moments, she decided enough time had passed. After primly patting the corners of her mouth with a lacy handkerchief and straightening her bonnet, she slid from the chair and left the establishment.

As she walked toward the stables, she made sure no one followed her. *One can never be too careful*, she thought.

She found the man sitting on a bale of straw behind the stable. He was partially obscured by shadow, yet she could tell he was a filthy mess. He wore a tattered, grey shirt that had likely been white at one time. His trousers were dark brown and rough spun. Bits of straw, leaves, and dried dirt clung to the worn fabric and were scattered about what little hair he had on his head. His thick beard probably crawled with lice, judging from the way he furiously scratched it.

"I heard you want information about Benjamin Campbell and his family," Maureen stated without preamble.

"Aye," the man said, retreating further into the shadows. "I am looking for someone who knows the lay of the place, who can tell me something about their habits."

"I can help you – for a price."

He laughed dryly. The man tossed a heavy leather bag to her. "That payment is for the information," he said. He shook another bag so she could hear the coins inside. He flung it to her and added, "This bag is for your silence."

Maureen easily caught the bags and suppressed a smile. If they contained as much gold as she guessed, she would have plenty of money to book a passage. She dared to peek inside the bags and gasped when she saw the gleaming contents. She might even have enough money to open a little shop in America.

She was so focused on the money that she did not notice the man was now standing in front of her. When she caught whiff of his soured body, she looked up and took a step back.

He held a shiny dirk in front of her face. "Be warned, lass. I will slit your throat from ear to ear if you betray me," the man said, a lethal promise in his voice.

She gulped involuntarily. "I hate the Campbells," Maureen hissed. "You need not worry about betrayal."

She slipped the money into her bag and retrieved a folded piece of parchment. "I made a map of the rooms as well as notes about Benjamin Campbell's schedule," she said, offering the parchment to him. "Do you require additional information?"

He took the map from her and tucked it into the

cracked leather sporran at his waist. He motioned to a bale of straw. "Aye, let us talk further, Mrs. Donnelly," he said. "As the former governess, you can tell me all about the children."

∞

THE NEXT MORNING, Richard MacDonald crouched low in the shrubs of the forest. If the former governess' information was accurate, Benjamin Campbell should be making his way toward Castle Fion's main stable for his morning ride.

Richard groaned as he shifted his weight. His knees aching, he must push past the pain and remember his purpose. He must not forget the suffering his family had experienced because of the Campbells. For centuries, the MacDonalds and Campbells feuded. It became far worse during the Rising, when the Campbells killed his people in their villages and on the battlefield at Culloden. After the Jacobites were defeated, the family followed the Crown's orders like the lapdogs they were. They stole MacDonald lands and reduced his family's holdings to a crumbling castle and a few acres of land not fit for man or beast.

The final insult came from Malcolm and Benjamin Campbell. Richard ground his teeth in fury as he recalled the sight of his brother and sister's lifeless bodies. Even after all these years, the image was burned into his brain. He would never forget.

Suddenly, a man appeared on the path leading toward the stable. His long auburn hair was unbound. His clothes were casual, definitely suited for riding. It seemed to Richard that the man moved with great ease, as if he had not a care in the world.

*That must be the bastard,* he thought, closing watching Benjamin. Reflexively, his hand clinched the hilt of the MacDonald blade tucked into his belt.

Benjamin laughed. He turned and stopped. A woman came into view. Richard could not hear what they were saying, but it did not matter. His focus was solely upon Benjamin.

He watched the pair walk toward the stable. They seemed to be having a lovely conversation. *Enjoy yourself while you can, lad,* he thought grimly, *for the hour of your death draws nigh.*

With difficulty, he stood and eased further into the shadows of the forest. The woman must be the new governess. What was her name again? Tilly Munro? Mrs. Donnelly did not have the pleasure of personally meeting the woman but knew a great deal about her. Apparently, there was a rumor that the woman might be more than a simple servant.

He did not care if Benjamin was having sexual relations with the new governess or any other woman, for that matter. He was encouraged to see, though, that Mrs. Donnelly's thorough knowledge of the man's habits was accurate. Benjamin appeared at the stable exactly when she indicated. Richard hoped the other information she provided was just as sound.

He carefully made his way deeper into the forest, heading for his makeshift camp. He was tired and uncomfortable in the shirt and trousers he wore. He looked forward to shedding the garments and donning his kilt as soon as he reached the camp. He would always prefer his kilt to these blasted English garments. The Act of Proscription made generations of Scots forget their heritage. Not him. He would always follow the old ways.

Richard kept those traditions alive at his home. Oh, how he looked forward to returning there, where he did not have to hide in the forest like an animal. He had been away for some time. He left the day after he buried his father. He should have stayed longer to tend to family matters. However, for too long, he had nursed the white hot flame of revenge. It was time to avenge centuries of horror inflicted on the MacDonald family by Benjamin Campbell and his forefathers.

He deeply regretted that innocent lives might be lost in his quest. His father taught him it was a necessary evil in battle, but he cared not for it. The fact was, he liked Maureen Donnelly.

They talked for nearly three hours. It was apparent that she hated Benjamin and his father Malcolm almost as much as he did. Still, she willingly shared extensive intelligence of the Campbell family, all for the price of a few gold coins. Would she run to Benjamin and reveal Richard's presence and intentions, if offered compensation?

He could not take the chance. When she turned to leave, he crept behind her and dispatched her as swiftly and quietly as he could. He made sure she did not suffer. He held her when she slipped from this world, not wanting her to die alone. He saw the fear in her eyes and whispered a prayer of deliverance into her ear. With great care, he buried her body in a grave behind the stable and hoped it would not be discovered until after he carried out his plan.

*Soon*, Richard thought.

# TWENTY SEVEN

AS TILLY MADE HER WAY TO THE STABLE, she calculated that she had been living in 1801 for two months. She was genuinely surprised. It did not seem as if she had been there that long. She remained unsettled that she did not know how to return to her own time, yet she grudgingly admitted she was happy.

Sure, the lack of plumbing and other modern conveniences was, at times, distressing. She really missed being able to take a nice bath, or even a quick shower, at least once each day. How could she ask the servants to heave buckets of hot water to her room for a daily bath? She tried it once and felt enormously guilty about the amount of effort it took. Thus, she adopted the custom of weekly bathing, with a daily wash from the basin of fresh water that Sarah provided. To live in this time, compromise was required with some things, and a good soak was one of them.

Despite the disadvantages of the plumbing situation, Tilly felt a lightness that she had not experienced since the accident. She was relieved that the pitying stares and whispered, sympathetic comments were confined to her own time. People knew a version of her story, yet they did not treat her differently here. After all, most had experienced equally profound loss and continued on with their lives. They had no other choice.

She reflected on her newfound situation as she surveyed her surroundings. It was so peaceful here. The air was clean. Utility lines did not scar the view. Airplanes did not streak overhead, leaving vapor trails and thundering noise. No, the only sound she heard now came from the red stag that stampeded through the forest. The first time she heard it, she nearly jumped out of her skin.

It had become her daily custom to take a walk around the grounds as soon as lessons were finished with the boys. Sarah was right all those weeks ago. The exercise and fresh air was great for her body and mind. Her favorite spots were the stable and chapel.

The stable reminded her of the little farm Alex and she once had. Their livestock consisted of chickens and goats, not horses. Still, the familiar smell of wild beast and fresh hay gave her a warm feeling. As she strode into the stable, Tilly inhaled deeply and could not resist smiling.

She was immediately greeted with a gentle "woof" from the little white terrier who patrolled the building. She knelt and scratched the happy dog behind the ears. She glanced up in time to see two puppies racing toward their mother. The terrier growled a warning. It seemed that Mommy wanted all the attention today.

"Grace is trying to wean the pups," a man said, emerging from the shadows. Tilly recognized him. He was the stablemaster, a sturdy Scot by the name of Graeme.

"I am sure Mr. Campbell would not mind if you took one of the pups," he said. Graeme leaned against a stall and gestured toward a scraggly black cat that groomed itself in the sunlight. "Grace is a better mouser than yon cat. Her pups should be too."

Tilly said nothing. While she would love to adopt Grace and her pups, she was not certain that she should be so firmly rooted in the current time. She might find a way home soon. How, she had no idea. So far, she found no clues or hints that suggested how she came to be in 1801.

She rose and moved toward one of the stalls. She

found that being around horses was a surprisingly fun experience for her. Tilly fancied one horse in particular. A white mare named Angel saw her and whinnied in anticipation. She produced an apple from her pocket, much to the delight of the horse. She stroked the side of Angel's face while the animal nibbled on the treat.

"You may ride her whenever you like, mistress," Graeme said. "She is the gentlest creature in the stable."

"Oh, thank you, but I do not know how to ride," she said, staring into the horse's soft brown eyes. If she did not know better, she would swear the horse smiled at her.

"You do not know how to ride?!" the stablemaster exclaimed in shock. He came to her side. "Do they not have horses in America?"

"I lived in a city," Tilly lied. "I used carriages. I never learned how to ride a horse."

"Well, we shall have to remedy that," Benjamin said as he exited the adjacent stall.

# TWENTY EIGHT

MUCH TO TILLY'S CHAGRIN, Benjamin was true to his word. That day, he placed her on Angel's back and led her around the castle grounds. He instructed her to return to the stable every day, at the same time, for proper lessons.

At first, the rides were brief. Unfortunately, with each passing day, the distance grew further. Then, at dinner one night, he informed her that the children's lessons were canceled the next day so that they might take a ride. She was worried but said nothing.

As instructed, she met him in front of the castle. Allan and Angus waved cheerily from their mounts, excited at the prospect of an adventure. She watched Benjamin tuck food and bottles of ale into his saddle bags, confirming her worst fears. Her 21st century body was not made to be jostled around on the back of a horse for hours on end. *Automobiles were invented for a reason*, she thought as he helped her onto the horse.

They headed for a road that hugged the rocky shores of the loch. When they reached a slight rise, she looked behind her. From this vantage point, the castle and surrounding forest was on full display. She drew her horse to a stop, enjoying the view. Its dark grey stones were no less forbidding, yet she felt a certain sense of home now when she gazed upon the castle.

"It is a fair view, lass," Benjamin commented, a contented smile forming upon his lips. "Whenever I am away for a long time, I feel such peace at the first sight of my home." He pointed to a turn ahead. "Come now. I want to show you a special place."

∞

AN HOUR LATER, they stopped on top of a windy ridge. Tilly did not know why Benjamin felt it would be the perfect picnic spot. When she turned to ask him, she noticed the angry expression upon his face. She said nothing, unsure what prompted the change in mood. At length, he moved his horse closer to hers so she could hear him over the wind. "Look in the valley," he said, pointing to a desolate area of gorse and heather.

She studied the scene. She noticed a crumbling rock wall and the remnants of a house, its roof collapsed long ago. One spot looked as if it held a garden at one time. Squinting, she saw a small cemetery in the distance. Did the place belong to some ancient ancestor?

"Iain MacIver's family owned this farm," Benjamin said. He grabbed the reins of his horse and motioned for Tilly and the children to follow him.

He led them to a trail that ended at a sheltered spot in the valley below the ridge. A small copse of trees remained where the rest of the land was bare. He deftly dismounted his horse and helped Tilly from hers. The boys hopped from their horses with ease. They did not seem to suffer the same ill effects as she.

Benjamin remained silent. He took their lunch from the saddlebags and handed a blanket to her. It was the same plaid blanket from their tryst. She decided that it was best to keep that knowledge to herself. Instead, she spread the blanket upon the ground. Using the food and drink as anchors, she secured it in the windy conditions. She sat onto the blanket as primly as she could with a corset digging into her ribcage.

"Da, we want to explore," Angus said, running up to his father. "Can we? Please?"

"Stay where we can see you," Tilly replied reflexively. Biting her lip, she looked at Benjamin, "Sorry. Force of habit."

A ghost of smile appeared on his lips. "You heard Mrs. Munro," he said. "Go."

"Tell me what happened to the MacIvers," she said when the boys were out of earshot.

He settled beside her on the blanket. "It is a long tale," he said, taking a swig of ale. "Do you wish to hear it?"

She nodded eagerly. She took a sip of the drink and looked at him in anticipation.

"As I told you, my father was always dedicated to the preservation of the estate," he said. "It became an obsession when my brother Allan died. Unfortunately for him, I did not share the same values as Allan and he."

"What do you mean?" she asked. After cutting the bread with the knife he provided, she handed him a slice along with a hunk of cheese.

He took the food and looked at her for a moment as if deciding how much to say. He relented. "My brother Allan was as ruthless as my father," he said. "God rest his soul, he did not care who he hurt or what he destroyed as long as the Campbell holdings were preserved."

"As you can imagine, my brother Allan made my father very proud," he said resentfully. Benjamin tore a bite of bread with his teeth and chewed it. He seemed to struggle with keeping his anger in check. "Of course, I care about the estate, but I care more deeply about the people. Without them, none of this matters."

He pointed to the ruins of the farm. "Iain's family lived there for five generations. We spent many summers roaming these hills and harassing the livestock. I grew up among what my father would call 'the common people.' I was never meant to be the keeper of the estate."

"And, then your brother was murdered," she said. She omitted the part about seeking vengeance. She did not want to pick at that wound. "What happened afterwards?"

"My father felt I was too young at 16 to be trusted with responsibility," Benjamin said. "He decided that he would train me for a few years and handle the family's affairs until I was ready." With undisguised resentment in his voice, he recounted the lessons his father taught him.

Malcolm feared his son would cast the estate into ruin through mismanagement. He set in motion a series of plans to make as much profit as possible. He hoped that, once his idealistic son saw the vast sums of money from the endeavors, he would be more easily swayed toward his father's point of view. "And, that is exactly how he said it – 'vast sums of money, my boy.' He thought it would be an encouragement for me," Benjamin recalled. "He did not understand that some people are not motivated by profit."

"The same idea continues in my time," Tilly said. "My husband spent so many years away from home, travelling all over the world to open restaurants for other people. He missed a good part of the children's early childhood."

Benjamin squeezed her hand. "You understand then why you cannot live your life based upon greed," he said. "Money does not bring true happiness. It can never fill the void in your soul."

"What did your father try, to make money?"

"At first, he harvested timber," he said. Benjamin motioned toward the treeless ridge from which they just came. "Naturally, the farms and cottages that stood in the way were cleared. Nothing could block progress. Then, he sold the Highland cattle that roamed the hills, replacing them with sheep."

"Someone needed to tend the wee beasts so he allowed a few of the crofters to remain," he continued. "Others moved south in search of work or took his offer of alternate accommodations in Deoch. After all, we would need blacksmiths, merchants, and other tradesmen to keep Castle Fion in operation."

"Forgive me, but I hardly think a lot of people are necessary," Tilly said, with a frown. "The family is not that large."

He laughed mirthlessly. "We had a great many guests then." He paused, as if an unpleasant memory flitted across his brain. "My father offered the castle as a country retreat for the English nobles. They came here for a grand Highland adventure. They killed our deer and birds and enjoyed our excellent whisky."

"Mr. Douglas said that your father became a duke as a result."

"Aye, he was renowned for his fine Scottish estate. When he married my mother, he spent every penny of her dowry to renovate the castle into a luxurious retreat for the many nobles whose favor he sought," Benjamin said. "And, they loved my father for it. He encouraged them to hunt the red stag and other game on his wild Highland lands. He catered to their every whim. He brought servants from London and France to lend an air of refinement and polish. His table was the finest in all of Scotland, prepared by a chef rumored to have served French aristocrats."

"It was a rumor my father started," he said, with a broad grin. "The chef was as Scottish as the heather and previously worked at an inn in London. Whenever the English asked him a question, he would reply in rapid Gaelic. The bastards were too stupid to know the difference."

Benjamin stood, checking the location of the boys. Spotting them some yards away, he returned to Tilly's side. "My grandfather Allan learned hard lessons during the '45," he said. "Times were very hard in Scotland. He had to tread carefully to avoid ruin for the family. My grandfather told my father that he must maintain the family's favorable position. We must always stay on the good side with the English."

"I take it you never came around to your father's point of view?"

"No. The man and I fought like cats and dogs from sun up to sun set. I despised him for what he did to people who were more like family to me than he ever could be."

"How did you convince him to let you manage the estate?" she asked. Based upon everything Tilly learned about His Grace, Malcolm Campbell, he did not seem to be easily swayed once his opinion was fixed.

"Mary and I were wed," Benjamin said. He cleared

his throat, visibly struggling to contain his grief. "She was my salvation in more ways than one."

"What advantage did your father perceive in your marriage? I doubt he would be interested in love."

"Oh, aye, my father would always look for the material gain in any arrangement," he said ruefully. "Mary MacDougall was the eldest daughter of Auld MacDougall, a powerful man in this region. It greatly pleased my father that our marriage would unite the MacDougalls and the Campbells. He believed it was a strategic move. He could never understand true love."

Tilly could not help but think of her own courtship with Alex. She took a long drink from the bottle and ran her finger around the rim, distracted by the ghosts of her former life.

Benjamin leaned forward and took the bottle from her. "Many people go through life never knowing love," he said. He took one of her hands and gently clasp it. "We are truly blessed."

She jerked her hand away. "Blessed!" she spat. "How can you say that? Your wife is gone. My husband is gone. My children…." She choked back tears. While she might think she buried the pain, it was always close to the surface.

He wrapped his arms around her and placed her head upon his shoulder. "I did not mean to imply the hurt is less," he said. "I miss Mary with every single breath, yet I am grateful that I knew her."

Stroking her hair, he asked, "Tell me, lass. If you knew what cruel fate would bring, would you turn away from Alex the first moment you saw him?"

She lifted her head and gazed into his eyes. "No," she admitted.

"We will survive this," he said. "We must – for their sakes."

She placed her head upon his chest and snuggled close. She knew it was an intimate gesture that she should probably avoid, but she did not care. Tilly craved the comfort it brought. "Did your father leave after your marriage?" she asked.

"He allowed me to take over different aspects of the estate's management, but he did not entirely trust me."

"What changed?"

Pointing toward his eldest son, he said, "When my son Allan was born, he told me I was ready. He said children always make a man more responsible." With a chuckle, he added, "They give you a reason not to cock things up."

"I suppose that is true, although I do not believe I would phrase it like that," she said with a laugh.

"He did not completely relinquish the reins, though. He split his time between England and here during the early years of my marriage. He kept a close eye on things, and Mr. Murphy sent regular reports of my activities when my father was not here. I had to prove I could at least maintain the income. In time, he was satisfied with my efforts and retired to his fine English estate, where he can keep his filthy nose out of my business."

Tilly shook her head. "I don't believe that a man like your father could resist meddling," she said. "He must send orders to you and try to impose his will, even if he is miles away."

"In the early years, I followed my father's orders like a dutiful son," he explained. "However, I knew the chief problem of maintenance was money, as it is with most things. If I could produce a certain amount of income, then my father might not notice *how* that income was generated. He would be content that the money flowed and would not ask too many questions."

"So, what are you doing to provide income?" she asked suspiciously. She hoped he was not engaged in anything illegal. Tilly was wrong.

He grinned broadly. "Whisky is a fine drink, aye?" Benjamin asked, a mischievous twinkle in his eyes.

She groaned. Illegal moonshine making was once common in the mountains of Western North Carolina. The tradition of bootleg liquor came from Scotland and Ireland when immigrants moved to America. She never thought she would meet its source.

"The family has always produced small batches of whisky for our personal use," he said naughtily. "I decided it could become a money-making venture after observing our English guests. They drank it in large quantities and always left with a cask or two when they returned home. They proclaimed it was the best whisky that ever touched their lips."

Tilly reluctantly extracted herself from the embrace. She wanted to see his face when he shared this particular tale. "Did you decide to sell it illegally?" she asked.

He feigned shock. "Why, no! I am a respectable gentleman," Benjamin said. "Imagine the shame that would befall the great House of Campbell!"

He lowered his voice, even though the boys could not hear, and said, "I officially sell a few casks and pay my taxes on the lot, like a good lad." He dramatically looked around him. "On the side, though, I have a larger operation that generates a great deal of income. The excise men look the other way."

"You bribe them?!" she exclaimed in disbelief.

He pursed his lips, sucking in air. "Oh, lass, we do not call it that," he said. Benjamin tried to look pious when he added, "I believe the Crown does not sufficiently compensate them for their tireless efforts. I simply wish to assist the poor men and their families. It is an act of Christian charity."

"You are a criminal!"

"Aye – and a right good one at that," he boasted, grinning wickedly. "I have earned enough money to bring back most of the families who my father evicted. They can set up shops in Deoch or return to farming, whatever they choose. I can also afford to keep my father in comfort and happiness in England, where he belongs. He entertains his fancy English friends at his estate there and regularly travels to London for politicking. He has all the money he needs to live a life of comfort and ease. The man has not set foot on this land in four years. I mean to keep it that way."

"You say that the castle has spies like Mr. Murphy," she said. "Doesn't he tell your father what you are doing?"

"Ah, Mr. Murphy," Benjamin sighed. "It takes a great deal of effort to conceal most things from him. I fear he knows more than I realize. I have a secret weapon, though, that helps me in my dealings with him."

"Oh? What?"

"My son Allan. Mr. Murphy fell in love with him the first time he held him. He would do anything for the boy."

"How does that keep him from saying something about your illegal activities?"

Benjamin stared at the ground for a moment as he collected his thoughts. "Mary first noticed his affinity for our son. The man knows how ruthless my father can be, and he saw how my father treated me," he said, his head lowered. "Mr. Murphy does not want that for Allan. As long as the estate runs smoothly, there is no need for my father to come here. I imagine our butler omits certain pieces of information to ensure that does not happen."

She had a new respect for the stern Mr. Murphy – and for Benjamin. She fully understood the potential sacrifice he made to have her there. One whisper from the butler would send his father racing back to the estate and undo all the careful work he had done over the last several years. "I am a complication, aren't I?" Tilly asked. "I could ruin everything for you."

Benjamin rose abruptly and yelled for the boys to

join them. He offered her his hand. "We have lingered too long," he said. "Let us away."

# TWENTY NINE

BENJAMIN, TILLY, AND THE BOYS RODE FOR SEVERAL MILES. Tilly was stunned at the great swaths of land completely stripped of both timber and inhabitants. She could not fathom how one's man greed could transform such a country yet knew it continued even during her day. Her admiration for Benjamin's efforts grew as she surveyed the damage caused by his father.

They stopped at a small farm so that their horses could rest and drink water. A woman emerged from the cottage and immediately broke into a run when she spotted Benjamin and the boys. She flung her arms around his waist and cried, "Oh, what a sight you are! You have not been here in weeks, my boy!"

Benjamin lifted the woman, eliciting a squeal of

joy. He released her from the embrace and gestured toward Tilly, "I would like to introduce you to Mrs. Tilly Munro."

"Oh, aye," the woman said as she appraised Tilly. "Iain has told me about the lass. It is a pleasure to meet you, dear. I am Fiona MacIver, Iain's mother."

Tilly bobbed a weak curtsy, which made the woman cackle. "You will drop in a moment," she said, taking her by the arm. "Come inside, child. Rest a bit."

Mrs. MacIver bade Benjamin and his sons to follow as she led them all inside the cottage. It was a cozy home comprised of a small kitchen to the right of the doorway, a sitting room to the left, and what was most likely the bedroom in the back. They gathered in the sitting room where a welcoming fire awaited them. Tilly immediately walked to the fireplace and warmed her cold hands.

Benjamin joined her. He watched Mrs. MacIver leave the room in search of refreshments. "She is like a mother to me," he whispered.

"She reminds me a lot of Iain," Tilly replied with a smile. "She seems to be a very friendly lady."

"Aye, she is wonderful."

They were interrupted by Mrs. MacIver. She

carried a tray with a plate of hot bannocks and mugs of whisky for the adults and tea for the children. Allan and Angus devoured the bannocks as they gulped the tea.

Benjamin and Tilly sat on a settee beside the fire. They enjoyed the refreshments while the woman informed Benjamin about the latest news from the farm. It seemed Mr. MacIver was in the fields, tending to a heifer and her calf. He intended to lead the animals back to the barn where they would be safer.

Upon hearing this, Benjamin announced that they would assist him. "Would you mind visiting with Mrs. MacIver for a bit while we help?" he asked Tilly as he beckoned the boys to join him.

"It would be a pleasure."

"He headed east, toward the stream," Mrs. MacIver added helpfully before the party walked out the door.

"Now, my dear, we can have a proper chat," Mrs. MacIver said, joining Tilly on the settee. She tucked an errant strand of her curly white hair into the little cap she wore on her head and smoothed her worn, wool skirt.

∞

IT BECAME APPARENT TO TILLY that the mother taught Iain everything he knew about interrogation. Their chat began innocently enough with a discussion of the weather and the approaching end of summer. As she expected, it was not long before the conversation became more personal.

"I understand that you have been a guest for a couple of months," she said. Without giving Tilly time to respond, she remarked, "And, I hear you have been teaching the children."

"Yes, ma'am."

"Do you enjoy the work?"

"Yes, ma'am. I have always loved teaching children."

"Ah, children are a great blessing from God," Mrs. MacIver said. "Iain was my only bairn. Benjamin seems like a second child to me. I love him as much as I do my own blood. Oh, and his wee bairns are like my grandchildren. They are such a joy!" She patted Tilly on the hand. "I do not know what I would do if any harm came to Benjamin or his children."

"I share the same concern. He has been so gracious to me," Tilly said. She leaned closer and placed her hand upon Mrs. MacIver's. "I would never wish harm upon Mr. Campbell or his family."

"Well, the Campbells have many enemies. One cannot be too careful."

"I have heard of the long feud with the MacDonalds. It seems treachery is everywhere."

"Aye, it is," Mrs. MacIver said thoughtfully. "Those of us who care for Benjamin and his kin must always be vigilant. You never know when the enemy may be near."

Tilly shifted in her seat. *You are an outsider, and you have done nothing to earn this woman's trust. Message understood.* She desperately wanted to shift the attention away from herself. The woman's piercing gaze was unnerving. "I understand that your husband was the factor when Mr. Campbell's father was here," she said. "What are your memories of Mr. Campbell – the father, I mean?"

Mrs. MacIver took a deep breath. "To understand the father, you must know more about his upbringing," she said. "He grew up in the years after the Rising. Times were much different than they are now."

"How so?"

"My mother told me stories that would raise the hair on your head," she said, pursing her lips. "After the Rising, the English spread across the Highlands like a plague of locusts. They murdered the men and raped the women. They burnt villages and destroyed fields ready for harvest. The Act of Proscription banned the speaking of our native tongue and wearing of the bonnie tartan. Our land could be seized on a whim. We had no recourse."

"Didn't the Campbells align with the English? The alliance should have protected the people here."

Mrs. MacIver's eyes grew watery. "My mother's family did not live on Campbell lands after the Rising," she replied. "They suffered greatly."

She wiped her eyes with an ivory handkerchief that she produced from the pocket of her apron. Tilly noticed the initials "MC" embroidered in pale pink thread upon one corner of the cloth. "When I was a child, I knew hunger and grief," she said. "It was a dark period of my life. Marrying Robert saved me from it."

Tilly squeezed the woman's hand. "You do not have to share the story if it is too painful," she said.

"No, I want you to know," Mrs. MacIver said, tucking the handkerchief into her pocket. "Robert worked for His Grace. We settled in a cottage near Castle Fion. It was like walking into the sunlight." She paused, lost in the memory. "Benjamin's grandfather Allan secured the estate by siding with the English. Everyone was safe, and the family kept its property.

Many people called him a traitor, though."

"Do you think he was?"

"In my youth, I would have," she said, smiling faintly. "As I grew older, I learned that you must sometimes do bad things to help people. We all dance along that line between right and wrong."

Tilly could not reconcile the woman's story with what she knew about the Campbell forefathers. "Based upon everything I have heard about the elder Campbells, they sound like men whose actions were more about their own advancement than protection of the people," she said.

Mrs. MacIver chuckled. "Aye, that may have been the primary goal, but the people benefited too," she said. "I never had to worry about the English killing my husband or burning down our farm. We always had food on our table and a little bit of money from Robert's work. The Campbell family's actions made that possible."

"Malcolm's father showed him what must be done to win favor with the English," she explained. "He taught His Grace how to use influence and gain power. By the time His Grace was old enough to manage the estate, he knew exactly what he must do."

"And, what did he do?"

"He found a woman with money. He was a very practical man. The Campbells may have owned a vast amount of property, but they lacked the financial resources necessary for the improvements His Grace wanted to make. He was elated to meet Eleanor. Oh, she was a great beauty, but, for him, her main attraction was the large dowry that came with her."

"I understand that he used the funds to renovate Castle Fion."

"Aye, he transformed the castle and hosted any influential noble who would accept an invitation. He catered to their every whim. His plan worked brilliantly. The English loved him."

Tilly's brow furrowed in frustration. "If the English enjoyed staying at the castle, then why did His Grace move the crofters?" she asked. "Surely, the nobles would not notice or even care about that."

"Eleanor Campbell's dowry provided funds for the improvements, not the upkeep," Mrs. MacIver said. "His Grace needed revenue to supply the castle with all the comforts that the English desired. He sold timber. He raised sheep. He did all sorts of things as he tried to generate enough income to keep the castle going. If anyone stood in the way, he removed them from their farms. It was of no consequence to him that the family had been there for generations."

She shook her head. "Benjamin – I mean, Mr. Campbell – told me about his father's actions," she said. "I just cannot believe someone would be so cruel."

"Rich men often think their actions are above contempt," Mrs. MacIver said. "They do what they want because no one stops them."

"Well, I am glad that the whisky business makes a fine profit," Tilly said wryly, rising her mug of whisky in silent salute. She noticed the shocked expression on Mrs. MacIver's face. "Mr. Campbell told me about it on the ride here. If it keeps His Grace from returning, then it is a fine endeavor."

Mrs. MacIver stared at her for several moments. She said, "If Benjamin trusts you enough to reveal the whisky business, then I suppose I can speak plainly with you."

Tilly already felt the woman was being rather forthright but said nothing. Instead, she nodded encouragingly.

"Allow me to provide a sketch of His Grace's character," she said. "Aye, his actions may have indirectly benefited some of us, but he never really gave a thought to anyone else. When my poor Robert became too weak, he forced us from the farm on which his family lived for years. His Grace shoved us into a tiny room above the stable in Deoch." She looked as if she just sucked on a lemon. "Oh, he gave us a pittance to get by and thought it was sufficient for all those years of faithful service. The day His Grace rode away from here was the happiest day of my life. Benjamin immediately moved us to this farm. My husband has dignity and feels like a man again."

"Why didn't Benjamin move you back to the old family farm?

"It was in terrible disrepair. This farm was in better condition. He did not want to burden Robert with a lot of projects. My husband would not have liked it if Benjamin sent teams of men to fix everything."

Mrs. MacIver stared fiercely into her eyes. "Benjamin has given the same opportunity to other families who were similarly discarded. He has tried to heal the wounds of the past. I shudder to think how life would be if His Grace returned."

Tilly took a long drink of whisky. She realized her own fate was equally tenuous. What would happen to her if the dreaded man returned?

∞

TILLY WAS EXTREMELY THANKFUL when Benjamin and his sons soon arrived with Mr. MacIver and the prodigal cows. After the livestock was safely corralled in the barn, the jovial party joined the ladies. Any tension between the women evaporated. To the casual observer, it seemed as if they had enjoyed a pleasant chat by the fire.

Tilly did a double take when Robert MacIver entered the room. The resemblance between father and son was remarkable. Like his son, he was a tall man with a bushy beard. His wavy, red hair was streaked with white, a sign of his advancing age. His hands were gnarled from arthritis, no doubt making some farm work difficult for him.

Robert was an affable man. He teased Allan and Angus about their cattle-wrangling skills. "Fiona, it took those boys a full 15 minutes to bring the heifer round," he told his wife, eyes watering from laughter. "Iain and Benjamin could gather a full herd in the blink of an eye when they were six years of age. I tell you; castle life has made the boys soft. They should stay with us for a few months."

The prospect of staying with the MacIvers seemed to be very exciting to the boys. They looked eagerly at their father. "I will consider it," Benjamin said cordially. "They do not spend as much time as they should on the farm."

The boys settled in front of the fire and listened to Robert's stories. Benjamin and Iain were very naughty as children. Tilly hoped the tales of their exploits would not inspire Allan and Angus to similar misadventures.

After a particularly embarrassing story involving a pretty girl from another farm, Benjamin cleared his throat and stood. He tugged at her elbow and said, "As much as we love visiting with you, I fear the hour grows late. We should return before it is dark." With a sharp look, he ended the protests from his sons.

The MacIvers accompanied the group outside, extending an invitation for a return visit. Robert retrieved the horses from the field where they were hobbled and helped Tilly mount her horse. He patted her on the leg and whispered, "Take care of my boy, Mrs. Munro."

She nodded, though perplexed by the comment. Mrs. MacIver's words still rang in her ears. Did the husband have a kinder view of her?

They waved goodbye and headed for a trail that Benjamin said would lead them back to the castle. Even though she was not looking forward to another long horseback ride, she felt her heart lift a little at the thought of returning home. *Home*, she repeated to herself. *Is Castle Fion my home now?*

∞

THE LITTLE PARTY RODE IN SILENCE for some time before Tilly reined her horse to a stop.

Benjamin swung around, a concerned expression on his face. "Are you unwell?" he asked.

"I am fine," she said, waving her hand. "Could we stop a moment?"

He looked ahead on the trail. "Let us make our way there," he said, pointing to a clump of trees in the distance. "It is a nice spot that is sheltered from the wind."

When they reached their destination, Benjamin helped Tilly from the horse. He retrieved the plaid blanket and sent the boys to play in the woods.

As she spread the blanket onto the ground and took a seat, she tried to gather her thoughts. She was not sure how to begin the conversation.

He stared expectantly at her. "Mrs. MacIver is like a second mother to me," he said defensively. "I hope she did not frighten you."

She shook her head. "She is a kind woman who means well." Tilly added, "She didn't say anything that I didn't expect to hear."

"Benjamin," she began, lightly placing her hand on his arm. "I wanted to thank you for what you have done for me. You gave me a place to stay, food and clothes. You allowed me to teach your children. It has been a gift."

"Are you vexed for some reason?"

"No, I am truly grateful. I see now how much you risked. Thank you."

They stared at each for a long time, unsure what to do next. She broke the silence. "You would not share so much with me if you thought I worked for your father," she said. "Who do you think I am?"

"I do not think you are a spy for my father. You are right. If I did, I would not have shown you these things today."

Something in his tone caught her attention. "Do you suspect I am a spy for someone else?" she asked. "Exactly how many enemies do you have?"

"The Crown could have sent you, thinking the excise men are not doing their job."

"No, you don't believe that. Who is it?" Sensing his reluctance, she added, "Well, If you don't tell me, I will just ask the servants when we return." She attempted to stand. "They are a great source of information."

He grabbed her skirt and tugged her onto the blanket. "Do you remember my tale about the MacDonalds?" he asked.

"Quite vividly."

He ran his hand through his hair. "When Cairen and James met their unfortunate demises, their father sought a truce with my family. He swore that the feud was over. No other MacDonald would raise a hand toward a Campbell, provided we swear the same." Benjamin sighed wearily. "He had one surviving heir, their older brother Richard. He was furious at his father but was forced to abide by the man's wishes."

"Do you think I could be a spy for that family, even though the feud is over?"

"When I returned to the castle with you, I learned the old man had died. Iain thinks Richard will seek revenge now that he is no longer bound by his father's rule."

"And, you think Richard sent me to gather information so he can strike?"

Benjamin was silent for several moments. He idly plucked a blade of grass and tore it to shreds. "Iain and I have considered it," he said honestly. "However, if I truly believed you were a spy for the MacDonald, I would not have brought you to the MacIvers' farm today."

He looked at her. "I know so little about you, yet you know so much about me," he said. "Tell me something, Tilly. Anything."

"My mother was a teacher like me," she said,

revealing the first thing that sprang into her mind. "She taught third grade at the local elementary school. I was an only child, so I guess it gave her a chance to experience what it was like to have lots of children."

"And your father?"

"He made furniture until the factory where he worked went out of business."

"Are they both living?"

"No. My dad died of a heart attack – I mean, his heart stopped working. Then, my mom died a few months later. The grief was too much for her. She was incomplete without him."

"You lost your parents, your husband, and your family. You are a strong woman, Tilly Munro."

"No more so than anyone here. When I hear how some people struggle to survive on a daily basis, I am deeply humbled," she said. Impulsively, she leaned forward and placed a light kiss on his cheek. "I see great strength in you too."

Her innocent kiss emboldened Benjamin. He swept Tilly into his arms and covered her lips with his, gently parting them with his tongue. Her heart thudded in her ears. How many times had she longed to kiss him like this? She moaned as she sank into her arms.

Abruptly, he pulled away from her. He scanned the area until he saw his children. They were running along the top of the ridge above them. They were completely oblivious to the passionate display.

Benjamin returned his gaze to hers. She saw a mixture of desire and fear in his eyes. "What is the matter?" she asked, using every ounce of strength to restrain herself.

"I apologize for my behavior," he said. "It was inappropriate of me to be so forward. A gentleman should conduct himself in a more respectable manner towards a lady." He paused and looked at her with such desire that her heart fluttered. "I must confess that, every night, I dream of kissing your lips and holding you in my arms."

A tiny tear traced the contour of her cheek. "I cannot pretend that I don't want you, Benjamin," she said, her voice raw with emotion. "I haven't felt this way in a long time. But, what happens to us? Do I go home? Do I stay here? What happens next?"

His face hardened. He looked as if someone poured cold water down his back. The flames of desire extinguished in his eyes. He grabbed her arm, easily lifting her from the blanket.

"I will not take you like a rutting stag," he said firmly. "You deserve to be treated like a lady."

She did not know exactly what that meant. She was about to ask him when he interrupted her.

"Come," Benjamin bade. "We should return to the castle before I change my mind."

# THIRTY

IT WAS NEARLY DARK when Benjamin, Tilly, and the boys reached the castle. Benjamin left Tilly and his sons at the entrance. He promised to return later. He told them that he wanted to see the horses to the stable and tend to some chores before dinner. In truth, he had a more personal errand that demanded his attention.

After delivering the horses to the stable, he made his way through the forest to the chapel. Benjamin slipped inside and took his usual seat at the first pew. He did not know why it was so important to be quiet, but it seemed like the right thing to do in a church. He bowed his head. He could hear the sound of his slow, steady breathing and the soft chirping of a bird outside the chapel. "Mary, I need your counsel," he whispered. "You always knew what to do."

He felt hot tears trickle down his face, leaving little trails through the dirt that accumulated there. He did not bother to wipe them away. "Tilly says she comes from the future – an outrageous proposition! Her ways are so foreign yet not offensive or coarse. She speaks in a manner that is unlike any woman with whom I have ever conversed. She tells me her own opinion, not one that was given to her by a man. I find her to be a fascinating person."

He admitted, "I found her in unusual circumstances." He chuckled softly. "Of course, you know what happened. I was lonely. I swear I never did anything like that when we were wed. I never even looked at another woman after I saw you, my bonnie bride."

He lifted his face and stared out the stained glass window. The setting sun illuminated the brilliant colors of gold, blue, and green in the glass. It was a beautiful sight. Benjamin could not resist smiling. "She is good with the children," he said. "Tilly has a gentle hand that reminds me greatly of you."

He removed a handkerchief from his pocket and wiped away the tears and grime on his face. For some reason he could not explain, he suddenly felt it was important to look presentable for Mary. "I will always love you," he promised. "You told me to find another wife. I thought you were mad to ask such a thing on your death bed. I never imagined that I would find someone who I could love, so I agreed that I would marry again. Now, I am surprised by the feelings I have for Tilly. I never believed it would be possible to love anyone else but you, my sweet Mary."

"Is it wrong to want to feel love again?" he asked. "Should I spend the rest of my life alone, in permanent mourning?" He swallowed hard. "Should I let Tilly into my heart or cast her away?"

He heard the leaves rustling in the trees outside the chapel. He watched the last rays of sunshine soften and then disappear into the night. Benjamin felt the air grow cooler as the evening approached. He sat very still and waited. If he was patient, she would come to him, just as she always did.

He felt a gentle hand upon his shoulder. He knew it was real. The spirit of his beloved was there. "I am listening, Mary," he said, his voice cracking with emotion. "Please – "

Deep within his soul, Benjamin heard the message. *Open your heart, my love, and a sign will appear.*

∞

IAIN PACED in front of the twin fireplaces in the housekeeper's office. Mrs. Keith and the maid Sarah sat on an old chaise, waiting expectantly. He knew they wondered why he summoned them, but he hesitated. How could he make the necessary inquiry without sounding like a worrisome old lady?

He turned to Sarah. "Mr. Campbell asked you to keep watch over our guest," he said. "What intelligence have you gathered about her?"

Sarah glanced nervously at Mrs. Keith, who nodded encouragingly. "I do not know what you want to hear, sir," she said. "I attend to milady's needs. We do not share confidences like boon friends."

Iain wearily rubbed his face. "Surely, she has given you some hint about her past," he said. He took a seat in a wooden chair beside the chaise. "Has she let slip how she came to be here?"

"She told me she was a governess, as she is now," Sarah said. Looking at Mrs. Keith, she implored, "Madam, I do not know what information he seeks."

Mrs. Keith patted the girl on the hand. "Mr. MacIver is milord's dear friend as well as his factor," she said. "I am sure he would have the same concern about any guest in our household." She cocked an eyebrow and asked Iain, "Wouldn't you, sir?"

"Aye, I keep close watch over the family," Iain said. "Their safety is my paramount concern."

Sarah seemed alarmed. "Do you think Mrs. Munro is a danger to the family?" she asked. "Should we all be on our guard?"

He shook his head. "No, child, that is not what I meant," Iain said. This was going to be harder than he thought. The last thing he needed was a maid who tiptoed around Mrs. Munro and jumped every time the woman said a word to her. "I wish to know more about her habits, her background. Let us begin with something simple. What does she do with her time?"

Sarah thought for a moment. "Before she began teaching the children, she spent a lot of time in the library," she said. "She examined every book. It was almost as if she was looking for something."

Iain found her comment most intriguing. "Do you know if she found it?" he asked.

"No, milady seemed most displeased after she had looked through all the books," the maid said. "Since she has begun teaching the children, I doubt she will have time to continue her search." She paused. "She is fond of walks to the chapel and the stable. She speaks often about how relaxing they are."

"Has she given any hint about her former home?"

"She sometimes speaks about her family. She is very sad and misses them."

Iain bowed his head, hoping it would look like a sign of respect for the dearly departed. In truth, he was impatient and frustrated. It was apparent to him that the maid had no new information. Sighing heavily, he stood. "I thank you for your time, ladies," he said, bowing slightly. "I would greatly appreciate it if you would continue to be watchful. If she reveals anything about her background, please report it to me straight away."

Mrs. Keith rose from her own seat and smiled faintly at Iain. "I assure you that my staff will be most attentive," she said. "Mr. Campbell and you need not worry."

"Aye, Mr. Campbell...." he hesitated. How should he phrase it? "Ladies, I would appreciate it if you would not mention this conversation to him or, for that matter, any of the other staff. As you say, madam, I am cautious around all guests because of my close relationship with the family. I do not want to unnecessarily raise alarm."

Iain knew Mrs. Keith was too tactful to question his motive. He accepted her nod as her vow of silence. Bowing again, he exited the room.

He made his way to the kitchen. With a little luck, Iain could persuade the grumpy cook to make him a late dinner. Perhaps a little food and a lot of whisky could divert his attention from the mystery of Tilly Munro.

# THIRTY ONE

TILLY AWOKE EARLY THE NEXT MORNING. She stretched, feeling the effects from yesterday's lengthy time on horseback. She was not sure if she could ever get used to all that jostling. Then, with a smile, she remembered the passionate kiss with Benjamin. She traced the outline of her lips with her fingertips. The man was a wonderful kisser.

Sighing, she pulled back the bed curtains and climbed out of bed. It felt as if, in the blink of an eye, she left behind a life filled with anguish and an uncertain future without the family she once had. In return, she gained a new life where she was surrounded by children once again. Tilly formed a bond with a man who she genuinely liked and respected. Could he feel the same way? Was this her future? Did she want to stay here? Would this life make her happy?

Before she could reach any conclusions, Sarah entered her room. The fireplace maid, as Tilly called her, was right on her heels and prepared a fire in the hearth. Judging from the frown on Sarah's face, she suspected the girl should have been in the room long before she awoke.

"Milady, you have risen early this morning," Sarah said as she helped Tilly into a robe. "It is barely dawn."

"I have been sleeping far too late. I should get out of bed earlier."

"Would milady like a tray brought to her room? Or, will you be dining in the breakfast room?"

"If it is not too much trouble, I would like to dine in the breakfast room."

Sarah cast a look at the other maid, who dropped a quick curtsy and fled the room.

As she helped Tilly dress, it was apparent that Sarah was in a fine mood that morning and chattered away about the goings on in the castle. Tilly listened absently until she heard mention of the tutor. "I am sorry. What did you say?" she asked.

While she arranged Tilly's hair, Sarah repeated, "The tutor arrived last night. His name is Daniel

Ramsey."

"Have you met him?"

"Aye," Sarah said, smiling shyly. Tilly thought she detected a slight blush on the girl's cheeks. "I prepared him a bit of dinner. He was so hungry after his journey."

"Does he seem to be knowledgeable?"

"Oh, aye," Sarah said. This time, her cheeks were a definite shade of red. "He is very fond of learning. He was most happy to hear that you taught me how to read. He told me he would love to continue my education."

Biting her lower lip, Tilly struggled to maintain her composure at the man's choice of words. "I am glad to hear that such a learned man is in our midst," she said. "I hope his knowledge can be a great benefit to Allan."

"I believe we can all learn from him," Sarah said, her tone suddenly serious.

Tilly feigned a cough to conceal the giggle that slipped past her lips. She thanked Sarah for her efforts and ran from the room, fearful she could no longer contain the laughter.

∞

TILLY WAS SURPRISED to find Benjamin waiting at the top of the stairs. "I hope you slept well, Mrs. Munro," he said pleasantly, offering her his arm.

"Yes, Mr. Campbell, thank you for your consideration," she responded in her most proper tone. When he turned toward the stairs, she asked, "Where are you taking me?"

"I find the state dining room to be too formal," he said. "Let us have our meal in the family's dining room."

He guided her down the stairs toward a smaller version of the formal state dining room on the second floor, where they had enjoyed their evening meals. She immediately recognized it as the first room she saw on her tour of the castle with Beth and Mr. Douglas. She chose to remain silent, lest she spoil the mood.

As she glanced around the room, she spotted subtle differences from the 21st century version. The walls were painted gleaming white, with gold molding along the high ceiling. Little vignettes of scenes from Greek mythology were hand-painted on the walls, replacing the gilded pictures that hung in her day. Twin marble fireplaces on opposite sides of the room provided warmth. The same wooden table that seated twelve stood in the center of the room. Overall, it was the coziest room she had seen in the entire home.

Benjamin placed her at the head of the table and took a seat to her right. He looked very fine this morning, in his tight, khaki knee britches and navy waistcoat. His shirt was open scandalously at the throat, revealing a hint of tan skin and coppery chest hair. She remembered what he looked like underneath that shirt and blushed slightly. Could he hear how loudly her heart was beating?

The footmen silently delivered several dishes to the sideboard and ladled small portions of each entrée onto plates that were then placed before Benjamin and Tilly. When they exited the room, Benjamin grabbed her hand and raised it to his lips. He released it before the door swung open again. She hoped the servants would not notice the rosy glow on her cheeks.

He was quick to dismiss the servants after they served the tea. He turned to her and said, "I thought they would never leave. I enjoy talking with you much more whenever we do not have an audience."

"I do not know if I will ever become accustomed to the presence of servants. They always seem to turn up at the most inopportune times."

"You read my mind," he mumbled as he stood. Gently caressing her cheek, Benjamin kissed her. "I have wanted to do that all morning."

"All morning?"

"Lass, I wanted to do that the moment I awoke."

Tilly understood Sarah's earlier giddiness. "Is this how proper courtship is conducted in 1801?" she asked.

He returned to his seat and answered, "No, some couples do not even kiss before marriage." With a broad grin, he added, "Given the nature of our first meeting, I hope you do not mind my unorthodox methods."

Her face burned and must have been an amusing shade of fuchsia. She shook her head, unable to form an intelligent reply. It was all very confusing.

"Do you have plans after you finish teaching the children?" he asked. "I thought we might take a stroll down to the loch."

She was relieved he did not suggest another horseback ride. Her spine would likely need a few days to heal. "I was not sure if my teaching would continue now that the tutor has arrived," she said.

"Ah, Mr. Ramsey," he said absently. "He will wish to spend some time with you. He should know about your educational progress so that he can form plans for future lessons."

"Will he teach *all* the children?" she asked

hesitantly. Tilly enjoyed teaching and hated to see it come to an end.

"Of course not," he said. "Mr. Ramsey will teach Allan for now. In a year or two, Angus can join him." Benjamin placed a light kiss on her hand. "I would greatly appreciate it if you would continue teaching the other boys."

She smiled. "I would like that very much," Tilly said happily. "And, yes, I would love to take a stroll to the loch after lessons are finished."

∞

AFTER BREAKFAST, Benjamin and Tilly went to the family library where the new tutor waited for them. Tilly noticed that the bespectacled man made notes in a pocket-sized, leather-bound journal as he surveyed the books upon the shelves. Hopefully, he did not find any deficits in the collection.

Daniel Ramsey was shorter than she. His light brown hair was held in place with a simple grey bow that matched his similarly-colored eyes. A dove grey coat and charcoal grey trousers were perfectly fitted to his slender frame. His well-polished black leather shoes had a fancy silver buckle that glinted in the sunlight. A smartly-tied knot topped the heavily starched shirt he wore. His outfit may not have been of the finest quality, yet she could tell that he took great care to be presentable.

He bowed deeply when he saw her. "Good day, madam," he said.

She offered a decent curtsy. Sarah had taught her well. "It is a pleasure to meet you, Mr. Ramsey." Gesturing toward the bookshelves, she commented, "I hope the selection of books meets with your approval."

He glanced at the full shelves and nodded. "It warms my heart to see parents who have a fine interest in knowledge," Mr. Ramsey said. "It will make teaching your children so much easier."

Tilly was about to correct him when Benjamin asked about the journey. The two men exchanged pleasantries before he told the tutor it was time to meet his eldest son. He asked Tilly to wait for them. He flashed a smile at her as they moved into the classroom next door. The simple gesture make her weak in the knees.

She strode to a window that offered the best view of the grounds. She watched one of the servants trim a shrub and glanced at the verdant forest. The view was gorgeous. Did the leaves provide a dazzling display of color here, as they did back home? She was surprised that she really wanted to see it. She did not find herself pining for North Carolina.

She did not want to ponder the reason for her change of heart. Instead, she recalled the conversation she shared with Benjamin yesterday and scanned the area again. This time, she observed the men who strolled around the grounds and along the edges of the forest. Were they always there? Or, had Benjamin increased their presence because of the MacDonald threat?

A movement to the left caught her eye. Tilly squinted. Was that a flash of tartan? She could not be certain. Shaking her head, she stepped away from the window. Maybe it was just the same sentry she encountered with Allan in the forest.

# THIRTY TWO

TILLY WAS PLEASED to learn how eager Mr. Ramsey was to learn the extent of Allan's knowledge. When he returned to the library for his meeting with her, the tutor asked very thorough, thoughtful questions. Then, he wanted to observe her when she began the day's lessons with the children. He sat in the back of the classroom, making occasional notes and smiling amiably at her. He was so quiet that she forgot he was there and completed the lessons with ease.

As the boys shuffled from the classroom, Mr. Ramsey pronounced Allan well prepared for his continued education. She suspected he was overly generous with his praise. After all, a look of concern crossed his face when she revealed the boy knew no Latin, Greek, or French.

The tutor's questions answered, Tilly went in search of Benjamin and found him in his study, talking with Iain. When she entered the room, he immediately put down the quill and rose from his seat. "I am sure you will decide what is best," Benjamin said to the factor, joining her at the door. "Mrs. Munro and I are going for a walk."

She took Benjamin's arm and noticed a frown on Iain's face. She let it pass.

∞

THEY WALKED IN COMFORTABLE SILENCE FOR SOME TIME. The air was crisp and cool. It felt like rain, not an uncommon thing in Scotland. Tilly could count on one hand the number of times the sun shone that summer. *Nothing like the South,* she thought ruefully.

"What are you thinking?" Benjamin asked.

"The weather is so different here," she said. "Where I come from, it is so hot and humid in the summer. When it rains, the temperature may cool for a few minutes. Then, it is just as hot as it was before the rain."

"Do you miss it?"

"Yes, I wish we had more sunshine here."

"No, I meant your home."

"I miss Beth."

"Please tell me about her."

"I'm not sure you would like her," she said. Seeing the bewildered look on his face, she said, "She is very blunt, and you sometimes have a problem with that."

"I am not used to women having strong opinions that are so freely expressed," he said, shaking his head. "And yet, I imagine such frankness would be refreshing in certain situations."

She stopped walking and stared at him. "Have I unwittingly succeeded in making a 19th century man appreciate women for their intelligence rather than their child-rearing skills?" she asked, incredulous.

Benjamin tossed back his head and laughed heartily. "Whenever I speak with you, I realize that I have much to learn, Tilly," he said. He nudged her ribs. "Now, tell me about your friend."

"We met when we were at college. We both worked as waitresses at a restaurant."

"What does 'waitress' mean?"

"It is someone who takes a patron's order and brings food and drink to that person. I guess it would be similar to the servants who bring our meals to us every day."

"You seem like a woman from a respectable home. Did you work because your parents were unable to provide for you?"

Once again, she found herself dealing with a difference in eras. In Benjamin's mind, women of good breeding only worked if their parents could not offer a better situation. She decided it was time to enlighten him. "I *did* come from a respectable home," she said. "Things are very different in my time. Women of all social classes are employed outside the home. Some even enjoy the jobs they have because it gives them a feeling of accomplishment."

"I apologize if I have offended you," he said sincerely. "I did not mean to imply that – "

"That only poor people work?" Tilly interrupted him, frowning. "Open your mind, Benjamin."

He started at her choice of words but said nothing. He squeezed her hand, and they resumed their walk. "Please tell me your story," he said.

"It was a difficult time," she continued. "Before I entered college, my father lost his job. They couldn't afford to send me to school on my mother's salary. I was lucky to get a few scholarships and earn some money as a waitress. Somehow, I scrapped together enough money for tuition."

She paused meditatively. "I would sometimes work until 3 in the morning. I studied 'til 5, slept a couple of hours, and then went to class. I don't know how I did so much on so little sleep. I suppose it prepared me for the twins."

"Was Beth in a similar situation?"

"Yes. Her father left her mother before Beth was born. Her life was a constant struggle."

He stopped walking and appeared to have difficulty processing her story. At last, he asked, "Assuming you are indeed from the future, why are women of good breeding forced to support themselves? Can they not marry well? Are there no genteel families who can assist those in need?"

Tilly sighed in exasperation. "In my time, a woman does not rely on a man to rescue her," she explained patiently. "We make our own way. We support ourselves as best we can. That's exactly what Beth and I did. We worked damn hard to get what we had."

"Madam, I sincerely apologize for my choice of words," Benjamin said, looking very contrite. "I fear I have upset you again. I want to understand the story you have told. It is unusual for my time."

"Is it? When have you had an honest conversation with a woman? Do you believe that someone like Mrs. Keith is not a respectable person because she is forced to work? Is she worth less in your eyes because she cannot spend her days embroidering pillows or taking turns around the garden?"

Benjamin jerked as if she had slapped him. "I spent my youth with the crofters. I did not spend a great deal of time with women," he said, lowering his head. "Mrs. Keith is a wonderful woman. I would be lost without her guidance and care for my family. I am deeply ashamed to admit my ignorance. Listening to you, I fear that I am just like my father."

Having spent time in this age, Tilly could understand how his opinions were formed. "You are already a better man than him," she said gently. She wrapped her arms around his waist. "You realize you have faults and will change them. Based upon everything you told me, he lacks both the ability to see his weakness and the desire to correct it."

"Lass, I sincerely hope you are right," Benjamin said. He placed a light kiss on her forehead. "Pray, educate me about the minds of women. I have much to learn."

∞

FROM THE ENTRANCE TO THE CASTLE, IAIN WATCHED Benjamin and Tilly with growing displeasure. The couple walked arm in arm, laughing and smiling. He was shocked to see his friend embrace her and place a kiss on her forehead. He snorted in disgust and made his way to the study.

He sat behind Benjamin's desk, reviewing the book of accounts. He read the same passage several times before he angrily slammed the book shut. He was most distressed at his friend's behavior.

Despite his best efforts, Iain learned nothing about the strange woman. No one had heard of any travelers in the area for months. He sent inquiries about any visiting Americans as far away as Glasgow to the south and Edinburgh to the east. No one fit Tilly's description. It was as if she really did materialize from the mist itself. He did not like it.

"What troubles you?" Benjamin asked as he strode through the doorway. His cheeks were flush, likely from his previous company rather than the chill in the air.

Iain carefully placed the quill in its holder. He tented his fingers and stared at his friend for a moment. "You seem most content with Mrs. Munro," he said coolly.

"Aye," Benjamin answered, taking a seat in a chair opposite the desk. "She is a remarkable woman."

"Mrs. Munro must be very remarkable indeed, for I understand you took her to meet my parents."

"Aye, what of it?" Benjamin asked defensively. "I hold your family in great esteem and wanted to introduce her to them."

"It was not long ago that you wanted your children to stay away from her. Now, you let her instruct them and are taking her on horseback rides to meet my family. She has free run of the castle. Why, I heard the two of you ate breakfast in the family's dining room this morning." Arching an eyebrow, Iain asked, "Do you plan to wed her next?"

"I may do as I please," Benjamin said, folding his arms across his chest. "I do not need permission from you or any other man."

"I know you well, my friend. Your heart aches because of Mary's unfortunate passing."

"What the bloody hell does that have to do with anything, Iain?" Benjamin roared, rising from the chair. He paced in front of the desk. "Do you think I am allowing Tilly to take advantage of me because I am lonely?"

"So, it is 'Tilly' now?" Iain asked. "You are very familiar with a woman you hardly know."

Benjamin placed his hands on the desk and leaned forward. "It is not like you to peck. Say it."

"We know nothing about her, yet you have let her

close to everything you hold dear. You grow fonder of her every day. I can see it. What has happened to my careful companion?"

"I am always careful," Benjamin scoffed. He pushed away from the desk and glowered at Iain. "It is true that we do not know from whence she came. I can see that she is a good person, though. She means no harm."

"You are blinded by your growing affection for her."

"And, you are wrong. If I thought there was any chance that she posed a danger to my family, I would toss her on a cart and send her to Glasgow this moment."

"What if I told you that I intercepted a message she sent to your father? It seems she has been his agent all this time."

Benjamin looked as if his heart plunged to his stomach. He fell into a nearby chair, deflated. "No," he whispered. "She cannot be. After all the time we have spent together, after all the intimate moments we shared…it cannot be true. How could it all be a lie?"

He stared at Iain, anguish written upon his face. "I tried to build a wall and keep her out, but she found her way inside," he said. "No, no, please say it is not true!"

Iain rose from his seat and walked around the desk. "You are the most stubborn person I know. If you hold this woman in such high regard, then would it matter if she worked for your father?" he asked. "Are you not confident that you have won her allegiance?"

He stared down at Benjamin, who had no reply. Shaking his head, he strode toward the door. "If you were secure in your affection for her, I would taste my own blood from the blow you delivered to me," he said. "You were too quick to believe my lie. Do not be so quick to believe hers."

Iain left Benjamin alone to consider his warning.

# THIRTY THREE

WITH THE ARRIVAL OF THE TUTOR, they had a new guest for dinner. Tilly supposed it was normally uncommon for servants to dine with their employers. Did Mr. Ramsey's position qualify him for a higher ranking on the food chain? Whatever the reason, she was excited at the prospect of getting to know the newest member of their household. She was further pleased to see that Benjamin continued to have the meals in the family's dining room, a much less stuffy location than the state dining room on the second floor.

Iain saw fit to join them. She suspected every new person was fresh fodder for the factor. The tutor would likely get the same interrogation she herself endured. Secretly, she was delighted by the prospect. *Let someone else squirm for a change,* she thought wickedly as she took a sip of wine.

Daniel Ramsey proved to be an interesting man with no reticence at sharing his life story. He was from Edinburgh. The sixth son of twelve boys, he knew at an early age that he had to find his own way in life.

He decided to pursue a life of piety within the church. He was fortunate that his mother worked for a respectable family who became his patrons. Years spent preparing for the endeavor instilled a great love of knowledge. Unfortunately, it could not take away his fondness for women and whisky, he informed them, with a wink to Tilly. Iain roared with laughter when he heard the admission.

As the tutor continued his tale, he absently smoothed the sides of his hair, this time held in check with a vibrant blue ribbon that stood in sharp contrast to his soft grey coat and the lace collar of his shirt. He had clearly dressed better for the evening's repast than his normal, dreary work-a-day attire. Tilly guessed the man was actually a dandy, something that would not agree with the austere accoutrements of a spiritual lifestyle.

He expressed great regret at leaving the church. After some inquiry with the local gentry, he found work as a private tutor in Edinburgh. Alas, he longed for a life outside the city after he travelled with a family to the Highlands. With one inhale of the fresh country air, he proclaimed that his soul belonged there. Fortunately, a colleague knew about the Campbell family's need for an instructor. He met His Grace, Malcolm Campbell, shortly thereafter and was most happy that he obtained employment at such a fine estate.

Daniel further complimented his new employer for allowing him time to visit friends on his way to the castle. "It was a most fortuitous visit, for they gave me a fine collection of books that your son will enjoy," he said. "I look forward to continuing the excellent work started by Mrs. Munro."

Benjamin smiled, yet seemed distant. She was puzzled by the abrupt change in his manner. He was so affectionate earlier in the day.

After the meal, she excused herself. She could tell the men wanted some time alone to discuss whatever it is men in the 19th century discuss over whisky. Tilly happily left them to their pursuits and hoped the company would brighten Benjamin's mood.

∞

TILLY WAS DELIGHTED when she heard two faint knocks on her door later that evening. Benjamin entered her room without comment and sat in his favorite chair. She was glad he did not spend the entire evening with Iain and Daniel.

"He seems to be a wise man," Benjamin said as he sank into the chair. "I think he will be a good tutor."

"Yes, I believe he will," Tilly said. She crossed the room to a table in the corner. "He will also be a great source of entertainment for the adults, particularly Iain."

"After you left, he told tales that would make you blush," Benjamin said, chuckling at the memory. "I must remember to limit his access to whisky, or I fear Allan will be educated in ways I did not intend."

She joined him by the fire and handed him a small glass. He stared at it before taking a tentative sip. He sighed with pleasure as the amber liquid rolled across his tongue.

She took a seat opposite him and sipped from her own glass. Tilly confessed, "I stole a bottle of whisky. I thought it would be nice to offer you refreshment when you returned to my room."

"I thank you for your consideration," he said, raising his glass to salute her.

Between the warmth of the blaze and the heat of the drink, they settled into a blissful state of contentment. Tilly savored the sense of family and comfort as they sat listening to the crackle and hiss of the logs.

"I like having you here, Tilly," Benjamin whispered.

Her heart fluttered like a school girl's at the raw emotion she saw on his face. "Benjamin, I-"

He interrupted by lifting her from the chair and enfolding her in his arms. "Please do not say anything," he said.

She relaxed in his embrace. With his strong arms wrapped around her, she felt peace. Tilly ran her hands down his back, enjoying the feel of his muscles. She remembered how wonderful they felt the night they made love. She drew back slightly so she could look up at him.

She savored the gentle caress of his hand and gazed deeply into his eyes. She did not resist when he leaned forward and gently kissed her. Her lips parted. She slipped her tongue into his mouth and tasted whisky. She moaned as she stood on her tips of her toes, eager to be as close to him as possible.

Tilly pressed her breasts against his chest and felt his arms tighten around her waist. She knew he felt every bit of the intense desire building between them. She should stop, yet she could not resist pressing her hips against his swelling manhood. Their night of passion blazed in her memory. She admitted that she secretly longed to experience it again.

"We must stop," he said breathlessly, pushing her away.

"Yes," Tilly said, though not entirely in agreement. "We shouldn't get carried away."

Groaning, he grabbed the glass and tossed back the remnants of the drink. "Why do you tempt me so?" he asked.

"What do you mean?" she asked in seeming innocence as she tried to wrap her arms around his waist.

He reluctantly extricated himself from her embrace. "I should not have come to your room tonight...or any night, for that matter," Benjamin said. "It is not proper."

Her face flushed. "We abandoned propriety the moment we met," she said defiantly. "Don't toss that in my face now."

She stood in front of him, forcing him to look her in the eyes. "You were different this afternoon," Tilly said. "Why are you so cold now?"

He stared at her so long that she thought he might not answer. "When we returned from our walk, I was reminded that we do not know each other as well as we should," Benjamin said. "I have allowed you certain liberties because of my growing comfort with you. Perhaps I have moved too quickly."

"You didn't seem to mind kissing me a few seconds ago!" she exclaimed, flinging her hands in disgust. "What the hell is your problem?"

She paced in front of the fireplace. "I don't understand you, Benjamin," she said. "You share your secrets with me. You introduce me to your family, even to your best friend's parents. You wouldn't do these things if you didn't trust me. Why second guess yourself? Are you afraid of your feelings?"

He returned to his seat and leaned forward. "Please tell me the truth," he said earnestly. "I must know how you *really* came to be here. If you are my father's agent, then tell me. If you work for another, confess. Let us be honest with each other. I must know if your feelings are true or part of a ruse. Please do not play with my affections, lass."

His words were like a blow to the stomach. *After all this time, we return to the same place*, Tilly thought. "Get out," she commanded.

"Tilly, I – "

She glared at him. "My name is Mrs. Munro, sir," she said, her voice trembling. "You should not address me so informally."

Benjamin nodded and slipped from the room.

∞

MR. MURPHY CAREFULLY CRACKED THE WAX SEAL and opened the letter that Daniel Ramsey presented to him earlier in the day. His extensive duties had not afforded him an opportunity to read it until this moment, no matter how much he desired. He bent closer to the lone candle on the table beside his bed. He smiled at the familiar handwriting.

> *My faithful servant,*
>
> *I thank you for your letter. You were right to alert me to the presence of the peculiar woman my son discovered in the forest. I share your concern about her. It is most unsettling.*
>
> *Let me speak frankly with you, my old friend. My son has a naïve view of the world. He thinks all people are good and trusts too easily. He is also grieving the loss of a beloved wife. He is an easy target for a cunning woman with matrimony on her mind.*
>
> *I know the post is not the most express means of communication. I give you leave to send a messenger with all haste if the situation becomes dire.*
>
> *With continued wishes for your health —*
>
> *Your Grace*

*Malcolm Campbell*

Mr. Murphy folded the letter and tucked it into a secret compartment he made under the table. The other servants probably suspected he sent news to His Grace. He did not want to give them proof.

He stared into the darkness of his room. The butler sincerely hoped that the rumors of growing affection between Mr. Campbell and Mrs. Munro were untrue. He feared the return of Malcolm Campbell almost as much as anyone else in the castle. *And, yet,* he thought, *I must protect dear Allan if she means us harm.*

Mr. Murphy frowned and rose from the bed. Before he could rest his head upon the pillow, he knew he must write a letter. He should thank His Grace for the generous offer and alert him to the arrival of the tutor. It was mundane news that would hopefully ease His Grace's mind, lest he worry about the governess and come to the Highlands. After all, no one wanted that visit.

# THIRTY FOUR

BENJAMIN SAT AT THE DESK IN HIS STUDY, staring at a ledger of tenant accounts. For the tenth time, he attempted to tally the column. His mind drifted once again before he reached the end. Irritated, he slammed the book closed and dropped his head into his hands.

For the last two weeks, Tilly distanced herself from him. She continued to teach his children and work with the new tutor. She was cordial to him at dinner and engaged in pleasant conversation with Iain and Daniel. However, she refused to answer her door when he visited her in the evening or address him directly whenever he spoke with her. She completely ignored him. To his chagrin, her cold demeanor chafed his pride.

Without question, their last encounter was the reason. Benjamin desperately wanted to know the truth, even if she was not the innocent woman she claimed to be. Iain was right. He allowed his feelings for her to cloud his judgment. *If I just knew who she was, I would know what to do,* he thought. Then, he remembered the whispered advice his wife's spirit gave him in the chapel.

"Then, show me the damn sign!" he exclaimed aloud, looking to the ceiling. "Mary, do not torture me!"

He jumped when someone knocked at his door. "Enter," he said.

Mr. Murphy walked into the room, accompanied by a flustered young man who would not meet Benjamin's gaze. "Milord, please forgive the interruption," the butler said. He cast a disapproving glance at the lad behind him. "Your father has sent an urgent message."

Benjamin motioned for the messenger to take a seat.

"Nay, milord," the man said. He gestured toward his dusty clothes. "I have been riding for three days and do not want to soil your fine furniture." He reached into his jacket pocket and produced a letter. His hand trembled slightly as he handed it to

Benjamin. "His Grace asked that I deliver this to you. He said I should not leave until you provide me with a reply."

"Mr. Murphy, please take this man to the kitchen and provide him with refreshment," Benjamin commanded, waving the men from his study.

The butler nodded and promptly escorted the man from the room.

Benjamin stared at the missive for a few moments. His father's correspondence never offered kind words and sincere wishes for health and happiness. Reluctantly, he broke the wax seal and opened the letter.

> *My son,*
>
> *I am most aggrieved by the information recently conveyed to me. You have taken in a wayward woman who is now acting as a governess to your children. It has been hinted that you may have developed an unnatural affection for her. It is outrageous!*
>
> *I cannot condone Mrs. Donnelly's horrifying behavior. You were right to dismiss her at once. However, hiring a replacement whose background is unknown greatly troubles me. This strange woman has no connections, no family, in the area. You found her wandering in the forest after her husband and servants were slaughtered by highwaymen.*

*I do not approve. While I understand the Christian duty to help those in need, you should have sent her on her way after a few days' stay. Why would you allow this woman to stay and teach your children? I fear the answer is most troubling.*

*I have heard she is a comely lass. Be on your guard, Benjamin. Women of nefarious character will take advantage of you and prey upon your affections. She may seek to ingratiate herself with your children in an effort to win your heart and fortune. A woman of unknown provenance is an unsuitable mate.*

*On that score, I am pleased to say that I have found a woman who is appropriate for the future heir of the Campbell fortune. She is a woman of great refinement and breeding. Her dowry is forty thousand pounds. Her family owns a lovely estate not far from Tinberry Hall.*

*I had hoped to forestall an introduction until your mourning passed. I intended for you to visit Tinberry Hall for a formal meeting with the lady. You have not been here in years, and I doubt you are raising your children to know that the Campbell family's reach extends beyond Castle Fion.*

*Given the intelligence I have received about this interloper, I am concerned you will make a foolish mistake. I have instructed my messenger to wait for a response from you. Is my intervention required? Is she more than a servant to you? Do you have plans to send her away?*

*You know me well enough, boy, to understand that an unacceptable response will send me to your door. I will bring the prospect with me. You may then settle your affections on a quality mate, not a fortune seeker from God knows where.*

*Do not disappoint me.*

*Your father,*

*Malcolm Campbell*

He tossed away the letter in disgust. The last thing he needed was a visit from his father. If Malcolm Campbell came to Castle Fion, Benjamin feared all his hard-won victories would be erased in a matter of days.

He rose from the desk and reached the door in four quick strides. When he flung open the door, he almost crashed into Iain. Seeing the concerned expression on his friend's face, Benjamin asked, "I take it you have heard about my father's messenger?"

"No," Iain said. "I come with other news."

Sighing heavily, he walked past the factor. "Let's us discuss it elsewhere," Benjamin said, making his way toward the castle's entrance. "I have a need to be away from this place."

# THIRTY FIVE

BENJAMIN AND IAIN RODE IN SILENCE until they reached a ridge that overlooked the loch. From this vantage point, they could see the little village of Deoch and the gently rolling mountains that were reflected upon the surface of the water. It was a view that always calmed Benjamin. He took several deep breaths of the clean, cool air and tried to slow the beating of his heart. He knew he must get his emotions in check before he made any hasty decisions.

He turned to Iain and asked, "What news do you have?"

"Our sentries found a camp in the forest," Iain said gravely. "It was some distance from the castle but too close for my comfort."

Benjamin had not expected this news. "Can you tell how recently it was used?" he asked, a cold chill of dread creeping up his spine. "Perhaps it was abandoned long ago."

Iain shook his head. "The embers from the fire were still warm," he said. "Whoever used the camp knew the sentries were near and ran. They found a trail leading away from the site. They lost it when the trail came to a stream."

"Could it be the MacDonald?"

"Aye, it is possible. It troubles me deeply."

"Have you received any reports from Deoch?"

"Not about Richard MacDonald."

He thought Iain's response was rather vague. "What have you heard?" he asked, eyes narrowing.

"Mrs. Donnelly disappeared. No one recalls seeing her leave the village. They found her things in her room. The innkeeper kept them as recompense for the unpaid bill. If she left for London, why would she have left her clothes and personal items?"

"Mrs. Donnelly's travelling habits are not my concern."

"They should be," Iain advised, his voice stern. "I found her sudden absence most vexing so I asked my men to investigate. This morning, they found a shallow grave behind the stable. They were able to identify the body from the ring she always wore. If you will recall, Mrs. Donnelly's wedding band was most unusual – a small ruby set in a band of silver thorns. She said it belonged to her late husband's mother."

"If someone robbed her, they could have taken the ring," Benjamin said. At the shake of Iain's head, his heart sank. Other proof must have been found for the factor to be so certain. "How did the woman die?"

"The men found a neat stab wound to the heart. The blow showed great efficiency, something a skilled warrior could have done."

"Someone like Richard MacDonald."

"Aye, I recall that he spent a few years in France as a mercenary. No one in Deoch reports seeing the man, but Mrs. Donnelly's death is too convenient. Everyone knew she worked at the castle. Could he have killed her to send a message to you?"

"I dismissed her months ago. She was of no consequence to me."

"It may be the reason why he killed her. He wanted you to know that he can take whoever he wants, whenever he wants."

"Why would he reveal himself prematurely? If he killed her, then he has lost the element of surprise."

Iain considered the observation. "Richard MacDonald has waited many years to exact his revenge," he said, at last. "I suspect he wants to slowly punish you. He will not strike in one swift blow. It will be death by a thousand tiny cuts."

"I trust you have increased security around the castle."

"Aye. I have doubled the guards and instructed them to keep a close eye on the children. If I were Richard MacDonald, I would attack them first."

"Please ask them to watch Tilly," he said. Iain was silent. "She deserves protection too."

"If she works for the MacDonald, she will not need it."

"Do you honestly believe that she does?" he asked, glaring at his friend. "She has not given us any reason to suspect her guilt."

"I am cautious around anything – or anyone – that I do not understand. Take heed. Mrs. Munro is equally troubling."

"You sound like my father," Benjamin said. With bitterness in his voice, he informed Iain about the contents of the letter. He was glad to see his friend was just as concerned as he was that Malcolm Campbell might return to Castle Fion.

"You must send her away at once!" Iain said urgently. "She could undo everything you have accomplished."

Benjamin said nothing as he coaxed his horse forward. Iain expected him to agree, yet he was greatly conflicted. He chose instead to delay the conversation.

They rode down the ridge into the green valley below and approached a small copse of trees. He dismounted from his horse and loosely tied its reins to a tree. He removed a bottle of whisky from his saddle bag. After taking a long swig, he offered the bottle to an appreciative Iain.

"I have lied," Benjamin said. "I have broken the law. I have concocted great schemes to subvert my father's plans. My life has been dedicated to the protection of this estate and its people."

"Aye, it has."

"For once, I want to do something for myself. Why is it wrong for me to be happy?"

Iain laid a gentle hand upon his friend's shoulder. "You cannot be happy if it meant destroying someone else's life," he said, smiling ruefully. "If your father knew half the things you have done, he would not allow you to manage the estate. It would be as it was before. Do you want that?"

Benjamin lowered his head. "No," he replied, his voice filled with sorrow. "It has been a long time since the people had hope."

"Aye, it has. You have given them a living. You have fed them when they had nothing to eat. You have provided them with shelter and let them pay their rent when they could, instead of demanding payment as your father would have," his factor said. "And, the crofters know, when your father dies, you will let them buy their farms. They can have a piece of earth that is their own. They stay because they know you will do right by them."

Benjamin walked away from Iain and looked at the valley before them. A farm had once stood there, its remnants evident by the crumbling rock fence and collapsed cottage. His father evicted the tenants to make way for the sheep that presently grazed on the fragrant grass.

"When I last spoke with her, I begged her to tell me who she was," he said, keeping his back to Iain. "She was angry and has not spoken with me since that evening. It rips apart my heart. I miss her. We used to have such wonderful conversations, unlike any I have ever experienced with a woman. I feel her absence keenly. What does that mean?"

"Do you love her, Benjamin?"

"I fear that I do."

"If you feel fear, then you must be in love," Iain said, laughing heartily. "I have found much fear in the presence of love."

Benjamin turned and cocked an eyebrow. "When have you known love?" he asked, surprised by the admission. "You have never courted a woman."

"Your attention was always turned toward Mary. What do you know of my life?" his friend asked. Iain's eyes grew uncharacteristically misty. "It was many years ago. She was a beautiful lass and wanted to wed. I was too stupid to see it. I thought we were having a bit o' fun. It was only after she told me she would marry another that I realized my true feelings for her. I begged her not to do it. Ah, it was too late."

"The day she wed a MacDougall, I stood on a hill above the church. My heart broke when the bells rang," he said, lost in memories of that day. "I watched them ride away, smiling and laughing. It was the last time I saw her alive. She died a year later while giving birth to a stillborn bairn."

"I am truly sorry, Iain."

"I often wonder if her life would have been better

with me than with the other man. Would she have survived? Would she have been happy?"

"Do not dwell upon the past, my friend. You cannot change it."

A ghost of a smile flitted across Iain's lips. "Wise advice," he said. "You should remember that when you think of Mrs. Munro. She is not Mary."

"No one will ever replace your beloved wife," Iain added. "Take care that you are not filling your heart with another just because you want to feel love again. You should only settle your affections upon someone who is worthy."

"Why would she be considered unworthy by anyone?" Benjamin asked. "Is it because she does not come from a fine family or have forty thousand pounds for a dowry?"

"You knew more about Mrs. Donnelly than you do Mrs. Munro!" his friend said. "With the governess, it was clear what her intentions were. We know not what Mrs. Munro seeks. She could have visited Richard MacDonald at the campsite and warned him. Or, she could still work for your father. His letter could be a ruse."

Benjamin shook his head. "I do not perceive guile," he said. "I believe her to be a kind woman."

"She may be a kind woman, but I do not see innocence in her eyes. Mrs. Munro has a secret."

"Dammit, Iain! She *does* have a secret. She said she is from the future. She does not speak of it to anyone. I imagine it is a heavy burden to be from another time and place."

"Do you believe her tale then?"

"I do not know what I believe anymore. I have never felt more confused in my life."

"Then, I urge you not to make any rash decisions. Take care in your actions, my friend. You have so much to lose."

He exhaled slowly. He felt no more settled now than he did when he first arrived at what was normally a peaceful spot. As he mounted his horse, he told Iain, "Thank you for your counsel. If you will excuse me, I would like some time to consider my decision."

Benjamin rode away without looking back at his friend. If this spot offered no solace, he knew of another place that might calm his restless spirit.

# THIRTY SIX

BENJAMIN PUSHED OPEN THE CHAPEL DOOR and winced at the sound of the creaky hinges. He mentally noted that he should send someone to grease them. He could not allow the grating sound to disturb the sweet silence.

To his astonishment, he saw Tilly sitting at the front pew. He took a seat beside her. He noticed that her eyes were red and puffy as if she had been crying. "What is the matter?" he asked.

Without looking at him, she replied, "Today was my wedding anniversary." She turned to face him. "Should I still celebrate such things even though my husband is dead?"

"Aye, of course," he said, daring to take her hand. Benjamin was relieved that she did not pull it away.

"If the day was a happy one, you should always remember it."

"It was. We were very much in love," she said. Tilly smiled weakly. "After the ceremony, Beth and her husband Randall bought us dinner and handed us a key to a fancy hotel room. We spent our first night there as husband and wife."

She sighed. "I always dreamt of having a big wedding with a poufy gown and large bouquet of flowers," she said. "Instead, I wore a blue dress that I bought for someone else's wedding and carried some wildflowers we picked along the highway."

"Why did you not have the wedding of your dreams?"

"We couldn't afford that kind of affair. And, Alex had been married before, so he wasn't interested. It seemed like a good idea at the time."

"You sound as if you regret it now."

"It saddens me more to think that I will never have that moment with my daughter Anna," she said, tears spilling down her cheeks. "Parents aren't supposed to die before their children. I feel as if I have this huge hole in my chest."

Benjamin gently brushed away her tears and said, "You rarely speak of your family. Would you like to talk about them?"

She accepted the handkerchief he handed her and wiped her eyes. "If I start talking about them, I am afraid I won't be able to stop!" she exclaimed in agony. She glanced up at him and reluctantly said, "Despite all the problems Alex and I had, our children were our top priority. We wanted them to have everything. My husband thought that meant material things. I believed they needed love and attention."

"It was tough at times to have twins," she continued. "I was a new mom. One baby would have been a challenge – but two at once? It was difficult."

"At least you did not have two boys," he teased. He was happy that his comment produced a smile.

"I'm not sure if I could have managed that! Your boys are a handful."

"Was your son John as mischievous as Angus or Michael?"

She thought for a moment before replying, "No, John was more like your son Allan. He could be boisterous as any child can, but he preferred being alone. He loved to sit in his room and play with building blocks and draw pictures."

"And, what was Anna like?"

"When she was a toddler, she was into everything. I constantly chased after her, taking away whatever object she found. She wanted to explore every nook and cranny of the house."

"Did she outgrow her inquisitiveness?"

"Not really. She loved to read and explore. Her favorite places were museums and parks. She had such a thirst for knowledge."

Benjamin wrapped his arm around her shoulders. "Please do not feel that you cannot speak about your family with me," he said. "They will always be a part of your life, just as Mary was a part of mine. Let us treasure the happy memories."

"I try to focus on the good times," she said. "I don't want to obsess over their tragic deaths. They deserve better than that."

"Aye, they do."

She stared at him. "How do you cope, Benjamin?" she asked. "It's not as if you have a support group or a psychiatrist you can visit in this time. How do you deal with your grief?"

He considered her questions for a moment before answering, "I do not have much choice in the matter. Many people depend upon my strength and leadership for their survival. I must put one foot in front of the other and keep moving. I do not have the luxury of mourning." He smiled ruefully. "When we met, you saw me in a rare, private moment. It was the first time I had allowed myself to grieve."

"We share a mutual heartache," she said. "If you want to talk, I will listen. Maybe we can figure out together how we are supposed to go on with our lives."

He dropped his head and allowed a single tear to escape his eye. "Thank you," he said. Benjamin felt the great weight of guilt on his heart. "I am sorry, Tilly. For everything."

She furrowed her brow. "Everything?" she asked.

"Aye. You have endured great hardship. I hope that my attitude has not made your life worse."

She wrapped her arms around him. Kissing him lightly on the cheek, she whispered into his ear, "You have given me hope, Benjamin."

Pulling her close to him, he savored the warmth of her supple body and inhaled the scent of her – jasmine, he thought. He closed his eyes. He decided he would allow himself a few moments of happiness before he turned his mind to more serious matters. In this quiet spot and in the safety of her arms, Benjamin found the peace he so desperately sought.

∞

AFTER DINNER THAT EVENING, Benjamin returned to his study and re-read his father's letter. Mr. Murphy found suitable accommodation for the messenger so a reply could wait until the morning. Unfortunately, he realized that he would not sleep until he put quill to paper and answered the correspondence.

He stared at the blank page for some time before the words came to him. He carefully scratched a brief reply and shook sand onto the page to dry the ink. Then, he sealed the document with a thick, red blob of wax, careful to affix his personal seal. Benjamin wanted it to be clear to his father that the words were his, no one else's.

His task complete, he extinguished the candles, banked the fire, and headed for bed. Benjamin fell into the deep slumber of an unfettered mind.

# THIRTY SEVEN

THE NEXT MORNING, Tilly descended the stairs and found the house in an uproar. Mr. Murphy scurried around the entrance, barking orders for the servants to make haste. She spotted a few horses outside the open front doors. Before she could ask what happened, she saw Benjamin.

He motioned for her to follow him to his study. He hurriedly closed the door behind them. "We received word that Iain's father, Robert, is dead," he said. "We do not know how. It is very mysterious."

"Do you think someone killed him?" she asked, shocked and terrified at the same time.

"I do not know," he said. He looked grim. "We are leaving for the farm now. It may be tomorrow before we return."

"Tell Iain I am so sorry for his loss," she said. "Is there anything I can do?"

They heard heavy footsteps coming toward the study. "Say nothing to the boys," he said. "Stay close to the castle, and you will be safe."

The door swung open. Iain stood in the doorway, his eyes bloodshot. "The horses are ready," he announced. He would not look at Tilly.

She moved forward anyway and tried to hug him. "Thank you, madam," he said gruffly as he pushed her away. He seemed surprised at her gesture. "We must be leaving. It will be a difficult journey."

She was unsure if he referred to the trip or the task of burying his father's body. Tilly managed a weak smile as she watched the men leave.

∞

IRONICALLY, THEY WERE BLESSED WITH A RARE SUNNY DAY. Daniel decided it would be the perfect time to have a practical lesson about botany. He found the appropriate books in the library and offered to include all of the boys if Tilly would not mind. Looking for any reason to be outdoors, she happily accepted.

She watched Daniel and Sarah walk in front of her, each carrying an armload of books into the garden.

They chatted amiably and laughed at some joke Sarah made. It appeared the two were quite taken with each other, as Tilly initially suspected.

The warm weather made Michael and Stephen a bit lax about specimen hunting. In no time, they drifted to the stream that ran beside the garden and tossed rocks into it. Daniel removed his stockings and dipped his feet in the cool water. Tilly noticed that Sarah looked away. Was it just as improper to see a man's ankles as it was to see a lady's?

She found Allan studying a leaf he held in his hand. As she spent more time with him, she found him to be a very quiet, observant child. He carefully compared the illustration in the book he carried to the actual leaf, a slight crease in his brow when he concentrated. His brother Angus looked over his shoulder, pretending to be equally fascinated by the subject.

When Tilly offered to help them find specimens, Allan suggested that they head into the forest. He knew the location of several oaks and other trees mentioned in the book. A hike in the woods sounded like an excellent idea in such fine weather. *We should be close enough to the castle that it is safe*, she thought fleetingly.

Of course, wherever Allan went, Angus followed. As the trio walked through the forest, Allan entertained them with stories of ghosts and fey who would hide in the woods and attack unsuspecting travelers. He pointed toward the chapel that stood at the end of the trail on which they walked. "They say a headless horseman sometimes rides this path," Allan said gravely. "He will not pass the chapel, for he fears to tread on holy ground."

She knew he meant to scare them and found it highly amusing. Judging from the wide-eyed look on Angus' face, Tilly feared his younger brother took the tales very seriously, though. She hoped the boy would not have nightmares tonight.

On the path ahead, a tall man blocked their way. Stringy hair retreated from the top of his head, with a few remaining greasy strands clinging to the sides and hanging limply on his shoulders. He wore a thick, greying beard that contained the remnants of a recent meal as well as an assortment of twigs and leaves. A threadbare kilt hung loosely around his thin frame. He wore no shirt.

Tilly could see the man's ribs poking through pale white skin smeared with dirt and glistening with sweat. He must have been living in the forest for some time, for she could smell the foul stench of unwashed flesh and rustic life in the wild.

It was the first time she had seen a man wearing a kilt since she arrived in this time. It was not the sexy sight described in romance novels. A distinctly lethal air surrounded the man. He was flesh and blood, not one of Allan's fey. She carefully stepped in front of the children, blocking them from view.

"I have no quarrel with you, woman," the man said. He smiled, revealing a set of rotting teeth. Pointing to the boys, he added, "I would like to have a word with the children."

Tilly felt Allan move behind her and grabbed his arm. "Whatever you have to say to them, you can say to me," she said, chin held high. She did not like the tone of his voice.

He stared at her as if he was considering something. He nodded his head and said, "I suppose it would serve to have someone who can tell the tale to Benjamin."

*That sounds ominous*, she thought. She mentally calculated how far they were from the others. It was highly unlikely that they could reach their party before the man caught them. She hoped fear did not show on her face.

"My name is Richard MacDonald," he said, taking a step toward her.

She involuntarily stepped back. *Oh, shit,* she thought.

"Benjamin and his father killed my sister and my brother. I promised my father I would not seek vengeance while he lived," he said. Richard took another step toward them and grinned with barely-concealed menace. "He never made me promise not to strike after he was dead."

His hand hovered over the hilt of a short sword hanging from his belt. He noticed Tilly staring at it. "It is the MacDonald dirk," Richard said, his fingers lightly tapping the hilt. "I have dreamt of this moment every single day for the last sixteen years. The boys will taste its iron before the sun sets this day."

Suddenly, he closed the distance between them and seized her arm. She screamed and yanked her arm free. Before she could flee, Richard swung his fist and struck her square in the jaw. Tilly saw a flash of stars and fell hard onto the ground. At that moment, she understood the phrase "knocked senseless." She struggled to remain conscious, placing a trembling hand upon her throbbing jaw.

"Stand aside, woman," the man commanded, trying to grab Allan. "I promise not to hurt you. I only want the children."

She stuck out her foot and tripped him. As he hurled forward, Tilly scrambled to her feet. She pushed Allan away from the man's grasp and frantically cried, "Run, boys! *RUN!!*"

She turned to her attacker. She needed to give the boys some time to escape. Of course, she knew she was no match for the man. She had to try something, though.

She planted her feet as she learned in self-defense class. Curling the fingers of her right hand firmly against her palm, she drove the heel of her hand with all her strength into the man's nose. With a sickening feeling, she felt his bones shatter.

He stepped away from her, blood gushing from his nose. "You bitch! You broke my nose!" Richard shouted in fury. He cursed her and the woman who brought her into this world as he clutched his nose.

She ignored his foul language and massaged her hand, knowing her blow hurt him more than it did her. Tilly turned and spotted Angus running at top speed down the trail. It brought a smile to her face until she realized that Allan had not followed his brother. He held a small dagger in his hand and intended to charge the MacDonald.

Even though tears streamed from his eyes, she could tell that Richard saw the boy. He was prepared for the attack. When Allan moved toward him, the man easily pushed the boy to the ground.

Judging from the fierce look on his face, his

vengeance would wait a few moments longer. Richard advanced toward her. It was obvious that his earlier promise would be broken.

Despite her instincts, she let him get close to her. Then, she kicked him in the groin. He doubled over, groaning loudly but managing to stay afoot. She moved to the right. She meant to snatch Allan and make a run for it.

Unfortunately, her attacker was faster. He clutched her left arm and pulled her toward him. His grip was like a vice. "I will kill you first, then send wee Allan to the devil where he belongs!" Richard roared, his foul breath on her face.

She pummeled his chest with her fists, all in vain, as she desperately tried to break free. She struggled to check the rising panic, knowing she needed to focus if they had any chance to survive. Then, her hand brushed against the hilt of the dirk. Now was not the time for a moral debate. The man would kill her and the rest of the Campbell family. Without hesitation, Tilly drew the blade from its sheath.

He held her so close that she instinctively recognized her targets were limited. She saw an exposed area. In one swift movement, she plunged the sword underneath his chin, jamming it into his brain. The shock of the blow reverberated down her arm. She tried to jerk away, but he did not release her.

Richard's eyes widened. His body tumbled backward, pulling her down on top of him.

They landed with a thud, knocking the wind out of her. Tilly took several deep breaths. She could feel the adrenaline coursing through her veins. Her heart beat so hard and loud against her chest that she feared it might explode.

She was on the verge of hysteria and desperately needed to calm herself, if only for Allan's sake. She looked up and discovered him staring at her. "You are safe now," she said, trying to keep her voice from shaking.

The boy pried Richard's filthy fingers from her arm and helped her to her feet. She stumbled as Allan led her a few feet away from the body and deposited her onto a rock. She was shaking from head to toe.

She looked down at her hands and saw the blood. She felt wetness on her cheeks. It must have splattered onto her face as well. *Suck it up, Tilly. You are about to go bat guano crazy, and it is not the time for such things!* she told herself.

"Madam, let me help you," Allan said, with great composure. He took a handkerchief from his pocket and gently wiped the blood from her hands and face. His hands did not shake. His calm steadied her.

"Are you alright?" she asked.

"Aye, I am well," he answered flatly. She could tell he was being brave for her. She wanted to hold him but suspected it might wound his pride.

His task complete, Allan returned the soiled handkerchief to his pocket. He strode to the body and lightly kicked the MacDonald's leg. The boy stared blankly at the man's face.

"Please come here, Allan," Tilly said. "You don't need to see that."

"No, I do," he argued. "This man wanted to kill my family – and you too, Mrs. Munro. I should remember him."

If the boy could be brave, so could she. She rose to her feet and walked toward Allan. She lightly placed her arm around his shoulders.

It was a gruesome sight. Richard MacDonald's lifeless eyes stared at the canopy of trees above them. Ruby red blood trickled down the sides of his mouth and out his broken nose. The sword was buried to the hilt under his chin. She did not realize how forceful the blow had been.

Despite what he said, no child should see this sight. Tilly turned Allan to face her. "Are you sure you are alright?" she asked again.

Before he could answer her, she heard racing

footsteps on the trail behind them. She wondered if their attacker might have others in his party. Apparently, Allan felt the same way, for he retrieved his dagger and stood at the ready. She stepped in front of him and prayed she had the strength to take on more assailants.

Two men charged up the trail and skidded to a stop when they saw the body lying on the ground. She recognized one of them as the sentry named Robbie. "Milord, have you and the mistress been harmed?" he asked.

Allan drew himself to his full height. "We are well," he replied, his voice strong. "Richard MacDonald cannot make the same claim."

The other man, a brawny fellow with hair as black as night, stepped forward and stared at the dead man's face. "Aye, the bastard will have a well-deserved dance with the devil tonight," he spat venomously. He kicked the corpse in the ribs. "Still, it does not serve the family to have a dead MacDonald on our lands."

"Do you think he had others with him, James?" Robbie asked the fellow sentry, worriedly scanning the forest.

"I do not believe so," James replied. For good measure, he unsheathed the blade he carried on his waistband. "Nevertheless, let us away to the castle. We can collect the body once milord is safe."

James whipped his head to the side. With a nod to Robbie, he grabbed Tilly and Allan. They all slipped behind a nearby tree.

Reflexively, Tilly wrapped her arm around Allan. *What now?* she wondered. Her nerves were frayed. Then, she heard it. People were running on the trail and getting closer by the second.

To her great relief, it was Sarah and Daniel. The pair halted when they saw the body.

Allan, the sentries, and she emerged from behind the tree, startling Sarah and Daniel. "It is just us," Tilly said shakily.

Daniel recovered and asked, "Did he hurt you or the boy?

"No," Tilly said, her voice coming out in a whisper. She took a deep breath. She spoke again. This time, the sound was stronger. "We are fine."

James stood beside Robbie who looked visibly shaken. "Are the rest of the children in the castle?" he asked Daniel.

"Aye," Daniel said. "Angus alerted us to the danger, so the children were ushered into the castle. More men are searching the forest, making sure the area is secure."

Sarah walked to the dead man's body. She took one look at the man's face and turned away. "It is Richard MacDonald," she said to Daniel. "This is very bad." She took a deep breath, briefly closing her eyes. Tilly thought the girl might faint.

When Sarah opened her eyes again, she seemed resolute. She pointed to Daniel. "Take Allan to the castle," she ordered. "Find Mr. Murphy and tell him his assistance is needed here. Ask Mrs. Keith to wait for us at the south entrance. Speak to no one else."

He stared vacantly at her. She snapped her fingers. "Quickly!" she said.

Daniel jumped. He moved toward Allan, but the boy refused to leave Tilly. Allan grabbed her arm and begged, "Please, I want to stay with you!"

She placed a trembling hand on his cheek. "I need you to protect your brothers and sister," she said with more calm than she felt. "Can you do that for me?"

Allan stood a little taller and tightly grasped the hilt of his dagger. He nodded to her before he marched with Daniel down the trail.

"How serious is the situation?" Tilly asked, looking from one person to another. Robbie and James stared at the ground, suddenly shy.

"Murder is always serious," Sarah answered vaguely.

"It was obviously an act of self-defense, but you are a stranger here," James said, at last. "There would be questions."

Tilly gulped. She remembered how primitive justice could be in this time. "Can we trust Mr. Murphy?" she asked.

"Aye, it is in the family's best interest to keep this secret," James said, a bemused smile lighting his face. "Mr. Murphy always does what is best for the Campbells."

Tilly noted that he said nothing about doing what was best for *her*.

∞

TILLY FELT STRANGELY DETACHED FROM HER BODY. Planted upon a rock, she could only watch as the others moved around the scene. It did not seem as unusual to them. For her, it seemed like watching a scene from a movie. A really terrifying movie.

If Mr. Murphy was shocked at the scene, he said nothing. He arrived with the still pale Daniel, who carried a large bundle of burlap.

She watched the butler take a brief moment to survey the scene. Then, Mr. Murphy took command of the situation as if nothing was out of the ordinary. *How many times has he handled something like this?* she could not help but wonder.

He told Daniel to go to the stable and find the stablemaster, Graeme. Daniel should return with a horse to carry the body. Graeme should bring three horses to the meadow outside the stable.

Before Daniel turned to obey his orders, Mr. Murphy seized the man by the collar and growled, "You say nothing of the errand you are doing, or you shall not live to see the morn!"

Swallowing hard, Daniel replied, "You can be assured of my silence, sir. I swear it upon my life." Then, he raced down the trail before Mr. Murphy could issue further threats upon his personage.

The butler spread the burlap beside Richard MacDonald's body. Robbie, James, and he lifted the dead man onto the cloth. They briefly considered whether or not they should remove the sword. They decided to leave it in place because its removal might make the scene very messy. The men tightly wrapped the body and left a handful of cloth at each end. Sarah kicked dirt over the blood stains on the trail, concealing the evidence of the dreadful deed.

When Mr. Murphy cleared his throat, Tilly came to her senses and looked at him. He had been speaking to her, though she did not hear a word. "Milady, perhaps it would be best if Sarah and you returned to the castle now," he repeated.

"What are you going to do?" she asked, pointing to the body. "No one must find him."

He walked over to her. Mr. Murphy gently guided her toward the trail, blocking her vision of the burlap bundle. "Milady, this is not the first time I have taken up the difficult business of the Campbell family," he said patiently. "Rest assured, I know a place where no one will ever discover Richard MacDonald."

She stared at him. Her life rested in his hands. Tilly could be executed for what she did – if not by the justice system, then by an angry MacDonald. Unfortunately, she had little choice but to trust him. The body must be moved right away. They could not wait until Benjamin returned, whenever that might be.

She clutched his arm. "Please...." she pleaded, unable to finish the sentence.

Lifting a hand to silence her, he leaned closer. "Milady, you saved the boy," Mr. Murphy whispered. "Let me save you."

A tear fell unchecked down her cheek. Tilly nodded and stumbled numbly toward the castle.

# THIRTY EIGHT

OUT OF ALL THE SHOCKING EVENTS OF THE DAY, Tilly was not at all surprised to see Mrs. Keith hurriedly approach them on the trail. Asking the housekeeper to wait was a ridiculous request. The woman's sturdy presence was a great comfort, almost like having a mother or dear friend present. Losing her family, traveling back in time, and now murdering someone – how much more could her mind take before it snapped like a twig?

The feel of the scratchy wool cloak that Mrs. Keith tossed over her shoulders brought Tilly out of the fog in which her brain descended. "You are properly covered," the woman was saying as she cinched closed the cloak. "A casual observer cannot see the bloodstains on your dress."

Sarah and Mrs. Keith each grabbed an arm for support and ushered her into a hidden entrance of the castle. She noticed that it led to the servants' area in the basement. *Looks like I will finally get that tour,* she thought humorlessly.

They took her to a room with two large fireplaces in which roaring blazes were already set. She spotted a copper tub to the right, filled to the brim with steaming water. The ladies hastily disrobed her, careful to tuck the stained dress out of her sight, and helped her into the tub. Mrs. Keith washed her hair while Sarah scrubbed all remaining traces of blood from her face, chest, and hands.

Normally, Tilly would be upset by such intimate attentions. At the moment, she felt lost in a haze of disbelief. Was this the moment when she would awaken from her nightmare? She would emerge from this strange time in which she found herself, with only memories of a weird dream about living in the 1800s. This could not be real.

She did not offer the usual murmur of thanks when they dried her and placed her in a clean gown. She merely stood there, lost in her thoughts. A man died by her hand. He was intent upon killing the boys and her, but he died because of her nevertheless. How was she supposed to live with it?

Shaking greatly, Tilly asked Mrs. Keith, "Where is

Benjamin?"

∞

IT WAS MIDDAY when the group arrived at the MacIver farm. Benjamin dreaded what he would find at the end of their journey. Robert taught him how to be a man. How could he face the loss of such a person? And, what if his death came because of the sins of the Campbell family? Could Benjamin live with that burden?

Benjamin spotted Fiona MacIver running from the cottage as they approached. He felt a knot form in the pit of his stomach. Had the poor woman been waiting for them, completely terrified?

She waved excitedly when she saw Iain. "I am so happy to see you!" his mother exclaimed. "You have brought your friends too!"

He furrowed his brow in confusion and looked at Iain. The man's mother did not seem upset. It was odd.

Iain dismounted from his horse and hugged his mother close. "When did it happen?" he asked, his voice raw with emotion. "I came as soon as I heard."

"Whatever do you mean, boy?" she asked. She lifted her hand to his forehead and lightly touched it. "Are you crazed with fever?"

When Robert MacIver emerged from the stable, the color drained from Iain's face. "Da? Are you flesh and blood?" he asked. "Or, does your spirit haunt us?"

Robert chuckled. "Are you daft? I am very much alive," he said. He glanced at Benjamin. "Lad, you are as pale as a ghost. What has happened?"

Benjamin's heart felt as if it stopped. He locked eyes with Iain and said, "You should stay with your family."

Iain would have nothing of it. "Like hell I will," he growled. He swiftly mounted his horse and barked at the men in their party. "You stay here and guard the farm. Do not leave until I return."

Mrs. MacIver balled her hands into fists and yelled in frustration, "Will someone tell me what has happened?"

The men dismounted from their horses and made their way to the stable. One of the men stopped in front of Mrs. MacIver and answered her with great sorrow in his voice, "It was a trick. The MacDonald is at the castle."

She fell to her knees and began to pray.

Benjamin choked back a sob and said, "Aye, pray that we make it in time." He tugged on the reins of his horse and coaxed it to a full gallop, with Iain hot on his heels.

# THIRTY NINE

THE RIDE BACK TO THE CASTLE was the longest of Benjamin's life. He felt sick. Would he return to find his entire family slaughtered? Would Tilly be safe? Images of their lifeless bodies flooded his imagination. He shook his head and tried to focus, knowing that such morbid thoughts would not make the journey end sooner. And yet, they served one purpose. He knew he would kill Richard MacDonald as soon as he found him.

It was dark when they arrived. He jumped from his horse and ran into the castle, shouting his children's names in rapid succession.

Mr. Murphy stopped him at the entrance. "Be quiet, milord," he hissed. "Everyone is sleeping. All is well."

Benjamin relaxed at the news but then noticed the worry upon the man's face. "What has happened?" he asked frantically.

Mr. Murphy guided him into the study. He poured two glasses of whisky, handing one to his liege and saving one for himself. To Benjamin's surprise, the man took a seat and slowly sipped the drink.

He had never seen the man sit, much less drink. The situation must be very grave. Benjamin paced in front of Mr. Murphy and waited as patiently as he could. His hands shook badly. "Tell me," he demanded, unable to wait another moment. The suspense was more than he could bear.

The butler stared solemnly into the glass. "The MacDonald killed two sentries," he said. "Then, he found Mrs. Munro, Allan, and Angus in the forest."

"Did he harm them?" Benjamin asked in desperation. He stopped pacing and stared at Mr. Murphy. He hoped his treasures were untouched.

"No. Mrs. Munro is a remarkable woman, milord. She protected the boys."

"Where is Richard MacDonald?" he asked. Unconsciously, Benjamin grasped the hilt of the blade attached to his belt. "I would like to have a word with him."

Mr. Murphy paused to take a long drink. "I fear that will not be possible as he is indisposed at the moment," he replied. "He is at the bottom of the old well."

Benjamin knew the spot. It was located near the ruins of the original castle. The well was long dry but no doubt functioned for centuries as the last resting place for many wayward souls. No one would ever think to look for a body there.

"Was he alive when you tossed him there?"

"No, milord, he most assuredly was not."

"Then, who killed him?"

"Mrs. Munro."

"What? How?" Benjamin asked as he collapsed into a chair, stunned. He expected the man was killed by one of his sentries or even Mr. Murphy. He never expected Tilly to do the deed.

"Mrs. Munro and the boys have been understandably distraught after the experience," Mr. Murphy said coolly, rising from his seat and placing the empty glass on the desk. "I suggest you speak with them in the morning. They can tell the tale."

Before the man could leave the room, Benjamin asked, "What will you tell my father?"

Mr. Murphy offered a slow, small smile. "I will tell him you have succeeded in finding two wonderful teachers for the boys," he said. With that, he silently slipped from the room and returned to his duties as butler.

∞

BENJAMIN KNEW HE SHOULD LET THE BOYS SLEEP, but he could not rest until he saw them in the flesh. He first stopped at Angus' room and found him snoring in his bed. He was relieved to see the boy had not suffered serious trauma.

His son Allan, on the other hand, was wide awake and waiting for his father. The boy was stoic until Benjamin hugged him. Then, Allan burst into tears as he recounted the horrifying tale.

It was his great desire to be a brave man. He hoped his father understood that he tried but was too small. "If Mrs. Munro had not been there, the bad man would have hurt the family, and it would have been all my fault," Allan cried, hot tears pouring down his reddened face.

"Oh, I know you showed great courage, lad," Benjamin said soothingly. "You did not run. You tried to help Mrs. Munro. I know you did. I am proud of you. What happened is not your fault."

The words seemed to comfort his son. He tucked

Allan into bed and watched him fall asleep. As he left the bedroom, he nodded at the guard who sat beside the fireplace. Mr. Murphy thoughtfully posted guards in each child's bedroom. He would sleep better tonight knowing that help was close at hand, though he suspected no other MacDonalds would come.

He almost lost two children today. Benjamin could not imagine what his life would have been like if the MacDonald succeeded. Tilly knew that pain – and he wanted to thank her for saving his sons.

# *FORTY*

BENJAMIN CLIMBED THE STAIRS TO TILLY'S ROOM. For the first time, it did not matter what anyone would think if they saw him. *Propriety be dammed*, he thought.

When he heard no answer to his knock, he entered the empty receiving room and proceeded directly to her bedchamber. All the while, he cursed his father for the maze of rooms one must navigate to reach the person one wanted to see. And, he desperately wanted to see her tonight.

He knocked on her bedchamber's door. She did not answer. The hour was very late. Sighing heavily, his thank you would have to wait until the morning. After everything she had been through that day, Benjamin did not wish to disturb her sleep.

With a disappointed heart, he made his way down the stairs. He found it odd that the guard sat outside the door to his rooms. Why didn't the man sit in his study? Shaking his head, he entered the room. He was too tired to question the man at this late hour.

When he entered his own bedchamber, he understood why the man kept a discreet distance. He found Tilly standing in front of the fireplace. She held a glass in her hand and stared upward at the shield hanging above the mantle. She turned when he walked into the room. He could tell she had been crying. He watched her drop the glass onto the floor, where it shattered into tiny pieces. Benjamin noticed how ragged her breathing was when she looked at him.

He rushed to her side, eager to be near her. With a trembling hand, he gently caressed her cheek. When she winced, he spotted the ugly purple bruise blossoming along her jawbone. At that moment, Benjamin was glad the MacDonald was dead, or he would have killed him a thousand times over.

"Thank you," he whispered. Despite his best efforts, he could not stop the tears from flowing.

Tilly gently wiped them from his cheeks. "Are the MacIvers safe?" she asked.

"Aye, they are both alive. The message was a trick

to lure us away from the castle."

"I am so glad they are okay," she said, with a relieved sigh. "We have had enough death today."

He nodded in agreement. He stared at the courageous woman who stood before him. "Thank you," he repeated. "If I live a hundred lifetimes, I will never be able to repay you for what you did."

She gazed deeply into his eyes. "I can think of one way you can repay me," Tilly whispered. "Right now, I don't care if you believe me. I just don't want to feel this pain. I killed a man today. He deserved it, but he is dead because of me." Tears tumbled down her cheeks. "My whole world is upside down. I am in a strange time, surrounded by people who don't know or trust me. I may never go home. I am so lost, so lonely."

He held her as sobs racked her body. "Please give me one more night, just one night," she pleaded. "Let me feel loved again."

He bent low, and she lifted her face to his. Their lips parted when they met, and the kiss immediately deepened. Her tongue slowly slipped into his mouth, a hot flame that seared him to the core. Benjamin's arms tightened around her. He let his hands explore the curves of her body and dared to caress her breasts. How many nights had he dreamed of touching her so intimately?

He could no longer resist the sweet pleasures of her flesh as he glided one hand down her back and grabbed her deliciously round bottom. Pulling her body against him, he wanted her to feel his growing excitement. He gasped when she wrapped her left leg around him and urged him closer. She drove him mad with desire.

Benjamin tugged at the cloth of her nightgown, gathering the hem into his hands. He withdrew from the kiss and looked into her eyes. Was she afraid? Did she want to stop? No, he only saw the growing need he himself felt. He smiled at her boldness when she took the garment from him and lifted it over her head, tossing it to the floor.

"You are the most amazing woman in the world," he murmured. He marveled at the beauty of her smooth skin which glowed in the soft firelight. He lowered his head and teased a nipple with his tongue. She arched her back, grabbing his head and entwining her fingers in his auburn hair.

In dismay, he understood how much their height difference had a negative effect on foreplay. He reluctantly withdrew from their embrace and led her toward the bed. He was shocked when Tilly shoved him onto it. She tugged at his boots, which seemed to be glued to his feet. With a chuckle, he helped her remove them. She ran her hands underneath his shirt and slipped it over his head. She bent to his breeches and stopped.

"Ah, how do you remove them?" she asked sheepishly. She plucked idly at a button and lifted an eyebrow.

He deftly undid the buttons and slid the breeches off his legs. He lay naked before her on the bed. She climbed on top of him, pressing her lovely flesh against his. It felt as if the full effect of his arousal burned against her cool skin like a hot brand.

Swiftly, he rolled her onto her back. Rising on one elbow, he stared at her. This time, it was not a dream. He wanted it to be real. He wanted her to want *him*, not the ghost of a dead husband. "Say it," he insisted.

"I want you," she whispered. "I want you, Benjamin Campbell."

They kissed. It was not just a kiss of desire, for there was plenty of that between them. It was a joining of body and soul. They poured their hearts into every touch. They stood on the edge of an abyss between life and death, an abyss that they had faced separately in the past. Tonight, Benjamin wanted to bridge the chasm with Tilly.

His fingers began a slow exploration of her skin. He flicked the nipple of her right breast with his tongue, alternately kissing and suckling. He gingerly brushed his fingertips over her goose-pimpled skin as he stroked her side and ran his hand down to her thighs. He ached with desire and felt her body rise to his touch. He loved the sound of her sweet moans.

She slid her hand down his firm stomach and wrapped her fingers around the throbbing heat of him. He shivered with pleasure at her touch. She stroked him, ever so slowly. Her lips parted, and her hot breath touched his cheek.

He could not endure another moment. Benjamin lifted on top of her and buried himself deep inside her. He quivered at the warm, moist heat that enveloped him. When she wrapped her silky legs around him and pulled him deeper inside her, he thought his heart would burst.

He moaned as Tilly's hands glided down his back and firmly cupped his buttocks. He plunged faster and deeper, unable to get enough of her. He had replayed their first coupling in his mind so many times that it felt like a dream. This moment was real, and he wanted to savor every kiss, every touch, and every sweet sensation.

He looked down at her. She was absolutely breathtaking. Her hair fanned away from her face onto the pillow, and her porcelain skin glowed. Her lips were full and lusciously red from their kisses.

They parted slightly as she licked her lower lip with the tip of her pink tongue. She stared back at him with hooded eyelids, her eyes dark with desire.

"Benjamin," she purred. She thrust upwards and moaned deeply.

He closed his eyes. He could feel her squeezing him, pulling him deeper inside her. He involuntarily quickened his pace. While his mind wanted to move slowly, his body had other designs. Since their interlude in the forest, he awoke so many nights in a cold sweat. He had been haunted by a desire that was not sated. Now, his hunger for her finally would be satisfied.

To him, it felt as if her body shared the same unfulfilled need. She matched him thrust for thrust. Her breasts brushed against his chest, deliciously torturing him.

He was exceedingly thankful that the castle walls were several feet thick, for they were unable to silence the intensity of their passion. He felt her spasm over and over again when she exploded in ecstasy. "Benjamin!" she cried, arching her body against his.

He could wait no longer. Overcome with bliss, he repeatedly cried her name. He shook violently at the exquisite release.

At length, their breathing returned to a normal

pace. Benjamin carefully slipped from her and moved to the side, where he scooped her into his arms. He smoothed her hair from her face. As he gazed at Tilly, his heart felt whole again.

∞

UNLIKE THEIR FIRST ENCOUNTER, THEY DID NOT DRIFT TO SLEEP. Benjamin held her tightly, afraid the spell would be broken. They exchanged soft kisses and gentle caresses. It was a rare moment of peace that he hoped would not end.

"Are you hurt, Tilly?" he inquired, inspecting the bruise upon her cheek.

"It was very passionate, but I do not believe you injured me," she teased, chuckling.

He lifted onto one elbow and stared at her. His eyes lingered on the deepening bruise. "If you do not want to discuss what happened in the forest, I understand," Benjamin said. He lightly touched her cheek. "Just tell me you were not seriously harmed."

She looked away, though she snuggled closer to him. "How do you live with killing someone?" she asked.

He sighed heavily and said, "I murdered someone. You defended the boys and yourself." Stroking her back, he tried to console her. "You need not feel any shame for what you did."

"Someone died at my hand," Tilly argued. "I know he would have killed us – and yet, I cannot forget the feeling of the blade piercing his skin or the terrible look on his face."

She buried her face in his chest and wept uncontrollably. Benjamin held her while she let the pain seep from her body.

When the tears began to ebb, he offered what little advice he had. "You will never forget what happened," he said. "You will find a way to live with it. Know this - killing is not who you are. It was an action you took to save lives. You did the right thing, even though it may not seem to be that way now."

"Can I stay here tonight?" she asked uncertainly. Tilly did not look at him.

The question was not as simple as it seemed. Was he ready to trust her? Did he dare let her into his heart? He might never know the truth about how she came to be here. Did it matter?

At last, Benjamin whispered, "Aye, lass. Where else would you go? This is where you belong."

# *FORTY ONE*

TILLY AWOKE to the sound of shuffling footsteps in the room. She squeezed Benjamin's arm, but he did not awaken. Surely, the guards around the castle would have sounded the alarm if something was amiss. She trembled slightly and hoped no one was there to slaughter them.

"Mistress, are you awake?" Mrs. Keith whispered, daring to crack the bed curtains ever so slightly.

Relieved, Tilly exhaled. She pulled the bedcovers tighter to conceal her nakedness. "What are you doing here, Mrs. Keith?" she asked.

"It is near dawn, milady," the housekeeper said. She pointed toward the window. "If you wish to steal away to your room before the household awakens, you must go now."

She dared not ask how Mrs. Keith knew she was in Benjamin's room. She followed the housekeeper's gaze and noticed the first rays of sunshine chasing away the night. The servants would begin their work at any moment. Delay would lead to detection.

Benjamin stirred beside her. "It is too early for propriety," he mumbled. "Leave some clothes for Tilly, and bring us breakfast later. I will see that the lady is properly tended."

"Milord, someone will see her leaving your room," the woman gasped in horror. "Think of milady's reputation!"

Tilly reluctantly freed herself from his arms. "Mrs. Keith is right," she said, sliding to the edge of the bed. "I should go."

He sat upright and rubbed the sleep from his eyes like a little boy. "No, you should stay," Benjamin replied. "To hell with everyone's opinions!"

She kissed him on the cheek and said, "I won't start this relationship with rumors and innuendo." Tilly thought a moment and amended her statement, "Well, at least not *more* rumors and innuendo."

Tilly hastily donned the nightgown that Mrs. Keith found in a ball beside the fireplace. They tiptoed out of the room, but not before hearing Benjamin violently curse the current social conventions.

∞

WHEN THEY RETURNED TO TILLY'S ROOM, Mrs. Keith and she found Sarah waiting for them. Her maid seemed unsurprised that she was not in her room as usual. Was it well known among the staff where she spent the night?

Sarah was well qualified to prepare her for the day, so the housekeeper should have returned to her duties. The woman stayed, though. In a moment, Tilly understood why.

Mrs. Keith's instructions were followed without comment. In no time at all, the ladies dressed Tilly in a black gown and seated her at the dressing table.

"What is to be done about the bruise?" the maid asked, surveying the angry splotch of purple and red along Tilly's jawbone.

Mrs. Keith produced a bag of cheesecloth from her pocket. Opening it carefully, she dipped her finger inside. She patted a white, powdery substance upon Tilly's face. Noticing their quizzical looks, she said, "It is flour."

The women giggled. "It should get you through breakfast as long as you do not wipe your face," Mrs. Keith said defensively. Her comment sent the women into a fit of laughter. Feigning frustration, she protested, "We haven't any face powder in the house, so what was I supposed to use?"

When they sufficiently recovered from their mirth, Mrs. Keith continued her work. Tilly would have preferred concealer and wondered if it had been invented yet. She thought it might exist in the big cities, but then again, didn't they put arsenic, mercury, and other toxic chemicals in early cosmetics? Flour may have been a safer option after all.

Inspecting her handiwork, Mrs. Keith seemed satisfied. "Let us discuss what happened," she said, putting away her makeshift cosmetic.

Tilly lowered her head. She did not wish to relive that terrible event.

Sarah gently raised her chin and shook her head. "Milady, you should tell Mr. Campbell to summon the cobbler as soon as may be," she said, in a serious tone. "Those slippers do not fit properly. You could have broken your neck!"

She glanced down at the crude slippers she wore. "Whatever do you mean?" she asked, confused. Her shoes were not the nicest pair she had ever worn but seemed to serve the purpose.

"Your slippers were so loose that you slipped on the trail and fell down an embankment," Mrs. Keith explained. "You got that nasty bruise on your face from the fall."

"Is that the story you are spreading?"

"Oh, aye," the housekeeper said, grinning broadly. "Mr. Murphy told the tale in the servant's hall during the evening meal. When the words come from his lips, it is considered gospel."

Tilly's eyes filled with tears. "Thank you," she said. She squeezed Mrs. Keith's hand and turned to Sarah, "You have both been so kind to me. Thank you so much."

"Milady, do not fret," Sarah said, patting her hand. "We will take care of you."

Those simple words warmed Tilly's heart more than Sarah could know. Taking a deep breath, she struggled to keep the tears from flowing down her cheeks and turning Mrs. Keith's floury concealer into a pasty mess.

∞

TILLY SMOOTHED HER HAIR before entering the family's dining room. They decided to leave it down this morning so that it could better conceal her bruise. While the official story seemed to quell most of the gossip, she was not inclined to be a spectacle.

She was delighted to see the boys sitting with Benjamin at the table. They turned when she entered the room and greeted her with huge smiles. In unison, they bid her good morning.

He guided her to a chair at the head of the table. He went to the sideboard and hastily prepared a heaping plate of food. The footmen must have been dismissed today.

As he placed the plate in front of her, he whispered in her ear, "You must be starving after last night." He chuckled at the blush on her cheeks.

Benjamin took a seat to her right. Michael grinned broadly at Angus but wisely held his tongue.

Angus entertained them with a story about the frog he found two days ago. Apparently, he chased one of the maids around the garden, threatening to drop it down her dress. Michael howled with laughter at the tale.

Tilly observed that Allan was very quiet, barely eating his food. She glanced at Benjamin who was also watching his son. They exchanged a look.

"Allan, I wanted to take Mrs. Munro to the old ruins today," his father said. "Would you like to join us?"

Angus and Michael cried in unison, "Can we come too?"

"No." He silenced the imminent protest with a look. "Will you go with us, Allan?"

His eldest son nodded and asked to be excused so he could prepare for the trip. Benjamin dismissed him. The boy left the room, head bowed and looking very defeated.

Tilly leaned forward. "He will be alright," she whispered, gently placing her hand on top of his.

He wrapped his hand around hers. They heard a small gasp from Michael and turned to see the boy staring at their hands.

Benjamin winked at his son as he withdrew his hand. "I find it hard to believe that you did not join in the fun," he said. "Tell me what wicked things you did."

Michael was not to be outdone by his brother. He proceeded to tell them about every bug and worm he found in the garden. His adventures dominated the conversation for the rest of the meal, offering a diversion from their concerns about Allan. Tilly hoped the trip to the ruins would lighten the boy's mood. It broke her heart to see the child so devastated by what happened. No one deserved to carry that burden.

# FORTY TWO

WHEN THEY ARRIVED AT THEIR DESTINATION, Tilly found that the old ruins were exactly that. Crumbling stone walls of a former castle were surrounded by a collection of cottages whose roofs long ago collapsed. Benjamin explained the area was the original seat to the Clan Campbell. It was abandoned in the 1600s after a fire destroyed half of the castle. The home they shared now was built to replace it.

He pointed to a rock wall three stories tall. "At the top of that wall, you would have found sentries patrolling the battlements," he said. "My ancestors had many enemies, the MacDonalds being the worst of the lot."

Allan snapped to attention. "Why were the

MacDonalds our enemies?" he asked eagerly.

Benjamin put his arm around his son's shoulders and explained, "They fought over property – cattle and land. Or perhaps someone would offend a member of the clan. Tempers ran high." He added, "It did not take much to start a fight."

Tilly beckoned them to join her. She found a nice spot overlooking the castle and spread a blanket on the ground for their picnic.

"The Campbells and MacDonalds have been foes for centuries, son," Benjamin continued as he sat close to Tilly. "What happened yesterday will be the last time our families fight."

"How can you be sure, Da? Will they not want revenge for the MacDonald's death?"

"They will not learn of his death. I promise you."

Allan frowned. "If he does not return, won't they suspect something has happened?" he asked. He idly broke apart a piece of bread Tilly handed him. "He must have told someone where he was going."

"Aye, he probably did. Richard MacDonald was not well liked, though. I believe many will be most happy when he does not return."

"What do you mean?" Tilly interrupted. It seemed odd to her that the man would not be missed.

"He was cruel," Benjamin said. "He charged exorbitant rents and had no qualms about turning out any tenant who could not pay, even in the dead of winter." He shook his head in disgust. "He treated his own family with equal brutality. I heard that he beat his wife and son. His kin definitely will not send any search parties for the man."

"It seems so many people know the truth – Mr. Murphy, Mrs. Keith, Sarah, Daniel, Graeme, James, and Robbie," Tilly said, nervously looking at Allan when she mentioned the nasty business of tidying up after their misadventure. "Can you trust them?"

"Do not forget the families of the sentries who were killed," Benjamin said. "They know the truth too. I only let the most trustworthy people near my family, Tilly. They will not betray me."

She realized his statement held special significance for her. She wished Allan was not there. She wanted to know if this meant he believed her. One look at Allan quelled further query.

The boy struggled to process what his father told him. "Why did the MacDonald come here?" he asked.

To Tilly's astonishment, Benjamin answered honestly, "Your grandfather and me killed his brother and sister."

Allan gasped in shock. "Why?" he asked. "Why

would you kill someone, Da?"

She did not fail to notice that the boy did not inquire about his grandfather's involvement in the murders. Perhaps such evil deeds were not beyond the realm of possibility with the man. She had better watch her back around Malcolm Campbell.

"They murdered your uncle," Benjamin answered, stirring Tilly from her thoughts. "We wanted them to pay for the crime they committed. I was 16 years old. I followed your grandfather's orders without question."

Placing his hand upon the boy's shoulder, he said gravely, "When I think about that night, I understand now it was the wrong thing to do. I cannot change what I did, no matter how much I regret it. My actions brought this trouble to the family. I hope you can forgive me." He looked at her then, silently communicating the same apology.

Allan flung his arms around his father. "I am sorry I could not defend the family, Da," he cried softly. "I tried."

Benjamin slowly rocked his son and whispered soothing words of comfort. Tilly moved to leave them alone but stopped when he placed a hand on her shoulder. He pulled her into the embrace with his free arm and she instantly relaxed. If Allan could find comfort and security there, so could she.

∞

BEFORE THEY LEFT THE RUINS, Benjamin insisted they visit the old well. "It will be real to you when you see it," he explained to them both.

The circular stone structure was unsound, so Tilly made sure they approached it with care. At one time, wooden boards were placed across the opening to protect anyone from an unfortunate accident. Over time, though, many of the boards rotted away. A large gap in the remaining boards was just wide enough through which someone could squeeze a body. She gulped at the morbid thought.

Tilly and Allan peered into the inky blackness of the well. "It is impossible to see anything down there," she said to Allan. Still, they knew Richard MacDonald's body lay at the bottom. The pair exchanged a look before mounting their horses. Benjamin was right. No one could find the man's body down there.

The mood on the return trip was much lighter. Allan appointed himself as her personal tour guide. He noted various landmarks they passed and mentioned the best places to find fresh water. The area was obviously a favorite spot. She noticed that Benjamin seemed visibly relieved. Clearly, the trip was meant as a salve for his soul as much as it was for theirs.

They returned to the stable and gave their horses to the groom. Allan snagged quick hugs from his father and Tilly before running toward the castle.

Benjamin took her hand as they slowly meandered through the garden. "Thank you for joining us," he said. "I know how much you hate horseback riding."

Tilly laughed. "It is not my favorite activity," she admitted. "I am glad you picked a gentle horse for me."

"Oh, aye, you must be very careful about what you put between your legs," he teased. He kissed her passionately, stealing away any reply she may have had.

Breathless, she managed to escape his kiss. "What if the servants see?" she asked primly. "Aren't we supposed to be more proper than this?"

As he wrapped his arms around her, Benjamin murmured against her lips, "As you say, to hell with propriety."

Tilly returned his kisses with fervor. She had no desire to return to the chaos inside the castle just yet. After such a surprisingly blissful day, why spoil it with reality?

∞

BENJAMIN DID EVENTUALLY RETURN TO THE CASTLE. He would like to ignore his responsibilities but knew that was impossible. After escorting Tilly to her room and stealing one last kiss, he reluctantly went to his study. He discovered Iain waiting for him.

"I understand you visited the old ruin," Iain said, handing him a glass of whisky. "Did it help the boy?"

"Aye, I believe it did," Benjamin replied, easing into the chair behind his desk. He studied his friend who obviously was not there to exchange pleasantries and enjoy the Campbell draught. "What troubles you?"

"I most sincerely apologize for failing you," Iain said, his voice shaking. "I thought I had enough protections in place so that we would know when Richard MacDonald arrived. I was wrong."

"Do not trouble yourself. The man was canny."

"No, no, it is my fault," the factor said as tears filled his eyes. "If something had happened to the children, I would never forgive myself."

"Nothing happened," he said firmly. "You posted sentries, and the man killed two of them. The MacDonald was determined to seek revenge. You could have put an army in front of him, and he still would have tried to fulfill his plan."

"It appears we only needed a woman, not an army. I am glad Mrs. Munro stopped him."

"I am too. Perhaps we misjudged her."

Iain nodded but said nothing. He sipped the glass of whisky, looking absolutely miserable.

Benjamin rose from his chair and took a seat beside his friend. Placing his hand upon the man's shoulder, he said, "I hold no ill will toward you. You did everything you could to protect my family, and I appreciate it."

"He could have killed my family too," Iain whispered. "I believed he had when we received the message. I was so focused upon my own kin that I forgot about yours."

"Enough! The MacDonald will no longer bring pain to this family. I will not have him destroy you. Your liege has said you did the best you could. Leave it."

Iain raised an eyebrow. "My liege, is it?" he asked in playful mockery. "Should I fall to one knee and thank you for your benevolence, milord?"

"If you did, I fear my heart would stop from shock."

Iain swallowed the last of the whisky and placed the empty glass on the desk. Sighing, he said, "I appreciate your forgiveness." He held up his hand to stifle Benjamin's protest. "I will not speak further on the subject. I promise."

Standing, he patted Benjamin on the shoulder. "Get some rest, my friend," he said. "One threat has passed. Let us enjoy a moment of peace before fate brings us another trial."

As he watched Iain leave the study, Benjamin sincerely hoped fate would leave him be. The latest trial was more than his heart could take.

# FORTY THREE

THE NEXT MORNING, Allan, Angus, and Michael waited for Tilly in the family's library. "Come quick, mistress," Angus beckoned as he grabbed her hand when she entered the room. "Mr. Ramsey has made an interesting discovery and wants to share it with us."

Chuckling, she followed Angus to the table where his brothers and the tutor were gathered. Daniel had located an old book in the family archives. Its age was evident from the worn leather cover and yellowed pages.

She was excited when she recognized it as the volume of family history that Benjamin wanted Allan to read. "Wonderful!" she exclaimed. "I am so happy we have a learned man in our midst. I am ashamed to say I cannot read Latin. You can reveal the mysteries of the text to us."

Daniel smiled at the compliment. "Oh, it is a fascinating work, milady," he said, carefully opening the book and turning the pages to a particular section of interest. "I was just about to share a story with the boys."

She walked around the table and stood beside Daniel so that she could get a better look at the page. Tilly inhaled deeply at the sight. "That picture!" she cried, pointing to the page. "It looks like a shield that hung in the inn where I stayed before I came here." She felt as if someone poured icy water down her back.

The tutor nodded absently. He ran a finger under the text, reading the words first in Latin and then translating them to English. The ancestor who documented the work told the story of the shield's origin. It came to the family after a fight with the MacDonalds.

"It proves those bastards have been cutthroats for centuries," Allan mumbled. Tilly gave him a stern look for his poor choice of words.

She felt the chill deepen when she realized the battle took place near the present day site of Mrs. Douglas' cottage. Didn't the woman tell them that the inn was located in Gleann A'bunadh, the same valley mentioned in the story? Fascinated, she listened closely as Daniel continued to translate it

Colin Campbell was the hero in the tale. Driven away by grief from the death of his true love, he fled abroad with a group of men. They became mercenaries who fought wherever fortune took them. Colin lived a bleak life for two long years. He eventually felt the pull of his homeland and decided to return.

Upon his arrival in the valley, Colin discovered villagers being attacked by a horde of MacDonald invaders. He and his men rescued them.

Unfortunately, he was unable to save the village's chieftain. The man's wife, a wise woman rumored to be a white witch, imparted a blessing upon Colin. She gave him the chieftain's shield as a talisman against harm. She called forth power from the earth and moon, imparting magic upon the metal. Carry it, she told him, and you will be safe.

He was moved by their plight so he promised protection and gave the villagers land, where they flourished. From the description of its location, it sounded like the beginning of the village of Deoch.

Colin credited the shield with bringing great fortune and luck to the family. Within days of his return to the Campbell castle, a woman arrived. It was her supposed demise that sent him away two years previously. To his delight, she was alive and restored to him. He immediately wed her, something he longed to do before she allegedly died. He would not let her slip from his grasp again.

In honor of the battle that brought him this mystical object, he erected a monument on the hill where he first looked down upon the valley and saw the battle. He personally designed the piece, using ancient symbols whose meaning was lost to time.

Tilly grew uneasy. Uneducated folk throughout time were a superstitious lot. However, the book's drawings of the shield and memorial greatly resembled the objects she saw at Gleann A'bunadh. The resemblance could not be a coincidence.

Daniel cleared his throat as he turned the page. Colin was a firm believer in the shield's power. He carried it with him in every battle. He claimed no arrow or sword ever harmed him whenever he had it. The day he did not carry it was the day he suffered a mortal blow. On his death bed, Colin reportedly entreated the family to always preserve the shield. It had been a great blessing to him.

Tilly reached forward and flipped the page to the original rendering of the shield. She studied it carefully. While the drawing showed the same primitive cross spread across the circular piece of metal, it lacked the symbols she saw the night she disappeared. If it was a mystical object, would the symbols only appear at certain times? Wasn't there a full moon that night?

"That shield looks like the one hanging above Da's fireplace," Angus said, pointing to the drawing. "He says it is really old and will not let us touch it."

The color drained from Tilly's face. She excused herself and left the library, hoping no one noticed her unease. After all this time, she could not believe the answer to her problem might be so near.

∞

TILLY CLIMBED ONTO A CHAIR that she dragged in front of the fireplace in Benjamin's room. Though she saw the object on her previous visit to her lover's room, she did not make the connection. After all of the events in the forest that day, an ancient armament hanging above the fireplace was not top of mind. *Plus, my brain was a little foggy from the whisky I was drinking,* she admitted.

She noticed scratches and gouges in the metal. The cross that spread across the front of the object looked similar to the one on the shield in her own time. It even bore the same Celtic knots on each end. Unfortunately, the intricate symbols she saw on that fateful night were missing. With a trembling finger, she dared to touch the shield. She half expected an electric shock yet only felt the coolness of the metal.

Sighing, she jumped from the chair and pushed it back in place. Tilly laughed to herself. So what if it was the same shield? The castle was filled with antiques. And, didn't Mrs. Douglas herself say the Campbell family loaned her objects for display at the inn? Maybe an old shield was one of them.

Still, it was unsettling to hear the tale and see something that looked so much like an artifact from her time. Could it be the supernatural object that would send her home? Isn't that how it worked in fairy tales? A magic portal would open at the right time, allowing her to return home or something preposterous like that? She could not stop staring at it. What if the shield really did have mystical powers?

She sank into the chair. "It is time to make a decision, girl," Tilly could imagine her friend Beth saying. If – and it was a BIG 'if' – the shield in front of her was the same object from the cottage and *IF* it could provide her with a way home, did she really want to return?

She considered the same question that she asked herself a thousand times yet could never answer. What was waiting for her? Her family was gone. She had no job. She sold the restaurant and the house.

She had no clear plan for the future. The negative column filled rapidly in her mental list of pros and cons.

Here, Tilly was a teacher, the very thing she wanted. She felt a growing attachment to Benjamin and his children, a feeling she never expected to have. If she stayed, she might have a family again. The scales were tipping highly in favor of staying.

"Do you love him?" she asked aloud, knowing Beth would ask the same question. "Do you love him enough to accept that he may never believe you?"

Honest at last, Tilly answered, "Yes." Sure, she wanted him to believe her, but would she let it be an obstacle to her happiness? She felt complete when she was with him and his family. Her life once again had purpose.

She made her decision. She would stay here. She would not look further for a way to return to her own time. Tilly exited the room before anyone found her there. She had no desire to explain the superstitious notions that caused the visit. It was nonsense, right?

*Just like time travel.*

∞

BENJAMIN AND TILLY DID NOT MAKE LOVE THAT NIGHT, preferring to snuggle close and discuss the happenings of the day. Oddly, it felt perfectly normal to her as she listened to him speak candidly about the business of the estate. She realized how strange it was to feel that anything was normal about a 21$^{st}$ century woman living in the 1800s.

She also understood that he walked a fine line. He tried to repeal the damage done by his father without alerting the man. She offered some suggestions, which seemed to ease his mind. Soon, he drifted off to sleep.

She was nearly there herself when the moon shone through the window. She watched a beam of light slowly climbed the wall and strike the silvery metal of the shield. Tilly gasped when the infinity symbol appeared in the top right quadrant. Slowly, another symbol – a fish - emerged in the lower left quadrant.

She stared in disbelief. She immediately recognized them as the same symbols she saw on the night she slipped through the mist and into Benjamin's arms. She waited for the other two to appear, but they did not. Almost as quickly as they appeared, the symbols vanished.

She carefully untangled herself from his embrace and slid from the bed. Tilly tiptoed to the fireplace. The story of a mystical shield was so fresh in her mind. It was possible that, on the verge of sleep, she dreamt that she saw the symbols. Squinting, she examined the metal. She did not see any hints of the symbols, only scratches from centuries of use.

"What is the matter?" Benjamin asked sleepily.

"Nothing," she answered breathlessly. "Go back to sleep."

Tilly took a seat beside the fireplace and stayed awake until the wee hours of morning, wondering if she imagined the sight.

# FORTY FOUR

TILLY RETURNED TO HER ROOM when she saw the first rays of dawn pierce the horizon. Though Benjamin would miss her presence, being alone was more important at the moment.

As she stealthily made her way from his room to her own, she was relieved that she seemed to be up before the servants. It was a bit too early for the fireplace maid to light the fire, and Sarah usually did not make an appearance until the sun was up. She might have a few moments to herself before the frenetic activity of the morning began.

Despite how tired she was, she had not been able to close her eyes. She was afraid she would miss the sight of the symbols if they reappeared on the surface of the shield. They did not.

Once in her bedchamber, Tilly flopped onto the bed and lay there for several moments. She could not believe what had happened.

All this time, she searched for some clue about how to return to her own time. Truth be told, she did not think it was possible. Then, she heard Daniel's fanciful story and saw the object in Benjamin's room

It was easy for her to decide to stay in that moment. On some level, she did not believe the shield really was her magic ticket back to the 21st century.

The appearance of the symbols on the shield cast everything into doubt. Perhaps there was a way to go back to her own time after all. When faced with a real opportunity, what should she do? What was her strongest conviction – that Benjamin loved her or that the shield offered her a way back home?

"I beg your pardon, milady," the fireplace maid said from the doorway. "I did not realize you would be awake. Should I send for Miss Sarah?"

"No, thank you," Tilly said. She rose from the bed and strode toward the window. She listened to the maid build a fire, a sound that was so familiar to her now. She closed her eyes and inhaled the first whiffs of smoke.

She thought how odd it was to grow so

comfortable with one's surroundings. In such a short time, she had adapted to the lack of plumbing and central heating. A warm fire was a necessity in a cold castle. Wearing long dresses instead of pants did not seem unusual. Donning a bonnet before leaving the castle – *the castle* – was normal.

*Strange how quickly I have adjusted,* she thought. She opened her eyes and surveyed the scene before her. It was so beautiful and so different from the view she had in North Carolina.

"Milady, you are awake!" Sarah exclaimed. "It is very early."

"I could not sleep last night."

"Are you unwell?"

"I am fine, although I would prefer to have breakfast in my room this morning. Would that be too much trouble?"

Sarah moved closer and stared intently at Tilly. "I will be happy to bring a tray to milady's room," she said. "Are you sure you are well? You look very pale."

"I am well, just tired."

Sarah nodded. She glared at the fireplace maid, who finished tending the fire, gathered her things, and rushed from the room.

"I will return in a few moments, milady," Sarah said as she exited the room. "Please rest until then."

Tilly managed a weak smile. She walked over to the bed and lay down again. This time, fatigue won over curiosity, and she fell into a deep sleep.

∞

AFTER YEARS SPENT WORKING THROUGH COLLEGE AND THEN RAISING TWINS, Tilly knew how to take a power nap. She felt refreshed and clear-headed when she awoke some thirty minutes later. Stretching, she emerged from the bed. She heard Sarah in the dressing room next door and beckoned her to enter.

"I was about to return to the kitchen, milady," she said. Sarah carried a heavy tray that she deposited onto a table beside the fireplace. "I thought you would sleep longer, so I did not want your food to be cold."

"Thank you very much for your consideration," Tilly said. She walked to the fireplace and took a seat in one of the overstuffed chairs.

Sarah poured a cup of tea and handed it to her. She added a liberal dose of cream and sugar. While she may have grown accustomed to some things, the bitter brew was not one of them. She plucked a freshly-baked scone from the tray and took a big bite.

She did love the scones, though.

"Will milady take a ride this morning?"

"No, I will not," Tilly replied. She needed time to think, and a horseback ride with Benjamin would be very distracting.

"I shall prepare another dress for you then," Sarah said as she made her way toward the dressing room. "If milady would like anything else, I will be happy to attend you."

Tilly frowned. Before Sarah could reach the doorway, she said, "Are *you* well this morning? You have been very formal with me."

She apparently struck a nerve. Sarah's lower lip quivered.

Tilly placed the cup of tea on the table and rushed to the maid's side. "Sarah, what is the matter?" she asked. "Has this business with Richard MacDonald upset you? Are you afraid?"

Sarah dissolved into tears. "No, milady. It is Daniel," she said between gasping sobs. "I am not fancy enough for him."

Tilly guided the maid back to the fireplace and forced her to take a seat in one of the chairs. She sat opposite her. "Is that why you were being so formal?" she asked. "Did you hope to change your personality for him?"

Producing a handkerchief from her apron pocket, Sarah dried her eyes. "Aye," she confessed. "I want to be more proper so that I can deserve him."

Groaning, Tilly took Sarah's hand. Seeing the shock on the maid's face, she concluded it was an overly familiar gesture. She did not care. "Did he tell you that you were improper?" she asked. If he had, she planned to throttle the tutor for his imprudence.

Sarah shook her head.

"Did he say you were not 'fancy' enough for him?"

Again, Sarah shook her head. "He is an educated man from Edinburgh. What could a poor maid from Devonshire possibly offer him?" she said, her voice filled with shame. "I did not know how to read until you taught me. I am no match for him."

At her last words, Sarah's crying renewed. Tilly squeezed the girl's hand. No matter *when* it was, some women always tried to mold themselves into a false image of the ideal woman. *What a stupid idea,* she thought to herself.

"You listen to me, Sarah," she said firmly. "You are not inferior to *any* man – and I don't believe for one second that Daniel Ramsey thinks that."

"You do not?"

"I have watched the two of you together. I see love."

"Milady, do you? Do you think he cares for me?"

"I do."

"The way Mr. Campbell cares for you?"

Tilly was taken aback. "What do you mean?" she asked.

Sarah grinned. "When he looks at you, he has a fire in his eyes," she said, blushing. "You can see that he wants you."

It was Tilly's turn to be flustered. "Well, I...." She completely lost her train of thought for a moment. "Well, Sarah, I am sure Daniel feels passionately toward you. He is not as demonstrative as some people are." She shook her head. "You don't need to worry about Daniel having a bad opinion of you. I believe he has the highest regard for you."

Sarah wiped the last of the tears from her cheeks. "Thank you," she said, lightly squeezing Tilly's hand. "You are a good friend, milady." She rose from her seat. "If you will excuse me, I will prepare your dress now." The girl left the room with a spring in her step.

She hated to see Sarah so upset, yet it warmed her heart to think a few kind words made that much difference. She returned to her morning repast.

Unfortunately, her maid's troubles were only a temporary diversion. Her thoughts raced back to the mysterious shield. What did the appearance of the symbols mean?

∞

WHEN TILLY DESCENDED THE STAIRCASE later that morning, she saw a maid speaking with an unfamiliar man in the foyer. He handed her a stack of letters, tapped the corner of his hat, and slipped out the door. The woman stared blankly at the documents in her hand.

"May I help you?" she asked the servant.

The woman flushed bright red and curtsied. "No, milady, I shall seek assistance from Mrs. Keith," she mumbled, lowering her eyes.

Tilly frowned. "Oh, don't be ridiculous," she said. "I can help you. What's wrong?"

The maid glanced nervously at the letters she clutched in her hand. "I cannot read, milady," she admitted. "I do not know who should receive these letters."

"Let me see them," Tilly said, extending her hand. When the servant refused to release the letters, she stepped forward and assumed the same firm tone she used with recalcitrant children. "You are wasting time.

Let me help you."

Reluctantly, the maid gave the letters to her. "Who are they for, milady?" she asked timidly.

Flipping through the small stack of four documents, Tilly read aloud the names. Mr. Murphy had two letters. Mrs. Keith had one. The last missive was for Benjamin.

"Milord is attending to a tenant matter," the maid said. "He told Mr. Murphy that he would return for dinner, milady."

"If you will leave the letter with me, I will make sure he gets it," Tilly offered. She noticed the worried expression on the maid's face. "I am sure Mr. Campbell would not mind me keeping the letter for him."

Chewing her lower lip, the maid considered the dilemma. Hesitantly, she held out her hand for the letters belonging to Mr. Murphy and Mrs. Keith. She curtsied again and scurried toward the basement to deliver the letters.

Tilly walked toward Benjamin's study, intent upon placing the letter on his desk. At the door, she stopped and glanced at the article. She recognized Malcolm's tight writing. She recalled the contents of the last letter she saw from the man. She stared at it for several moments. Seized by sudden and unexplainable curiosity, she turned and raced up the stairway to her room.

∞

TILLY LOCKED THE DOOR TO HER BEDCHAMBER. She had no desire for Sarah or any of the other maids to enter the room and find her doing what she was about to do. Her heart pounded in her ears and hand trembled slightly as she grabbed a candle from the mantel. She tilted it into the fire that burned in the hearth until the wick was alight. Gently, she returned the candle to its silver holder and carried it to the desk beside the window.

She examined the thick blob of wax that sealed the pages. She knew it would crack if she popped open the letter. For a few seconds, she gingerly waved the wax seal over the flame, praying that the dry paper would not ignite. Testing the wax with her fingernail, she was pleased to discover that it was pliable. With a small knife she found in the drawer of the desk, she separated the wax from the paper without cracking the seal. If she was very careful, she should be able to reseal the wax. Benjamin would be none the wiser.

She delicately unfolded the letter and read it:

> *My son Benjamin,*
>
> *It was with great joy that I received your message about the new governess. I am exceedingly pleased to*

*hear that she is of no consequence to you. As you learned with Mrs. Donnelly, many women will seek the comfortable arrangement that marriage to you will bring. You are wise to withhold your affections until you can find a suitable match.*

*I am glad that you view her employment as temporary. You are right. You can find a governess who possesses greater skills elsewhere. Please inform me if your search is not fruitful. I have many contacts who may be of assistance. After all, we found Mr. Ramsey. I am sure we can find a proper governess.*

*I do have one piece of unfortunate news. In my last letter, I spoke of a young woman who would make an excellent match for you. Sadly, she is now betrothed to another. Be not distressed by this news. I have other candidates who are worthy.*

*I am encouraged to hear that you too may have found a good prospect. Please do not settle the matter before consulting with me. While I know country women can be very charming, let us use this opportunity to further the Campbell cause. A union with a woman who has a large dowry and property could be most advantageous.*

*You need not send a response with the messenger. He has strict instructions to return at once. We are of the same mind in this matter, and it does my heart glad to hear it.*

*Your father,*

*Malcolm*

Tilly placed the letter on the desk. She did not bother to wipe away the tears that tumbled down her cheeks.

*How could Benjamin say such awful things?* she thought. All this time, she believed they were falling in love. With every kiss and every touch, he seemed to affirm that belief, yet he told his father that she was of no consequence and that he had already found another prospect. Who was this woman? Was a meeting with a tenant a ruse so that he could visit her now? Were they laughing about Tilly at this very moment?

More importantly, what would happen to her? Benjamin said her employment was temporary. When did he plan to cast her out? Where would she go?

She sniffed loudly, not caring that it was most unladylike. For a really long time, she did not feel as if she had a place in the world. After the tragedy of her family's passing, she was numb. A year later, things started to make sense again. Tilly was ready to move on with her life, knowing that she would always carry the scars with her.

She never expected that a silly little trip to Scotland would result in being flung back to 1801. She certainly did not think she would meet a wonderful man and his family. She never planned to fall in love again. Tilly had — and what was she supposed to do about that?

# FORTY FIVE

IAIN PACED OUTSIDE THE FAMILY'S DINING ROOM. He could hear the boys gathered around the table, chatting about their day. He enjoyed listening to the innocence of the conversation. He longed for the days when the most pressing matter in his life was deciding what trick to play on an unsuspecting person.

He glanced up in time to see Tilly descending the stairs with Benjamin. He noted how content his friend looked. He hoped what he was about to do would not erase the feeling.

"Madam, you look well this evening," he said formally, bowing as they approached. "May I speak with you in private before dinner?"

Ignoring Benjamin's quizzical look, he led Tilly to

the library. Iain made sure the door was firmly closed. While he knew she would relay the entire conversation to Benjamin at the first opportunity, he had no desire to share it with the rest of the household.

They took seats beside one of the windows that provided dim light for the room. Iain did not bother to light candles. He did not intend for the chat to be of long duration. Exhaling slowly, he said, "I must thank you for what you did in the forest. It was very brave."

Tilly shrugged and said, "Bravery was not an option. He made clear his intent to kill the boys." She paused. "Did you think I would abandon them in favor of my own survival?"

"I had hoped you were better than that," he replied, smiling humorlessly. "It took extraordinary courage to face the man. The MacDonald was a great warrior, so killing him was no easy task."

"And, he was a heartless bastard, if you will excuse my language," Iain added. He gestured toward the bruise on her jaw. "Does it hurt?"

Tilly shook her head and stared down at the floor.

"Richard MacDonald was consumed by revenge," Iain said. "Do not let this event cripple you, Mrs. Munro. You did what you must and should feel no remorse for that. Make no mistake. He would have killed those children - and you too."

A tear trickled down her cheek. "Do you know how many times people have told me not to be 'consumed' by something?" she asked resentfully. "It was hard enough surviving after Alex, John, and Anna died. This is terrible."

"Were they your husband and bairns?"

"Yes. I am sure Benjamin told you the story. Do *you* believe me?"

Iain shifted in his seat. "I have long questioned your reason for being here," he said. "Your story is beyond any imagining."

"It is the truth, although I have no way of proving it to you or anyone else," she said. "I desperately wish I could. It would make things so much easier."

He chuckled. "Would it?" he asked. "Your position would not change. You would still be trapped in another time."

"Why did you want to speak with me?" Tilly asked, tilting her head to the side. "I doubt you wanted to give comfort or discuss time travel."

Iain shook his head. Benjamin mentioned that the woman was very blunt. He supposed it was time to dispense with the pleasantries. "I wanted to caution you against offering false hope," he said.

"False hope?" she asked in confusion. "What do you mean?"

"When Mary died, a cloud descended upon this house," Iain explained. "The family was devastated by the loss. I was uncertain if they could recover. Then, you arrived, and everything changed." His tone softened. "You must see that Benjamin is falling in love with you. The children increasingly look to you as a mother, especially after what happened in the forest. If you share the same affection, then I wish you well."

He gave her hand a firm squeeze that conveyed a clear warning. "However, if your intentions are not pure, leave this place immediately. Do not play games with their hearts."

He retrieved a small leather bag from his jacket pocket and gingerly shook it. "I have a fair sum of money that will get you to Edinburgh," he said. "I have contacts there who can help you secure a position as a governess."

He turned the bag in his hand so that she could hear the clink of the gold. "You could have a position with a good family," Iain said. "You might even find a nice husband there. All you must do is take the money and leave."

He watched the play of emotions on Tilly's face. He saw outrage give way to quiet resignation. "You strike me as a practical woman," he said. "You came into this household with nothing. I give you the opportunity to leave with some dignity."

She stood abruptly and stared down at him. "I thank you for your offer," she said. "How is it you people say this? May I speak plainly with you?"

Iain nodded. He was deeply intrigued by what she might say.

She paced, appearing to gather her thoughts with each step. "Contrary to what you may think, I have never had ulterior motives for being here," Tilly said. She stopped in front of him. Her eyes filled with tears. "I lost my family too. I know how devastating it has been for them. You only want to protect them, and I appreciate that. But, know this. I don't wish to hurt Benjamin or his children – *ever*."

"You say that Benjamin has fallen in love with me. Well, I'm not sure if that is true," she said. "He has never expressed it to me, and I have good reason to believe that I'm nothing more than a fling to him. Do you know that word – *fling*?"

Iain shook his head.

"It means a casual dalliance – nothing serious."

"Benjamin is not the sort of man to toy with a woman's affections."

"I wish I could believe you," Tilly said. She lowered her head, her voice barely a whisper. "I thought he cared for me. I was wrong."

Iain placed the bag in his pocket and beckoned her to return to her seat. "I did not wish to upset you," he said. "I only wanted to offer you an alternative path, if you felt your present course was not desirable."

She took a seat beside him. He could see the uncertainty in her eyes. "I have not been lucky enough to have a family," he said. "Benjamin and I grew up together, and his children seem like my own. I am sure you can understand why I am protective of them."

"I have watched the two of you together, and I see great love there," he said. Iain held up his hand to silence her. "As you say, let us speak plainly. If you believe that your affection is unrequited, then allow me to be of assistance. I can give you enough money to travel to Edinburgh and live comfortably there until you find an establishment."

"Why would you help me? Do you want rid of me that badly?

Iain chuckled and said, "I have enjoyed your company these past few months, Mrs. Munro." He removed the bag from his pocket and again offered it to her. "The money is in payment for the education you provided to the children. And, more importantly, I want to thank you for the protection you gave Allan and Angus. *That* debt is one I can never repay. If you are ever in need of anything, you need only ask. I am forever at your service, madam."

Tilly pushed away his hand. "Keep the money for now," she said. "I haven't decided what I am going to do. I would appreciate it if you wouldn't mention this to Benjamin."

He nodded as he returned the bag to his pocket and eased from his seat. Iain extended his hand, helping her from the chaise in a most gentleman-like manner. He placed her hand in the crook of his arm and winked at her. "Aye, I would ask the same of you, Mrs. Munro," he said. "Benjamin would be sorely vexed to know of this conversation."

They made their way toward the door. When his hand touched the doorknob, he noticed that she had stopped and was staring at the moonlight streaming through the window.

"Did Benjamin tell you where he found me?"

"Aye, I know the place well – Gleann A'bunadh. I have often thought it would make a fine place for a cottage."

"Could you take me there tomorrow?"

Iain cocked his head in confusion. "Why would you want to go there?" he asked.

"When you cannot figure out what to do, sometimes it is best to go back to the beginning," Tilly replied cryptically. "Can we ride there in the morning?"

"Aye, will you meet me at the stable at ten?"

Tilly nodded. She opened the door and whispered, "Remember – do not tell anyone."

Iain followed her as she made her way to the dining room. He was not sure which was more perplexing – her uncertainty about Benjamin or her request to visit a secluded valley.

∞

BENJAMIN STUDIED IAIN AND TILLY THROUGHOUT THE MEAL. To his dismay, they offered no clues about their conversation. In fact, they both seemed more at ease with each other than they had ever been. His friend entertained her with tales about their childhood adventures, roaming the Campbell lands and generally being rambunctious little boys. Daniel shared stories about growing up in Edinburgh. The children were in awe of their humble instructor's rowdy life on the city streets. To the casual observer, it seemed like an ordinary family meal. He was most unsettled.

He planned to ask Iain about the chat after dinner. They would have an opportunity to talk privately then, since the tutor usually retired to his room. Unfortunately, Daniel choose this evening to pull Benjamin aside and ask for a word in his study. He hoped the man was not tendering his resignation.

They took seats by the fire. Benjamin offered him a drink, which the man declined. "I trust you find your new position to be satisfactory," he said. "My son Allan speaks highly of your teaching skills."

"Aye. I am most grateful for the opportunity you have extended to me," Daniel said, nervously rubbing his hands on his breeches. "I am not sure if it is my place to interfere. I wanted to speak with you about Mrs. Munro."

Benjamin became uneasy. "Please speak freely, sir," he said. He took a sip of his drink.

"In the library, she became distressed at a story we found in yon book," he said, gesturing toward the volume of family history that Mr. Murphy had previously delivered to Benjamin's desk. "I found it most peculiar that a simple story could upset her."

"Please show me," Benjamin said. He lit candles in the holders around the desk so they could have sufficient light.

The tutor flipped through the brittle pages until he came to the story about the shield. "She said it looked like one that hung in an inn where she stayed before she came here," Daniel explained. "I doubted the Campbells would relinquish such a treasure but said nothing. She seemed agitated to learn its history. I do not know why."

Benjamin read the story and found nothing remarkable about it. Had he not heard many stories about mystical things and places during his childhood? Intrigued, he returned to the page with a drawing of the object in question.

"She seemed alarmed when your son Angus told her about the shield in your room," Daniel mentioned. He closed the book. "Perhaps I am overly sensitive. Not everyone has grown up hearing stories of Celtic mythology."

"I am sure you are right," Benjamin said distractedly. "I thank you for sharing the information nevertheless."

The tutor bowed slightly and scurried from the room without further comment. Benjamin chuckled. He presumed Daniel wanted to see Sarah before she retired for the evening. It had not escaped his notice that the shy maid and tutor were fond of each other.

Returning his attention to the book, he opened it and easily found the story. He examined the drawing. Shaking his head, he admitted that he could see the resemblance to the shield that hung above the fireplace in his bedchamber. The ancestor who wrote the story probably invented it to create an interesting history for the object. It was likely the work of someone's overactive imagination.

He set aside the book and stared at the pile of letters on his desk. He knew he should attend to some matters of business before he visited Tilly. Of course, now that her name had crossed his mind, he could think of nothing else. He struggled to focus his attention to the task at hand as he flicked through each document.

When he happened upon his father's letter, all thoughts of pleasure fled from his mind. He stared at the rigid handwriting and could feel himself tense involuntarily. Even though the man was not standing before Benjamin in the flesh, Malcolm had a powerful effect.

He flipped over the letter and was about to break the wax when he noticed something odd. His father always pressed the distinctive Campbell seal into the wax. As he examined the wax, he noticed that the impression was blurred. The wax barely held the pages together. Looking closer, he saw the paper's edges were singed near the seal.

"Murphy!" he bellowed. He came around the desk in three quick strides and flung open the door. "Murphy!"

The flustered butler scurried down the hallway. "Milord, is something amiss?" he asked.

"Aye, something is amiss," Benjamin replied. He waved the letter in front of the man. "What can you tell me about this letter? It is from my father."

"It arrived this morning. A maid told me Mrs. Munro helped her with names, for the maid cannot read."

"A servant's literacy is not my concern at the moment. Did the maid give the letter to you?"

"No, milord. Mrs. Munro took the letter from the maid and said she would give it to you," the butler said, clearing his throat. "Given recent events, I saw nothing inappropriate about allowing her that liberty. Was I incorrect?"

Benjamin shook his head. "Thank you, Mr. Murphy," he said. "I do not require further assistance." He turned and walked into the study, slowly closing the door behind him. Did Tilly open the letter?

He sank into a chair beside the fireplace. Why would she want to read a letter from his father? With ease, he cracked the seal and read the contents. Groaning aloud, he crumbled the letter and dropped his head into his hands. If Tilly read the letter, then what must she think of him?

∞

BENJAMIN FOUND HER sitting beside the fireplace in her receiving room. He could tell that she had been crying.

"Tilly, are you unwell this evening?" he asked, hoping the source of her tears was not that blasted letter.

If looks could kill, then he would have been struck dead on the spot. The piercing glare she shot his way immediately told him that she had indeed read the letter. "Please allow me to explain…" he began, racing to her side.

"We never should have slept together," she said hotly. "It has led to nothing but ruin for us both."

He fell to his knees in front of her. "Please do not speak of such things," Benjamin pleaded. "Finding you has been a great blessing to my family and me."

When he placed his hand upon her knee, she angrily flung it away. "Don't pretend that I mean something to you!" Tilly exclaimed angrily. "I read your father's letter. I am nothing to you. The sooner I leave, the better. Then, you can get a real governess to teach your children."

She pushed out of the chair and moved away from his reach. "Who is this fine prospect you have found?" she asked. "Does my presence interfere with your ability to court her?"

He dropped his head and closed his eyes. *Lord, give me strength,* he thought but dared not speak aloud.

He stood in front of her and forced her to look him at him. "If I thought of you only as a servant, you would not be enjoying the comforts of our guest quarters," Benjamin said practically. "You would be amongst the other servants. You would not be treated as favorably as you are. And, you most certainly would not share my bed."

He watched her face flush red with anger. "Please do not take offense, Tilly," he said. "I merely wish to illustrate to you that I hold you in the highest regard. I do not view you as a servant in my household. You have a place of honor in my heart."

She remained silent so he seized upon the opportunity to plead his case. "I swear upon on the lives of my children that there is no other woman except you," Benjamin said. "I told my father those things because he threatened to come here. Of all people, you know how devastating his interference would be."

It broke his heart to see her cry. "Yes, I do," Tilly said. "Benjamin, you cannot be with someone like me. Your father will eventually find out. What will you do? Will you risk everything for me?"

He stared at her. He knew a thousand things that he should say but could not bring himself to speak the words. He wanted to scream that he would move heaven and earth to be with her. He hesitated for a moment too long

She spoke the truth. If he pursued a relationship with her, his father could not travel fast enough to Scotland. The man would be furious.

His inner turmoil must have registered upon his face. Tilly smiled grimly as if she understood what he was thinking. Shaking her head, she eased past him and opened the door to the adjoining room. She softly closed it behind her.

Benjamin did not follow.

∞

BENJAMIN COULD NOT SLEEP. His conversation with Tilly tore a hole in his heart. Why had he hesitated in telling her the feelings that reached the depth of his soul? He knew only the most sincere professions of love and fidelity would win her heart, but he was unable to utter the words. He could not fathom a life worth living if Tilly was not in it. Was he prepared to gamble the estate and its people on love? Would he risk everything to be with her?

And, lest he forget her mysterious background. Could he take her hand in marriage without any hope of knowing from whence she came? Could he accept her and love her without that knowledge? He was stuck between the proverbial rock and a hard place.

He sipped a glass of whisky as he sat in a chair beside the fireplace of his bedchamber. Idly, he glanced up at the shield hanging above the mantel. Studying the object, he mentally compared it to the one from the drawing in the old book about his family's history. There were a great many relics strewn about the castle. It could be another ordinary souvenir from a battle long ago. In fact, the whole story could be the fancy of an ancestor who wanted to add a bit of color to the family history.

Benjamin was intrigued about the location of the battle, the valley known as Gleann A'bunadh. It was the same valley where Tilly came into his life and changed it forever.

He vividly recalled that fateful night. The campsite was an excellent location because of its proximity to the stream that ran through the valley. He promised Iain that he would not venture far. He needed time alone. Mrs. Donnelly's naked offer pushed him past the breaking point. If he spent another moment in the castle, he would go mad.

He had listened to the birds singing in the trees and heard the soft trickle of water from the stream. He had closed his eyes, relishing the solitude. He must have sat that way for hours before he noticed night had fallen. The moon was full, painting the forest in a pale silvery light. As a cold mist rose from the forest floor, he built a small fire to chase away the chill. He did not try to stop the tears when they began to flow.

He had not allowed himself to cry since Mary died. The loss he felt was almost crippling. His family needed him to be strong. In the stillness of the forest, Benjamin let his grief take over. He cried for her, for the life they would never have. She would never see wee Maggie grow into a woman or share in the daily adventure of Stephen's rowdy childhood. His wife would not watch the boys become men. Sweet Mary's passing was a great tragedy and waste of a precious life.

Then, Tilly appeared like an apparition in the mist. He really believed his mind had lost all grasp of reality. He did not care. He greatly enjoyed the escape from the gut-wrenching pain.

Jolting him from his revelry, a log broke free and

tumbled toward the edge of the hearth. It sent a spray of red embers onto the rug. He stomped the hot cinders before the rug was singed. It was an abrupt return to the present.

He shook his head. He admitted that he remained unsure if her tale was true. Could someone travel through time? Of course, Benjamin could not determine any other possible explanation. She was not an agent sent by the MacDonalds for she would not have killed their leader. He did not see any mark upon her head that would indicate severe injury, so he doubted her story came from physical trauma. And, he could not picture his father picking her as a spy. She was completely guileless.

He turned his gaze to the shield. Was it really a mystical object? Tilly thought a similar shield hung in her chambers…in her time. Could it have guided her to him?

He had not bothered to draw the curtains. When a sliver of moonlight danced across the surface of the shield, he thought he saw the figure of a fish etched into the metal. He moved closer to the mantel, carefully examining the surface. As quickly as it appeared, the symbol vanished. He questioned if his eyes deceived him.

Benjamin sat in the chair in front of the fireplace and stared at the shield until the first beams of light broke across the horizon. He had waited all night for the symbol to reappear. It never did.

# FORTY SIX

TILLY STARED INTO THE LOOKING GLASS while Sarah fixed her hair. She noticed the dark circles under her eyes had deepened after another sleepless night. With amusement, she observed her exhausted countenance on this day resembled her 21$^{st}$ century look.

She spent the entire night debating about what to do. She had half-heartedly searched for a way home in the last few months. During one of her daily hikes around the grounds, she found what she believed was the trail from the castle to the valley. She did nothing upon making the discovery, though. She had no indication that the spot held a clue to her return. Besides, wasn't she happy? Didn't she enjoy being with Benjamin and his family?

As outrageous as it was, she found herself enjoying each new day. The opportunity to be with children once again was precious. Tilly loved teaching them, even though they were sometimes a handful. And, if she was honest, she fell in love with their father.

Her relationship with him felt natural. She never struggled to *like* Benjamin. His manner was easygoing with her, even though she knew he carried great responsibility on his shoulders. He made her laugh. He made her forget *when* she was. With her late husband, it was never this easy. They constantly fought to be together, until she no longer wanted to fight.

In the end, she had been unable to decide her next move. It was the same dilemma she faced in her own time. She seemed frozen in place by indecision. Then, the tragic encounter happened with Richard MacDonald. Afterward, all thoughts of wandering alone in the forest disappeared. She no longer felt the need. Her relationship with Benjamin seemed to be closer than ever.

Now, everything had changed. The letter from his father cast doubt on the depth of Benjamin's feelings. Her presence could ruin everything, even if he really did care for her.

She remembered the shiny symbols on the shield. It could be the link between the two times. Could the shield offer her a passage home?

"Milady, you are in poor spirits today," Sarah said, interrupting her thoughts. "Are you well?"

"I am in good health, Sarah," Tilly replied, mentally noting how easily she fell into the speech patterns of the 19th century. "I simply have troubles weighing upon my mind. Do not fret."

"I understand, milady," she said. She looked very serious. "May I speak in confidence with you?"

"Let us sit in front of the fire, Sarah," she said as she moved toward the fireplace in the dressing room and motioned for Sarah to take a seat. Smiling, she was pleased that the young maid had learned to relax in her presence and immediately took the offered seat without objection.

"Daniel has proposed marriage," Sarah announced.

*Wow, that was fast,* Tilly thought. "Do you want to marry him?" she asked.

"Oh, aye, milady. Very much," Sarah said, blushing and grinning broadly.

"Then, what is the problem?"

"If I marry, I must leave the service."

"Why? A woman can work and be married."

"Is it that way in America?" Sarah asked, confused. "Can a woman work and have a family there?"

Tilly silently cursed the slip of tongue. She wanted to reply that it was commonplace – in her time. The lot of women was much different in the 19th century. While Benjamin never made her feel inferior, many women could not make the same claim. Opportunities were very limited for women like Sarah. The prospect of losing a treasured position was very upsetting. "Please forgive me," she murmured. "I sometimes forget that life is different here."

"What should I do, milady?" Sarah asked in desperation.

She stared at Sarah for some time before answering. "We all make sacrifices for love," she said. "You must ask yourself if marriage to him is worth losing a position as a lady's maid."

She could not bear the heartbroken expression on the maid's face. "I do not know how long I shall be here, but please know this. As long as you are my maid, you can have your position. It matters not to me if you are wed or unwed," Tilly said.

She held up her hand when she saw the jubilant look on Sarah's face. "Now, I cannot make a promise for what happens if you are not my maid," she said.

"I can only speak for your current situation."

Sarah dared to squeeze her hand. "I understand, milady, and thank you very much!" she said. Her mind at greater ease, she rose from her seat and asked, "Since today is Sunday, does milady plan to attend services with the family?"

"No, I would like to go for a ride."

Nodding, Sarah found the makeshift riding outfit they had assembled. It was nothing smart or fashionable, just another black dress similar in design to the others in her wardrobe. She only wore it when she rode, though, limiting the horse stench to one dress. Tilly slipped into the garment and lamented the lack of modern washing machines.

Once she was properly dressed, she dismissed Sarah who seemed eager to leave. The maid probably wanted to share the good news with Daniel and accept his marriage proposal. She did not have the heart to tell her that her position as a lady's maid would soon end, if the shield worked its dubious magic.

*No sense spoiling another person's happiness*, Tilly thought as she made her way down the stairs.

∞

TILLY FOUND IAIN WAITING FOR HER AT

THE STABLE. He had already saddled the horses and was astride a handsome black stead. She nodded to him as the groom helped her mount the kindly mare who had become her ride of choice.

They made their way toward the valley in silence. She was glad Iain did not question her motive for choosing this unorthodox route. She begrudgingly admitted she was unsure if her theory was correct. It was madness to believe a silver shield could be a portal between two times. *Don't you usually need a time machine for that?* she thought.

When they reached the valley, Iain broke the silence. "We have reached our destination, though I know not why you picked this place," he said, shifting in the saddle. He stared at her. "You believed you could find answers here. Do you feel enlightened?"

"At the moment, I do not," she said, laughing. "Will you help me from my horse?"

Iain smiled but said nothing. Her adventures with horseback riding must be a source of amusement. Well, she hoped her theory was accurate. Then, her days of using horses for transportation would be a distant memory.

She took a few tentative steps while she tried to bring life back into her shaky legs. Tilly looked up at the hill and saw the familiar monument. It was definitely the right spot. Closing her eyes, she listened carefully. She could only hear the heavy breathing of the horses and low buzz of insects in the grass. Inhaling, she smelled grass, earth, and pine from the nearby forest. In the distance, the trickle of a stream gurgled faintly.

"You said you owed me a debt that can never be repaid," she said, opening her eyes and turning to face Iain. "If I asked you for a favor, would you help me with it?"

"Aye, milady," he replied. He offered a very courtly bow. "I am your servant."

"The moon will be full tonight, correct?"

"Aye."

"Will you please make sure my horse is saddled and left in her stall tonight?"

Iain furrowed his brow. "Why?" he asked.

"The less you know, the better," Tilly said. "Will you do it?"

"Should I also place the gold and some provisions in the saddle bags?" he asked. Oddly, he seemed disappointed with her plan.

"No, with any luck, that will not be necessary."

"Madam, I do not understand the game that you play," Iain said, disapproval evident in his voice and on his frowning face. "It is not safe to travel without money or food. It is especially unsafe for a woman to travel alone – and even worse, at night!"

She placed her hand upon his arm and forced a smile. "I do not intend to travel beyond this valley," Tilly said. "If I have not returned to the castle by dawn, please come here and collect my horse." Seeing the growing anger on his face, she hastily added, "If my plan is unsuccessful, then I will seek your help with a trip to Edinburgh. That is all I can tell you at this moment. Does that ease your mind?"

"No, it does not," Iain said. It was clear that he became more agitated by the minute. "Please allow me to escort you. It is not safe."

She shook her head. "No," she said firmly. "I have stated my requirements. This is the payment I ask for the debt you say you owe me. Will you honor your promise? Or, were those empty words?"

She noted with some satisfaction that her remarks offended him. Right now, she did not care if she hurt his feelings. Tilly was prepared to say whatever was necessary to get her way.

"My words were not empty, madam," Iain said, squaring his shoulders. "I will do as you request, though it pains me. If you change your mind, I will be glad to accompany you this evening."

"And, I request one more favor."

"Does milady want a pistol?" he asked, amused but somewhat serious.

Tilly chuckled. "No," she said. She walked toward her horse. "You cannot tell Benjamin."

"Milady, I can assure you that will not happen," he vowed. "He would be most aggrieved that I allowed a woman to travel unaccompanied at night."

She was grateful when Iain helped her onto her horse without judging her lack of horseback riding skills. She looked down at him as he placed her foot in a stirrup. "Come the morning, Benjamin will be relieved to know I am gone," Tilly said sadly. "Do not fret, Iain. All will be well."

"If you are gone, many will miss you," he said. Without further comment, he mounted his horse and turned the beast toward the road leading to the castle.

Tilly took one last glance at the valley before urging her horse to a trot. She hoped she would be able to find it again in the darkness.

# FORTY SEVEN

LATER THAT AFTERNOON, Iain walked into the castle. He remained most perplexed by Mrs. Munro's strange request. He spent the day contemplating it and could not comprehend its meaning. Lost in thought, he was oblivious to the servant who followed him. When the man was forced to step in front of Iain to get his attention, he heard that Benjamin wanted to see him in his study.

He knew his friend was in a serious mood after taking one look at the glum expression on Benjamin's face. Without comment, he accepted the offered glass of whisky and joined the man beside the fireplace.

"What troubles you?" Iain asked, taking a sip of the fiery liquid.

Benjamin recounted the tale of the old shield and

the symbol that briefly flashed upon its surface. He then told Iain about the letter from his father and Tilly's reaction. "She believed every word that bastard wrote," he said ruefully. "She does not know the man as we do. You know everything I told him was a lie."

"Was it?" Iain asked. He studied his friend. "Do you wish to risk everything for this woman?"

Benjamin stared into his glass, absently swirling the liquid. "I love her, Iain," he said. "I would risk much if I pursued her, though."

"Aye, you would. Can you stand firm against your father?"

Benjamin shrugged. "I do not know," he said. "I have accomplished so much. If Tilly became my bride, would he allow me the same freedom I have enjoyed these many years? I have managed the estate well and brought him more revenue than when he was master of the estate. Would that be enough?"

Iain shook his head. "You will not know the answer until you confront your father," he said. "You must be prepared for the worst. If he disapproves, you must be willing to walk away from the estate and start anew." He chuckled. "Perhaps you could travel to America, where Tilly lives."

"She insists she is from the future. I cannot travel there."

"You cannot? You believe the shield is a mystical object. It could transport you to another time and place where you could be free from the cumbersome burden of your father."

It was Benjamin's turn to laugh. "I would have to travel hundreds of years into the future to escape that man!" he said.

"You will never have peace until the questions are settled," Iain said, turning serious. "If you believe she is from another time, and you have a link to her old life, you must offer her a choice to return. And, you must decide if you are prepared to anger your father in pursuit of her."

"I do not want her leave," he said, defeated. "I wish there was some way to keep her here and satisfy my father at the same time."

"Of all people, you know that life is never that simple. You have a hard choice to make, my friend," Iain said, placing a hand upon Benjamin's shoulder. "I promised that I would not share the information, but I feel it is important. She asked me to take her to Gleann A'bunadh this morning."

"Why?"

"She told me it sometimes helps to return to the beginning. You met in that valley. You saw the symbol on the shield, and you told me that she was greatly distressed when she heard the story about it. Could she too imagine it offers her a way to her own time, if her outrageous tale is true?"

"Did she ask anything more of you?"

"Aye, she asked me to saddle a horse for her this evening. She also wanted to confirm that a full moon would shine tonight."

"The moon was full the night she appeared in the mist."

"Tales of fairies and strange apparitions often occur by the light of the full moon, do they not?" Iain joked.

"This is no laughing matter," Benjamin said crossly. "If she truly believes the shield will take her home, she plans to leave tonight."

Iain stared at his friend and said gravely, "You do not want her to stay, if she is not meant to be here."

"How do I know the shield will work?" Benjamin asked, frustrated. "Does one deliver some incantation or make a pagan sacrifice to call forth a means for her return?"

"The story in your family's book said nothing of those things," Iain said. "If a goat's slaughter was a necessary component to its power, I am sure your ancestor would have vividly described the ritual." He paused as he remembered something from the tale. "You said a white witch gave the shield to Colin Campbell after a battle at Gleann A'bunadh. Could it be possible that the shield's power is tied to that valley? The spell may only work at that location."

"Aye, it might explain why she remained here and did not return to her own time when I saw the symbol," Benjamin said. "The connection between times may only exist in that valley."

He stared into the fire for several moments before turning to Iain. "Gleann A'bunadh is an easy ride," he said. "I could take Tilly and the shield there tonight. It is the only way to settle the question."

"It would settle the question about how Tilly came to be here. It does not address your father's reaction to your romance," Iain said, shaking his head. "We always return to that. What are you prepared to do for love?"

When his friend did not answer, Iain continued, "You must ask yourself that question before you go further. You must also consider whether or not you truly believe her. Magic shields and women travelling through time? It is the stuff of fanciful stories told to children at bedtime. It is not supposed to be real."

"Benjamin, what will you do if you both go to that

valley, and the shield does not work? What if her tale is the stuff of fantasy?" he asked. He leaned closer and stared intently at his friend. "What if she is nothing more than a confused woman who has no connections, no family or friends? Are you willing to overlook her past in favor of building a future together?"

"What if we go to the valley, and the shield *does* work?" Benjamin said, a note of fear in his voice. "Do you think she will return to her own time, Iain? Do I offer anything here?"

"You are a foolish man," Iain said. "I believe that she loves you very much. She only wants to hear the words from you." He rose from his seat and placed the empty whisky glass on the table. "I will have the horses ready for you both this evening. If you wish to proceed, bring the shield and the woman to the valley."

He made his way to the door and paused, his hand on the doorknob. Turning, he said, "Make your decision – and live with the consequences."

Iain did not bother to stay for Benjamin's reaction.

∞

BENJAMIN SPENT THE REST OF THE AFTERNOON IN HIS STUDY, TRYING TO MAKE A DECISION. His head told him one course of action would be most prudent. His heart vehemently disagreed. When Mr. Murphy knocked on the door and informed him that dinner was ready, he was no closer to a decision than he was at the beginning.

He slowly made his way to the family's dining room. He was not surprised that Tilly did not join him for dinner. She had been avoiding him ever since that blasted letter arrived, choosing to eat her meals in her chamber and hiding there when not teaching his children. Based upon what Iain told him, she might be preparing for her clandestine escape that evening.

He posted a guard at the stable and would be alerted if she chose to leave. What would he do if she did? He wished he could have more time to think about the choices that lay before him. He knew the great risk involved, yet he could not imagine life without her.

The last few months seemed like a rebirth to him. He felt as if the cloud that descended after Mary's death was lifted. He even noticed a change in his children, who were once again carefree and happy. It was not from the passage of time, for he knew it never healed wounds. No, time only taught you how to make peace with the pain and resume your life. The happiness he and his family felt could only be attributed to a restoration of spirits brought on by the love and care of a mysterious woman.

As he absently sampled the dishes the footmen placed before him, Benjamin understood that he had no choice. He must face the ire of his father. He simply could not live without Tilly, and he could not imagine telling his children that they must do the same. Like it or not, they had all come to rely on her as a member of their family. Her absence would be as deeply felt as the loss they endured when Mary died.

Now, he moved to the next question posed by Iain. Did he believe her? He shook his head. It was beyond all imagining that a simple shield could be a device that transported her from over two hundred years in the future back in time to 1801. That was the story she expected him to believe, though.

Benjamin had repeatedly analyzed her behavior and admitted nothing in her manner, her speech, or her stories gave him any indication that she was dishonest. She was unwavering in her declaration that she came from the $21^{st}$ century.

He tossed his napkin onto the table. He decided there was only one way to settle the matter.

"My apologies, sir," Benjamin said, noting the shocked expression on the butler's face. "I am not hungry this evening and will retire to my chamber."

He strode toward his bedchamber. He would collect the damn shield and take Tilly to the valley.

Then, maybe they would know once and for all whether or not she came from the future.

"This is madness," Benjamin mumbled as he opened the door to his bedchamber. He walked to the fireplace and was surprised to see a chair in front of it. Looking up, he gasped in shock. The shield was gone.

# FORTY EIGHT

TILLY PULLED THE WOOL CLOAK TIGHTER AROUND HER to chase away the chill. She wished she had the forethought to bring a blanket that might have offered some protection against the wet grass on which she sat. Of course, it was hard enough sneaking out of the castle with a metal shield. Bringing more supplies would have been impractical. She could not have managed it without Sarah's help and sincerely hoped the poor girl would not get into trouble.

She glanced at the object in question, which she placed on the ground in front of her. Tilly hoped her theory was accurate. Otherwise, she would feel awfully foolish about sitting in the middle of a grassy field, waiting for some sign. What if she was stuck in the 1800? Shaking her head, she tried to push aside that depressing thought.

Unfortunately, it could not be so easily dismissed. If she had not read that damn letter from Malcolm Campbell, she would not have been troubled by the prospect of staying. She fell in love with Benjamin and believed he felt the same way. It was a silly fantasy. His true feelings were right there in print.

Tilly looked up at the sky. She could not remember seeing so many twinkling stars in the inky black canvas of night. In her time, light pollution blurred the evening sky unless she travelled into the country. Smiling, she remembered that was one of the reasons her husband and she picked their farmhouse. It was inconvenient to town, yet the location gave them an opportunity to raise the children in an environment that provided natural surroundings.

She giggled despite the gravity of the situation. Gleann A'bunadh definitely offered the rustic splendor Alex and she wanted back home. She had grown accustomed to the sounds that filled the air, all the familiar noises of life in the 19th century – red stag running through the forest, insects whizzing through the air, an owl hooting in a tree. She did not miss the sound of airplanes overhead, the roar of car engines, or the ringing of cell phones that plagued modern life. She relaxed in this environment.

She looked across the field and saw nothing. She should stop thinking about the things she liked in this time. She wanted to leave, right?

What did she miss about the 21st century? Tilly closed her eyes and thought of all the modern conveniences. She planned to take a hot bath and soak for hours as soon as she returned. What a luxury it would be to switch on the tap and instantly have water! Oh, she had never considered a toilet to be a thing of beauty until she spent months using a chamber pot. What else?

Maybe she would order a pizza and enjoy it right there in the tub. Mozzarella cheese and mushrooms with crushed red pepper flakes sprinkled on top, all on a thin crust lightly covered with fresh tomato sauce. Her mouth practically watered at the thought.

*Beth.* She missed her friend so much. It would be wonderful to be with her old friend again, someone with whom she could discuss anything. Beth was always there to offer help whenever she needed it.

They had been through dark times together. Beth never left. She was a faithful friend.

*Unlike Benjamin,* she thought resentfully. The whole time they were together, did he woo another woman? Was she nothing more than a servant, one who would be replaced soon? Maybe Tilly was just a lovely roll in the hay, a physical release. No doubt, the other woman chose to remain chaste before marriage.

*Stop it!* she commanded herself. She must not think

of him. Why did it matter? She would be gone, and he could marry someone who suited his father. His new wife and he would raise the children and manage the estate.

Embarrassed, she admitted the idea of another woman raising the children and enjoying Benjamin's affections deeply hurt her. He would carry on just fine without her. In fact, if he picked the right woman, he might be better off. His new wife might bring a bit of money to the marriage, which would satisfy Malcolm Campbell. Hell, Benjamin might even fall in love with her.

She gritted her teeth in frustration. She must stop thinking about him and turn her mind toward her own time. *Focus,* she thought. *What will you do when you go back?*

She took a deep breath. Her life felt frozen for the last year. This trip was meant to be the first step toward restarting her life. With the sale of the restaurant and house, she had some money to start over in another town. Beth and Randall had a cottage on Sullivan's Island. They probably would not mind if she stayed there for a while.

Teaching Benjamin's children had reignited her love of education. She could find a job at one of the schools in the Charleston area. She would have a fresh start. Yes, Tilly could build a new life. In time, she might even be happy.

She opened her eyes and watched the moon as it slipped from behind a fluffy white cloud. It cast a pale, silvery light upon the cold metal of the shield. One by one, the symbols slowly appeared in each quadrant of the battered armament - a fish, an infinity symbol, triangles, and a caldron with legs protruding from it.

She squinted through the soft mist that drifted across the valley. Stumbling to her feet, her mouth fell open at the sight. Mrs. Douglas' slate-roofed cottage emerged from the mist. The windows were ablaze with *electric* lights. Cars filled the parking lot. If she listened carefully, she could hear canned laughter from a show playing on a television inside the inn.

"I am not crazy!" Tilly shouted as she jumped with joy. "It is real!"

"Holy mother of God!"

She spun around at the exclamation. She found Benjamin standing three feet behind her, his face ghostly pale and eyes wide.

"What the hell are you doing here?" she asked, closing the distance between them.

"Can you smell the bread?" Benjamin asked. He pulled his gaze away from the scene and stared at her in shock. He seemed eager for proof that he too was not insane.

Despite her previous thoughts about him, she could not help feeling a twinge of relief that he was here. Finally, she could show him the truth. "Yes, I do," Tilly said. "Mrs. Douglas makes it every evening." She took a moment to inhale deeply. "It smells like banana bread."

"It is an intoxicating aroma."

"Well, she is a great cook."

He shifted uneasily. "Tilly, I…." he began.

She pressed her finger to his lips. "Don't say anything, Benjamin," she said. "I will leave. You can return to your life."

"I do not want to return to my former life," he said, grabbing her hand. "You have brought me a happiness that I never thought I could experience again."

"The letter –"

"The letter was a lie! I had to say those things to my father. I did not want him to come to Castle Fion."

Tilly wrenched away her hand from his and turned her back to him. She looked longingly at the cottage.

All she had to do was walk across the field and leave Benjamin forever. He would just be another page in a history book. She did not need this anguish again.

She hesitated. "Nothing will change if I stay," she said. "He will still come."

"I know," he said, resignation creeping into his voice. "I also told him those things because I wanted more time with you. I did not want our relationship to begin in a rush."

Her romance with Alex was a whirlwind. She could appreciate Benjamin's desire, but it did not change the simple fact. "I am not a suitable prospect," she said.

"To hell with 'suitable prospects,' Tilly! I want a woman by my side who I love and respect. And, I think you want the same of your husband."

Benjamin stood in front of her, blocking the view of the cottage. "I do not pretend to know the intimacies of the relationship you had with Alex. From what you have told me, I cannot believe it was as it is with you and me," he said. "I have never felt such a kinship with another person, save my friendship with Iain. Did you feel this with him?"

"No," she said softly. Tilly could not look him in the eyes. "It is so easy with you."

He caressed her cheek and lifted her face so that she had to meet his gaze. "You are the strongest person I have ever met," Benjamin said. "If you are standing by my side, I can overcome any obstacle."

"Even your father?"

"Aye, even Malcolm Campbell," he replied. "As I rode to this valley, I feared that you would be gone. It frightened me more than I can express. I would rather face his disapproval than live a life without you."

He dropped to his knees at her feet. His face was raw with emotion. Bowing his head, he said huskily, "You have a choice now, Tilly. You may return to your own time. All you have to do is cross this field."

"You could come with me," she said hopefully. "We could go back to the castle and get the children. We could all go to the future. We could have a nice life there. I could show you wonderful places and things. You could leave behind all this struggle and worry."

He shook his head. "You can never escape struggle and worry in any time," Benjamin said ruefully. "I cannot leave the estate to the whim of my father. I have a responsibility to take care of these people. My home is here."

"My heart tears in two at the idea of you leaving," he whispered. "I do not know how I shall endure another heartbreak. I will survive, though, if I know that you want to go home and that you will be happier there. You can return to your own time. It has been your wish these many months." He swallowed hard as his eyes filled with tears. "Or, you can stay here. I love you, Tilly Munro."

"You do?" she asked in disbelief.

"With my whole heart," he said. He clutched her hands. "Stay with me as my wife. Be the mother to my children – *our* children. Please choose the life we can give you in *this* time. I vow to you that I will make it worth the sacrifice. Please choose us. Please choose *me*."

Tilly felt hot tears tumble down her cheeks. She had a difficult choice. Until a few moments ago, she felt it was one she would never have to make. "Do you know what you ask?" she said, between sobs. "I would have to ride a stinky horse if I stayed here!"

He laughed, glad for a moment's levity. "If it would please milady, I would carry you everywhere you wanted to go," Benjamin promised. "Your feet would never touch the ground, and your bottom would never sit on a horse."

"In your time, I am regarded as a second-class citizen," she said soberly. "How can I accept that teaching, raising children, and managing Castle Fion are my only career options?"

He furrowed his brow as he considered her remark. "I cannot change the ways of my world," he said. "I can only pledge that, in all matters of our family, you will be my equal partner."

Tilly sniffed loudly and glanced at the cottage. "Could I live without Beth?" she asked aloud. As she remembered her best friend, a jolt of pain shot through her heart.

Beth was like a sister to her. If she stayed, she would lose the last person she considered to be a part of her old family. This time, though, it would happen because Tilly chose it. Beth would not be ripped away by a freak accident.

He squeezed her hands, bringing her attention to him. "I know that she meant a great deal to you," he said tenderly. "If you stay here, I will be your friend. You can trust in me as you did her."

Tilly could not find the right words to say. She cast another look at the cottage.

"You have no reason to stay here," Benjamin said miserably, releasing her hands. "I should let you go."

"I am not looking for a substitute family for the one I lost," she whispered as she touched his cheek. "No one will ever replace John and Anna. Spending time with your family gave me hope for the future, though." She smiled faintly. "I know you did not believe me until this moment. Even so, you opened your home to me and took care of me when I needed you most. Thank you."

A single tear trickled down his cheek. "I will always treasure the time that I had with you, Tilly Munro," he said. He rose to his feet and stepped aside, dropping his head in defeat.

She managed a weak smile. She took a step forward and then stopped. She turned to face him. Benjamin may be the physical embodiment of the great Scottish laird from all those silly romance novels. In the months she had known him, she discovered that he was so much more than that. Simply put, she could not envision a world in which she could not talk with him or hold his hand. If she returned to her time, she would lose him forever. He would become nothing more than a side note in the Campbell family history.

*Please forgive me, Beth*, she silently said to herself, hoping her friend could somehow hear her wish. Stealing one last look at the cottage, Tilly walked back to him. She brushed away the tears on his cheeks. "I love you too, Benjamin Campbell," she said. "I choose you – now and forever."

As they kissed, the cottage faded into the mist.

And, the symbols vanished from the shield.

# FORTY NINE

TILLY STOOD IN FRONT OF ONE OF THE WINDOWS IN BENJAMIN'S BEDCHAMBER. She watched him as he slept soundly in his bed – or was it now *their* bed? After their return to the castle, they made love and spent hours talking about their future together. It was a future she never imagined happening. How could she?

She turned back to the view. Streaks of purple and blue slashed the horizon as the first rays of sunshine pierced the sky over the verdant mountains. The leaves on the trees in the forest were just beginning to show signs of the gradual turning from rich green to vibrant red and orange. Seeing the seasons change in a foreign country would be a new and different experience.

Of course, from this point forward, everything would be new and different. Her world was about to change in ways she never dreamt possible. After enduring a hellish year, she emerged on the other side and stumbled into a new life with a new family. It only took a walk across a misty field and into the arms of a 19th century Scotsman to make it possible.

She pulled the shawl tighter around her shoulders. Her one regret was leaving her friend Beth. The woman was always by her side, always steadfast and true. It would have been her friend who told Tilly to make this jump. It would have been Beth who said happiness was the most important thing, right?

Unfortunately, she would never know how Beth truly felt when her friend realized the absence was not temporary. Tilly's heart ached at causing her friend pain, for she knew better than anyone the agony of loss. However, she could not deny the powerful love she felt for Benjamin and his children. Turning her back on another shot at happiness was not an option.

The life she had in the 21st century was over. She enjoyed moments of pure joy – seeing happiness on her parents' faces when she graduated from college, meeting her future husband Alex for the first time, holding her children after they were born, and watching John and Anna take their first steps. She also experienced deep, heartbreaking pain at the loss of her parents and her family. All of those moments made her the person she was. While that part of her life had ended, she would carry those memories with her forever.

She moved away from the window and returned to the bed. Tilly snuggled close to Benjamin, trying not to wake him. She was unsuccessful.

"Good morning, my love," he murmured into her ear as he placed a kiss upon her neck.

"Good morning," Tilly whispered. "Welcome to a new day."

# EPILOGUE

*Deoch, Scotland*
*Mrs. Douglas' cottage*
*January 2019*

BETH STOOD AT THE DOORS LEADING INTO THE GARDEN. It was almost dark. She sipped a glass of Mrs. Douglas' fine whisky while she watched a cold, freezing rain pelt the windows.

She could not believe that she was back in Scotland, this time without her best friend. She longed for her beloved friend to walk back into her life. She spent the last several months waiting. She just knew she would get a phone call, informing her that Tilly had been found, alive and well. All would be explained and forgiven.

The call never came. The police, helpful locals, the

Douglases - everyone searched for weeks and did not find a single trace. Beth stayed as long as she could, but she eventually accepted reality. She returned home with a broken heart.

Her life swiftly changed after she fell into her husband's arms at the airport. She could hardly believe anything that happened since her return from Scotland. How did things go so badly, so fast?

She refilled her glass. She found herself in a similar predicament as Tilly. What do you do when the life you planned is over?

Beth decided to return to the scene of the crime, so to speak. The Douglases were adamant that she return to Scotland. They had shown some of her work to the duchess, who was interested in hiring her for some marketing assistance. With no other options at home, she figured, why not? It would have been a bad idea, except Beth desperately wanted to be close to Tilly in whatever twisted way she could.

She looked out over the field, wishing her friend was there. Tilly would know what she should do. She closed her eyes and let the tears trickle down her face.

Behind her, the infinity symbol flashed upon the shield that hung above the fireplace. Beth did not see it.

.

# LIKE THE WRITER?

Search for more novels from *C. Renee Freeman* on Amazon. Available in both e-book and paperback versions.

Enjoy works from the *Through the Mist* series:

*Through the Mist: Restoration*

*Through the Mist: Adrift (a novella)*

*Through the Mist: Reunion*

*Through the Mist: Reflection*

*Through the Mist: Redemption*

…and more novels to follow with the series.

Also, for something completely different, check out a contemporary romance, *Love at the Woolly Bookworm Shop*. Set in a small town in North Carolina, follow the story of Peg Alexander. She returned to her hometown after a shocking divorce and built a wonderful life for herself. Her world is turned completely upside down when John Sweeney returns. Find out what happens next.

# ACKNOWLEDGEMENTS

To H., your unwavering support and friendship made this book possible. Thank you for enduring endless discussions about the story and patiently offering suggestions whenever it needed a tweak. I never could have created this world without you.

To G., thank you for patiently waiting whenever Mommy delayed a walkie or did not provide a belly rub as quickly as you would have liked. Yes, I included you in the book, as promised.

And last, but certainly not least – thank you to everyone who reads my books. You are awesome!

# ABOUT THE AUTHOR

C. Renee Freeman lives in a small town located in the mountains of Western North Carolina. She has written six books, five in the *Through the Mist* series and one contemporary romance, *Love at the Woolly Bookworm Shop*.

Writing gives her an opportunity to escape into another time and place. When she is not writing, she enjoys cooking, reading, spending time with her dogs, and researching topics for her next book.

She begins each book by asking questions. What drives people to do the things they do? What would it be like to live that person's life?

You can learn more about the goings-on in the writer's life by checking out her website, creneefreeman.com, or visiting her on Facebook.

Made in the USA
Columbia, SC
22 January 2024

30798309R00283